Books by Judith McNaught

JUDITH McNAUGHT

Someone to Watch Over Me

POCKET BOOKS

New York   London   Toronto   Sydney

Pocket Books
A Division of Simon & Schuster, Inc.
1230 Avenue of the Americas
New York, NY 10020

This book is a work of fiction. Names, characters, places and incidents are products of the author's imagination or are used fictitiously. Any resemblance to actual events or locales or persons, living or dead, is entirely coincidental.

Copyright © 2003 by Eagle Syndication, Inc.

Originally published in hardcover in 2003 by Atria Books

This Pocket Books paperback edition June 2011

POCKET and colophon are registered trademarks of Simon & Schuster, Inc.

For information regarding special discounts for bulk purchases, please contact Simon & Schuster Special Sales at 1-866-506-1949 or business@simonandschuster.com.

The Simon & Schuster Speakers Bureau can bring authors to your live event. For more information or to book an event contact the Simon & Schuster Speakers Bureau at 1-866-248-3049 or visit our website at www.simonspeakers.com.

Cover design by Lisa Litwack.
Photos © Lisa Spindler Photography Inc./Getty Images; city © Douglas Pearson/Jupiter Images

Manufactured in the United States of America

10 9 8 7 6 5 4 3 2 1

ISBN 978-1-4516-4834-8

FOR SPENCER SHELLEY

Dearest Spence,

In keeping with tradition, I want very much to give you a letter of advice like the one I wrote for your brother in the dedication of my last book. But I can't. I'm so awed by your charm and entranced by your laughter, that I can't wait until you're older so that I can ask you for advice. How do you make people smile whenever they look at you? I know where you got your eyes, but where did you get your joy? Where did you get so much magic?

I have so many questions to ask you, but you're only two now, so I'll have to wait for my answers. The only thing I know for certain is that you're going to chart your own course through life. And if that course happens to be one that causes great trepidation in the hearts of your parents, then you can count on me to soothe things over. In the meantime, I will give you this one little piece of grandmotherly advice: Don't let any of us change you.

ACKNOWLEDGMENTS

I write novels about exceptional men, men of great character, wit, compassion, and strength. In real life, I've known men like that. One of them was Gayle Schroder; he was my friend. The other was Michael McNaught; he was my husband. All of us who loved these two extraordinary men miss them terribly. In life, they were admired and cherished by us; now it is their memory that lights our lives—and our way. How blessed we are to have known them at all.

Writing a novel is a prolonged, solitary endeavor for me. I survive it only with the support and empathy of my family and close friends. Thank you, Clay, and Whit, and Rose, for understanding the lack of phone calls and visits, and never complaining. I love you so much for that! Thank you, Carole LaRocco and Judy Schroder and Cathy Richardson, for being such steadfast friends.

Writing a novel like this one also requires the advice and assistance of many people with knowledge of my subject— or it requires only one person with vast knowledge, endless contacts, and limitless patience. In this case, Steve Sloat. Steve, you've been a prince. I can't thank you enough.

CHAPTER I

"Miss Kendall, can you hear me? I'm Dr. Metcalf, and you're at Good Samaritan Hospital in Mountainside. We're going to take you out of the ambulance now and into the emergency room."

Shivering uncontrollably, Leigh Kendall reacted to the insistent male voice that was calling her back to consciousness, but she couldn't seem to summon the strength to open her eyelids.

"Can you hear me, Miss Kendall?"

With an effort, she finally managed to force her eyes open. The doctor who had spoken was bending over her, examining her head, and beside him, a nurse was holding a clear plastic bag of IV fluid.

"We're going to take you out of the ambulance now," he repeated as he beamed a tiny light at each of her pupils.

"Need . . . to tell . . . husband I'm here," Leigh managed in a feeble whisper.

He nodded and gave her hand a reassuring squeeze. "The state police will take care of that. In the meantime, you have some very big fans at Good Samaritan, including me, and we're going to take excellent care of you."

Voices and images began to fly at Leigh from every direction as the gurney was lifted from the ambulance. Red and blue lights pulsed frantically against a gray dawn sky. People in uniforms flashed past her line of vision—New York State troopers, paramedics, doctors, nurses. Doors swung open, the hallway flew by, faces crowded around her, firing urgent questions at her.

Leigh tried to concentrate, but their voices were collapsing into an incomprehensible babble, and their features were sliding off their faces, dissolving into the same blackness that had already devoured the rest of the room.

WHEN LEIGH AWOKE AGAIN, it was dark outside and a light snow was falling. Struggling to free herself from the effects of whatever drugs were dripping into her arm from the IV bag above her, she gazed dazedly at what appeared to be a hospital room filled with a riotous display of flowers.

Seated on a chair near the foot of the bed, flanked by a huge basket of white orchids and a large vase of bright yellow roses, a gray-haired nurse was reading a copy of the *New York Post* with Leigh's picture on the front page.

Leigh turned her head as much as the brace on her neck would allow, searching for some sign of Logan, but for the time being, she was alone with the nurse. Experimentally, she moved her legs and wiggled her toes, and was relieved to find them still attached to the rest of her and in reasonably good working order. Her arms were bandaged and her head was wrapped in something tight, but as long as she didn't move, her discomfort seemed to be limited to a generalized ache throughout her body, a sharper ache in her ribs, and a throat so dry it felt as if it were stuffed with sawdust.

She was alive, and that in itself was a miracle! The fact that she was also whole and relatively unharmed filled Leigh with a sense of gratitude and joy that was almost euphoric. She swallowed and forced a croaking whisper from her parched throat. "May I have some water?"

The nurse looked up, a professional smile instantly brightening her face. "You're awake!" she said as she quickly closed the newspaper, folded it in half, and laid it facedown beneath her chair.

The name tag on the nurse's uniform identified her as "Ann Mackey, RN. Private Duty," Leigh noted as she watched the nurse pouring water from a pink plastic pitcher on the tray beside the bed.

"You should have a straw. I'll go get one."

"Please don't bother. I'm terribly thirsty."

When the nurse started to hold the glass to Leigh's mouth, Leigh took it from her. "I can hold it," Leigh assured her, and then was amazed by how much effort it took just to lift her bandaged arm and hold it steady. By the time she handed the glass back to Nurse Mackey, her arm was trembling and her chest hurt terribly. Wondering if perhaps there was more wrong with her than she'd thought, Leigh let her head sink back into the pillows while she gathered the strength to talk. "What sort of condition am I in?"

Nurse Mackey looked eager to share her knowledge, but she hesitated. "You really should ask Dr. Metcalf about that."

"I will, but I'd like to hear it now, from my private duty nurse. I won't tell him you told me anything."

It was all the encouragement she needed. "You were in shock when you were brought in," she confided. "You had a concussion, hypothermia, cracked ribs, and suspected injuries to the cervical vertebrae and adjacent tissue—that's whiplash in layman's terms. You have several deep scalp wounds, as well as lacerations on your arms, legs, and torso, but only a few of them are on your face, and they aren't deep, which is a blessing. You also have contusions and abrasions all over your—"

Smiling as much as her swollen lip would allow, Leigh lifted her hand to stop the litany of injuries. "Is there anything wrong with me that will need surgery?"

The nurse looked taken aback by Leigh's upbeat attitude, and then she looked impressed. "No surgery," she said with an approving little pat on Leigh's shoulder.

"Any physical therapy?"

"I wouldn't think so. But you should expect to be very sore for a few weeks, and your ribs will hurt. Your burns and cuts will require close attention, healing and scarring could be a concern—"

Leigh interrupted this new deluge of depressing medical minutiae with a grin. "I'll be very careful," she said, and then she switched to the only other topic on her mind. "Where is my husband?"

Nurse Mackey faltered and then patted Leigh's shoulder again. "I'll go and see about that," she promised, and hurried off, leaving Leigh with the impression that Logan was nearby.

Exhausted from the simple acts of drinking and speaking, Leigh closed her eyes and tried to piece together what had happened to her since yesterday, when Logan had kissed her good-bye in the morning. . . .

He'd been so excited when he left their Upper East Side apartment, so eager for her to join him in the mountains and spend the night with him there. For over a year, he'd been looking for just the right site for their mountain retreat, a secluded setting that would complement the sprawling stone house he'd designed for the two of them. Finding the right site was complicated by the fact that Logan had already completed the drawings, so the site needed to be adaptable to the plans. On Thursday, he'd finally found a piece of property that met all his exacting qualifications, and he'd been so eager for her to see it that he insisted they should spend Sunday night—their first available night—in the existing cabin on the land.

"The cabin hasn't been used in years, but I'll clean it up while I'm waiting for you to get there," he promised, displaying an endearing enthusiasm for a task he'd always avoided. "There isn't any electricity or heat, but I'll build a roaring fire in the fireplace, and we'll sleep in front of it in sleeping bags. We'll have dinner by candlelight. In the morning, we'll watch the sun rise over the tops of the trees. Our trees. It will be very romantic, you'll see."

His entire plan filled Leigh with amused dread. She was starring in a new play that had opened on Broadway the night before, and she'd only had four hours of sleep. Before she could leave for the mountains, she had a Sunday matinee performance to give, and that would be followed by a three-hour drive to a cold, uninhabitable stone cabin, so that she could sleep on the floor . . . and then get up at dawn the next day.

"I can't wait," she lied convincingly, but what she really wanted to do was go back to sleep. It was only eight o'clock. She could sleep until ten.

Logan hadn't had any more sleep than she, but he was already dressed and eager to leave for the cabin. "The place isn't easy to find, so I drew you a detailed map with plenty of landmarks," he said, laying a piece of paper on her nightstand. "I've already loaded the car. I think I have everything I need—" he continued, leaning over her in bed and pressing a quick kiss on her cheek, "—house plans, stakes, string, a transom, sleeping bags. I still feel like I'm forgetting something . . ."

"A broom, a mop, and a bucket?" Leigh joked sleepily

as she rolled over onto her stomach. "Scrub brushes? Detergent?"

"Killjoy," he teased, nuzzling her neck where he knew she was ticklish.

Leigh giggled, pulled the pillow over the back of her head, and continued dictating his shopping list. "Disinfectant . . . mousetraps . . ."

"You sound like a spoiled, pampered Broadway star," he chuckled, pressing down on the pillow to prevent her from adding more items to the list. "Where is your sense of adventure?"

"It stops at a Holiday Inn," she said with a muffled giggle.

"You used to love to go camping. You were the one who taught me how. You even suggested we go camping on our honeymoon!"

"Because we couldn't afford a Holiday Inn."

With a laugh, he pulled the pillow away from her head and rumpled her hair. "Leave straight from the theater. Don't be late." He stood up and headed for the door to their bedroom suite. "I know I'm forgetting something—"

"Drinking water, candles, a tin coffeepot?" Leigh helpfully chanted. "Food for dinner? A pear for my breakfast?"

"No more pears. You're addicted," he teased over his shoulder. "From now on, it's Cream of Wheat and prunes for you."

"Sadist," Leigh mumbled into the pillows. A moment later she heard the door close behind him, and she rolled onto her back, smiling to herself as she gazed out the bedroom windows overlooking Central Park. Logan's enthusiasm for the mountain property was contagious, but his lighthearted mood was what mattered most to her. They'd both been so young, and so poor, when they got married thirteen years ago that hard work had been a necessity, and then it had become a habit. On their wedding day, their total combined assets were eight hundred dollars in cash, plus Logan's new architectural degree, his mother's social connections, and Leigh's unproven acting talent—that, and their unflagging faith in each other. With only those tools, they'd built a wonderful life together, but during the last few months, they'd both been so busy that their sex life had been almost nonexistent. She'd been immersed in the preopening craziness of a new play, and Logan had been consumed with the endless complexities of his latest, and biggest, business venture.

As Leigh lay in bed, gazing out at the clouds gathering in the November sky, she decided she definitely liked the prospect of spending the night in front of a roaring fire with nothing to do but make love with her husband. They wanted a baby, and she suddenly realized that even the timing was right for conception tonight. She was dreamily imagining the evening that lay ahead when Hilda walked into the bedroom wearing her coat and carrying Leigh's breakfast tray. "Mr. Manning said you were awake, so I brought you breakfast before I leave," Hilda explained. She waited while Leigh struggled into a sitting position; then she handed her the tray containing Leigh's ritual breakfast fare—cottage cheese, a pear, and coffee. "I've tidied up after the party. Is there anything else you'd like me to do before I go?"

"Not a thing. Enjoy your day off. Are you planning to stay in New Jersey at your sister's tonight?"

Hilda nodded. "My sister said she's had very good luck at Harrah's lately. I thought we might go there."

Leigh suppressed a grin because, as far as she'd been able to tell, Hilda had absolutely no human weaknesses—except one for the nickel slot machines in Atlantic City. "We won't be back here until late tomorrow afternoon," Leigh said as a thought occurred to her. "I'll have to go straight to the theater, and Mr. Manning has a dinner meeting that will last until late in the evening. There's really no need for you to be here tomorrow night. Why don't you spend two days with your sister, and check out some of the slot machines at the other casinos?"

The suggestion of two consecutive days off threw the housekeeper into a total state of inner conflict that reflected itself on Hilda's plain face and made Leigh stifle another grin. In the War Against Dirt and Disorder, Hilda Brunner was a militant, tireless general who marched into daily battle armed with a vacuum cleaner and cleaning supplies, her foreboding expression warning of an impending assault on all foreign particles. To Hilda, taking two days off in a row was tantamount to a voluntary retreat, and that was virtually unthinkable. On the other hand, if she did as Leigh suggested, she would be able to spend two full days with her sister at the nickel slot machines. She cast a glance around the immaculate bedroom that was her personal battlefield, trying to assess in advance the extent of damage likely to occur if she were absent for two entire days. "I would like to think about it."

"Of course," Leigh said, struggling to keep her face straight. "Hilda," she called as the German woman bustled toward the door.

Hilda turned in the act of belting her brown coat around her waist. "Yes, Mrs. Manning?"

"You're a treasure."

LEIGH HAD HOPED to leave the theater by four o'clock that afternoon, but the play's director and the writer wanted to make some minor changes in two of her scenes after watching the matinee performance, and then they argued endlessly over which changes to make, trying out first one variation, then another. As a result, it was after six when she was finally on her way.

Patchy fog mixed with light snow slowed her progress out of the city. Leigh tried to call Logan twice on his cellular phone to tell him she was going to be late, but either he'd left his phone somewhere out of hearing or the cabin was beyond range of his cellular service. She left voice mail messages for him instead.

By the time she reached the mountains, the snow was falling hard and fast, and the wind had picked up dramatically. Leigh's Mercedes sedan was heavy and handled well, but the driving was treacherous, the visibility so poor that she could only see fifteen feet in front of her car. At times it was impossible to see large road signs, let alone spot the little landmarks Logan had noted on his map. Roadside restaurants and gas stations that would normally have been open at ten P.M. were closed, their parking lots deserted. Twice, she doubled back, certain she'd missed a landmark or a road. With nowhere to stop or ask for directions, Leigh had little choice except to keep driving and searching.

When she should have been within a few miles of the cabin, she turned into an unmarked driveway with a fence across it and switched on the car's map light to study Logan's directions again. She was almost positive she'd missed a turnoff two miles back, the one Logan had described as being "200 feet south of a sharp curve in the road, just beyond a little red barn." With at least six inches of snow blanketing everything, what had seemed like a little barn to her could just as easily have been a large black shed, a short silo, or a pile of frozen cows, but Leigh decided she should go back and find out.

She put the Mercedes into gear and made a cautious U-turn. As she rounded the sharp curve she was looking for, she slowed down even more, searching for a gravel drive, but the drop-off was much too steep, the terrain far too rugged, for anyone to have put a driveway there. She'd just taken her foot off the brake and started to accelerate when a pair of headlights on high beam leapt out of the darkness behind her, rounding the curve, closing the distance with terrifying speed. On the snow-covered roads, Leigh couldn't speed up quickly and the other driver couldn't seem to slow down. He swerved into the left lane to avoid plowing into her from the rear, lost control, and smashed into the Mercedes just behind Leigh's door.

The memory of what followed was horrifyingly vivid— the explosion of air bags, the scream of tortured metal and shattering glass as the Mercedes plowed through the guardrail and began cartwheeling down the steep embankment. The car slammed against several tree trunks, then hurtled into boulders in a long series of deafening crashes that ended in one, sudden, explosive jolt as five thousand pounds of mangled steel came to a bone-jarring stop.

Suspended from her seat belt, Leigh hung there, upside down, like a dazed bat in a cave, while light began exploding around her. Bright light. Colorful light. Yellow and orange and red. Fire!

Stark terror sharpened her senses. She found the seat belt release, landed hard on the roof of the overturned car and, whimpering, tried to crawl through the hole that had once been the passenger window. Blood, sticky and wet, spread down her arms and legs and dripped into her eyes. Her coat was too bulky for the opening, and she was yanking it off when whatever had stopped the car's descent suddenly gave way. Leigh heard herself screaming as the burning car pitched forward, rolled, and then seemed to fly out over thin air, before it began a downward plunge that ended in a deafening splash and a freezing deluge of icy water.

Lying in her hospital bed with her eyes closed, Leigh relived that plunge into the water, and her heart began to race. Moments after hitting the water, the car had begun a fast nosedive for the bottom, and in a frenzy of terror, she started pounding on everything she could reach. She located a hole above her, a large one, and with her lungs bursting, she pushed through it and fought with her remaining strength to reach the surface. It seemed an eternity before a blast of frigid wind hit her face and she gulped in air.

She tried to swim, but pain knifed through her chest with every breath, and her strokes were too feeble and uncoordinated to propel her forward more than a little bit. Leigh kept thrashing about in the freezing water, but her body was going numb, and neither her panic nor her determination could give her enough strength and coordination to swim. Her head was sliding under the surface when her flailing hand struck something hard and rough—the limb of a partially submerged fallen tree. She grabbed at it with all her might, trying to use it as a raft, until she realized that the "raft" was stationary. She pulled herself along it, hand over hand, as the water receded to her shoulders, then her waist, and finally her knees.

Shivering and weeping with relief, she peered through the dense curtain of blowing snow, searching for the path the Mercedes would have carved through the trees after it plunged off the ridge. There was no path in sight. There was no ridge in sight either. There was only bone-numbing cold, and sharp branches that slapped and scratched her as she clawed her way up a steep embankment she couldn't see, toward a road she wasn't sure was there.

Leigh had a vague recollection of finally reaching the top of the ridge and curling her body into a ball on something flat and wet, but everything after that was a total blur.

Everything, except a strange, blinding light and a man—an angry man who cursed at her.

LEIGH WAS ABRUPTLY JOLTED into the present by an insistent male voice originating from the side of her hospital bed. "*Miss Kendall?* Miss Kendall, I'm sorry to wake you, but we've been waiting to talk to you."

Leigh opened her eyes and gazed blankly at a man and woman who were holding thick winter jackets over their arms. The man was in his early forties, short and heavyset, with black hair and a swarthy complexion. The woman was considerably younger, slightly taller, and very pretty, with long dark hair pulled back into a ponytail.

"I'm Detective Shrader with the New York City Police Department," the man said, "and this is Detective Littleton. We have some questions we need to ask you."

Leigh assumed they wanted to ask about her accident, but she felt too weak to describe it twice, once for them and again for Logan. "Could you wait until my husband gets back?"

"Gets back from where?" Detective Shrader asked.

"From wherever he is right now."

"Do you know where he is?"

"No, but the nurse went to get him."

Detectives Shrader and Littleton exchanged a glance. "Your nurse was instructed to come straight to us as soon as you were conscious," Shrader explained; then he said bluntly, "Miss Kendall, when did you last see your husband?"

An uneasy premonition filled Leigh with dread. "Yesterday, in the morning, before he left for the mountains. I planned to join him there right after my Sunday matinee performance, but I didn't get there," she added needlessly.

"Yesterday was Monday. This is Tuesday night," Shrader said carefully. "You've been here since six A.M. yesterday."

Fear made Leigh forget about her injured body. "Where is my husband?" she demanded, levering herself up on her elbows and gasping at the stabbing pain in her ribs. "Why isn't he here? What's wrong? What's happened?"

"Probably nothing," Detective Littleton said quickly. "In fact, he's probably worried sick, wondering where you are. The problem is, we haven't been able to contact him to tell him what happened to you."

"How long have you been trying?"

"Since early yesterday morning, when the New York State Highway Patrol requested our assistance," Shrader replied. "One of our police officers was dispatched immediately to your apartment on the Upper East Side, but no one was home."

He paused for a moment, as if to make certain she was following his explanation; then he continued, "The officer spoke with your doorman and learned that you have a housekeeper named Hilda Brunner, so he asked the doorman to notify him as soon as she arrived."

Leigh felt as if the room were starting to rock back and forth. "Has anyone spoken to Hilda yet?"

"Yes." From the pocket of his flannel shirt, Shrader removed a notepad and consulted his notes. "Your doorman saw Miss Brunner enter your building at two-twenty that afternoon. He notified Officer Perkins, who then returned to your building at two-forty P.M. and spoke with Miss Brunner. Unfortunately, Miss Brunner didn't know exactly where you and your husband had planned to spend Sunday evening. Officer Perkins then asked Miss Brunner to check the messages on your answering machine, which she did. Seventeen messages had accumulated on your answering machine between Sunday at one-fourteen P.M. and Monday at two-forty-five P.M., but none of them were from your husband."

He closed his notebook. "Until now, I'm afraid we haven't been able to do much more than that. However," he added quickly, "the mayor and Captain Holland both want you to know that the NYPD is going to assist you in every way we can. That's why we're here."

Leigh eased back against the pillows, her mind falling over itself as she tried to grasp what seemed to be a terrifyingly bizarre situation. "You don't know my husband. If he thought I was missing, he wouldn't stop at calling our apartment. He'd call the state police, the governor, and every police department within a hundred fifty miles. He'd go out searching for me himself. Something has happened to him, something terrible enough to—"

"You're making too many assumptions," Detective Littleton interrupted firmly. "He might not have been able to use a telephone or go out looking for you. The blizzard knocked out telephone and electrical service in a one-hundred-mile radius, and in many areas, it still hasn't been restored. Almost a foot and a half of snow fell, and none of it is melting. Snowdrifts are eight feet high in places, and the plows have only been able to clear the main roads. The side roads and private roads up here are mostly impassable."

"The cabin doesn't have any electricity or phone service, but Logan would have had his cell phone with him," Leigh told her, growing more frantic with each moment. "He *always* has it with him, but he didn't try to call me, or warn me to stay home, even though he must have known I was driving into a bad storm. That isn't like him. He would have tried to call me!"

"He probably couldn't use his cell phone," Detective Littleton argued with a reassuring smile. "Mine doesn't work very well up here. You said the cabin doesn't have electricity, so even if your husband's cell phone was working, it's possible he decided to leave it on a charger in his vehicle, rather than take it inside. The blizzard came on very suddenly. If your husband was taking a nap, or doing something else, when it started snowing, it might have been too late to get to his car and his phone when he finally realized there was a problem. The snowdrifts are unbelievable."

"You could be right," Leigh said, clinging fiercely to the fairly plausible theory that Logan was safe but unable to use his phone or dig his Jeep out of the snow.

Shrader removed a pen from his pocket and opened his notebook again. "If you'll tell us where this cabin is, we'll go out there and look around."

Leigh gazed at both detectives in renewed alarm. "I don't know where it is. Logan drew a map so I could find it. It doesn't have an address."

"Okay, where is the map?"

"In my car."

"Where is your car?"

"At the bottom of a lake or a quarry, near wherever I was found. Wait—I can draw you another map," she added quickly, reaching for Detective Shrader's notebook.

Weakness and tension made Leigh's hand shake as she drew first one map and then another. "I think that second one is right," she said. "Logan wrote notes on the map he drew for me," she added as she turned to a fresh page and tried to write the same notes for the detectives.

"What sort of notes?"

"Landmarks to help me know I was getting close to the turnoffs."

When she was finished, Leigh handed the notebook to Shrader, but she spoke to Littleton. "I might have gotten the distances a little wrong. I mean, I'm not sure whether my husband's map said to go eight-tenths of a mile past an old filling station and then turn right, or whether it was *six*-tenths of a mile. You see, it was snowing," Leigh said as tears choked her voice, "and I couldn't—couldn't find some of the landmarks."

"We'll find them, Miss Kendall," Shrader said automatically as he closed his notebook and shrugged into his jacket. "In the meantime, the mayor, the police commissioner, and our captain, all send you their regards."

Leigh turned her face away to hide the tears beginning to stream from her eyes. "Detective Shrader, I would appreciate it very much if you would call me Mrs. Manning. Kendall is my stage name."

NEITHER SHRADER nor Littleton spoke until they were in the elevator and the doors had closed. "I'll bet Manning went out looking for her in that blizzard," Shrader said. "If he did, he's already a Popsicle."

Privately, Samantha Littleton thought there were several, less dire possible explanations for Logan Manning's absence, but it wasn't worth arguing about. Shrader had been in a foul mood for two days, ever since Holland pulled him off the homicide cases he was working, and sent Sam and him to Mountainside. She couldn't blame Shrader for feeling angry and insulted at being turned into what he regarded as "a celebrity baby-sitter." Shrader was a dedicated, tenacious, overworked homicide detective with an outstanding record for clearing his cases. She, on the other hand, was new to Homicide and, in fact, had only transferred to the Eighteenth Precinct two weeks before, when she'd been temporarily assigned to Shrader until his regular partner returned from sick leave. Sam understood and even shared Shrader's frustrated urgency about the cases piling up at the Eighteenth, but she prided herself on her ability to deal with frustrations without inflicting them on others. Masculine displays of irritability and outrage, like the ones Shrader had been indulging in for two days, struck her as being amusing, adolescent, or mildly annoying—and, occasionally, all three.

She'd chosen a career in a field dominated by macho men, many of whom still resented the encroachment of women into what had been their domain. But unlike some other women in law enforcement, Sam felt no compulsion to make her male colleagues accept her, and absolutely no desire to prove she could compete with them on their own level. She already knew she could.

She'd grown up with six rowdy older brothers, and she'd realized as a ten-year-old that when one of them shoved her, it was futile to try to shove him back harder. It was far easier, and far more satisfying, to simply step aside. And then stick out her foot.

As an adult, she'd converted that tactic to a mental one, and it was even easier to execute because most men were so disarmed by her pretty face and soft voice that they foolishly mistook her for a sweet, ornamental pushover. The fact that men underestimated her, particularly at first, didn't faze Sam in the least. It amused her and it gave her an edge.

Despite all that, she genuinely liked and respected most men. But she also understood them, and because she did, she was serenely unperturbed by their foibles and antics. There was little they could say to shock or anger her. She'd survived life with six older brothers. She'd already heard and seen it all.

"God dammit!" Shrader swore suddenly, slapping his hand on the elevator wall for emphasis.

Sam continued fastening her jacket. She did not ask

him what was wrong. He was a man who'd just cursed and then hit an inanimate object. It followed that he would now feel compelled to explain the unexplainable. Which, of course, he did.

"We'll have to go back upstairs. I forgot to ask her for a description of her husband's vehicle."

"It's a white Jeep Cherokee, brand-new, registered to Manning Development," Sam told him, digging her gloves out of her pockets. "I called DMV a little while ago, just in case Mrs. Manning couldn't talk much when she finally came around."

"You called DMV on your cell phone?" Shrader mocked. "The phone that doesn't work up here in the mountains?"

"The very same one," Sam admitted with a smile as the elevator doors opened. "Mrs. Manning needed some sort of explanation for her husband's absence, and that was the most reassuring one I could think of at the moment."

The lobby of Good Samaritan Hospital was deserted except for two maintenance men who were polishing the terrazzo floor. Shrader raised his voice to be heard above the noisy machines. "If you're going to get all soft and gooey every time you talk to a victim's family, you won't last two months in Homicide, Littleton."

"I've made it two weeks already," she replied brightly.

"If you hadn't transferred to Homicide, I'd be back at the Eighteen, doing my job instead of sitting on my ass up here."

"Maybe, but if I hadn't transferred, I would never have had the chance to work with someone like you."

Shrader shot her a suspicious glance, searching for signs of sarcasm, but her smile was perfectly pleasant. "Logan Manning doesn't even qualify as a missing-person case. He's a misplaced person."

"And you think it's my fault that Captain Holland sent us up here?"

"You're damned right." He pushed his shoulder against the exit door, and the blast of arctic wind nearly blew both of them back a step. "The Mannings are VIPs. The mayor and Commissioner Trumanti are both personal friends of theirs, so Holland decided he'd better send someone 'with social polish' to deal with Mrs. Manning."

Sam treated that like a joke. "And he thinks I have it?"

"That's what he said."

"So, why did he send you along?"

"Just in case there was any actual work that needed to be done." Shrader waited for her to return his insult, and when she didn't, he began to feel like a bad-tempered jerk. To even out the score, he poked fun at himself. "And also because he thinks I have a great ass."

"Did he say that, too?"

"No, but I saw him checking me out."

Sam couldn't help laughing. Shrader knew his appearance was anything but attractive; in fact, it was downright daunting to strangers. Although he was only five feet six, he had massive shoulders that were disproportionately large for his short body and that complemented his thick neck, square head with wide jowls, and piercing deep-set brown-black eyes. When he scowled, he reminded Sam of an angry rottweiler. When he wasn't scowling, he still reminded Sam of a rottweiler. Privately, she'd nicknamed him "Shredder."

Back upstairs, on the third floor of the hospital, a young doctor was standing at the foot of Leigh's bed, reading her chart. He left quietly, closing the door behind him. The additional morphine he'd ordered was already seeping through Leigh's veins, dulling the physical ache that suffused her body. She sought refuge from the torment in her mind by thinking about the last night she'd spent with Logan, when everything had seemed so perfect and the future had seemed so bright. Saturday night. Her birthday. And the opening night of Jason Solomon's new play.

Logan had given a huge party afterward to celebrate both occasions. . . .

CHAPTER 2

"**B**ravo! Bravo!" Six curtain calls and the applause was still at a deafening roar. The cast was lined up onstage, taking their bows one at a time, but when Leigh stepped forward, the cheers rose to a wild crescendo. The houselights were up, and Leigh could see Logan in the front row, on his feet, clapping and cheering with enthusiastic pride. She smiled at him, and he gave her a thumbs-up.

When the curtains closed, she walked to the wings where Jason was standing, his face beaming with triumph. "We're a smash hit, Jason!" she said, giving him a hug.

"Let's take another bow, just you and me this time," he said.

Jason would have taken curtain calls all night until the last theatergoer left his seat. "Nope," Leigh said with a grin. "We've both taken enough bows."

He tugged on her hand, a happy thirty-five-year-old child—brilliant, insecure, sensitive, selfish, loyal, temperamental, kind. "C'mon, Leigh," he cajoled. "Just one more little bow. We deserve it." The crowd began chanting, "Author! Author!" and his grin widened. "They really want to see me again."

He was in an ecstatic mood, and Leigh looked at him with a mixture of maternal understanding and awe. Jason Solomon could dazzle her at times with his intellect, hurt her with his insensitivity, and warm her with his gentleness. Those who didn't know him thought of him as a glamorous eccentric. Those who knew him better generally regarded Jason as a brilliant, irritating egocentric. To Leigh, who knew him, and loved him, he was a complete dichotomy.

"Listen to that applause," he said, tugging on her hand. "Let's go out there . . ."

Helpless to resist him in this mood, Leigh relented, but stepped back. "Go for it," she said. "I'll stay here."

Instead of releasing her hand, he tightened his grip and dragged her with him. She was off balance when they emerged from the wings, and her surprised resistance was plain to see. The moment of unplanned confusion struck the crowd as wonderful. It made the two biggest names on Broadway seem endearingly human, and the riotous applause was joined with shouts of laughter.

Jason would have tried to coax her into taking yet another bow after that one, but Leigh freed her hand this time and turned away, laughing. "Don't forget the old adage—" she reminded him over her shoulder, "Always leave them wanting more."

"That's a cliché," he retorted indignantly.

"But true, nonetheless."

He hesitated a moment, then followed her backstage, down a hallway crowded with elated cast and busy crew members, who were all trying to congratulate and thank each other. Jason and Leigh stopped several times to participate in the congratulatory hugging.

"I told you the twenty-eighth was always my lucky day."

"You were right," Leigh agreed. Jason insisted on opening all his plays on the twenty-eighth including *Blind Spot*, even though as a general rule, Broadway plays did not open on Saturdays.

"I feel like champagne," Jason announced as they finally neared Leigh's dressing room.

"So do I, but I need to change clothes and get this makeup off right away. We have a party to attend, and I'd like to get there before midnight."

A theater critic was congratulating the play's director, and Jason watched him closely for a moment. "No one will mind if we're late."

"Jason," Leigh reminded him with amused patience, "I'm the guest of honor. I should make an effort to get there before the party is over."

"I suppose so," he agreed, dragging his gaze from the critic. He followed her into her flower-filled dressing room, where the dresser was waiting to help Leigh out of the cheap cotton skirt and blouse she'd been wearing in the last act.

"Who are these from?" Jason asked, strolling over to a gigantic basket of huge white orchids. "They must have cost a fortune."

Leigh glanced at the immense bouquet. "I don't know."

"There's a card attached," Jason said, already reaching for the florist's envelope. "Shall I read it?"

"Could I stop you?" Leigh joked. Jason's nosiness was legendary. Behind the folding screen, Leigh stepped out of her clothes and into a robe; then she hurried over to her dressing table and sat down in front of the big lighted mirror.

With the open envelope in his hand, Jason caught her gaze in the mirror and gave her a sly smile. "You've evidently acquired a serious suitor with big bucks. Come clean, darling, who is he? You know you can trust me with your sordid secrets."

His last sentence made Leigh laugh. "You've never kept a secret in your life, sordid or otherwise," she told his reflection in the mirror.

"True, but tell me who he is, anyway."

"What does the card say?"

Instead of telling her, Jason handed it to her so she could read it herself. "LOVE ME," it said. Leigh's brief frown of confusion gave way to a smile as she put down the card and began removing her stage makeup. "It's from Logan," she told him.

"Why would your husband send you one thousand dollars' worth of orchids with a card asking you to love him?"

Before replying, Leigh finished spreading cream over her face and began wiping off her makeup with tissues. "When Logan told the florist what to write on the card, the florist obviously misunderstood and forgot to put a comma after the word 'love.' It should have read, 'Love comma Me.' "

A bottle of Dom Pérignon was chilling in a bucket, and Jason spotted it. "Why would Logan call himself 'me' instead of calling himself 'Logan'?" he asked as he lifted the bottle from its icy nest and began unpeeling the black foil from the bottle's neck.

"That's probably my fault," she admitted with a quick, rueful glance at him. "The Crescent Plaza project has been consuming Logan for months, and I asked him to relax a little. He's trying to be more playful and spontaneous for my sake."

Jason gaped at her in laughing derision. "Logan? Spontaneous and playful? You can't be serious." He poured champagne into two flutes and put one on the dressing table for her; then he settled himself onto the little sofa at her left, propped his legs on the coffee table, and crossed his feet at the ankles. "In case you haven't noticed, your husband thinks a five-star restaurant is just a badly lit conference room with forks. He thinks a briefcase is an indispensable fashion accessory, and he depreciates his golf clubs."

"Stop picking on Logan," she told him. "He's a brilliant businessman."

"He's a brilliant *bore*," Jason retorted, clearly enjoying the rare opportunity to joke about someone he actually admired and even envied. "If you wanted playfulness and spontaneity in a man, you should have had an affair with *me* instead of turning to this orchid guy for those traits."

She flashed him an amused, affectionate look and ignored his reference to the orchids. "You're gay, Jason."

"Well, yes," he agreed with a grin. "I suppose that could have been an impediment to our affair."

"How's Eric?" Leigh asked, deliberately changing the subject. Eric had been Jason's "significant other" for over six months—which almost set a longevity record where Jason was concerned. "I didn't see him out front tonight."

"He was there," Jason said indifferently. He shifted his foot from side to side, studying his shiny black tuxedo loafers. "Eric is becoming a bit of a bore, too, to tell you the truth."

"You are very easily bored," Leigh said with a knowing look.

"You're right."

"If you want my opinion—"

"Which, of course, I don't," Jason interrupted.

"And which, of course, I'm going to give anyway—If you want my opinion, maybe you should try to find someone who isn't so much like you that he seems predictable and boring. Try going with someone who depreciates his golf clubs for a change."

"Someone who is so gorgeous that I could overlook his boring traits? As a matter of fact, I do know someone like that!"

He was being so agreeable that Leigh shot him a suspicious look before she tossed a tissue into the wastebasket and began putting on her regular makeup. "You do?"

"Yes, indeed," Jason said with a wicked grin. "He has thick light brown hair streaked blond from the summer sun, beautiful eyes, and a great physique. He's a little too preppy-looking for my tastes, but he's thirty-five, and that's a good age for me. He's from an old aristocratic New York family that ran out of money long before he was born, so it was up to him to restore the family fortune, which he's managed to do single-handedly . . ."

Leigh finally realized he was describing Logan, and her shoulders began to shake with laughter. "You're a lunatic."

Jason's short attention span led him from romance to business without a pause between. "What a night!" he sighed, leaning his head back against the sofa. "I was right to change your lines in the last scene of the second act. Did you notice how strongly the audience reacted? One minute everyone was laughing; then they realized what you were actually going to do and they ended up crying. In the space of a few lines, they went from mirth to tears. Now that, my darling, is brilliant writing—and brilliant acting, of course." He paused for a sip of champagne and, after a moment of thoughtful silence, added, "After I see the matinee tomorrow, I may want to change a little of the dialogue between you and Jane in the third act. I haven't decided."

Leigh said nothing as she quickly applied the rest of her makeup, brushed her hair, and then disappeared behind the screen to change into the dress she'd brought to the theater. Outside the dressing room, the noise level had risen dramatically as actors, crew members, and people with enough influence to obtain backstage passes all began leaving the theater by the rear door, laughing and talking as they headed off to celebrate the night's triumph with friends and families. Ordinarily, Jason and she would be doing the same thing, but today was Leigh's thirty-fifth birthday, and Logan was determined that it not take second place to the play's opening night.

She emerged from behind the screen wearing a deceptively simple red silk sheath with tiny beaded straps at the shoulders, matching high heels, and a jeweled Judith Leiber evening bag that dangled from her fingers by a narrow chain.

"Red?" Jason said, grinning as he slowly stood up. "I've never seen you wear red before."

"Logan specifically asked me to wear something red to the party tonight."

"Really, why?"

"Probably because he's being playful," Leigh said smugly; then uncertainty replaced her jaunty expression. "Do I look all right in this?"

Jason passed a slow, appraising glance over her gleaming, shoulder-length auburn hair, large aquamarine eyes, and high cheekbones; then he let it drop to her narrow waist, and down her long legs. She was pretty, but certainly not gorgeous, and not even beautiful, he observed. And yet in a roomful of women who were, Leigh Kendall would have drawn notice and attracted attention the moment she moved or spoke. In an attempt to define her powerful presence onstage, critics likened her to a young Katharine Hepburn or a young Ethel Barrymore, but Jason knew they were wrong. Onstage, she had Hepburn's incomparable glow and she had Barrymore's legendary depth, but she had something else, too, something infinitely more appealing and uniquely her own—a mesmerizing charisma that was as potent when she was standing in her dressing room, waiting for his opinion about her attire, as when she was onstage. She was the most even-tempered, cooperative actress he'd ever known; and yet there was a mystery about her, a barrier, that no one was allowed to cross. She took her work seriously, but she did not take herself seriously, and at times her humility and sense of humor made him feel like a towering, temperamental egotist.

"I'm starting to wish I had a pair of jeans and a sweatshirt on," she joked, reminding him that she was waiting for an opinion.

"Okay," he said, "here it is—the unvarnished truth: Although you aren't nearly as gorgeous as your husband, you are remarkably attractive for a woman."

"In the unlikely event that that was meant to be a big compliment," Leigh said, laughing as she opened the closet door and removed her coat, "thanks a lot."

Jason was truly stunned by her lack of perspective. "Of course it was a compliment, Leigh, but why would you care how you look right now? What matters is that an hour ago, you convinced four hundred people that you are actually a thirty-year-old blind woman who unknowingly holds the key to solving an unspeakable murder. You had every member of that audience squirming in his seat with terror!" Jason threw up his hands in bewildered disgust. "My God, why would a woman who can do all that give a damn how she looks in a cocktail dress?"

Leigh opened her mouth to reply; then she smiled and shook her head. "It's a girl thing," she said dryly, glancing at her watch.

"I see." He swept the dressing room door open and stepped aside in an exaggerated gesture of gallantry. "After you," he said; then he offered her his arm and she took it, but as they started down the back hall, he sobered. "When we get to the party, I'm going to ask Logan if he sent you those orchids."

"I'd rather you didn't worry yourself or Logan about that tonight," Leigh said, keeping her tone light. "Even if Logan didn't send them, it doesn't really matter. We've taken precautions—I have a chauffeur-bodyguard now. Matt and Meredith Farrell lent him to me for six months while they're away. He's like a member of their family when they're home in Chicago. I'm very well protected."

Despite Leigh's reassuring words, she couldn't completely suppress a tremor of anxiety about the orchids. Recently, she'd received some anonymous gifts, all of them expensive and several with blatant sexual overtones, like a black lace garter belt and bra from Neiman Marcus and a sheer, extremely seductive nightgown from Bergdorf Goodman. The small, white cards that accompanied the gifts bore short, cryptic messages like, "Wear this for me" and "I want to see you in this."

She'd received a phone call at home the day after the first gift was delivered to the theater. "Are you wearing your present, Leigh?" a man's soft, cajoling voice had asked on the answering machine.

Last week, Leigh had visited Saks, where she'd purchased a robe for Logan and a little enamel pin for herself, which she'd tucked into her coat pocket. She had been about to step off the curb at Fifth and Fifty-first Street with a crowd of other pedestrians when a man's hand reached forward from behind her, holding a small Saks bag. "You dropped this," he said politely. Startled, Leigh automatically took the bag and dropped it into the larger one containing Logan's robe, but when she looked around to thank him, either he'd retreated farther back into the crowd of pedestrians or he was the man she saw walking swiftly

down the street, his overcoat turned up to his ears, head
bent against the wind.

When she got home with her purchases, Leigh realized
her own small bag from Saks was still in her coat pocket,
where she'd originally put it. The bag the man had handed
her on the street contained a narrow silver band, like a
wedding ring. The card said "You're mine."

Despite all that, she was certain the orchids in her
dressing room were from Logan. He knew they were her favorite flower.

IN THE ALLEY BEHIND THE THEATER, Leigh's new chauffeur-bodyguard was standing beside the open door of a limousine. "The show was a big hit, Mrs. Manning, and you
were terrific!"

"Thank you, Joe."

Jason settled into the luxurious automobile and nodded with satisfaction. "Everyone should have his very own
bodyguard-chauffeur."

"You may not think so a moment from now," Leigh
warned him with a rueful smile as the chauffeur slid behind
the steering wheel and put the car into gear. "He drives like
a—" The car suddenly rocketed forward, throwing them
back against their seats and barging into heavy oncoming
traffic.

"Maniac!" Jason swore, grabbing for the armrest with
one hand and Leigh's wrist with the other.

CHAPTER 3

Leigh and Logan's apartment occupied the entire twenty-fourth floor. It had a private elevator lobby that functioned as an exterior "foyer" for their apartment, and Leigh inserted her key into the elevator lock so that the doors would open on her floor.

As soon as the elevator opened, the sounds of a large party in full swing greeted them from beyond her apartment's front door. "Sounds like a good party," Jason remarked, helping her out of her coat and handing it to Leigh's housekeeper, who materialized in the outer foyer to take their coats. "Happy birthday, Mrs. Manning," Hilda said.

"Thank you, Hilda."

Together, Jason and Leigh stepped into the apartment onto a raised marble foyer that offered a clear view of rooms overflowing with animated, elegantly dressed, beautiful people who were laughing, drinking, and nibbling canapés from trays being passed around by a battalion of waiters in dinner jackets. Jason instantly spotted people he knew and headed down the steps, but Leigh remained where she was, struck suddenly by the beauty of the setting, its portrayal of the success and prosperity that Logan and she had achieved together in their individual careers. Someone spotted her then and started a loud chorus of "Happy Birthday to You!"

Logan arrived at her side with a drink that he placed in her hand and a kiss that he placed on her mouth. "You were fantastic tonight. Happy birthday, darling," he said. While their guests watched, he reached into his tuxedo jacket pocket and produced a Tiffany box tied with silk ribbon. "Go ahead and open it," he prodded.

Leigh looked at him uncertainly. "Now?" Normally Logan preferred privacy for sentimental moments, but he was in a boyishly carefree mood tonight.

"Now," he agreed, his eyes smiling into hers. "Absolutely, now."

It was either a ring or earrings, Leigh guessed, judging from the size and shape of the cream leather box that slid out of the robin's egg blue outer box. Inside was a spectacular ruby-and-diamond pendant in the shape of a heart. Now she understood why he'd wanted her to wear something red. "It's magnificent," she said, incredibly touched that he had spent so much money on her. No matter how much money Logan made, he felt almost guilty about spending it on anything that wasn't likely to become a profit-making asset or at least a tax deduction.

"I'll help you fasten the chain," he said, lifting the glittering pendant from its case. "Turn around." When he finished, he turned her back around so that their guests could see the magnificent pendant, lying just below her throat. The gift earned a round of applause and cries of approval.

"Thank you," Leigh said softly, her eyes shining.

He looped his arm around her shoulders and laughingly said, "I'll expect a more appropriate thank-you later, when we're alone. That bauble cost two hundred and fifty thousand dollars."

Stunned and amused, Leigh whispered back, "I'm not sure I know how to express a quarter of a million dollars' worth of gratitude."

"It won't be easy, but I'll make some helpful suggestions and recommendations, later tonight."

"I'd appreciate that," she teased, watching his gaze turn warm and sexy.

He sighed and put his hand under her elbow, guiding her down the marble steps to the living room. "Unfortunately, before we can take care of that very important matter, we have a few hours of obligatory socializing to perform." On the bottom step, he paused and looked around. "There's someone here I want you to meet."

As they wended their way slowly through the noisy, crowded rooms, greeting their guests, Leigh was struck anew by the almost comic contrast between Logan's friends and business acquaintances and her own. Most of Logan's friends were members of New York's oldest and most influential families; they were bankers and philanthropists, judges and senators, all of them with "old" money. Quiet money. They were expensively but conservatively attired and impeccably behaved, with wives who matched them perfectly.

In comparison to them, Leigh's friends seemed absolutely flamboyant; they were artists, actors, musicians, and writers—people who equated "fitting in" with being overlooked, and that was anathema to them. The two groups didn't avoid each other, but neither did they mingle. While Leigh's friend Theta Berenson expounded on the merits of a new art exhibit to her group, the huge yellow feathers on her hat continually brushed against the ear of the investment banker behind her. The banker, who was a friend of Logan's, irritably brushed the feathers aside while he continued discussing a new strategy for portfolio reallocations with Sheila Winters, a highly respected therapist. Leigh and Logan had met with Sheila a few times to smooth out conflicts in their relationship a couple of years earlier; in the intervening time she had become a dear friend. When she looked over for a moment and saw Leigh, she blew a kiss and waved.

Although Logan and Leigh stopped frequently to chat with their guests, Logan didn't allow his wife to linger long. He was searching for whoever it was that he wanted her to meet. "There he is, over there," Logan said finally, and immediately began guiding Leigh toward a tall, dark-haired man who was standing completely by himself at the far end of the living room, looking at an oil painting that was hanging on the wall. His bored expression and aloof stance made it very obvious he wasn't interested in the artwork, or in the party, for that matter.

Leigh recognized him at once, but his presence in her home was so unlikely that she couldn't believe her eyes. She stopped short, staring at Logan in horrified disbelief. "That can't be who I think it is!"

"Who do you think it is?"

"I think it's Michael Valente."

"You're right." He urged her forward, but Leigh was rooted to the floor, staring at Valente, aghast. "He wants to meet you, Leigh. He's a big fan of yours."

"Who let him in here?"

"I invited him," Logan explained patiently. "I haven't mentioned him to you before, because the deal isn't finalized, but Valente is considering putting up *all* the venture capital for the entire Crescent Plaza project. I've had several meetings with him. He has a genius for putting together highly lucrative business deals."

"And for avoiding prosecution afterward," Leigh retorted darkly. "Logan, he's a criminal!"

"He's only been *convicted* of wrongdoing once," Logan said, chuckling at her indignant reaction. "Now he's a respectable billionaire with an incredible track record for turning risky commercial projects, like Crescent Plaza, into wildly successful ones that make a fortune for everyone."

"He's a felon!"

"That was a long time ago, and it was probably a bum rap."

"No it wasn't! I read that he pleaded guilty."

Instead of being annoyed, Logan gazed at her mutinous expression with amused admiration. "How have you done it?"

"Done what?"

"Maintained the same rigid, wonderful values you had when we first met?"

" 'Rigid' doesn't sound like a good thing to me."

"On you," he said softly, " 'rigid' is a wonderful thing."

Leigh scarcely heard that as she looked around the room. She spotted Judge Maxwell and Senator Hollenbeck, who were standing against the wall behind the buffet—as far as they could physically get from where Valente was standing. "Logan, there isn't a man in this house with a reputation to safeguard who is anywhere near Michael Valente. They've gotten as far away from him as they can."

"Maxwell is no saint, and Hollenbeck's closets have barely enough room for all his skeletons," Logan said emphatically, but as he looked around, he reached the same conclusion that Leigh had reached. "It probably wasn't wise to invite Valente."

"What made you do it?"

"It was an impulse. I phoned him this afternoon to discuss some contractual details for Crescent Plaza, and I mentioned that your play was opening tonight and we were having a party afterward. He mentioned the play, and he said he was a big fan of yours. I knew there wasn't a seat to be had in the theater tonight, so I compromised and invited him to the party instead. I had so many things going on I didn't stop to consider that his being here might be awkward, particularly for Sanders and Murray. Will you do me a favor, darling?"

"Yes, of course," Leigh replied, relieved that Logan was at least acknowledging the problem.

"I've already spoken with Valente tonight. If you don't mind introducing yourself to him, I'll go over and soothe Sanders's and Murray's offended sensibilities. Valente drinks Glenlivet—no ice, no water. See that he gets a fresh drink, and play hostess for a few minutes. That's all you have to do."

"And then what? Leave him there by himself? Who can I possibly introduce him to?"

Logan's dry sense of humor made his eyes gleam as he glanced around the room, looking for possible candidates. "That's easy. Introduce your friend Claire Straight to him; she'll tell anyone who'll listen about her divorce. Jason and Eric already look ready to strangle her." At that moment, Claire, Jason, and Eric all looked up, and Logan and Leigh waved to them. "Claire—" Logan called, "don't forget to tell Jason and Eric all about your lawyer and how he sold you out. Ask them if you should sue him for malpractice."

"You are an evil man," Leigh said with a giggle.

"That's why you love me," Logan replied. "It's too bad that Valente isn't gay," he joked. "If he was, you could fix him up with Jason. That way, Jason would end up with a lover *and* a permanent backer for all his plays. Of course, that would make Eric jealous and even more suicidal than usual, so that's probably not a good idea." He resumed his thoughtful surveillance of their guests until Theta's yellow-feathered hat captured his notice. "I suppose we could introduce him to Theta. She's ugly as sin, but Valente has a fabulous art collection, and she's an artist—allegedly."

"Her last canvas just sold for one hundred seventy-five thousand dollars. There's nothing 'alleged' about that."

"Leigh, she painted that thing with her elbows and a floor mop."

"She did not."

Logan was laughing in earnest, and he covered it by lifting his glass to his mouth. "Yes, she did, darling. She told me so." Suddenly his delighted gaze shifted to an attractive blonde standing with the same group. "The Valente problem is solved. Let's introduce him to your friend Sybil Haywood. She can tell his fortune—"

"Sybil is an astrologer, not a fortune-teller," Leigh put in firmly.

"What's the difference?"

"That depends on whom you ask," Leigh said, feeling a little put out with Logan's blanket joking dismissal of her friends, and Sybil in particular. Leigh paused to nod and smile graciously at two couples nearby; then she added, "Sybil has many famous clients, including Nancy Reagan. Regardless of whether you believe in astrology, Sybil is as committed to her field and her clients as you are to yours."

Logan was instantly contrite. "I'm sure she is. And thank you for not pointing out that my friends and I are as boring as dust, and our conversations are predictable and tedious. Now, do you think Sybil would take Valente off our hands as a favor and spend a little time with him tonight?"

"She will if I ask her to," Leigh said, already deciding that the plan was a viable one.

Satisfied that a compromise had been worked out, Logan gave her shoulders a light hug. "Don't stay away from me too long. This is your big night, but I'd like to be as much a part of it as I can."

It was such an openly sentimental thing to say that Leigh instantly forgave him for joking about her friends and even for inviting Valente. As Logan brushed a kiss on her cheek and left, Leigh glanced in Valente's direction and discovered he was no longer looking at the painting. He had turned and had been staring directly at them. She wondered uneasily how much of their debate he had witnessed and if he'd guessed that he was the cause of it. It wouldn't have taken much imagination on his part, Leigh decided. She suspected that whenever Valente managed to intrude on respectable social gatherings, most hostesses probably reacted with the same resentment and reluctance that Leigh felt right now.

CHAPTER 4

Hastily smoothing the expression of distaste from her face, Leigh moved sideways through the crush of guests until she reached Sybil Haywood's group. "Sybil, I need a favor," she said, drawing the astrologer aside. "I have an awkward social problem—"

"You certainly do," Sybil agreed with a knowing grin. "Virgos can be very difficult to deal with, especially when Pluto and Mars are—"

"No, no. It's not an astrological problem. I need someone I can trust who can deal with a particular man—"

"Who happens to be a Virgo—" Sybil stated positively.

Leigh adored Sybil, but at the moment, the astrologer's fixation on astrology was driving her crazy. "Sybil, please. I have no idea what his astrological sign is. If you'll take him off my hands and chat with him for a few minutes, you can ask him your—"

"Valente is a Virgo," Sybil interjected patiently.

Leigh blinked at her. "How did you know?"

"I know, because when the Senate was investigating

him last September Valente was asked to give his full name and date of birth. The *Times* reported on his testimony, and the reporter noted that Valente was actually testifying on his forty-third birthday. That told me he was a Virgo."

"No, I mean how did you know that Valente is my 'awkward social problem'?"

"Oh, that," Sybil said with a laugh as she passed a slow, meaningful glance over all the other guests within view. "He does stand out in this crowd of politicians, bankers, and business leaders. There's not another criminal in the entire place for him to socialize with— Actually there are probably a lot of criminals here, but they haven't been caught and sent to prison like he was."

"You could be right," Leigh said absently. "I'm going to introduce myself to him. Would you get him a drink and bring it over in a couple of minutes so I can escape gracefully?"

Sybil grinned. "You want me to socialize with a tall, antisocial, semihandsome man who happens to have a murky past, a questionable present, and fifteen billion dollars in assets, probably all from ill-gotten gains? Is that it?"

"Pretty much," Leigh admitted ruefully.

"What shall I bring him to drink? Blood?"

"Glenlivet," Leigh said, giving her a quick hug. "No ice, no water, no blood."

She watched Sybil begin working her way toward one of the bars, and with reluctant resignation, Leigh pasted a smile on her face and wended her way toward Valente. He studied her with detached curiosity as she approached, his expression so uninviting that Leigh doubted he was actually "a fan" of hers or even that he particularly wanted to meet her. By the time she was close enough to hold out her hand to him, she'd noted that he was at least six feet three inches tall with extremely wide, muscular shoulders, thick, black hair, and hard, piercing amber eyes.

Leigh held out her hand. "Mr. Valente?"

"Yes."

"I'm Leigh Manning."

He smiled a little at that—a strange, speculative smile that didn't quite reach his eyes. With his gaze locked onto hers, he took her hand in a clasp that was a little too tight and lasted a little too long. "How do you do, Mrs. Manning—" he said in a rich baritone voice that was more cultured than Leigh had expected it to be.

Leigh exerted enough pressure to indicate she wanted her hand released and he let it go, but his unnerving gaze remained locked on hers as he said, "I enjoyed your performance very much tonight."

"I'm surprised you were there," Leigh said without thinking. Based on what she knew of him, he didn't seem the type to enjoy a sensitive theatrical drama with a lot of subtleties.

"Perhaps you thought I'd be knocking off a liquor store, instead?"

That was close enough to the truth to make Leigh feel exposed, and she didn't like it. "I *meant* that opening night tickets were virtually impossible to get."

His smile suddenly reached his eyes, warming them a little. "That's not what you meant, but it's charming of you to say so."

Leigh clutched at the first topic of common interest that came to mind. With an overbright smile, she said, "I understand you're thinking of going into some sort of business venture with my husband."

"You don't approve, of course," he said dryly.

Leigh felt as if she were being maneuvered into a series of uncomfortable corners. "Why would you think that?"

"I was watching you a few minutes ago when Logan told you I was here, and why I'm here."

Despite the man's unsavory background, he was a guest in her home, and Leigh was a little mortified that she'd let her negative feelings about him show so openly. Relying on the old adage that the best defense is a good offense, she said very firmly and politely, "You're a guest in my home, and I'm an actress, Mr. Valente. If I had any negative feelings about any guest, including you, you would never know it because I would never let them show."

"That's very reassuring," he said mildly.

"Yes, you were completely mistaken," Leigh added, pleased with her strategy.

"Does that mean you *don't* disapprove of my business involvement with your husband?"

"I didn't say that."

To her shock, he smiled at her evasive reply, a slow, strangely seductive, secretive smile that made his eyes gleam beneath their heavy lids. Others might not have noticed the nuances of it, but Leigh's career was based on subtleties of expression, and she instantly sensed peril lurking behind that come-hither smile of his. It was the dangerously beguiling smile of a ruthless predator, a predator who wanted her to sense his power, his defiance of the social order, and to be seduced by what he represented. Instead, Leigh was repelled. She jerked her gaze from his, and gestured to the painting on the wall, a painting that Logan wouldn't have let hang even in a closet under ordinary circumstances. "I noticed that you were admiring this painting earlier."

"Actually, I was admiring the frame, not the painting."

"It's early seventeenth century. It used to hang in Logan's grandfather's study."

"You can't be referring to that painting," he said scornfully.

"I was referring to the frame. The painting," she advised him with a twinge of amused vengeance, "was actually done by my husband's grandmother."

His gaze shifted sideways, from the painting to her face. "You could have spared me that knowledge."

He was right, but Sybil's arrival saved Leigh from having to reply. "Here's someone I'd like you to meet," she said a little too eagerly, and introduced the couple. "Sybil is a famous astrologer," Leigh added, and immediately resented his look of derision.

Undaunted by his reaction, Sybil smiled and held out her right hand, but he couldn't shake it because she was holding a drink in it. "I've been looking forward to meeting you," she said.

"Really, why?"

"I'm not sure yet," Sybil replied, extending her hand farther toward him. "This drink is for you. Scotch. No ice. No water. It's what you drink."

Eyeing her with cynical suspicion, he reluctantly took the drink. "Am I supposed to believe you know what I drink because you're an astrologer?"

"Would you believe that if I said it was true?"

"No."

"In that case, the truth is that I know what you drink because our hostess told me what you drink and asked me to get this for you."

His gaze lost some of its chill as it transferred to Leigh. "That was very thoughtful of you."

"Not at all," Leigh said, glancing over her shoulder, wishing she could leave. Sybil gave her the excuse she needed. "Logan asked me to tell you he needs you to settle some sort of debate about the play tonight."

"In that case, I'd better go and see about it." She smiled at Sybil, avoided shaking Valente's hand, and gave him a polite nod instead. "I'm glad to have met you," she lied. As she walked away, she heard Sybil say, "Let's find somewhere to sit down, Mr. Valente. You can tell me all about yourself. Or, if you prefer, *I* can tell you all about yourself."

IT WAS AFTER 4 A.M. when the last guest departed. Leigh turned out the lights, and they walked across the darkened living room together, Logan's arm around her waist. "How does it feel to be called 'the most gifted, multitalented actress to grace a Broadway stage in the last fifty years'?" he asked softly.

"Wonderful." Leigh had been running on excitement until they walked into their bedroom, but at the sight of the big four-poster bed with its fluffy duvet, her body seemed to lose all its strength. She started yawning before she made it into her dressing room, and she was in bed before Logan was out of the shower.

She felt the mattress shift slightly as he got into bed, and all she managed to muster was a smile when he kissed her cheek and jokingly whispered, "Is this how you thank a man for a fabulous ruby-and-diamond pendant?"

Leigh snuggled closer and smiled, already half asleep. "Yes," she whispered.

He chuckled. "I guess I'll have to wait until tonight in the mountains for you to properly express your gratitude."

It seemed like only five minutes later when Leigh awoke to find Logan already dressed and eager to leave for the mountains.

That had been Sunday morning.

This was Tuesday night.

Logan was lost somewhere out in the snow . . . probably waiting for Leigh to do something to rescue him.

CHAPTER 5

By ten-thirty Wednesday morning, Leigh's anxiety was almost beyond bearing. Detective Littleton had phoned three hours earlier to say that although the map Leigh had drawn hadn't been of much help the night before, she and Detective Shrader were already on the road again, following it through the mountains. She promised to call again as soon as they had anything to report.

All other incoming telephone calls were obviously being held by the hospital switchboard, because sometime during the night, someone had put a pile of phone messages on her nightstand. With nothing else to do to occupy her time, Leigh reread the phone messages that she'd only scanned earlier.

Jason had phoned six times; his next-to-last message had been frantic and curt: "The hospital switchboard is holding your damned calls, and you can't have visitors. Tell your doctors to let me up to see you and I can be there in three hours. Call me, Leigh. Call me first. Call me. Call me." He'd evidently called again, immediately after he'd hung up, because the time on the next message was only two minutes later. This time he wanted to reassure her about the play: "Jane is holding her own in your role, but she's not you. Try not to worry too much about the play." Leigh hadn't given a thought to the play or to her understudy, and her only reaction to Jason's message was a sense of amazement that he could imagine she'd care what happened to the damned play right now.

In addition to Jason's messages, there were dozens of telegrams and phone calls from business and personal acquaintances of Logan's and hers. Hilda had called, but the housekeeper had left no message except "Get well." Leigh's publicist and her secretary had both called, asking for instructions as soon as Leigh felt up to calling them.

Leigh continued leafing through the messages, finding a little bit of comfort in everyone's genuine concern—until she came to the message from Michael Valente. It read, "My thoughts are with you. Call me at this number if I can be of help in any way." His message instantly struck her as being too personal, very presumptuous, and completely inappropriate, but she realized her reaction was based more on her negative reaction to the man himself, than on what he'd said.

Unable to endure inactivity any longer, Leigh put the messages down, shoved the table with her untouched breakfast tray aside, and reached for the telephone. The hospital switchboard operator seemed startled and awed when she identified herself. "I'm sorry if you've been overloaded with phone calls," Leigh began.

"We don't mind, Mrs. Manning. That's what we're here for."

"Thank you. The reason I was calling," Leigh explained, "is that I wanted to be certain you aren't holding any calls that might come from the police department or from my husband."

"No, no, of course not. We would let the police through at once, and we all know your husband is missing. We'd never hold his call. Your doctor and the two police detectives from New York City gave us complete instructions about handling your calls. We're to put through any caller who says they have any information whatsoever about your husband, but we're to take messages from all other callers, except reporters. Calls from reporters are to be transferred to our administrator's office, so he can handle them."

"Thank you," Leigh said, weak with disappointment. "I'm sorry to cause you so much trouble."

"I've been praying for you and your husband," the operator said.

The sincerity and simplicity of that almost made Leigh cry. "Don't stop," she said, her voice strangled with fear and gratitude.

"I won't, I promise."

"I need to make some long distance calls," Leigh said shakily. "How can I do it from this phone?"

"Do you have a telephone credit card?"

Leigh's credit cards, wallet, and electronic phone book had all been in her purse in her car, but she knew her telephone credit card number by heart because she used it often. "Yes, I have one."

"Then all you have to do is dial nine for an outside line and use your card in the usual way." Despite what the detectives had said, Leigh tried to call Logan on his cell phone. When he didn't answer, she called Hilda to see if she'd heard anything, but the worried housekeeper could only repeat what she'd told the detectives.

Leigh was in the process of calling Jason when a hospital staff nurse bustled into her room and interrupted her. "How are you feeling this morning, Mrs. Manning?"

"Fine," Leigh lied as the nurse checked the tubes and containers attached to Leigh's body.

"Haven't you been using your morphine drip?" she asked, her expression puzzled and accusing.

"I don't need it. I feel fine." In truth, every inch of her body, from her toes to her hair, either ached or throbbed, and the nurse undoubtedly knew that. She stared at Leigh in frowning disbelief until Leigh finally relented and added, "I don't want the morphine because I need to be alert and sensible this morning."

"You need to be free of pain and resting comfortably so that your body can heal," the nurse argued.

"I'll use it later," Leigh promised.

"You also need to eat," she commanded, pushing the table with Leigh's breakfast tray up close to the bed.

As soon as she left, Leigh moved the breakfast tray out of the way and reached for the telephone. She woke Jason up.

"Leigh?" he mumbled sleepily. "Leigh! Jesus Christ!" he sputtered coming awake. "What the hell is going on? How are you? Have you heard from Logan? Is he all right?"

"There's been no word from Logan," Leigh said. "I'm okay. A little sore and banged up, that's all." She could feel Jason's conscience warring with his self-interest as he fought against his urge to demand to know when she could return to the play. "I need a favor," she said.

"Anything."

"I may want to hire my own people to help search for Logan. Who should I call to arrange it? Private detectives? Do you know anyone like that?"

"Darling, I can't believe you have the slightest doubt. How do you think I caught Jeremy cheating on me? How do you think I avoided paying off that charlatan who claimed—"

"Could you give me the name of the firm and the phone number?" Leigh interrupted.

By the time Leigh got a pen out of the drawer beside her bed and wrote down the phone number on the back of a telegram, she was hurting so badly she could scarcely think. She hung up and lay back against the pillows, concentrating on breathing without intensifying the pain in her ribs. She was still doing that when the nurse who'd been in the last time returned to her bedside and saw the untouched breakfast tray. "You really must eat, Mrs. Manning. You haven't eaten anything in days."

Leigh's private duty nurse had been much easier to ignore, but she'd gone home to sleep and wasn't due to return until evening. "I will, but not now—"

"I insist," the nurse countered as she moved the portable table over Leigh's lap. She whisked the plastic covers off the dishes. "What would you like first?" she inquired pleasantly. "The applesauce, the wheat germ with skim milk, or the poached egg?"

"I don't think I could swallow any of those things."

Frowning, the nurse glanced at the little list beside the tray. "This is what you ordered last night."

"I must have been delirious."

Evidently the nurse agreed, but she would not be deterred from achieving her goal. "I can send someone down to the cafeteria. What do you normally like to eat for breakfast?"

The simple question filled Leigh with such longing for her old life, her safe, lovely routine, that she felt the sting of tears. "I usually have fruit. A pear—and coffee."

"I can handle that," the nurse said cheerfully, "and I won't have to send someone down to the cafeteria, either."

She'd barely left the room when Detectives Shrader

and Littleton walked into it. Leigh shoved herself upright. "Did you find the cabin?"

"No, ma'am. I'm sorry. We have no news to report, just some more questions to ask you." He nodded toward the breakfast tray. "If you were about to eat, go ahead. We can wait."

"The nurse is getting me something else," Leigh said.

As if on cue, the nurse arrived, pushing a cart that bore a gigantic basket of pears nestled in gold satin and entwined with gold ribbon. "This basket was out at the nurses' station. A volunteer brought it up and said it was for you. These aren't just pears, they're works of art!" she enthused, removing a huge, glossy pear from its golden nest and holding it up to admire. She peered at the basket from all sides. "There doesn't seem to be a card. It must have fallen off. I'll look around for it," she said as she gave the pear to Leigh. "I'll leave you alone with your visitors now."

The pear in her hand reminded Leigh of her last conversation about breakfast with Logan, and her eyes filled with sentimental tears. She cupped it in her hands, brushing her fingertips over its smooth skin while she thought of Logan's skin, his smile; then she held it to her heart, where all her other memories of Logan were stored, safe and alive. Two tears slipped between her lashes.

"Mrs. Manning?"

Embarrassed, Leigh brushed the tears away. "I'm sorry—It's just that my husband always teases me about being addicted to pears. I've had one for breakfast almost every day for years."

"I imagine a lot of people know about that?" Detective Littleton asked casually.

"It's not a secret," Leigh said, laying the pear aside. "He's joked about it from time to time in front of people. These pears were probably sent by my housekeeper, or my secretary, or even more likely, by the market that gets them for me when I'm home." She nodded toward two brown vinyl chairs. "Please—sit down."

Littleton pulled the chairs over to Leigh's bed while Shrader explained the situation. "Your map wasn't as helpful as we'd hoped it would be. The directions were a little contradictory, the landmarks missing or obscured by snowbanks. We're checking with all the realtors in the area, but so far, none of them know anything about the house and property you've described."

A thought suddenly occurred to Leigh—a solution so obvious that she was dumbfounded they hadn't thought of it themselves. "I know I was close to the cabin when I had the accident. Whoever found me on the road will know exactly where that was! Have you spoken to him?"

"No, we haven't spoken to him yet—" Shrader admitted.

"Why not?" Leigh burst out. "Why are you wandering all over the mountains, trying to follow my map, when all you have to do is talk to whoever rescued me?"

"We can't talk to him, because we don't know who he is."

Leigh's head was beginning to pound with angry frustration. "He can't be very hard to locate. Please ask the ambulance drivers who brought me here. They must have seen him and talked to him."

"Try to be calm," Shrader said. "I understand why you're upset. Just let me bring you up to date on the situation with your rescuer."

Sensing that the situation was more complex than she'd thought a few moments before, Leigh tried to do as he asked. "All right, I'm calm. Please bring me up to date."

"The man who found you Sunday night brought you down the mountain to a little motel on the outskirts of

Hapsburg called the Venture Inn. He woke up the motel's night manager and told him to call nine-one-one. Then he convinced the manager that you'd be better off in a room with a heater and blankets until help arrived. After the two men carried you into a room, your rescuer told the manager that he was going back to his vehicle for your belongings. He never returned. When the night manager went looking for him a few minutes later, his vehicle was gone."

Leigh's anger drained out of her body, leaving her limp and despondent. Closing her eyes, she leaned her head against the pillows. "That's crazy. Why would anyone do something like that?"

"There are several possible explanations. The most likely one is that he was the same guy who ran you off the road. Afterward, he felt guilty, so he went back to see if he could find you. Once he found you, he started worrying about being blamed for the accident, so he made sure you were in good hands at the motel, then split before the police and ambulance arrived. Whether he was actually the guy who ran you off the road or not, he definitely had some reason for not wanting to talk to the police.

"The motel manager told us the guy was driving a black or dark brown four-door sedan—a Lincoln, he thought—an old one, and pretty battered up. The manager is in his seventies, and he didn't notice much else, because he had his hands full trying to help get you out of the vehicle. His recollection of the driver is a little better, and he's agreed to work with one of our sketch artists in the city tomorrow. Hopefully, they'll come up with a decent likeness that we can use if your husband still hasn't turned up."

"I see," Leigh whispered, turning her face away. But all she could really see was Logan's happy expression as he kissed her good-bye Sunday morning. He was out there somewhere—hurt or snowbound, or both. Those were the only alternatives Leigh was willing to consider. The possibility that Logan might already be beyond help or rescue was too shattering to contemplate.

Detective Littleton spoke for the first time, her tone hesitant. "There's one more thing we wanted to ask you about—" Leigh blinked back the tears burning her eyes and forced herself to look at the brunette. "This morning, Officer Borowski came back on duty after his regular days off, and he notified us that you reported a stalker in September. It was Officer Borowski who took down the information, and he thought we ought to know. Has the problem continued?"

Leigh's heart began to thud in deep, terrified beats that resounded up and down her body, and fear made her voice shake so badly it was nearly inaudible. "Are you thinking that a stalker ran me off the road, or that he might have done something to my husband?"

"No, no, not at all," Detective Littleton said with a warm and reassuring smile. "We're only trying to be helpful. The main roads are clear now, and the side roads are being cleared. Phone and electric service has been reinstated except in a very few isolated areas where they're still working on the lines. Your husband is bound to turn up any minute now. We thought you might like us to see what we can find out about the identity of your stalker while we're still working with you. If you don't want us to—"

"I'd appreciate it if you would," Leigh said, clinging to Detective Littleton's explanation because she wanted to believe it.

"What can you tell us about your stalker?"

Leigh described the events that had worried her.

"You said he sent you orchids," Littleton said when Leigh finished. "Have you looked at any of the cards on these flowers?"

"No."

Littleton stood up and went to the white orchids first. "They're from Stephen Rosenberg," she said, reading the card.

"He's one of the backers of the play," Leigh told her.

One by one, Littleton began reading Leigh the messages and names on the other cards. When she was halfway through, she nodded toward the stacks of phone messages and telegrams on Leigh's nightstand. "Have you looked those over carefully?"

"Most of them," Leigh said.

"Would it be all right if Detective Shrader goes through them while I'm doing this?"

It was fine with Leigh, but Shrader didn't look very enthusiastic as he began going through the stack. When the name on the last bouquet was also one Leigh recognized, Littleton picked up her jacket and Shrader stood up, too, trying to finish his own task on his feet. He was reading one of the last messages when his entire attitude underwent a sudden, unpleasant transformation. He stared at Leigh, studying her as if seeing her in an entirely new, and unflattering, light. "So, I guess Michael Valente is a good pal of yours?"

The expression on his face, and even on Littleton's, made Leigh feel soiled by association.

"No, he is not," Leigh stated emphatically. "I met him for the first time at a party celebrating the play's opening Saturday night." She didn't want to say more, didn't want to mention that the party had been at her home, and she especially didn't want them to know that Logan had been discussing a business deal with Valente. She didn't want to say anything to make these detectives think Logan was anything but a thoroughly upright businessman and loving husband who was missing. Which he was.

Both detectives seemed to accept her explanation. "I

imagine you attract a lot of creeps and kooks when you're a big star," Shrader said.

"It goes with the job," Leigh said, trying to joke and failing miserably.

"We'll let you get some rest now," he said. "You have our cell phone numbers if you need to reach us. We're going to try following your map again. Normally, it's easy to locate the site of an accident like yours, but there's so much snow piled up along the sides of the road that it's difficult to spot the indications we're looking for."

"Call me if you find out anything—anything at all," Leigh pleaded.

"We will," Shrader promised. He held his temper in check while Littleton stopped at the nurses' station and asked about the card that was missing from the basket of pears. He held his temper while the nurse looked for it and couldn't find it, but when he reached the bank of elevators, he unleashed it on Sam. "What you did in there was completely senseless! You scared the shit out of her with that stalker crap. She didn't buy your reasons for asking. She knew exactly what you were thinking."

"She's not stupid. Pretty soon she'd have remembered him, and then she'd have been terrified that he could be responsible for what's happened," Sam retorted. "It's better that she knows *we've* already thought of it and are following up."

"Following up what?" he scoffed. "Her stalker is still in the romantic, gift-giving stage, which is probably where he'll stay until someone else catches his eye. Secondly, stalkers aren't spontaneous—they fantasize about the moment they'll come out in the open. They plan and they fantasize, and they don't like deviating. They don't decide to make their move in the middle of an unexpected, unpredictable blizzard, unless they could plan for that, too—which is not possible."

The arrival of the elevator distracted him, and when Sam saw that it was empty, she tried to explain her reasoning. "Don't you find it odd that her husband vanished on the same night that she was nearly killed—and then mysteriously rescued? That's just too many coincidences."

"Are you suggesting one stalker is behind all that? How many stalkers do you think she has?"

Sam ignored his sarcasm. "I think it's possible he could have been following her when he saw her car go over the embankment, and he stayed there to rescue her." Once she said it aloud, Sam wished she hadn't, because even to her it sounded ludicrous.

"That's your theory?" he mocked. "A stalker who turns into a knight in shining armor?" Without waiting for a reply, he said, "Now, let me give you *my* theory: Manning got stuck in the blizzard and for one reason or another, he can't get out. Mrs. Manning lost control of her car in the same blinding snowstorm and went off the road. Here's why I like that theory: *The same thing happened to hundreds of people in that blizzard on Sunday!* Here's why I *don't* like your theory: It's improbable. In fact, it's outlandish. In short, it sucks."

Instead of resenting his accurate summation, Sam looked at him for a moment, and then she laughed. "You're right, but please don't soften your opinions for my sake."

Shrader was a man, therefore being "right" was both a compliment—which immediately improved his mood—and also a very high priority. "You should have discussed your theory with me before you inflicted it on Mrs. Manning," he pointed out, but in a more pleasant voice.

"I didn't develop it until after we got here," Sam admitted as the elevator doors opened on the first floor. "It was the pears that finally sent me in that direction. They represent a personal knowledge of her habits—'insider' information—and there wasn't a card with them. Then, when I saw how strongly Mrs. Manning reacted to them . . ."

"She told you why she reacted that way."

They were already partway across the lobby when Sam decided to make a detour, which Shrader incorrectly assumed was to the ladies' room. "I'll meet you at the car," she told him.

"Prostate trouble?" he joked. "You already stopped on the way upstairs."

Sam walked over to the reception desk, where several new floral arrangements were waiting to be delivered to patients' rooms. She showed her badge to an elderly volunteer with blue tinted hair and a name tag that said she was Mrs. Novotny. "Was a big basket of pears delivered here this morning?" Sam asked her.

"Oh, yes," the volunteer said. "We were all marveling at the size of those beautiful pears."

"Did you happen to notice the truck or car that delivered them?"

"As a matter of fact, I did. It was a black car—the kind movie stars drive—I know, because two teenagers were sitting right over there at the time, and they were admiring it. One boy said it cost at least three hundred thousand dollars!"

"Did they mention what kind of car it was?"

"Yes. They said it was a . . ." She paused, deep in thought, and then she brightened. "They said it was a Bentley! I can describe the man driving it, too: He was wearing a black suit and a black hat with a visor on it. He carried the pears in here and put them on my desk. He said they were for Mrs. Leigh Manning, and he asked me to please see that she gets them as soon as possible. I told him I would."

Sam felt completely foolish for obsessing over what was obviously an innocuous basket of expensive fruit delivered in a chauffeur-driven Bentley. Shrader had been totally right. "Thank you very much, Mrs. Novotny, you've been very helpful," Sam assured her automatically, because she thought it was important to make every cooperative citizen feel as if they'd been valuable. It was a way of saying "thank you for being willing to get involved."

Mrs. Novotny was so flattered that she tried to be even more helpful. "If you want to know anything else about the man driving that car, you could ask the person who sent the pears, Detective."

"We don't know who sent them," Sam said over her shoulder. "There was no card with them."

"The envelope fell off."

Something about the way she said that made Sam stop and turn.

Mrs. Novotny was holding a square envelope in her hand. "I was planning to send this upstairs to Mrs. Manning with a volunteer, but they've been busy all morning. Almost all the beds here are filled because of the blizzard. Lots of folks fell, or got in car wrecks, or had heart attacks from shoveling snow."

Sam thanked her profusely, took the envelope, and continued across the lobby. She opened the envelope, not because she expected to discover anything meaningful inside it, but because she'd already embarrassed herself with Shrader and upset Mrs. Manning over the basket of fruit that it should have been attached to. She removed a small folded sheet of engraved stationery from the envelope and read the handwritten message on it. Then she stopped in midstride. And read it twice more.

Shrader had gotten their car out of the lot and it was at the curb just outside the main doors. Puffs of exhaust were pumping out of the tailpipe and a hard, thin coat of frost had already built up on the windshield. He was scraping it off with his credit card—an entertaining procedure with the windshield wipers running at top speed and his knuckles bare. She waited in the car until he got in and began blowing on his cold hands and rubbing them together; then she offered him the folded note. "What's that?" he asked between puffs on his fingers.

"The note that came with Mrs. Manning's pears."

"Why are you giving it to me?"

"Because you're cold," she said, "and I think this will . . . electrify you."

Shrader clearly thought that was unlikely, and he demonstrated that opinion by ignoring the note and continuing to rub his hands together. When he finished, he put the Ford into gear, looked in the rearview mirror, and pulled away from the curb. Finally, he reached for the note, casually flipped it open with his thumb, and as they neared a stop sign at the pedestrian crosswalk, Shrader finally allotted it a sideways glance.

"Holy shit!" He slammed down on the brake so hard that Sam's seat belt locked and the rear end of the car fishtailed on the icy drive. He read it again, then he slowly lifted his big dark head and gazed at her, his brown eyes bright with wonder and anticipation—a very happy rottweiler who'd just been given a juicy sirloin. He shook his head as if to clear it. "We've got to call Captain Holland," he said, pulling the Ford over to the curb. Chuckling silently, he punched numbers on his cellular phone. "What a coup, Littleton! If Logan Manning doesn't show up soon—healthy and hale—you've just handed NYPD a case that's going to make you a heroine and Holland the next police commissioner. Commissioner Trumanti will be able to die a happy man." Into the phone he barked, "This is Shrader. I need to talk to the captain." He listened for a moment, then said, "Tell him it's an emergency. I'll hold on."

He took the phone away from his ear long enough to press the *mute* button; then he announced, "If you weren't already Holland's fair-haired angel, you'd be that from now on."

Sam suppressed a jolt of alarm. "What do you mean, I'm his 'angel'?"

Shrader gave her an abject, hangdog look. "Forget I said that. Whatever is between you and Holland is none of my business. It's real clear now, though, that you've got more going for you than just your looks. You've got tremendous instincts, you've got tenacity, you've got ability! That's what matters."

"What matters to me at this moment is that you implied Captain Holland has some sort of partiality for me, and I want to know why you think that."

"Hell, everybody at the Eighteen thinks that!"

"Oh, gee, that makes me feel much better," she said sarcastically. "Now answer my question or I'll show you 'tenacity' like you have never—"

The person on the other end of the phone said something, and Shrader held up his hand to silence Sam's outburst. "I'll hold on," he said; then he looked at Sam, gauging the degree of determination in her facial expression, and decided he believed her threat. "Consider the evidence," he said, after pressing the *mute* button again. "You're a rookie detective, but you wanted Homicide at the Eighteen and you got Homicide. We've got cases coming out the wazoo, but Holland doesn't want to give you any of those cases; he wants a nice clean case to start you out on. You need a permanent partner, but Holland won't assign you to just anybody. He wants to pick your partner *personally—*"

Sam grasped at the only lame explanation she could come up with at the moment. "Holland is handling assignments for everyone right now, since Lieutenant Unger's position is still open."

"Yeah, but Holland hasn't assigned you to a partner, because he wants to make sure your partner is someone real nice, someone you're 'compatible' with."

"Then how could he have picked you?"

Shrader grinned at her gibe. "Because he knows I'll 'look out for you.'"

"He told you to look out for me?" Sam gaped at him in shocked disgust.

"In exactly those words."

She digested that for a moment; then she shrugged in pretended disinterest. "Well, if that's all it takes to make everyone think there's something odd going on, then you're all a bunch of gossipy old women."

"Give us a break, Littleton. Take a look at yourself—you're not exactly the typical female cop. You don't swear, you don't get mad, you're too proper and ladylike, and you don't *look* like a cop."

"You haven't *heard* me swear," Sam corrected him, "and you haven't *seen* me get angry yet, and what's wrong with the way I look?"

"Nothing. Just ask Holland and some of the other guys at the Eighteen—they think you look real fine. Of course, the only other female detectives at the Eighteen are a lot older than you and fifty pounds heavier, so they don't have a lot to compare you with."

Sam shook her head in disgust and hid her relief, but his next statement jarred her and ended that momentary respite. "Since you want to know the whole truth," he said, "according to the grapevine over at headquarters, you've got some sort of clout—friends in high places—something like that."

"That's just typical," Sam said, managing to look scornfully amused. "Whenever a woman starts succeeding in a male-dominated profession, you guys would rather attribute her success to anything, *anything*, except ability."

"Well, you got plenty of that," Shrader shocked her by saying; then he broke off abruptly as Holland finally took his call and evidently began by chewing Shrader out for holding on and running up his cellular phone bill.

"Yes, sir, Captain, I know—probably five minutes. Yes, sir, Captain, but Detective Littleton discovered something I felt you'd want to know about immediately."

Since Shrader was the senior detective on the case, and also "in charge of her," Sam expected him to take some sort of credit for her discovery, or at least to claim the satisfaction of telling Holland about it himself, but to Sam's surprise, Shrader handed the phone to her with a wink. "Holland says this had better be good."

By the time Sam disconnected the call, she had no doubt that Captain Thomas Holland thought her information justified an expensive phone call.

In fact, he thought it warranted the full and immediate use of *all* of the NYPD's available personnel and resources.

"Well?" Shrader said with a knowing grin. "What did Holland say?"

Sam handed his phone back to him and summarized the conversation. "Basically, he said that Mrs. Manning is going to get more help from the NYPD in the search for her husband than she ever imagined."

"Or wanted," Shrader said flatly. He glanced up at the hospital in the general direction of the third floor and shook his head. "That woman is one *hell* of an actress! She fooled me completely."

Sam automatically followed his gaze. "Me, too," she admitted, frowning.

"Cheer up," he advised her as they pulled away from

the curb. "You've made Holland a happy man, and by now, he's on the phone with Trumanti, making the Commissioner a happy man. By tonight, Trumanti will make the mayor a happy man. The biggest problem for all of us," he said as he put the car into gear, "will be keeping what we've got a secret. If the Feds get wind of it, they'll try to find some way to muscle in on the case. They've been trying to nail Valente on a dozen charges for years, but they can never make them stick. They aren't going to be happy when the NYPD succeeds where they've failed."

"Isn't it a little too early for all this ecstasy?" Sam said. "If Logan Manning turns up alive and well, there is no 'case.'"

"True, but something tells me that isn't going to happen. It's time for lunch," he added after a glance at the clock on the dashboard. "I owe you an apology for shooting holes in your theory earlier. I'll buy you a hamburger for lunch."

His extraordinary offer made Sam do a double take. Shrader was so cheap that everyone at the Eighteenth joked about it. In the few days they'd been in the mountains together, he'd already stuck her for several cups of coffee and vending machine snacks at the hospital. In view of that, and his earlier attitude about her "theory," Sam decided on a revenge she knew would torture him: "You owe me a *steak* for dinner."

"Not a chance."

"I know just the place. But first, Captain Holland wants us to make some phone calls to the local authorities."

CHAPTER 6

Unable to endure the thought of eating or more badgering on the subject from her nurse, Leigh hid two pieces of toast and the pear in the drawer of her nightstand; then she lay back, contemplating what the detectives had said and done. After a few minutes, she made a decision and phoned her secretary.

Brenna answered the telephone in Leigh's Fifth Avenue apartment on the first ring. "Is there any news about Mr. Manning?" Brenna asked as soon as Leigh finished reassuring her about her own condition.

"No, not yet," Leigh said, trying not to sound as despondent as she felt. "I need some phone numbers. They won't be in the computer. They'll be in a small address book in the right-hand drawer of my writing desk in the bedroom."

"Okay, which numbers?" Brenna said, and Leigh could picture the efficient little blonde snatching up a pen, poised as always to respond to any request.

"I need Mayor Edelman's direct line at his office and his

private number at home. I also need William Trumanti's number at his office and his home. He'll be listed either under his name or under 'police commissioner.' I'll hold on while you get them."

Brenna was back on the phone so quickly that Leigh knew she must have sprinted to and from Leigh's bedroom. "Is there anything else I can do?" Brenna asked.

"Not right now."

"Courtney Maitland has been here several times," Brenna said. "She's absolutely convinced you're dead and that the authorities are covering it up."

Under normal circumstances, the mere mention of the outspoken teenager who lived in Leigh's building would have made her smile, but not then. "Tell Courtney that the last thing she and I talked about was how she feels about her father's new wife. That should convince her I'm alive and talking."

"I'll call her right away," Brenna said. "I arranged for a private duty nurse for you as soon as I heard about your accident. Has she been there?"

"Yes, thanks. I let her go this morning, but I should have kept her an extra day."

"Because you aren't feeling well enough yet?"

"What?" Leigh's mind was already on the phone calls she wanted to make. "No, because she was easier to intimidate than the staff nurse."

MAYOR EDELMAN was leaving for a meeting when Leigh called, but his secretary told him Leigh was on the phone, and he took her call immediately. "Leigh, I'm so sorry about what's happened. How are you?"

"I'm fine, Mayor," Leigh replied, fighting to keep her voice steady. "But there hasn't been any word about Logan yet."

"I know. We've asked the state police to help out, and they're doing their best, but they have their hands full up there." He paused and said very kindly, "Is there anything else I can do to help?"

"I realize this is an imposition—that it isn't even the responsibility of the New York City Police Department—but there are only two detectives up here looking for Logan, and time is slipping away. Is it possible to get more people up here to help with the search? I'll be glad to reimburse the city for the extra manpower, or any expenses involved—cost is of no importance."

"It's not entirely a matter of cost. There are some jurisdictional issues involved from the NYPD's standpoint. Commissioner Trumanti can't send an 'invasion party' into the Catskills without being asked to participate in the search by the local municipalities who have jurisdiction up there."

To Leigh, that sounded like pure trivia—the etiquette of law enforcement—and she had no time for it. "It's eighteen degrees outside, Mayor, and my husband is somewhere out there, missing. The FBI has jurisdiction everywhere. I'm thinking about calling them."

"You can certainly try," he said, but Leigh knew from his tone that he didn't think she had any hope of getting the FBI to involve themselves in the search. "It's my understanding there are many people still missing in that blizzard, Leigh, but they're believed to be safe and simply unable to dig their way to a main road or use a telephone. Why don't you call Bill Trumanti, and let him update you?"

"I was going to do that next. Thank you, Mayor," Leigh said, but she didn't feel particularly grateful to him. She was frantic, and she wanted more than sympathy and excuses. She wanted help, or at least suggestions for how she could get help.

Commissioner Trumanti wasn't available when she

tried to reach him, but he returned her call a half hour later. To Leigh's enormous surprise and relief, Trumanti offered her a great deal more than mere suggestions; he was preparing to provide the full support and resources of the NYPD to help find Logan. "The jurisdictional issues the mayor mentioned are already being resolved as we speak," he said. He paused for a moment and put his hand over the phone, spoke a few unintelligible words to whoever was there, then returned to his conversation with Leigh. "I've just been advised that Captain Holland's detectives up there have contacted the local municipalities and they've all agreed to let the NYPD join in their search-and-rescue efforts. In fact, their attitude is 'the more help, the better.' As you know, Leigh, that was one hell of a blizzard, and the local agencies and authorities have been working around the clock, trying to assist their residents."

Leigh was so relieved she felt like weeping.

"According to the weather forecast," he continued, "we should be getting a break very soon. I've just approved the use of NYPD helicopters to begin searching for the cabin as soon as the ceiling lifts and visibility improves to a safe level. There's a lot of area to cover, so don't get your hopes up too quickly. In the meantime, you have two of Captain Holland's excellent detectives up there right now, and they'll follow up on any leads that come along."

"I can't thank you enough," Leigh said feelingly. She and Logan knew Commissioner Trumanti and his wife socially, but not nearly as well as they knew the mayor, and the mayor hadn't offered her much help at all. In view of that, she'd expected less, not more, help from Commissioner Trumanti, yet he was turning out to be a truly forceful, determined ally—a genuine godsend. Leigh decided to ask if he thought she should also contact the FBI. "I told

Mayor Edelman I was thinking of asking the FBI for help—"
she began.

Trumanti's reaction was so negative that Leigh wondered if he'd taken it as an insult to the NYPD and to him personally. "You'd be wasting your time, Mrs. Manning," he
interrupted, turning formal and chilly with her. "Unless
there's something you haven't told our detectives, there's not
one shred of evidence, not one tiny detail, that would point
to a crime of any kind in connection with your husband's disappearance, let alone a *federal* crime that would warrant
calling in the *Federal* Bureau of Investigation."

"I've had a stalker—" Leigh began.

"Who I understand has confined his activities—his
very *minimal* activities—to a geographic area that is entirely within the NYPD's jurisdiction. No *federal* law has
been violated. In fact, I'm not sure the NYPD would be
able to charge him with anything other than making a nui-
sance of himself at this point."

Every time he emphasized the word "federal," Leigh felt
somehow that she was being severely reprimanded, and by
the person whose help and allegiance she needed most. "I
see. I was only trying to think of ways to be helpful," she
said with deliberate humility. She would have crawled to
Trumanti on her knees if that's what it took to secure his
help for Logan. "Is there anything else you could suggest
that I ought to do?"

His tone underwent a definite change for the nicer.
"Yes," he said. "I want you to rest as much as you can, and
take good care of yourself, so that when we find Logan, he
doesn't blame us for worrying you."

"I'll try to do that," Leigh promised. "I may be going
home tomorrow."

"Are you well enough to leave the hospital?" he said,
sounding shocked.

Leigh evaded that question but told him another truth: "Hospitals make me feel helpless and depressed."

He laughed. "Me, too. I hate the damned places. I don't start feeling good until I get to go home."

At that last, belated moment, Leigh finally remembered Trumanti had been waging a long fight with prostate cancer, a fight he was rumored to be losing. She tried to think of something adequate to say and had to settle for saying, "Thank you for everything. You're being incredibly kind."

CHAPTER 7

"I want to go home tomorrow," Leigh told her physician when he stopped in to see her at five that afternoon.

He peered at her over her chart, his expression as implacable as hers. "That's not possible."

"But I was able to get out of bed several times today, and I walked down the hall this afternoon. I'm sure I don't need this neck brace. I'm fine," Leigh insisted.

"You're not fine. You had a serious concussion, you have fractured ribs, and we don't know yet if you need that neck brace."

"I'm hardly in any pain at all."

"That's because you're being given powerful painkillers. Have you looked at your body beneath that hospital gown?" he demanded.

"Yes."

"Have you seen your face in a mirror?"

"Yes."

"How would you describe what you see?"

"I look like I've been in an accident."

"You look like a living eggplant." When her expression remained stubbornly determined, he changed tactics. "Reporters and photographers have been hanging around downstairs, hoping for a look at you. You don't want anyone to see you looking like this, do you? You have a public image to preserve."

Leigh was in no mood for a lecture on the importance of her public image. It was already Wednesday, and the helicopters wouldn't be able to fly tomorrow if the weather didn't improve. She wanted to help the police narrow down the search by finding the spot where her car went over the embankment. She could not endure another day of helpless inactivity and enforced bed rest. Her body hurt everywhere, but her mind was clear and she needed to be able to act.

Her doctor mistook her silence for assent. "You know I only have your best health interests at heart. You simply are not well enough to be discharged."

"Let's pretend I'm an ordinary blue-collar worker," Leigh proposed smoothly. "I have a family to support and no money to cover what my HMO policy won't pay. If that were true, Dr. Zapata, when would you discharge me?"

His gray brows snapped together.

"Would it have been yesterday?" she prompted.

"No," he said.

"Then when?" she persisted.

"This morning," he said. "You've made your point, Mrs. Manning."

Leigh instantly felt like a witch. "I'm very sorry. That was rude of me."

"Unfortunately, it was also completely on point. I'll sign your discharge papers after I stop in to see you in the morning—provided you agree to leave here in an ambulance."

As soon as he left, Leigh tried to call Brenna, but her secretary had already started for home. With an hour to waste, Leigh made her way slowly and painfully to the chair opposite her bed. She eased herself onto it and began leafing through the magazines and newspapers she'd gotten earlier from a volunteer who was pushing a cart with reading materials. Leigh was trying to rebuild her strength.

At six-thirty, she put the newspapers aside, crept back to her bed, and called Brenna at her home number. "I have a favor to ask," she began. "It's a little out of the ordinary—"

"I don't care," Brenna interrupted swiftly. "Just tell me how I can help."

"I'm being discharged in the morning. Could you bring me some fresh clothes?"

"Of course. Anything else?"

"Yes, rent a four-wheel-drive vehicle and drive that up here. Park it somewhere close to the hospital, then take a cab the rest of the way. I'm required to leave the hospital in an ambulance," Leigh explained, "but I'm not going to stay in it. We'll let the ambulance go as soon as we get to the rental car."

"And then what?" Brenna asked uneasily. "I mean, if you need an ambulance in order to leave the hospital, shouldn't you stay in it back to the city?"

"We're not going directly back to the city. The police can't follow my map, but I should be able to find the place where I went off the road. The cabin where I was supposed to meet my husband has to be very close to that spot."

"I understand," Brenna said, "but I'm really worried about you, and—"

"Brenna, please! I need your help." Leigh's voice broke with exhaustion and fear, and when Brenna heard it, she capitulated at once.

"I'll take care of everything," she promised fiercely. "Before you hang up," she added, "there's something I want to say. I hope you—you won't take this in the wrong way."

Leigh leaned her head against the pillows and braced herself to hear something she didn't want to—the normal outcome, in her experience, of any statement that began with someone suggesting that the listener *not take it the wrong way.* "What is it?"

"I haven't worked for you very long, and I know you have hundreds of friends you could turn to, so I'm very pleased . . . well, flattered . . . that you're counting on me . . . when you have so many other people . . ."

"Brenna," Leigh said with a weary smile, "I hate to disillusion you, but I have hundreds of *acquaintances* I can't trust, and only a few true friends I can completely trust. Two of them are on the other side of the globe, and one of them is lost in the mountains. Everyone else—casual friends, acquaintances, and people I've never even met—are already under siege from the media. The newspapers are full of misinformation, speculation, and wild innuendos, and they're getting that stuff from my so-called friends and close acquaintances."

Brenna fell silent, obviously trying to think of another explanation, but there was none. "That's very sad," she said softly.

It was also the least of Leigh's worries. "Don't dwell on it. That's simply the way life is for people like me."

"Thank you for trusting me; that's all I wanted to say."

Leigh closed her eyes. "Thank you for being—for being you."

When Brenna hung up, Leigh gathered the last of her strength and made her final phone call of the night. It was to her publicist, Trish Lefkowitz. She gave Trish a quick, unemotional update on the situation, and once Trish had offered words of sympathy and encouragement, the publicist got straight down to business: "Do you feel up to giving me some instructions about how you want me to handle the press? Up until now, I've been winging it."

"That's why I'm calling. I'm going to be discharged in the morning, but I'm not going directly home, and I don't want reporters following me. Brenna and I are going to drive up into the mountains to look for the place where I had my accident."

"That's crazy. You can't possibly be well enough—"

"If I can find it, it will help narrow down the search."

"Men!" Trish exploded. The publicist's long string of unsatisfactory relationships was turning her into an outspoken man-hater. "Logan is probably camping out in some cozy snowbound cabin, with a farmer's wife baking him cookies, while we're all going crazy with worry and you're trying to rescue him."

"I hope you're right," Leigh said.

Trish sighed. "Me, too. Now, let me think, how can I distract the media so you can make your getaway . . . ?"

Leigh waited, picturing the publicist pushing her shoulder-length black hair behind her right ear, then slowly twisting the end of a lock and tugging on it while she contemplated the situation. In happier days, Leigh had teasingly warned her that the entire lock of hair was going to drop off in her hand one day.

"Okay, here's the best way. I'll call the hospital's spokesman—his name is Dr. Jerry-something. I'll have him notify any members of the press who are hanging around the hospital that you're being released in the morning and will be leaving by ambulance to come home. Then I'll arrange for an empty ambulance to leave the hospital, and hopefully, they'll chase it all the way back to New York City. How's that sound?"

"It sounds good. One more thing—notify the media that I'll give a press conference at home tomorrow tonight."

"You're kidding! Do you feel up to that?"

"No, but I need their help and cooperation. A police artist is working up a sketch of the man who found me after my accident. We can hand out the drawing if it's ready. I also want to try to put a stop to the rumors I read in two newspapers tonight that Logan's disappearance is merely the result of some sort of marital squabble. The NYPD has volunteered to get actively involved in the search, but newspaper articles like those will make the police look— and feel—foolish."

"I understand. Can I ask how you look?"

"I look okay."

"No bruises on your face, or anything? I'm thinking about cameras."

"I need a public forum; it doesn't matter how I look."

Trish's silence on the other end of the telephone punctuated her adamant disagreement with that statement, but she sensed it was useless to argue. "I'll see you tomorrow evening," she said.

CHAPTER 8

The telephone calls had exhausted Leigh, but they had also kept her mind occupied. However, when she turned off the lights and closed her eyes, her imagination took over, tormenting her with the horrors that might have befallen Logan. She saw him tied up in a chair being tortured by some demented stalker. . . . She saw him frozen to death in his car . . . his lips blue, eyes glazed and staring.

Unable to endure the agony of those images, Leigh tried to draw strength and hope from memories of the past. She remembered their simple wedding in front of a bored justice of the peace. Leigh had worn her best dress and a flower in her hair. Logan had stood beside her, managing to look elegant, handsome, and self-assured, despite the fact that he was wearing a threadbare suit and their combined assets amounted to eight hundred dollars.

Leigh's grandmother hadn't been able to scrape together the cost of an airline ticket to attend the wedding, and Logan's mother was so opposed to the marriage that they hadn't told her about it until the day after. But despite all that—despite their virtual poverty, the absence of friends and family, and the uncertain future ahead of them, they'd been happy and infinitely optimistic that day. They believed in each other. They believed in the power of love. For the next several years, that was all they had—each other and a great deal of love.

Images of Logan flipped through Leigh's mind like slides in a projector . . . Logan when they met, young, too thin, but dashing, worldly, and wise beyond his years. He'd taken her to the symphony on their first date. She'd never been to the symphony, and during a pause in the music, she'd clapped too soon, thinking the piece was over. The couple in front of them had turned and given her a disdainful look that doubled her mortification, but Logan hadn't let the incident pass. At intermission, he leaned forward and spoke to the older couple. In that polished, disarming way of his, he said congenially, "Isn't it wonderful when we're first introduced to something we love? Remember how good that felt?"

The couple turned in their seats, and their frowns became smiles, which they directed at Leigh. "I didn't like the symphony at first," the man confided to her. "My parents had season tickets and they dragged me along. It took quite a while to grow on me." The couple spent intermission with Leigh and Logan and insisted on buying them a glass of champagne to celebrate Leigh's first symphony.

Leigh soon discovered that Logan had a particular way of dealing with snobby, standoffish, critical people, a way that disarmed them and converted them into friends and admirers. Logan's mother often said that "there is no substitute for good breeding," and Logan had it in abundance—a natural, unaffected kind of good breeding.

For their second date, Logan suggested Leigh choose how they spend the evening. She decided on a little known off-Broadway play by a new young playwright named Jason Solomon. Logan closed his eyes and dozed off during the third act.

Because Leigh was a drama student at New York University, she'd been able to get backstage passes. "What did you think of the play?" Jason Solomon asked them when Leigh finished the introductions.

"I loved it," Leigh said, partly out of courtesy and partly out of her all-encompassing love of everything related to the theater. In truth, she thought most of the writing was excellent, but the acting was only fair, and the lighting and direction were poor.

Satisfied, Jason looked to Logan for more praise. "What did you think of it?"

"I don't know much about theater," Logan replied. "Leigh is the expert on that. She's the leading drama student at NYU. If my mother had been here tonight, you could have asked her opinion. It would be more meaningful than mine."

Instantly insulted by Logan's lack of enthusiasm, Jason lifted his chin and eyed Logan scornfully down the length of his nose. "And you think your mother's opinion would carry weight because she's—what? A successful playwright? A theater critic?"

"No, because among her circle of friends there are several influential patrons of the arts."

Leigh didn't realize it at the time, but Logan was dangling the slim possibility of a financial backer under Jason's nose. All Leigh knew was that the playwright became slightly ingratiating, but was still resentful. "Bring your mother to my play," he said. "Let me know when you're planning to come, and I'll see that you have front row tickets."

As they left, Leigh said, "Do you think your mother would enjoy his play?"

Grinning, Logan put his arm around her shoulders. It was the first time he had touched her in a personal way. "I don't think my mother would set foot in this theater unless the city of New York was on fire and this was the only fire-proof building."

"Then why did you let Jason Solomon think she might?"

"Because you're a gifted actress and he's a playwright who is badly in need of people who can actually act. I thought you might want to drop in here next week, if the play doesn't close before then, and volunteer your services."

Warmed by his praise and distracted by his touch, Leigh nevertheless felt compelled to point out the truth: "You have no way of knowing whether I can actually act."

"Yes, I do. Your roommate told me you're 'gifted.' In fact, she said you're some kind of prodigy and you're the envy of the entire drama school."

"Even if all of that were true—which it isn't—Jason Solomon wouldn't hire me. I don't have any professional credentials."

Logan chuckled. "From the looks of this place and the quality of the acting, he can't afford to hire anybody *with* professional credentials. And, I said 'volunteer' your services—free of charge. After that, you'll have credentials."

It wasn't that easy to break into the business; it didn't work that way; but Leigh was already falling in love with Logan Manning, and so she didn't want to debate with him about anything that night.

Outside the theater, he hailed a taxi, and when the driver was absorbed with midtown traffic, Logan put his arm around her shoulders again, drew her close, and kissed her for the first time. It was an amazing kiss, filled with all the deep infatuation Leigh was feeling herself, an expert kiss that left her feeling not only dazed and overheated, but also uneasily aware that in this, as in most everything else, Logan Manning was a lot more experienced and worldly than she was.

He walked her to the dingy apartment building on Great Jones Street, where she shared a one-bedroom apartment on the fifth floor. Outside her apartment, he kissed her again, longer and more thoroughly this time. By the time he let her go, Leigh felt so euphoric that she knew she wouldn't be able to sleep for hours. She waited just inside her apartment, listening to him bounding down the flights of stairs to the street level; then she opened the door and dreamily walked down the same stairs he'd descended.

Logan hadn't taken her to get anything to eat after the play, which was an omission she would wonder about later, but at that moment all she knew for certain was that she was deliriously happy and ravenously hungry. The grocery market on the corner was only a few doors away, and it was open all night, so Leigh went there.

Angelini's Market was narrow, but very deep, with creaking linoleum floors, terrible lighting, and the pervasive smell of kosher pickles and corned beef emanating from a deli counter that occupied the entire left wall. The right wall was crammed with shelves of canned and boxed goods from floor to ceiling. Wooden crates of fresh produce and cases of soft drinks were stacked in the center, leaving only a narrow aisle on either side to reach the refrigerators and freezers at the rear of the store. Despite the market's unprepossessing appearance, the Italian pastas and meats in the deli section were wonderful and so were the small homemade frozen pizzas.

Leigh took the last shrimp pizza from the freezer and put it into the store's microwave; then she went to the crates of produce, looking for pears.

"Did you find your shrimp pizza?" Mrs. Angelini called from behind the cash register at the deli counter.

"Yes, I'm heating some of it right now. I got the last one in the freezer," Leigh said as she located a wooden box of pears. "I always get the last one—I guess I'm just lucky," she added, but she was thinking of Logan, not pizza.

"Not so lucky," Mrs. Angelini replied. "I only make one shrimp pizza at a time. I make them for you. You're the only one who asks for them."

Leigh looked up, a pear in each hand. "You do? That's very nice of you, Mrs. Angelini."

"Don't bother looking through those pears; we got better in the back. Falco will bring them." Raising her voice, she called to Falco in Italian.

A few moments later, Falco emerged from the store-room, wearing a stained apron over his shirt and jeans and carrying a small bag. He walked past Leigh without a glance and gave his mother the bag, from which she extracted two large pears. "These are for you," Mrs. Angelini told Leigh. "These are the best of all."

Leigh retrieved her heated pizza from the microwave, slid it back onto its cardboard dish, and covered it with its original plastic wrapping; then she headed for the cash register, where she properly admired pears so shiny that they looked polished. "You're always so nice to me, Mrs. Angelini," she said with a smile, trying very hard to convey some sort of warmth and cheer to the long-suffering woman. Mrs. Angelini's oldest son, Angelo, had been killed in a gang fight long before Leigh moved to the neighborhood. Her youngest son, Dominick, was a thoroughly likeable, gregarious young man who used to help out in the store all the time, but then, one day, he disappeared. Mrs. Angelini said Dominick was away at school, but Leigh's roommate—a native New Yorker—said that in their neighborhood "away at school," meant "away at Spofford," New York's Juvenile Detention Center, or away at one of the state prisons.

Soon after Dominick "left for school," Falco started working in the store, but the only thing Falco Angelini had in common with his outgoing, younger brother was a record—and not at Spofford, either. Based on what Leigh's roommate overheard in the store one day, Falco had spent several years in Attica for killing someone.

Even if Leigh hadn't known that, Falco would have made her extremely uneasy. Silent and forbidding, and over six feet tall, he moved through the store like a towering specter of impending doom, his expression ice cold and distant, his powerful shoulders seeming to crowd the narrow aisles. In jarring contrast to his thick black eyebrows and full beard, his skin had a ghostly pallor that Leigh's roommate said was from being in prison. His voice—on the rare occasions when he spoke—was hard and brusque. He made Leigh so uneasy that she actually avoided looking at him whenever possible, but there were times when she caught him watching her, and it made her even more uncomfortable.

Mrs. Angelini, however, seemed almost comically unaware of Falco's fierce features and intimidating demeanor. She called orders to him like a drill sergeant and referred to him affectionately and possessively as "my Falco," and "my *caro*" and "my *nipote*." Leigh figured that since she had already lost two of her boys, it was probably natural that Mrs. Angelini would treasure the remaining one, regardless of his very obvious character flaws and social shortcomings.

As if Mrs. Angelini knew what Leigh was thinking, she smiled sadly as she counted out Leigh's change. "If God had given me a choice," she confessed with a nod toward the front of the store, where Falco was stocking shelves with canned goods, "I think I would have asked Him for daughters. Daughters are easier to raise."

"I'm not sure most mothers would agree with you,"

Leigh joked uneasily. She was uncomfortable with the topic, sad for Mrs. Angelini's sadness, and eternally disconcerted by Falco Angelini's presence. Picking up her purchases, Leigh politely said good-bye to Mrs. Angelini, then she called a hesitant good-bye to Falco—not because she wanted to speak to him, but because she was a little afraid of snubbing—and therefore offending—him. Leigh was from a quiet, small town in Ohio, and she had absolutely no experience with ex-convicts, but it seemed to her that deliberately offending an ex-convict—particularly one who'd been in prison for killing somebody—was probably an unwise, even dangerous, mistake.

She was preoccupied with those thoughts as she walked out of the market and started down the street, so she was taken completely by surprise when two menacing-looking young men materialized from the shadows and stepped purposefully into her path. "Well, well, look what came out of the market," one of them said as he reached into his jacket pocket. "You look good enough to peel and eat."

A knife! He had a knife! Leigh froze like a deer caught in the headlights of an oncoming car. Her one idiotic thought was that she mustn't be killed now, not now when she'd just found Logan. Suddenly, Falco Angelini erupted from the market behind her and began taunting the youth holding the long, thin blade. "Do I see a knife?" he jeered. "Do you know how to use it, shithead?" Opening his arms wide, Angelini invited Leigh's would-be attacker to lunge at him. "You can't earn your bones cutting up little girls. Try cutting up a grown man. Cut *me* up. Come on, asshole, try it!"

Mesmerized, Leigh saw the second youth pull a knife out of his pocket just as the first one lunged. Angelini sidestepped the attack, grabbed the assailant's arm and yanked it back over his shoulder with a sickening bone-breaking sound that sent the youth stumbling backward into the alley, howling in pain. The second attacker was more skilled, less rushed, than his companion, and Leigh watched in paralyzed horror as he circled Angelini in a half-crouch, his blade flashing beneath the streetlamp. Suddenly the blade shot upward, Angelini stepped back, and the older boy screamed in pain and fell to his knees, clutching his groin. "You sonofabitch!" he whimpered, glaring at Angelini, trying to roll onto his side and get up.

While he was trying to get to his feet, Falco grabbed Leigh's arm and yanked her unceremoniously backward, into the doorway of the market. She stayed there, frozen, until both youths had taken off down the street and then disappeared into an alley. "We—we—we should call the police," she stammered finally.

Angelini scowled at her and pulled off the apron he'd been wearing. "Why?"

"Be . . . because we might be able to pick out their pictures. I'm not sure I could do it alone, but between the two of us, we might be able to identify them."

"All punks look alike to me," he said with a shrug. "I can't tell one from another."

Rebuffed, Leigh leaned forward and peered apprehensively in the direction of her apartment building. "I don't see any sign of them. They're probably a mile away by now." She glanced awkwardly at Angelini, trying to hide her fear of walking home alone. "Thank you for coming to my rescue," she said, and when he didn't reply, she stepped out of the doorway.

To her vast relief, he stepped forward, too. "I'll walk you home." He waited a moment for her to react and mistook her nervous silence for a dismissal. "Maybe you'd rather walk alone," he said, turning away.

Completely unnerved, Leigh actually clutched his arm to pull him with her. "No, wait! I'd like you to walk with me! I just didn't want to cause you any more trouble, Falco."

Her involuntary gesture seemed to amuse him, or perhaps it was what she'd said that amused him. "You haven't caused me any trouble."

"Other than almost getting you killed back there."

"I was not in any danger of being killed by those—" Whatever profanity he'd had in mind, he checked the words.

Encouraged by the communication they'd established, Leigh said, "I really think we should call the police."

"Suit yourself, but leave me out of it. I don't have time to waste on cops."

"How do you expect the police to protect us if citizens won't cooperate? Among other things, it's every citizen's duty . . ."

He shot her a look filled with such withering disdain she felt like sinking into the sidewalk. "What planet are you from?"

"I'm from Ohio," Leigh replied, so completely off balance that she could not form a better reply.

"That explains it," he said flatly, but for the second time in the last few minutes, she thought she heard a glimmer of amusement in his voice.

He walked her to her building, up four flights of stairs to her apartment door, and left her there.

HER NARROW ESCAPE from violence that night put a permanent end to Leigh's solitary nocturnal trips to Angelini's Market, but she continued to go there during the day for her groceries. On her next visit, she told Mrs. Angelini about her brush with danger, but instead of being proud of Falco, the poor woman was upset. "Ever since he was a little boy, he finds trouble and trouble finds him."

A little taken aback, Leigh looked around for her rescuer, and spotted him just inside the storeroom at the back of the store, stacking boxes. "I wanted to thank you properly," she announced, coming up behind him. He stiffened, as if startled; then he turned slowly and looked down at her, his black brows drawing into an impatient scowl, his thick black beard concealing the rest of his expression. "For what?" he said shortly.

He seemed somehow more distant and daunting than ever, his body taller and more massive than before, but Leigh was determined not to let any of that faze her. Ex-convict or not, he had risked his life to save hers, and then he had walked her home to make certain she got there safely. That was true gallantry, she thought, and as the word popped into her mind it crossed her lips. "For being so gallant," she explained.

"Gallant?" he repeated ironically. "Is that what you think I am?"

Despite Leigh's determination to stand her ground and not be thwarted in expressing her gratitude, she took a tiny, cautious step backward before she nodded emphatically. "Yes, I do."

"When did they let you out of your playpen, yesterday?"

Frustrated, Leigh put up her hand to stop any further argument. "My mind is made up. Don't try to change it, because you can't. Here," she said, holding out her other hand. "This is for you."

He eyed the gift-wrapped box she was holding as if it were a container of rat poison. "What's that?"

"A memento of the occasion. Open it later and find out for yourself." When he refused to reach for it, she stepped around him and put it on the bottom rung of an old wooden stepladder, next to some textbooks. "Are those yours? What are you studying?"

"Law," he said sarcastically, and Leigh choked on her laugh, horrified that her laughter would give away the fact that she knew he'd been in prison. And, unfortunately, it did. "If you're finished slumming," he said shortly, "I've got work to do."

"I didn't mean—" she said, backing out of the room. "I'm sorry for interrupting. I'll just—"

"Leave?" he suggested.

She never knew if he'd opened the gift she'd given him. But she had a feeling that if he had opened it, he wouldn't have liked or wanted the small pewter figure of a knight in armor she'd found in an antique shop. He never addressed a voluntary word to her after that, but at least when he saw her, he nodded curtly, acknowledging her presence. If she spoke to him first, he answered, and Leigh always smiled at him and said hello.

A few weeks after Falco had frightened off her attackers, Logan and she went to Angelini's for late-night snacks. Leigh introduced Logan to Mrs. Angelini; then she saw Falco and introduced the two men. After that, Mrs. Angelini always asked Leigh about her "young man." Falco never referred to Logan by any name or description, and not long afterward, he vanished completely. Mrs. Angelini said Falco had "gone back to school."

LYING IN HER HOSPITAL BED, Leigh thought of all that because the night she'd nearly been attacked had been the most terrifying experience of her life—until now, when Logan was missing. Then as now, she'd felt the same sense of terrifying helplessness, the feeling that she should have been more prepared, should have been able to anticipate this and safeguard Logan and herself from it.

CHAPTER 9

eigh's doctor, her nurse, and the hospital's administrator escorted her down in a wheelchair to an ambulance backed up to the rear entrance of the hospital. Brenna was waiting for her there, wearing a heavy jacket and red woolen cap. "Security says the coast is clear," she told Leigh.

The security guard standing beside her nodded. "Most of the press people left when they heard you were being discharged this morning," he told Leigh with a grin. "Two of them hung around though, hoping for a look at you. They gave me ten bucks to tip them off when you were leaving, so I pointed out that empty ambulance you arranged for; then they hopped in their cars and went after it. I figure they're sixty miles ahead of you by now."

Leigh asked Brenna to give him twenty dollars more for being so helpful. Two paramedics tried to help her out of the wheelchair, but she waved them away. "I can do it myself," she insisted, wincing with pain as she slowly eased herself into a standing position. All she'd done that morning was sign some autographs for the staff on her floor, shower, and get dressed, but she was already feeling weak and shaky. Mentally, however, she was alert and filled with purpose. The prospect of retracing her path and locating Logan in the next few hours had her geared up and ready to go the distance.

Brenna got into the ambulance behind her, and the vehicle began moving slowly down the driveway. "Where's our car?" Leigh asked.

"About two miles down the highway, at the American Legion Hall. I've already told the ambulance driver to take me there so I can get my car. He knows where the place is."

Shortly afterward, the ambulance slowed and turned into a parking lot filled with enough deep potholes to rock the vehicle and make Leigh grit her teeth in pain. "Are you okay?" Brenna asked worriedly.

Leigh slowly expelled her breath and nodded. "The hospital gave me some painkillers to take with me, but I don't want to use them because they make me feel woozy. I need to be completely focused and clearheaded right now. Would you help me up?" Leigh added as the vehicle drew to a stop.

One of the paramedics got out and went around to the rear of the ambulance to help Brenna down. He opened the doors, saw both women on their feet, and stepped back, staring at them. "I promised I'd leave the hospital in an ambulance," Leigh explained to the young man, "and that's exactly what I've done. However, I did not promise to stay in it all the way to Manhattan."

"I can't let you do this, Miss Kendall!"

Leigh managed a little smile and held out her hand to him for help. "You really don't have any choice."

"But—"

"If you make me jump down from this thing," she warned lightly, "the jolt will probably kill me." She stepped forward, and left with no other choice, the paramedic reached up to help her. The ambulance driver came around to see what was causing the delay, and Leigh held up her hand to halt his outburst. "There's no point in arguing," she told him.

They helped her into the silver Chevrolet Blazer Brenna had rented. "My secretary has your names," Leigh told them with a grateful smile. "She'll arrange for you to have four tickets to *Blind Spot* next Saturday night."

Normally, the promise of complimentary tickets to a sold-out Broadway play made even the most jaded New Yorker extremely happy, so Leigh was understandably taken aback when both men looked a little disappointed.

"If it wouldn't cause you any extra trouble," the driver said after exchanging a glance with his companion, "we'd rather wait until you're starring in the play again, Miss Kendall."

They were so young, and they saw so much suffering and horror, that Leigh had to restrain an impulse to pat his cheek. "Then, I'll arrange for that," she promised. "Brenna will call you when—when everything is back to normal," she finished. *Normal.* . . .

Leigh clung fiercely to the concept; she yearned for it—prayed for it as Brenna started the Blazer's engine.

CHAPTER 10

Snowbanks piled as high as the Blazer's hood, and sometimes its roof, lined the main highways and made the secondary roads so narrow that it was often difficult to squeeze two cars heading in opposite directions past each other.

For the first hour, nothing looked particularly familiar to Leigh except some major landmarks she'd noticed soon after she reached the mountains, landmarks she'd already been familiar with from her few previous trips to the Catskills. However, the deeper into the mountains they went, the more unfamiliar the landscape became and the more uncertain she was of the directions Logan had given her. Three hours after they started searching, Brenna insisted they stop for lunch and pulled into a McDonald's. "Has anything seemed familiar since we passed that little gas station back there?" she asked as they waited at the drive-up window for their order.

"I might as well have been driving blindfolded in a tunnel that night," Leigh said bleakly. "The visibility was so bad that I could only see a few feet beyond my headlights." She pressed her fingers to her temples, trying to massage away the tension and anxiety that made her head feel as if it were going to explode. "I should have been concentrating harder on Logan's directions, but I was concentrating on keeping the car on the road. And Logan's instructions weren't the kind you'd normally give someone. He was so excited about our 'mountain hideaway' that the map and directions he gave me were more like a treasure hunt—"

Leigh stopped herself from repeating that explanation yet again to Brenna. "Even so," she said bitterly, "I should be able to remember if the directions said to turn right when I was *four-tenths* of a mile past the stoplight in Ridgemore, or *four* miles past it! When I wrote the directions for the detectives on Tuesday, I thought I remembered everything important. But now, I'm not sure of that or anything else."

"You have to stop beating up on yourself," Brenna warned.

Leigh couldn't stop, but she tried not to do it aloud, for Brenna's sake.

After two more hours of searching and turning back whenever Leigh thought she might have recognized something, everything was beginning to look familiar to her. In desperation, Leigh began systematically exploring side roads and private roads, and even driveways, looking for the cabin Logan had described. She was prepared to explore every overgrown, rutted path that might have been a driveway long ago—but the snow made that impossible.

Several times they nearly got stuck, but Brenna was surprisingly skilled at handling the heavy four-wheel-drive vehicle—a skill she said she acquired growing up on her parents' farm. Brenna's ability to maneuver the Blazer through snowbanks, and the change that occurred in the weather that afternoon, were the only two positive events in an otherwise heartbreaking day. Shortly after they stopped for lunch, the sun appeared. In the space of an hour, the heavy clouds parted, the sky turned a brilliant blue, the temperature climbed above freezing, and the snow began melting.

In addition to bringing Leigh some clothes to wear, Brenna had also brought her a handbag with some spare items she'd found at Leigh's apartment. The sunglasses came in especially handy because they hid the tears that began gathering in Leigh's eyes and spilling over with increasing frequency as the afternoon wore on.

"If you're going to be on time for the press conference tonight," Brenna said, "we need to turn around and head back to the city pretty soon."

Leigh heard her, but she was craning her neck to see down a lane that had a steep drop-off. "Slow down—" she said excitedly, and Brenna stepped on the brake, slowing the Blazer to a crawl. "There's a house down there; I can see the roof." At the end of the steep drive, Leigh caught a glimpse of a large old house with a green roof, but Logan had said the only dwelling on their property was a tiny, three-room cabin, and its roof was gray slate. "That's not it," Leigh said bleakly. In the wake of her frustration and disappointment, a burst of anger swept over Leigh. "I haven't seen the helicopters Commissioner Trumanti was supposed to send out here today. What is he waiting for, anyway—summer?"

"The sky could be full of helicopters," Brenna pointed out gently, "but if they were over the next rise or around the next bend, we probably wouldn't be able to see them."

"Are you sure your cell phone is turned on?" Leigh asked.

Brenna kindly refrained from pointing out that they'd already had this discussion several times that day. "Positive. I checked it again when we stopped to use the rest room."

"I'd like to call Detective Shrader and Detective Littleton. I left voice mails for them this morning with your cell phone number, but maybe they didn't get my messages."

"My cell phone is in my purse on the seat behind us." As she spoke, Brenna tried to stretch her right arm between the front seats, but the purse was beyond her reach. "I'll have to pull over," she added, glancing in the rearview mirror.

"No, I'll get it," Leigh said, "keep driving." Leigh drew a deep breath, bracing for the pain in her ribs, and slowly, awkwardly, managed to twist herself around in the front seat and reach behind her for the purse. Brenna's purse was the size of a large airline carry-on bag, but the phone was on the top. Leigh's hand shook as she pressed the tiny keypad and put the phone to her ear.

Detective Shrader answered her call right away. "Have you had any news about my husband?" she asked him without preamble.

"No. If we did, I would have called you at the phone number you left on our voice mails this morning. Where are you now?"

"I'm in the mountains, trying to find the roads I took on Sunday."

"Having any luck?"

It took several seconds before Leigh could make herself admit the truth aloud. "I have no idea where I was, or where I was supposed to be."

Instead of commenting on that, Shrader said, "In your phone message this morning, you mentioned you were planning to give a press conference at your apartment tonight. Is that still on?"

When Leigh said that it was, he told her the police artist had a sketch of Leigh's rescuer ready to hand out to the media at the conference. "Detective Littleton and I could be there tonight and bring it with us," he volunteered. "It might be helpful to you to have representatives from the NYPD present—"

"I hadn't thought of that," Leigh admitted, but she decided to decline. "I truly appreciate your willingness to drive back to the city tonight, but I would rather you stay in the mountains and keep searching for my husband."

"Detective Littleton and I can drive to the city tonight and drive straight back up here early tomorrow morning to resume the search. We can always use the overtime."

"In that case, thank you, I'd like you to be at the press conference. One more thing," Leigh said swiftly. "Commissioner Trumanti said he was going to send helicopters to help with the search, but I haven't seen any of them today."

"Two of them have been in the air since noon, more will arrive tomorrow, but until the snow melts, the choppers can't cover as much territory as you think. The problem is, snow-covered roofs all look pretty much alike from the air, so they have to fly low and slow."

"I hadn't considered that," Leigh said, but she couldn't keep the despondency from her voice. Nature itself seemed to have declared war on her on Sunday.

"In case you haven't caught a weather report lately, this sunshine is supposed to stick around for another day or two. We have a team searching the roadsides for signs a vehicle went over the embankment and more searchers are due to arrive tomorrow. If the snow keeps melting the way it did today, we should be able to find the spot where you went off the road very quickly. Once we find that, the helicopters will be able to narrow down their search area for the cabin. Try not to worry," he finished. "Your husband was planning to stay in an old house with no power and no phone. If the road out of there is impassable, then he's built himself a nice fire and he's been waiting for us to figure out how to get him out of there."

Leigh thought that sounded completely unlike Logan. He'd have hiked through the snow to the main road the next morning, if for no other reason than that he'd have been worried about Leigh. "You're probably right," she lied.

"You'd better start back to the city right now," Shrader said. "If you intend to be there when that press conference starts, you're cutting it pretty close."

Thoroughly depressed, Leigh touched the red *disconnect* button on Brenna's cell phone. "Detective Shrader said we need to start back right away," she said, staring out the window at the snow-covered mountains dotted with towering pine trees. Somewhere up in these hills, she'd lost her car, and her husband, and nearly her life. She felt as if she were dangerously close to losing her grip on sanity, as well.

"Are you all right?" Brenna asked softly.

"I'm fine," she lied. "Everything's going to be okay," she added, trying to make herself believe that. "Logan is perfectly safe. We'll all laugh at this someday."

A MILE BEHIND THEM, in an unmarked Ford, Shrader glanced at Sam Littleton. "She's going to turn around and go home." Moments later, the silver Blazer passed them going in the opposite direction, heading toward the city. In his rearview mirror, Shrader watched the Blazer until it rounded a curve; then he made a leisurely U-turn and drove slowly along, no longer following the vehicle at all. "Considering how many times they've passed us on the road today," he said with a smirk, "it's amazing they haven't made us."

"That Blazer is one of the few clean vehicles in the Catskills," Sam murmured, studying the map in her lap that

Leigh Manning had given them Tuesday night. "The rest of us all look alike—filthy." With a sigh, she folded the map and slid it into a plastic evidence bag. "This morning, she seemed to be trying to follow roughly the same directions she gave us in the hospital. Then, around noon, she started backtracking and retracing her route in wider circles."

"Yeah, and after that, she started sightseeing. She figured we might follow her today, so she decided to take us for a ride—literally. You owe me a quarter, by the way."

He held out his hand, and Sam looked at his open palm and then at his smug profile. "For what?"

"Because I said that following her wasn't going to get us anywhere, but you thought she could be up to something interesting."

"Call me suspicious, but when I notice a badly injured, supposedly frantic woman getting out of an ambulance in a deserted parking lot on an open highway and then climbing into a vehicle that heads north instead of south, it just naturally sparks my interest."

"Ante up," he persisted. "Where's my quarter?"

"I'll deduct it from the seven dollars and forty-three cents you owe me for your M&M's and Cokes this trip."

"What?" he exclaimed, giving her his ferocious doggie look. "I don't owe you seven-forty-three, Littleton. I owe you six-forty-three."

Sam smiled at him. "Right, you do. And don't forget it."

CHAPTER II

Trish Lefkowitz was waiting in the apartment's outer foyer when Leigh and Brenna finally stepped out of the elevator, five minutes late for the press conference. "My God!" the publicist burst out, rushing forward to take Leigh's arm, "you look positively awful, Leigh. Which, in a way, is perfect," she added, always thinking of the public-relations value of everything. "Those reporters will take one look at you and be dying to help you."

Leigh scarcely heard her. She was looking around at the elegant black marble foyer with its carved gilt console tables and silk-covered Louis XIV chairs. Everything was exactly the same as when she left it on Sunday, except that now Logan was missing from her life. So nothing was the same.

A concealed door on the far left of the foyer, used for deliveries, led directly into the kitchen area. Brenna, Trish, and Leigh used that door to enter the apartment. Hilda was carrying glasses on a serving tray and she nearly dropped it at the sight of Leigh's bruised face and bedraggled appearance. "Oh, Mrs. Manning . . ." she burst out. "Oh, my. Oh—"

"I'm okay, Hilda. I just need to comb my hair," Leigh added as she carefully removed her arms from the coat Brenna had brought her. Based on the commotion in the living room, she gathered that quite a few members of the press were present.

"A little lipstick wouldn't hurt," Trish put in, reaching for the mirror and cosmetics she'd brought to the kitchen for exactly this purpose.

"Just a hairbrush," Leigh said absently, smoothing the wrinkles from the black slacks and sweater she was wearing. "Okay, I'm ready," she said after running a brush through her hair.

With Trish on one side of her and Brenna on the other, Leigh walked into her living room. Only six nights before, it had been filled with laughing people who'd come to help her celebrate one of the most wonderful nights of her life. Now the room was filled with staring strangers who'd come to pry, to observe, to record, and then report the lurid details of her living nightmare to the public. Strangers, all of them, except for Detectives Shrader and Littleton, who had just arrived.

"How are you feeling, Miss Kendall?" a reporter called.

"Give us a moment to get settled," Trish told them all.

She'd positioned a chair in front of the fireplace for Leigh to use, and Leigh sank down onto it, not because she was physically unable to stand, but because her entire body was beginning to quake. Somehow, the presence of the reporters and photographers in her home made Logan's disappearance seem even more macabre and more . . . real. She looked up at them and reluctantly signaled the start of the interview by saying, "Thank you for coming—"

Her words set off a volley of blinding camera lights and an instant barrage of questions: "Have you heard from your husband?" "Is there any truth to the rumor that he's been kidnapped?" "When was the last time you saw him?" "Do the police know who ran you off the road?" "How are you feeling, Miss Kendall?" "Is it true that the two of you had been discussing divorce?" "What are the police doing?" "Do they have any suspects? Who found you the night of your accident? Was it an accident or do you think it was deliberate?" "When are you planning to return to your role in *Blind Spot*?"

Leigh held up her hand to stop the questions. "Please, just listen to what I have to say—I'll tell you everything I know as quickly as I can." The room grew silent, except for the whirring of the video cameras. She told them why she had been driving into the mountains Sunday night, and she gave them the details of her accident. "As you know, the police haven't been able to identify the man who found me on the side of the road," she finished, "but they have a police artist's sketch and they'll give it to you tonight."

"Why haven't the police been able to find your car?"

"I'll let them explain that to you," Leigh said weakly as a wave of dizziness swamped her. She tried to focus on Shrader and saw him nod that he'd deal with their questions about the police investigation. "I invited you here not only to answer your questions," Leigh continued, "but also because I need your help. Please put that sketch in front of the public. Someone out there will surely recognize the man in that sketch. He knows where my accident happened, and—wherever it was—it's near the place I was supposed to meet my husband. I'd also like you to have a description of my husband's car . . ." Leigh paused again, feeling very strange, very clammy, and she sent a silent appeal for help to Detective Littleton, who was standing off to the side, her face a mixture of what appeared to Leigh to be alertness and curiosity. "Will you give these people the information about Logan's car, and anything else they can use to help us?"

"Yes, of course, Mrs. Manning," Detective Littleton said promptly, drawing several admiring looks from the males in the room.

Detectives Littleton and Shrader took over at that point and answered questions for the next ten minutes. Leigh listened until they were finished, but she was gripping the arms of her chair toward the end, trying to stay upright while the room began to recede and revolve. She reached a shaking hand up to her forehead just as a reporter from one of the newspapers suddenly addressed her. "Miss Kendall, can you think of any reason why your husband might not want to be found? Business problems, or—?"

Leigh frowned at him, trying to keep his face in focus. "That's ridiculous."

"What about the rumors that your marriage wasn't as idyllic as you'd like the public to believe—that, in fact, he was involved with another woman?"

Leigh mustered all her strength and looked straight at him. "My husband is a wonderful man, and a loyal and loving husband." With quiet dignity, she added, "I cannot believe you would soil his reputation, or deliberately hurt and humiliate me at this moment, by commenting on what are nothing but ugly, unfounded rumors."

Trish Lefkowitz decided it was time to put an end to the press conference. "Okay, people!" she announced, "that's it for tonight. Thank you for coming. Right now, Miss Kendall needs to get some rest."

Several reporters tried to ask one more question, but Trish firmly and pleasantly cut them off. "No more questions tonight. I'll contact you with updates every time we have anything at all to tell you." So saying, she went to the front door of the apartment and opened it, standing there while they put away their recorders and notepads, packed up their cameras, and filed out.

With her hand braced on the back of her chair for support, Leigh managed to stand up and thank each of them individually for coming, but when Trish finally closed the door behind the last straggler, she sank back onto the chair. Shrader was on his cell phone, so Leigh spoke to Littleton. "Thank you for being here, and for . . . everything. Would you like some tea or coffee?" she added. "I'll have a cup with you."

"Thanks, coffee would be great," Detective Littleton replied, and Leigh marveled at how fresh and rested the pretty brunette always looked. She glanced around for Hilda and saw her standing on the sidelines, surveying the damage to her perfect living room. "Hilda, would you bring coffee for all of us?"

Shrader snapped his cell phone closed. "Never mind the coffee," he said to Hilda. "We'll take our coats instead." He turned to Leigh, his expression intense and energized. "A state trooper may have located the place where you went off the road. He was writing up a motorist on a speeding violation tonight when he happened to notice a bunch of freshly broken tree limbs leading down from the embankment where he was standing. The snow plows had piled up a lot of snow along the side of the road there, so he couldn't see any tire tracks or inspect the guardrail for damage, but he knows there's an old quarry somewhere down at the bottom."

He paused to put on the heavy jacket Hilda was holding. "We've already got a couple NYPD units up there right now," he added, "and I'll arrange for more to be on hand first thing in the morning. Littleton and I will grab a few hours' sleep and be up there when things start happening. We'll call you as soon as we know anything."

Leigh wasn't interested in recovering her car; she was interested in recovering her husband. "If that's the place where I had my accident, then the cabin can't be far away. I don't understand why everything has to wait until morning."

"Because it's too dark to accomplish anything more tonight," Shrader pointed out patiently. "The state trooper tried to go down the embankment, using his flashlight, but it's very steep and treacherous underfoot, especially at night. As soon as we get some daylight, we'll be able to tell very quickly if he found the right place. And if he did find it, our teams will start combing the surrounding area by air and on the ground."

"But we're losing so much time, waiting for morning—" Leigh protested again, wringing her hands.

"A few hours isn't going to make much difference if your husband found shelter from the storm."

"But what if he didn't?" Leigh argued.

Shrader's answer made her wish she hadn't asked the question. "In that case," he replied matter-of-factly, "after five days, a few hours more isn't going to make any difference." He looked impatiently at Detective Littleton, who was slowly putting on her jacket, her gaze fixed on Leigh. "If the state police have actually found the place where you went off the road," he added, starting for the door with Littleton finally following, "then the map you gave us at the hospital was way off. The location the trooper pinpointed tonight is at least twenty miles away from where your directions sent us. Then again, this may not be the right spot at all, so don't get your hopes up too high."

Littleton walked up the foyer steps, pulling on her gloves; then she paused at the front door and turned to Leigh. "The best thing you can do now, Mrs. Manning, is to go to bed and stay there until you hear from us in the morning. Several times tonight, you looked as if you were going to pass out."

"You did," Trish said as soon as the front door closed behind the two detectives. "Brenna and I are going home now," she announced, already heading for the coat closet, "and *you* are going to eat something and go straight to bed. Brenna said you barely touched any food today."

"That's right," Brenna confirmed; then she turned to Hilda and deftly shifted Leigh into the care of the loyal housekeeper: "She hasn't eaten, Hilda, and she hasn't taken her pain pills either. They're in her purse."

"I'll look after her," Hilda promised. She ushered Brenna and Trish out of the apartment; then she went to Leigh, who had sunk back onto her chair. "I made dinner for you earlier, and I'll bring it to you on a tray, along with your medicine, after you're in bed. Here, let me help you up, Mrs. Manning."

"Thank you, Hilda," Leigh said, too exhausted and weak to protest. She stood up and trailed slowly along in the wake of the bustling housekeeper.

"I'll turn your bed down first," Hilda said over her shoulder.

Turning the bed down required the removal of the elaborate designer pillows that covered nearly half the mattress and obscured much of the Queen Anne headboard. Normally, Hilda made the nightly removal of the pillows into a ceremonial procession that both amused and fascinated Leigh. First, an armload of fringed pillows were removed and carried into the linen closet, followed by two armloads of pillows with tassels, followed by two more armloads of pillows trimmed with miscellaneous braids, cords, and rickrack. In the morning, the entire loving ceremonial procession began again, in reverse.

That night, however, Hilda broke with her usual tradition in a way that made Leigh realize how truly pained the housekeeper was by Leigh's situation. "I'll just clear these pillows out of your way," Hilda announced; then she bent over the bed, braced her hands on the pile, and with a single mighty shove, she sent most of them tumbling off the bed onto the floor on the opposite side. She dispatched the few remaining pillows by bracing her knee on the mattress and swatting the malingerers onto the floor; then she straightened and pulled back the fluffy white duvet. "I'll warm up your dinner while you get ready for bed," she said, and Leigh nodded, already on her way into her dressing room.

Too exhausted to contemplate a shower, Leigh pulled off her slacks and sweater. She was reaching for a nightgown when Hilda walked past the open doorway carrying the thick, down-filled pillows that were used on the bed at night. The housekeeper stopped in her tracks and let out a muffled cry of anguish at the sight of Leigh's battered body. "Oh no! Oh, Mrs. Manning! You poor thing—you should be in the hospital!"

"I'm just bruised up, that's all," Leigh said. She was so touched by Hilda's anguished expression that she started to give her a reassuring hug; then she changed her mind out of fear for her fractured ribs. Gingerly, Leigh lifted her arms and began easing the nightgown over her head. When she could see again, Hilda was gone. Relieved that she didn't have to conceal what a difficult and painful ordeal the simple act of walking was right then, Leigh clamped her right arm over her aching ribs, then limped slowly and awkwardly across the room to the bed.

Alone in the bed she'd always shared with Logan, she gazed at the achingly familiar room, remembering the last time he'd been here with her. She closed her eyes and she could visualize him, standing beside the bed, exactly as he'd been on Sunday morning, his voice teasing as he pressed a good-bye kiss on her cheek. *"I've already loaded*

*the car. I think I have everything I need—house plans,
stakes, string, a transom, sleeping bags. I still feel like I'm
forgetting something . . ."*

*"A broom, a mop, and a bucket? . . . Disinfectant?
Mousetraps?"*

He nuzzled her neck, trying to tickle her, and she
pulled the pillow over her head so he couldn't.

"Leave straight from the theater. Don't be late," he said
as he headed for the door.

But Leigh continued her joking chant of practical ne-
cessities, *"Drinking water . . . food for dinner . . ."*

The memory of that happy, halcyon morning finally
demolished the iron grip Leigh had been keeping on her
rampaging emotions, and tears began to stream in hot tor-
rents down her cheeks. "Oh, darling," she sobbed, turning
her face into the pillows, "wherever you are, stay safe for
me. Please, please stay safe."

She never knew if Hilda actually brought in a dinner
tray, but sometime during the night, she thought she felt
someone smooth the covers over her and brush the hair off
her face. She wanted it to be Logan, needed it to be Logan,
and so she let herself believe it had been—just for a little
while. After all, pretending was what she did best.

CHAPTER 12

The ringing of the telephone jolted Leigh awake at eight o'clock the next morning. In another part of the house, Hilda answered it on the second ring, and Leigh stared fixedly at the little red light glowing on the phone beside her bed.

All of the apartment phones had three separate telephone lines—a main line, her private line, and Logan's private line—and this call had come in on the main line. Since the police had her private phone number, she knew the call wasn't from them, but she clung to the hope that someone was calling with news of Logan. Praying that the little light would start blinking, indicating that Hilda had put the caller on hold and was coming to get her, Leigh waited, watching it. Moments later it went out, and she climbed out of bed, her hopes dashed, her tension already beginning to mount.

By the time she finished showering and washing her hair, the telephone was ringing incessantly, and each call jangled her nerves a little more. The face that looked back at her in the mirror at her dressing table was pale, bruised, and haunted. Her face, but not her face—another thing that was familiar to her and yet completely alien, just like her life today, and every day since she'd first awakened in the hospital.

The stitches in her scalp and the stiffness in her arms made the simple act of blowing her hair dry into an uncomfortable, awkward challenge that seemed to take forever. In her closet, she reached for the first sweater on the nearest shelf, a brown one; then she hesitated. The shelf beside it held a cherry red sweater. Logan had asked her to wear red to the party Saturday night because he'd bought her rubies, which of course were also red. Leigh decided to wear red today. Maybe if she did that, their lives would somehow pick up where they'd left off Saturday night. Maybe it would change her luck if she put on something bright and cheerful. She put on the red sweater and the wool slacks that matched it.

By eight-forty-five, when Leigh left the bedroom, the phone was ringing almost nonstop. Normally the sight of her living room, with its polished parquet floors, soaring marble colonnades, and expansive views of Central Park, gave Leigh's spirits a lift, but that morning it was just another meaningless space that was rendered lonely and bizarre by the disappearance of one of its owners. Leigh heard Brenna's voice coming from the kitchen, at the other end of the apartment, so she went there.

The kitchen was a large inviting room with an island in the center and a wide window. Its weathered brick walls and arched fireplace made it seem cozy and rustic, despite the commercial-size stainless steel appliances that lined the walls. Brenna was standing near the refrigerator, talking on the telephone and making notes on a pad; Hilda was at the stove, stirring something in a pot. She saw Leigh in the doorway and stopped to pour her a cup of coffee. "I'm making your breakfast," she said.

When Brenna finished with the caller, Leigh motioned her over to the table to join her. Eyeing the spiral notebook in Brenna's hand, she said, "Who do I want to hear about?"

Brenna began scanning the pages of neatly written notes. "Sybil Haywood said to tell you she's working on your astrological chart and she should have some guidance to offer you very soon. Courtney Maitland wants to come up and visit you as soon as you 'can possibly bear some company.' Senator Hollenbeck called to tell you that he's at your service. Judge Maxwell called to say . . ." Leigh's attention wandered during the long list of well-wishers, but she listened closely again as Brenna came to the end and said, "Dr. Winters called yesterday and again early this morning. She said to tell you that she's holding you in her thoughts, and that she would like to come and see you to help 'keep the vigil' whenever you want company. She also phoned in a prescription for you, and she wants you to start taking it immediately."

"What sort of prescription?"

Brenna hesitated and then said very firmly, "She said it's an antianxiety medication. She said she knows you won't like the idea, but it will help you to think clearly and stay calm right now, when you most need to do both."

"I'm calm," Leigh said.

Brenna's doubtful gaze shifted to Leigh's hands on the table. They were clasped together and clenched so tightly that the tops of her fingers were white. Leigh hastily unclasped them. Brenna continued, "I sent Joe O'Hara to the pharmacy to pick up the prescription."

It took Leigh a moment to realize that Joe O'Hara was her new chauffeur-bodyguard. Not only had she forgotten his name in the chaos of the last few days, she'd forgotten that Matt and Meredith Farrell had insisted on loaning O'Hara to her before they left on their world cruise. He was staying at their New York apartment, but he was supposed to drive Leigh about in the Farrell limousine and protect her from further approaches by her stalker.

"I may as well warn you," Brenna added with a sigh, "he's a little upset that we didn't ask him to drive the Blazer for us yesterday."

Leigh lifted her hands in helpless admission of the embarrassing truth. "That would have been a good idea. I just—forgot he existed."

"If you ask me," Hilda angrily announced, "that man doesn't know his place! He's supposed to drive you when *you* want him to, not when *he* decides he should." She banged a pot to emphasize her opinion. "He's just a chauffeur."

Leigh forced herself to focus on the matter at hand before it resulted in more disharmony in her already disharmonious life. "I understand what you're saying, Hilda, but he's not used to being 'just a chauffeur.' He's worked for the Farrells for years, and they think of him as a very loyal member of their family. They told him to look after me while they were gone, and he's probably going to take that very seriously, particularly right now when—when things are so mixed up." She was about to say more when the service door into the kitchen from the elevator foyer was flung open, and she half rose in her chair, stifling a cry of nervous shock.

"Sorry, I guess I shoulda knocked," Joe O'Hara said, striding into the kitchen wearing a heavy black overcoat with the collar turned up over his ears.

A thick-shouldered, heavyset man about five feet ten inches tall, he had the lumbering gait of a grizzly bear and an almost-ugly face that looked as if it had taken serious poundings in either the boxing ring or street brawls. His appearance didn't daunt Hilda, however. She glared at him over her shoulder and snapped, "Don't you come into my kitchen without wiping your feet!"

A flash of surprised annoyance made the chauffeur look almost threatening as he glared first at the irate woman across the room and then at his shiny shoes. Dismissing the entire matter with a shrug, he hung his overcoat in the closet and approached the kitchen table carrying a little white bag from the local pharmacy in his meaty fist. "Mrs. Manning," he said, his gravelly voice tinged with calm resolution. "I realize you don't know me, and you probably don't want a stranger underfoot at a time like this, but your husband and Matt Farrell both told me to look after you and make sure you stay safe."

Leigh had to tip her head all the way back in order to see him, and since that made her neck hurt, she motioned him to sit next to Brenna. "When you walked in just now, you startled me. It's not that I don't want you here," she finished.

"No need to apologize," he told her, settling his broad frame onto a chair that looked a little too small for him. "But I have to tell you that if you'd let me drive you into the mountains Sunday, instead of driving there yourself, you might not be sitting here grittin' your teeth so no one will notice how bad you hurt."

"Thank you for making my effort unnecessary," Leigh replied, not at all certain whether she liked him or not.

Her reprimand sailed over the chauffeur's head. "Yesterday, you shoulda called *me* and let me do the driving. You two women got no business driving around the mountains in the snow by yourselves. You coulda got stuck!"

"Well, we obviously didn't," Brenna pointed out.

"Yeah, lucky for you. But if you had, what would you have done, hiked off for help while Mrs. Manning huddled alone in the car, hurt and sick and trying to stay warm after it ran out of gas?"

"They would have managed just fine," Hilda informed him sharply as she stirred the contents of the pot on the stove.

Leigh observed the uneasy, heated exchange taking place between her three employees as if from a great distance, her entire being focused on the telephone and the clock on the opposite wall. When Logan's private line suddenly lit up and began to ring, she shoved Brenna back in her chair and bolted for the phone, her injuries forgotten. "Hello," she burst out breathlessly.

The male voice on the other end was deep and unfamiliar. "Mrs. Manning?"

"Yes, who is this?"

"Michael Valente."

Leigh slumped against the wall, unable to hide her disappointment. "Yes, Mr. Valente?"

"I'm sorry to disturb you. From the sound of your voice, I assume you haven't had any word yet about Logan?"

"No. Nothing."

"I'm sorry," he said again. He hesitated a moment and then said, "I know this isn't good timing, but Logan has some documents I need. He had them with him at your home when he called me from there Saturday afternoon. I'm only a few blocks away. Would it be at all possible for me to stop by and get them?"

"I have no idea where they are," Leigh said, disliking the idea of anyone going through Logan's things when he wasn't there.

"They are the plans and a prospectus from another project of mine that Logan borrowed."

The documents were his property, not Logan's. He was making that courteously but abundantly clear. Leigh swallowed her resentment and disappointment that the call wasn't from or about Logan. "I see. Then come over and get them."

"Thank you very much. I'll be there in twenty minutes."

Leigh forced herself away from the supporting wall, hung up the phone, and looked around at the occupants of the kitchen. A few moments ago, they had merely been employees who seemed to be bickering over nothing, but as she looked at the three tense faces etched with raw anxiety, sympathy, and concern for her, her heart melted. They truly cared; they wanted to help in whatever way they could. She had a thousand acquaintances, but she knew she couldn't count on their discretion or their silence. She knew from experience that Hilda and Brenna were completely trustworthy, and she had a feeling that Joe O'Hara probably was, too. Right now, those three people were her closest friends and allies, her family.

She gave them a wan smile, but disappointment over the phone call she'd answered made her face even paler, and Brenna noticed it. She opened the bag from the pharmacy, removed the prescription bottle, and held it toward Leigh. "Leigh, Dr. Winters was insistent that you take these."

Leigh gently but firmly pushed the bottle away. "I don't like drugs that affect my mind. I don't need them. Later, if I feel that I do, I'll take them. I promise."

Satisfied that the pill issue seemed to be resolved, O'Hara tackled the issue that was foremost on his own mind. "If you've got a spare room I could use, I think it would be a good idea if I stayed here until things settle down."

Leigh's apartment had sixteen rooms, including two small suites that were intended to be used as "servants' quarters," one of which Hilda occupied. The other was vacant, but Leigh felt a sudden, almost superstitious need to keep everything exactly as it had been before Logan disappeared. So long as everything stayed the same, his absence was only temporary, but making a change—that might encourage or imply permanence. "That's very nice of you, but I'm not alone. Hilda stays here."

His reply made Hilda whirl around and glower. "I'm real sure Hilda could beat up an omelet or wallop the dust right out of a rug," he mocked, "but until your husband comes back, I really think you need a man around here to deal with people problems. The lobby's crawling with reporters, you got fans lined up out on the sidewalk, and you got a stalker who knows your husband is out of the way now. There's no telling when somebody's gonna pay off your doorman or find some other way to sneak up here, but sooner or later, it's gonna happen." Sensing that Leigh was wavering, he quickly played his trump card. "I'm sure your husband would expect me to stay here and look after his womenfolk," he stated emphatically, and to Leigh's shock, he cast a benevolent look around the room that encompassed indignant, self-sufficient Hilda and displeased, independent Brenna in the category of "womenfolk" O'Hara felt obliged to protect.

Somewhere in her frantic mind, Leigh noted that O'Hara had a small, startling knack for diplomacy and wily persuasion, because he'd scored his win as soon as he deftly turned his wishes into Logan's wishes. "You're probably right, Mr. O'Hara. Thank you very much."

"You're welcome. And please call me Joe," he reminded her. "That's what Meredith—I mean, Mrs. Farrell—calls me."

Leigh nodded as she shifted her attention to Hilda, who was placing two bowls on the place mat in front of her. "What is this?" Leigh asked, staring at a bowl containing a thick white substance that looked like gritty paste. Beside it was a smaller bowl of nasty-looking brown lumps that made Leigh's stomach churn.

"It's Cream of Wheat and prunes," Hilda said. "I heard Mr. Manning say that was what you were going to have for breakfast from now on." When Leigh continued to stare blankly at her, she added, "I heard him say it on Sunday morning, just before he left for that place in the mountains where you were supposed to meet him."

The achingly sweet memory washed over Leigh. *"No more pears,"* Logan had teased her. *"You're addicted. From now on, it's Cream of Wheat and prunes for you."* Tears blurred Leigh's vision, and without realizing what she was doing, she put her arms on the table around the two bowls, encircling them, trying to gather them to her and protect the happy memory. Her head fell forward, and her shoulders began to shake with helpless weeping that embarrassed her and alarmed the people in the kitchen. Trying to gain control and make light of what had happened, she turned her face away and brushed the tears from her cheeks with her right hand. With her left hand, she reached toward Brenna and opened her palm. Brenna understood and put one of Sheila Winters's prescription pills in it.

"I'm sorry," she told the three of them. They looked at her with such intense, speechless sympathy that she had to blink back a fresh surge of tears.

"I'll fix you your usual breakfast," Hilda announced, relying as always on domestic matters to achieve balance in an otherwise unbalanced, disorderly world.

"I think I'll eat this one today," Leigh said, giving in to a fresh rush of painful sentimentality as Brenna got up to answer yet another call on the main line.

CHAPTER 13

With her gaze riveted on the kitchen clock, Leigh forced down part of her breakfast while she tried to gauge how long it would take for Shrader and Littleton to determine if the state trooper had actually found the location of her accident.

In Brenna's office in the next room, the phone continued to ring incessantly, and each time Brenna answered a call, Leigh tensed, waiting. . . . When Brenna finally reappeared in the kitchen, holding a cordless phone in her hand, Leigh jumped up from the table and nearly overturned her chair, only to have Brenna quickly shake her head and explain, "It's Meredith Farrell. They've just heard about your accident and everything. I thought you might want to talk to her."

Leigh nodded and took the call. The shipboard satellite hookup was poor, and there was the usual brief delay that caused both parties to either talk at the same time or stop and wait unnecessarily to see if the other person was finished speaking. Meredith volunteered to cancel their trip and fly back to New York, and Matt Farrell offered the services of a large investigative firm that was among the companies he owned. Leigh declined both offers and thanked them sincerely. She was certain the Farrells' offer to cancel their trip had been a courtesy that they knew she would decline, but she was surprised and touched by it nonetheless.

After that call, she went into the living room and sat down at her desk, waiting for something to happen. Within moments, Brenna walked in to give her news she didn't want: "Horace down in the lobby just called and said that Mr. Valente is here. I told Horace to send him up. Do you want to go into the other room and let me handle him?"

Leigh very much wanted to do exactly that, but she did not want anyone touching anything in Logan's study unless she herself was there. "No, I'll take care of it," Leigh said as a buzzer announced the arrival of her unwanted visitor at her door.

Brenna let him in and automatically offered to take his coat. To Leigh's dismay, he shrugged out of it and handed it to her, which evidently meant he intended to stay longer than the time it would take to find his papers and leave. Leigh had no intention of granting Michael Valente a social visit, but as he strode swiftly down the foyer steps and crossed the living room toward her, it was a little difficult to believe the tall, immaculately groomed, athletically built man striding toward her was a criminal. Dressed in an exquisitely tailored dark blue suit, pristine white shirt, and a navy blue and dark gold silk herringbone tie, he looked like an expensively dressed Wall Street banker. But then, so had John Gotti.

As he came toward her, he subjected Leigh to the same sort of intense scrutiny he'd focused on her the night of her party, and she found it just as discomforting and overly personal. She stood rigidly while he finished inspecting every feature on her face at close range, but she ignored his hands when he held them out to her and said quietly, "How are you holding up?"

"As well as can be expected," Leigh said politely but impersonally.

He slid his rejected hands into his pants pockets, an odd smile lurking at the corner of his mouth, and said absolutely nothing, which made Leigh feel awkward, rude, and ill at ease. In that state of momentary uncertainty, she felt compelled to add something. "I feel better than I look," she said.

"I'm sure you must," he said with his ghost of a smile. "I've seen faces that looked worse than yours—but their owners weren't breathing."

Leigh figured he'd probably seen a lot of dead people, at least one of whom he'd killed himself, and she turned abruptly toward Logan's study. "I'm not certain what you're looking for, but—"

"Leigh!" Brenna burst out, running into the living room, while Hilda and Joe O'Hara both crowded into the kitchen doorway. "Detective Shrader is on the telephone! It's important."

Leigh grabbed for the closest telephone, one that was on an end table next to the living room sofa. "Detective Shrader?"

"Mrs. Manning, we're pretty sure we've found the spot where you went off the road. There are some boulders near the top of an embankment with fresh black paint on them, and there's a path of broken branches down the embankment. There's a small clearing at the bottom and we've just determined there's water under the snow and ice there. We've also detected a large mass of metal in the water, and we've called for trucks with winches—"

"What about my husband!" Leigh burst out. "He has to be somewhere close to there!"

"We've got search teams on the way to the area; they'll start circling out over—"

"I'm coming out there. Where are you?"

"Look, why don't you just stay by the phone. It will take you several hours to—"

"I want to be there!"

Michael Valente touched her sleeve. "I have a helicopter—"

Leigh's momentary annoyance at his interruption gave way to dizzying gratitude. "Detective Shrader," she said into the phone, "I have use of a helicopter. Tell me where you are—" As she spoke, Leigh looked wildly about for paper and a pen. Valente reached for the phone with one hand and into his jacket pocket for a pen with the other. "I'll get the directions," he told her. "Go and get ready to leave."

As Leigh rushed for the bedroom, she heard him say into the phone, "Exactly where are you, Detective?"

It took Leigh several painful minutes to pull on her boots, and when she emerged carrying her coat and gloves, Valente was already standing in the foyer with his coat on, flanked by Brenna and Hilda. He frowned as he watched her walking toward him; then he took her coat from her. "Stand still, and let me do the work," he instructed, and then he drew each sleeve over her arm, rather than merely holding the coat behind her.

The procedure took only moments, but to Leigh it seemed much longer. She was already out the door with him when she called over her shoulder to Brenna and Hilda, "I'll phone you as soon as I know anything."

"Don't forget," Brenna said.

In the elevator, Leigh felt Michael Valente's eyes on her, but she was so grateful to him that she was able to ignore his scrutiny and even managed to give him a wan smile as she said, "Thank you very much for what you're doing."

He dismissed that without reply. "A couple of reporters were hanging around the entrance to your building," he said instead. "I had your secretary phone my driver and tell him to bring my car around to the service entrance. Where is it?" he asked as they stepped out of the elevator.

"Follow me." The elevators were blocked from the view of people on the street by a veritable forest of potted trees in the lobby, and Leigh carefully stayed behind them as she turned right, toward the rear of the building. They emerged into an alley blocked by two identical black Mercedes limousines with chauffeurs standing at attention beside each of the vehicles' open passenger doors.

Valente's car was in the rear. His chauffeur was a clean-cut man in his early thirties, who looked like a Secret Service agent who ought to be driving a dignitary's car. Joe O'Hara, with his bulky body and prizefighter's broken face, looked as if he should be driving a former convict's car. Valente started to steer Leigh toward his own car, but O'Hara stepped purposefully into his path. "I'm Mrs. Manning's driver," he informed Valente.

"I have my own car and driver," Valente said shortly, starting to step around him.

"Then you can take your car and lead the way, but Mrs. Manning rides with me."

At his confrontational tone and manner, Valente's chauffeur suddenly started forward. "Is there a problem here, Mr. Valente?"

"There is going to be," O'Hara warned with a surprisingly sharp edge to his voice.

"Get the hell out of the way—" Valente said in a low, explosive voice.

"Please!" Leigh cried. "We're wasting time." She

looked at Michael Valente, her eyes pleading. Her life had become a dark, dangerous, unknown sea that she had to navigate, and at the moment, O'Hara was the only slightly familiar person in it. She rather wanted him with her. "My husband told Mr. O'Hara to stay with me. I'd like to let him do that."

To her surprised relief, Valente capitulated immediately, but the look he gave O'Hara was distinctly unpleasant. "Get in and drive," he said shortly, holding the door himself for Leigh.

CHAPTER 14

Seated next to Valente's pilot, wearing thick padded headphones to muffle the roar of the rotors, Leigh anxiously scanned the scene below. The state police had blocked off the mountain road, men were swarming over the steep snow-covered incline, and trucks with winches were backed up on the shoulder. Police cars from the NYPD and the state police lined both sides of the road, and several police helicopters were flying slow circles over the hills nearby, undoubtedly searching for the cabin that Leigh believed was near the site of her accident.

Valente's voice came through her earphones, calm, matter-of-fact, and strangely reassuring. "They've found something in the water down there, and they've already got the winches connected to it." To the pilot, he said, "Put us down on the road, behind the tow trucks."

"It's going to be tight, Mr. Valente. There's a wider spot a half mile back where the trees aren't so close to the road."

"Mrs. Manning can't walk that far. Put us down behind the trucks," he ordered.

It occurred to Leigh that if the helicopter crashed because it got hung up in tree limbs, none of them were going to be able to walk anywhere for a very long time, but caution was not a priority of hers at that moment.

The helicopter rotors were still whipping snow into a white typhoon when Valente came around to her side and lifted her down. His eyes narrowed when she bent forward, clutching her midriff. "How bad are your ribs?"

"Not bad," Leigh lied, trying to catch her breath. "Small fractures." With O'Hara on her left and Valente on her right, Leigh looked around for the two New York City detectives. Detective Littleton was standing in the road, a phone pressed to one ear, her hand covering the other, her ponytail blowing in the wind. Shrader was on the shoulder of the road, opposite the tow trucks, talking to a New York City officer. He saw Leigh, ended his conversation, and started toward her. "Good morning, Mrs. Manning—" he said politely; then he recognized Valente, and Shrader's expression turned positively hostile.

"Have your helicopters found any sign of the cabin yet?" Leigh asked.

"No," Shrader said curtly, his gaze riveted on Michael Valente's face. When he finally shifted his attention to Leigh, he looked at her with such icy contempt that she felt as if she'd committed a crime merely by being in Valente's presence.

"Are you certain you've found my car?" she asked.

His gaze flicked to Valente. "At this moment," he informed her sarcastically, "I'm not certain of anything." Without another word, he turned on his heel and strode toward the tow trucks, but first he stopped to say something to the officer he'd been talking to earlier. The officer nodded and walked in the direction of Michael Valente's helicopter.

Put off by Shrader's attitude, Leigh stayed where she was, partially shielded from the wind by Joe O'Hara and Valente, while the winches on both trucks revolved slowly, haltingly, grinding almost to a stop, then moving abruptly again as they slowly dragged the dead weight of an unseen object through the trees and up the incline. Leigh thought of walking over to the edge of the road to get an early glimpse of what she knew was going to be her car, but she stayed where she was, reluctant to go near Shrader in his current mood. She watched the helicopters searching the ridges to her right; then she glanced to the left and saw the police officer in an intense conversation with Valente's helicopter pilot. The pilot was retrieving books and documents from inside the plane and showing them to him. "What is he doing?" she asked Valente, motioning to the officer.

Valente looked in the direction she indicated. "He's hassling my pilot," he replied flatly.

Based on his attitude, Leigh assumed that being hassled by the police was probably a regular routine for him. "Oh," she said lamely.

"Mrs. Manning—" Shrader motioned for Leigh to join him. "Is that your vehicle?"

With inexplicable feelings of dread, Leigh walked slowly to the edge of the embankment and looked down at the tortured metal remains of what had once been her car. No longer oblong and shiny black, the Mercedes was burned to bare metal in places and mangled into a shape that vaguely resembled a squashed cube. "Yes," she said. "That's my car."

Valente came up behind her and looked over the embankment. "Jesus Christ!" he said softly.

Tearing her gaze from the automobile that had nearly been her temporary casket, Leigh focused on the helicopters searching the distant skyline. "How long do you think it will be before they find the place I was supposed to meet my husband?"

"It's hard to say. Could be any minute, or it might take hours or even longer."

Before she could say anything, one of the officers shouted that Shrader had a radio call, and he turned his back on her and strode off. Praying that the call involved news of Logan, Leigh watched Shrader walk over to a patrol car, reach in through the open window, and take out the police radio. He listened for a moment; then he twisted around sharply and looked up at the horizon to the northeast. Leigh followed his gaze. One of the helicopters had narrowed its circle and was swooping lower and lower, flying in very tight circles. "They've found something!" she burst out, grabbing Valente's arm in her excitement. "Look—over there, at the helicopter farthest away. He's flying low, and the other helicopters have started over there toward him. They've found Logan. I think they've found Logan!"

Shrader finished talking on the radio and tossed it onto the front seat of the car; then he trotted over to her. "One of our pilots thinks he's found the house. Small stone cabin with a light gray slate roof. He thinks he can make out a stone well, too—like a little 'wishing well' near the cabin. Did your husband mention anything about a wishing well?"

"Yes!" Leigh exclaimed. "Yes, he did. I'd forgotten about that!"

"Okay, then," he said, turning to motion to Littleton. "Let's go!" he shouted. He started toward their car, and Littleton trotted to it from the opposite direction, getting in on the driver's side.

Leigh tried to run after him and nearly passed out on the third step from the streaks of pain in her ribs. "Wait," she called, grasping her midriff. "I want to go with you."

Shrader turned, frowning at the delay, as if he'd forgotten she had an intense personal interest in the search. "It would be better if you wait here."

"I want to go with you," Leigh repeated angrily.

He glanced around, saw the police officer who'd been "hassling" Valente's pilot earlier, and motioned him over. After a brief conversation, Shrader continued toward his own car, and the police officer walked over to Leigh. The name tag on his jacket said he was "Officer Damon Harwell."

"Detective Shrader said you can ride with me," Harwell told her; then he turned a scathing look on Valente. "You're finished here, Valente. Get that bird off the road before I impound it."

Leigh was dimly embarrassed by Harwell's treatment of the man who had kindly flown her to the site, but all of her concentration was centered on Logan. Logan was close. He was near.

O'Hara's interest was Leigh. "I'm going with Mrs. Manning," he warned the officer. "I'm her bodyguard."

"Fine," Harwell said with a shrug, and turned away.

Leigh was in a desperate hurry to leave, but when she turned to thank Valente and tell him good-bye, she realized he was unmoved by Harwell's threats. His next words confirmed that. "Would you like me to go with you?" he asked calmly.

The last thing Leigh wanted to do was to subject him to any more humiliation or cause him any trouble with the police. "I'll be all right," she said. "Thank you so much for everything."

Ignoring both her gratitude and her statement that she'd be all right, he looked at her intently and repeated his question. "Would you like me to go with you?"

The truth was that Leigh would have liked to take an

army with her; the more able men to find Logan and get him out of there, the better. She cast an uneasy glance at Harwell, who'd gotten into his squad car and started the engine. "I don't think that would be a very good idea."

"I think it would be," he said, guessing at the reason for her reluctance and overriding it.

Leigh decided he was right, and as she slid into the backseat of Officer Harwell's car, she said as courteously as she could, "Officer Harwell, Commissioner Trumanti assured me I would have the full cooperation of everyone in the NYPD. And Mr. Valente is with me."

Harwell said nothing until they were under way; then he flipped on the siren and glanced at Valente in the rearview mirror. "You must feel right at home back there, Valente," he said with a malicious smile. "You're usually in handcuffs, though, aren't you?"

Too horrified to hide her reaction, Leigh glanced sharply at Valente. He was calmly phoning his pilot and giving him instructions, but his eyes were riveted on the back of Harwell's head, and the expression on his face was lethal.

CHAPTER 15

One after another, police vehicles from the site of Leigh's accident flew past them, light bars flashing and sirens blaring, en route to the cabin. Leigh leaned forward and angrily asked Harwell, "Did Detective Shrader tell you to go this slow, or are you doing it just to be unpleasant?"

"Detective Shrader's orders, ma'am," Harwell replied, but Leigh could see his smirking face in the rearview mirror, and she knew he was enjoying her frustration—probably because she'd forced him to take Michael Valente along.

"Why would he give you an order like that?"

"I really couldn't say."

"Take a guess!" O'Hara snapped.

"Okay. My *guess* is that Detective Shrader doesn't know what he's going to find, or if he's going to find anything, and he wants a little extra time to look around and assess the scene. Family members and civilians get in the way." As he spoke, he flipped on his turn indicators. "This is it."

A mile after the turnoff, he pulled to a stop in the middle of a narrow mountain road crowded with police cars, including some from surrounding communities. The cabin was nowhere in sight, but a steep, narrow lane led from the road, down through the trees, and then disappeared around a bend.

Harwell got out of the car. "You stay here!" he ordered her, shouting to be heard above the roar of a hovering helicopter and the wailing siren of an approaching ambulance. "I'll let you know what they've found."

Police officers wading through the chest-high snow had created a passage of sorts with their bodies, and Leigh stood between O'Hara and Valente, watching Harwell make his way down the deep, slippery channel. More police officers arrived and trooped through the snow, but no one reappeared from around the bend below.

Leigh counted each second, waiting for someone to come up and tell her something, and when no one did, she began to feel as if she were going to explode into a million pieces.

Beside her, Valente was scowling down the lane; then he swore under his breath and looked at her. "How badly are you hurt?"

"What?"

"Your ribs?" he clarified. "Can you handle the pain if I lift you up and carry you down there?"

"Yes!" Leigh said. "But I don't think you—"

Before she could finish, Valente put one arm beneath her knees, curved his other arm around her shoulders, and lifted her into his arms. He looked at O'Hara and nodded toward the steep path. "You go first, and I'll walk in your footsteps. If I start to slip, try to brace me."

The plan worked, and a few minutes later, Leigh finally had an unobstructed view of the entire scene. The picturesque stone cabin stood in a clearing at the end of the driveway, just as Logan had described it to Leigh. Fifty yards from the cabin, the land dropped off sharply, and a horde of policemen were working their way slowly downward through the trees.

Another officer was stationed on the cabin's porch, peering inside through the open doorway. He turned in surprise as Valente put Leigh down behind him.

"You can't go in there," he informed her. "Detective Shrader's orders."

"I'm Mrs. Manning," Leigh argued. "I want to know if my husband is inside!" She was prepared to try to push past him, but Detective Littleton appeared in the doorway and answered her question. "There's no one here, Mrs. Manning. I'm sorry," she added. "I was planning to go up to the road and tell you myself, as soon as we finished a preliminary search of the area."

Devastated, Leigh sagged against the doorframe. "This must be the wrong place. . . ."

"I don't think so. There are some things inside that may belong to your husband. I'd like you to tell me if you can identify anything." As she stepped aside to allow Leigh past, she looked at Valente and politely said, "You'll have to wait out here, sir."

Inside, the empty little cabin was as bone-chillingly cold as the interior of a freezer, and almost as dark. Dampness had permeated the stone floors and walls, and the only available light came through a small, grimy window on her right. Leigh blinked, trying to adjust from the dazzling brightness outside to the gloom within.

To her left, two doorways off the main room opened into a kitchen and bathroom respectively, and opposite her, a third doorway, in the corner, opened into a room Leigh assumed was a bedroom. Adjoining that doorway, to the right, and occupying most of the wall directly in front of her, was a fireplace, its stones blackened with decades of accumulated soot. Lying on the floor in front of it, Leigh saw a dark green sleeping bag, still rolled up and neatly tied. She rushed over to it and bent down to see it better; then she looked over her shoulder at Littleton and Shrader, who were standing side by side. "This looks like one of ours!"

"Are you certain it's yours?" Shrader asked.

Sleeping bags all looked pretty much alike to Leigh and she hadn't actually seen this one for years. "I think so. I'm not positive."

"Do you and your husband own more than one sleeping bag?"

"Yes, we have two of them. They're identical."

Looking for something more identifiable, she stood up and walked into the empty bedroom; then she glanced into the bathroom, which was also empty. Unaware of how closely she was being observed, Leigh went into the kitchen next. A big, old-fashioned porcelain sink on steel legs stood against the far wall, an open paper bag on the floor beneath it. Spread out on the drain board were items Logan had bought for the day. Leigh felt a lump in her throat as she looked at the boxes of Logan's favorite crackers, an open package of cheese, and a deli sandwich still wrapped in plastic wrap. In addition to the bottled water Leigh had asked for, he'd also brought a bottle of champagne and a bottle of chardonnay. Because he'd wanted to celebrate the occasion with her that night. . . .

Lined up on the windowsill above the sink was a roll of paper towels, a bottle of liquid detergent, a box of wooden matches, and a can of insecticide. A new broom with the price tag still attached was propped against the wall near the back door.

Everything Leigh saw reminded her poignantly of

Logan and their conversation the morning he left, but until she stepped closer and looked into the sink, she had clung to the frail hope that this was the wrong place, that Logan was still safe and snug in some other cabin. Two Baccarat crystal wineglasses in the sink robbed her of her last comforting fantasy.

She turned to Shrader and Littleton, her eyes filled with anguish. "The glasses are ours." Driven by a sudden, overpowering urge to search for Logan and rescue him herself, she brushed past the two detectives and returned to the bedroom. She was reaching for the closet door when Shrader barked, "Don't touch anything, Mrs. Manning!"

Leigh jerked her hand back. "Did you look in the closet? Maybe Logan is—"

"Your husband isn't in there," Detective Littleton assured her.

"No, of course not," Leigh said, but she was rambling now, talking to stop herself from thinking about the unthinkable. "Why would Logan hide in a closet? He was obviously here, though, and he—" She broke off as a sudden realization gave her momentary hope. "But his car isn't here. He must have gone somewhere else—"

Shrader ruthlessly demolished her logic and her hope. "Your husband was driving a white Jeep, wasn't he?" When Leigh nodded, he shrugged and said in a matter-of-fact voice, "Well, when I stand in the doorway over there and look out, all I see are a whole lot of white hills. A white Jeep, covered in a few inches of snow, could look just like one of those."

That was the last thing Leigh wanted to hear anyone say. She wrapped her arms around herself and concentrated on not losing her grip on her emotions. In the living room, she went over to the window and watched the police searching the wooded hillside. They weren't really looking for Logan down there, she realized. Logan had disappeared almost six days ago. They were looking for his *body.*

Her own body began to shake so hard she had to clutch the window frame to keep herself from sliding to the floor. "It was so cold the night of the blizzard," she whispered brokenly. "Did he have wood to build a fire? I haven't seen any wood. I hope he wasn't cold—"

"There is plenty of wood stacked outside the kitchen door," Detective Littleton tried to reassure her.

Leigh wasn't reassured. She'd just realized the implications behind Shrader's warning. "Why don't you want me to touch anything?" she whispered.

"Since we have no idea what happened to your husband," Shrader said, "we're following standard procedure—"

It was Michael Valente who lost control—his temper erupted against Shrader and he brushed past the startled officer on the porch. "You're either a sadist or a moron!" he said, stalking into the house and going to Leigh's side. "Listen to me," he told her. "That asshole doesn't know any more about what happened to Logan than you do! There's a chance he's snowbound somewhere else, waiting for someone to dig him out. Maybe he got hurt and can't walk out on his own. Whatever the case, the best thing you can do now is let me take you home. Let the police do whatever it is they think they need to do here."

Surprisingly, Detective Littleton seconded that idea. "He's right, Mrs. Manning. It would be best if you left now. We have a wide area to search, and we'll phone you in the city the instant we find any clue to what happened here."

Leigh stared at her, sick with fear that Valente had alienated both detectives so completely that they'd never tell her anything. "Do you promise you'll call, no matter what?"

"I promise."

"Even if it's just to tell me you don't know anything else?"

"Even then," Littleton agreed. "I'll call you tonight." She walked to the doorway and waited for Leigh and Valente to step outside on the porch; then she nodded at one of the police officers standing there. "Officer Tierney here will drive you back to your helicopter, just tell him where it is."

When they left, Sam Littleton motioned to another NYPD officer standing nearby, brushing packed snow off his legs and jacket. "Get some rolls of crime-scene tape and start blocking off the area from that point there—" She pointed to the end of the driveway visible from the house.

"Don't you want it up at the road, too?"

"No, it would only arouse curiosity and invite attention, but I want an officer stationed up there around the clock until CSU has been here and gone. No one gets down here without permission from Detective Shrader or me."

"Got it," he replied, turning to leave.

"One more thing—Ask one of the local departments if we can borrow a generator. We're going to need lights and heat down here."

"Anything else?"

Sam gave him a beguiling smile. "Since you asked, two cups of hot coffee would be very nice."

"I'll see what I can do."

SHRADER WAS ON THE PHONE with Holland, making arrangements for a crime scene unit to be sent to the cabin ASAP. When he finished his call, he gave Sam a ferocious scowl, which, on Shrader, looked so much like his happy face that Sam wasn't certain whether he was amused or angry. "Valente called me an asshole!" he exclaimed, and Sam realized he was actually delighted.

"He did," she agreed, "—and you were."

"Yeah, but you know what I found out?"

Sam shoved her hands in her pockets and grinned. "That he also thinks you're a sadistic moron?"

"Besides that."

Sam tipped her head to the side. "I give up. What else did you discover?"

"The Feds call Valente the Ice Man—but I found out he has a warm, soft, sensitive spot. It's Mrs. Logan Manning. Our people are going to find that very interesting." He crouched down in front of the fireplace and took a pen out of his pocket. "I don't know how she's made it as an actress onstage."

"You don't think she can act?" Sam uttered in surprise.

Shrader gave a sharp bark of laughter. "Hell, yes, she can act! She gave us an Academy Award performance in the hospital and again right here. The problem is she doesn't seem to remember her lines. In the hospital Wednesday morning, she got all righteous and indignant when I asked her about Valente's phone message. Today, two days later, she shows up in his private helicopter and he carries her down here in his arms."

Since they'd already covered this topic on the way here from the accident site, Sam said nothing.

"In order to be a good liar, you've got to have a good memory," Shrader declared as he poked around in the ashes. "This looks like ordinary wood ash to me, probably oak. The problem with Mrs. Manning," he continued, "is that she not only has a bad memory, she also has a real bad sense of direction. She was twelve miles south of here when her car went over the embankment, and she was heading south, not north. That means . . . what?" He looked over his shoulder and lifted his brows, waiting for Sam to fill in his verbal blank.

"Is this a quiz?" she said with amusement. "It means it looks as if she was on her way back home, not on her way here, when she went off the road."

"Right. Now, what bothers you about this place? Anything stand out?"

It dawned on Sam that this was the first case they'd started on together, and that Shrader was truly trying to get a sense of how observant she was. "There are several things that stand out. First, someone swept this floor very clean, very recently, which is why you didn't bother to keep everyone out of here. You already knew CSU wouldn't be able to get any footprints off this stone, not only because it's been swept, but because it's too uneven."

"Good. What else?"

"You let Valente walk in here, in the impossible hope that CSU could somehow lift a partial print of his shoes and that they'd match up with a print somewhere else on the stone floor in here."

"So I'm a dreamer."

"By the way, in case you didn't notice, Mrs. Manning left at least a partial print on that window."

He pushed himself to his feet, dusted off his hands, and tucked the pen in his pocket. "She put her hand on the frame, not the glass. I was watching."

"I think her hand slid over onto the glass when she turned around."

Shrader's eyes narrowed. "If you're certain, make a note of it."

"I will." Turning, she walked into the kitchen. "Are you going to say anything to Tierney? He let Valente get past him and walk in here."

"You bet your sweet ass I am! Sorry—no personal, inappropriate, or offensive sexual connotation was intended."

"None taken," Sam assured him gravely, but her mind was on the glasses in the kitchen sink. Those glasses seemed as odd to her as the single sleeping bag seemed to Shrader, and she said that aloud.

"What bothers you about the glasses?" he asked.

"Why are they in the sink? The bottles of water weren't opened, neither was the bottle of champagne or the bottle of chardonnay. So if the glasses were unused, why did he put them in the sink?"

"He probably figured they'd be safer there, less likely to get broken."

Sam didn't argue.

CHAPTER 16

The brief jubilation of thinking she'd found Logan, followed by the shattering reality of finding only a deserted cabin, had drained Leigh's mental and physical strength to an unprecedented low. Lying on a living room sofa, wrapped in an afghan, she watched CBS 2 News reporting that day's discovery of the cabin. . . .

"Police have roped off the area and a full-fledged investigation is under way at the scene," Dana Tyler, one of the coanchors, reported. "In the meantime, hopes of finding Logan Manning alive and unharmed grow dimmer. Our reporter, Jeff Case, was at One Police Plaza this afternoon, where NYPD commissioner William Trumanti had this to say regarding the investigation. . . ."

Leigh listened for anything new, but Trumanti said only that they were following up several leads and that kidnapping had been ruled out because no ransom demand had ever been made. Leads, Leigh thought wearily. They had no leads. Shrader and Littleton were as clueless about Logan's whereabouts as everyone else. Commissioner Trumanti finished his brief statement, but the reporters weren't through. "Is it true that Leigh Kendall was flown by helicopter to the site this morning?"

"That's correct."

"Did the helicopter belong to Michael Valente, and did he accompany her?"

At the mention of Valente's name, Commissioner Trumanti's expression hardened. "That is my understanding."

"How does Valente figure into all this?"

"We don't know yet," Trumanti said, but his words and his tone seemed to imply that wherever Valente was involved, there was something sinister that needed to be investigated.

Leigh felt a brief spurt of angry energy at the sheer injustice of that remark, but she'd already exhausted her supply of anger on the unsubstantiated rumors and lurid speculation she'd read in the day's newspapers. That morning, *The New York Times* had run a story alongside a picture of Logan and her at a charity fund-raiser with a headline that asked, "Manning Missing: Tragedy, Foul Play, or High Drama?" The accompanying article included comments from an "official source" that hinted at the possibility that Logan's disappearance was some sort of publicity stunt.

The *Post* had found out about Leigh's stalker and was building a case for "kidnapping by stalker." To promote interest in that theory and lend credence to it, the *Post* included a detailed "profile" of Leigh's stalker created by some expert on celebrity stalkers.

The *National Enquirer* had another theory, and they splashed it across the front page of their latest issue as if it were fact, not fiction of their own invention: "MANNING-KENDALL MARRIAGE ON THE ROCKS BEFORE MANNING DISAPPEARED." According to the *Enquirer*'s "undisclosed sources," Leigh had been planning to file for divorce because she "was fed up with Logan's infidelities." In the same article, "a friend close to the couple" was quoted as saying that Logan had refused to give up the woman with whom he'd been having an affair.

The *Star* favored that theory, but according to the *Star*, Logan's secret lover was a man, not a woman, and the two of them had been spotted holding hands in Belize.

Until that morning, the media had at least been forced to limit their speculation and occasional slander to Logan and Leigh, but now they had rich new fodder in Michael Valente, and they were having a feeding frenzy. Photographs of him were splashed across the front pages of the evening newspapers, along with Logan's and hers. The articles about Valente centered on his unsavory background and past run-ins with the justice system, but they were also delving into his relationships with women. According to one article, he'd been involved with the daughter of the head of one of New York's crime families before he embarked on several closely guarded relationships with "unnamed, married socialites."

Leigh's only reaction to all that was a vague sense of guilt because he'd been dragged into the ugly limelight merely for having committed an impulsive act of kindness to aid a virtual stranger. Proof again that no good deed goes unpunished.

She reached for the television's remote control and turned the set off; then she picked up the large framed photograph she'd put on the coffee table earlier so she could see it.

Logan's handsome face smiled back at her from the deck of the forty-five-foot sailboat he'd rented for a weekend last summer to celebrate their anniversary. Leigh was in front of him, at the helm, ready for her first sailing lesson. One sail was unfurled, his hands were on the wheel beside hers, and the breeze was blowing their hair. In the photograph, they were both laughing because Logan had persuaded a passerby to snap the photograph and, although it looked as if they were sailing, the truth was, they were still tied up at the dock.

Tenderly, Leigh traced her finger over the image of his beloved face, remembering the way his skin felt to her touch. He hadn't shaved that weekend, and beneath her finger now, she could almost feel the curve of his jaw and the roughened texture of his skin with its two-day growth of beard.

In her memory, she could hear his laughter that halcyon summer day as he stood behind her at the helm. "Where to, Captain?" he'd asked, brushing a kiss on the nape of her neck.

Leigh closed her eyes against the hot tears gathering there and pressed the photograph to her heart. "Wherever you are, darling," she whispered.

CHAPTER 17

Hilda was on a ladder, dusting the tops of doorframes, when the telephone rang at eleven-fifteen Saturday morning, and so it was Joe O'Hara who answered the kitchen phone and took the call from Dr. Sheila Winters. He recognized her name immediately, partly because she'd phoned in a prescription for Leigh Manning a few days before, but also because Brenna had several times referred to her as a very close friend of the Mannings.

"I'd like to speak to Mrs. Manning," Dr. Winters told him.

O'Hara hesitated and then reluctantly recited the excuse Hilda, Brenna, and he had been told to make to anyone who called with a similar request. "I'm sorry, Dr. Winters, but Mrs. Manning isn't taking phone calls today. She's resting."

Callers—except for reporters—always accepted that and politely left messages, but not this caller. As if she'd picked up on O'Hara's reluctance to brush off her call, she began chatting with him. "Who is this?"

"Joe O'Hara. I'm Mrs. Manning's chauffeur."

"I thought it might be you! You're also a bodyguard, aren't you?"

"If necessary, yes."

"Leigh and Logan told me how happy they were to have you working for them for the next few months. As things stand right now, I'm especially glad you're there." She was so warm, and genuinely concerned, that Joe instinctively liked and trusted her. "Is she really resting?" Dr. Winters asked abruptly.

Joe leaned back and peered past the dining room into the living room, where the subject of the discussion was staring at a framed photograph of her husband on a sailboat, her face so tense and forlorn that it was heartbreaking.

"She isn't resting, is she?" Dr. Winters guessed from his hesitation.

"No."

"I'd like to come over and see her this morning. Do you think that would be a good idea?"

"Maybe so," he said; then he remembered Brenna's saying she wished Dr. Winters had been allowed to come over yesterday, and he strengthened his reply. "Yes," he said. "I do."

"How could we work it out?"

Joe tucked his chin close to the phone and lowered his voice. "Well, if you were to tell me that you're coming over this morning—and that you won't take no for an answer when you get here—then I'd have to tell Mrs. Manning that, and I don't think she's in any condition to put up much of an argument about anything right now."

"I see," Dr. Winters said with a smile in her voice, and then she became very stern and coolly professional. "This is Dr. Winters," she informed him as if they hadn't already been talking, "and I'm coming over in a few minutes to see

Mrs. Manning. Please tell her that I will *not* take no for an answer when I get there!"

"Yes, ma'am. I'll give her the message," O'Hara said. He was hanging up the phone when Hilda's gruff voice made him twist around in surprise. "Who were you talking to?"

"Dr. Winters. She insisted on coming over. She said she won't take no for an answer."

Hilda glared at him in disdain. "Sure, and this dustcloth I'm holding is really a hand puppet!"

O'Hara glowered back at her. "You callin' me a liar?"

"I'm calling you a meddler!" she retorted, but she marched around him and down the back hall to the laundry room without threatening to expose him or spoil his plan.

O'HARA STROLLED into the living room and cleared his throat. "I'm sorry to disturb you, Mrs. Manning," he lied.

The woman on the sofa hastily swiped the tears from her wet cheeks before she looked around at him. "Yes, Joe?" she said, making an ineffective effort to smile a little and look composed.

"Dr. Winters just called. She said she's coming over in a few minutes—"

"Did you tell her I wasn't seeing anyone and that I was resting?"

"Yep. I told her that. But she said she will not take no for an answer when she gets here."

Leigh was surprised for a moment, then annoyed, and then resigned. "That sounds just like Sheila," she sighed, and when he looked uneasy, she added, "Don't worry about it. I should have talked to her days ago. She's a very dear friend."

"It'll do you a lot of good to talk to a close friend," he predicted.

Leigh didn't think anything could do her much good, but Sheila was the one person she could be completely honest with. Among other things, Sheila Winters had recognized the pitfalls Logan and Leigh were facing in their relationship, and she'd steered them around them.

In the early years of their marriage, it had been Leigh who made most of the money, with Logan contributing his Social Register background and a driving desire to see her succeed that surpassed Leigh's own. After using all of his family's social connections to ensure that Leigh came into personal contact with anyone who was influential in Broadway theater, Logan single-mindedly devoted himself to restoring the Manning family's fortune, which had been squandered by his grandfather during a lifetime of gambling debts and harebrained business schemes.

A love of gambling was a Manning family trait, but, with the exception of Logan's grandfather, the Manning men also possessed sound business judgment. Logan's great-great-grandfather, Cyrus Manning, had carved a comfortable little empire in the canning industry, only to invest everything in a huge gamble on textiles, followed by another, even bigger gamble on oil. Like him, Logan was always willing to gamble on the next big venture. And like old Cyrus's, Logan Manning's gambles nearly always paid off.

By the time he and Leigh celebrated their eleventh wedding anniversary, Logan had succeeded far beyond anyone's expectations, and Leigh's theatrical career had made her into an international star. She wanted to start taking more time off between plays and reduce her appearances during a show's run, but Logan couldn't understand her logic. No matter how well one of his own ventures did, he was driven to expand, to reinvest in another, often riskier venture. He wouldn't stop and he couldn't slow down. His drive to succeed came with an enormous personal cost, and the price to Logan was sixteen-hour workdays, months without even a short vacation, and weeks without making love.

When one of his smaller gambles failed to pay off shortly after their eleventh wedding anniversary, Logan was so stressed over it that Leigh finally insisted they go for some counseling. The therapist she selected was Dr. Sheila Winters, a stunning thirty-seven-year-old blonde who had built a thriving Park Avenue practice by specializing in the treatment of highly successful, overstressed people, including several acquaintances of Logan's and Leigh's.

To Leigh's delight, Sheila Winters lived up to her reputation for intelligent insight, humor, and quick creative solutions tailored to the special idiosyncrasies of her illustrious clients.

After only a few sessions, she prescribed a weekend vacation home as a partial and practical cure for Logan's inability to relax. "Logan, you're one of those people who requires a total change of scene in order to get your mind off your work," the psychiatrist said. "But if you aren't within easy commuting distance of your office in the city, Leigh will have trouble dragging you away. A beach house on Long Island would provide a nice change of scene, but it's too close to the city, and too easy for Logan to spend his days at the beach club or on the golf course talking business with the same people he sees in Manhattan during the week." After a moment's thought, she told both of them, "If I were you, I'd consider a place somewhere upstate— maybe in the mountains."

It had been obvious from the first that Sheila truly liked and admired Logan, and that she somehow empathized with his unwavering desire to succeed, and so it was no real surprise to Leigh when the psychiatrist recommended that Leigh assume most of the responsibility for initiating romance. "Light some candles, turn on soft music, and push him into the shower when he gets home," she told Leigh with a smile. "He's smart, he'll get the idea. He has no sexual problems, other than overwork."

She turned and looked sternly at Logan. "For the first few weeks, Leigh will be in charge of reminding you that there's more to enjoy in life than work, but it's up to you to make the most of the opportunities for intimacy that she offers you. I understand that achieving great financial success requires enormous dedication and a willingness to take the sort of risks that can occupy all your thoughts. I even admire most of the sacrifices you've been willing to make in order to succeed, but it's a serious mistake to take risks with your marriage to further your financial goals." The sense of humor that made her particularly popular with her clients suddenly asserted itself. "You know, Logan, men who neglect their wives because they're too busy making money usually end up with no wife—and with only *half* their money."

Unlike some therapists who refused to see members of a couple separately, Sheila preferred to give her clients a few minutes with her individually before or after each session. At the next session, when Leigh was alone with her, Sheila surprised her by revealing a little bit about herself: "I may seem a little too tolerant of Logan's driving ambition to succeed, and perhaps I am," she said. "If so, it's because I'm from a similar background. According to what you told me, Leigh, you grew up in a family where there was never enough money, but the kids you went to school with weren't much better off than you. As a result, you didn't grow up with a profound sense of shame and inferiority because you could never fit in with your peers. Logan and I grew up like that. We're both from old, respected New York families, and we both went to all the 'right' private schools, but after school, we went home to a life that was shabby-genteel at best, and everyone knew it. We couldn't vacation with our schoolmates, we couldn't dress like them, or be like them in any way. Psychologically, we'd both have been far better off if we'd gone to public schools and been allowed to hang around with ordinary kids from ordinary families like yours."

The session was over and they both stood up. Leigh smiled fondly at her and gave her a quick, impulsive hug. "You could never have been 'ordinary,' Sheila."

"Thank you. That's a lovely compliment coming from an extraordinary woman like you." She turned and looked at the appointment book lying open on her desk. "There's really no need for you to see me again, but if you could persuade Logan to come a few more times, I'd like to try to relieve him of some of that shame he's been carrying around since childhood."

"I'll urge him to do that," Leigh promised.

It had taken Logan two years to design the weekend retreat of their dreams and then to find the perfect spot for it, but Leigh hadn't minded that in the least. The endless hours they'd spent talking and planning and revising the drawings had brought them closer together. The weekends they'd spent scouting for just the right location had provided a lovely change of pace for both of them, which was really what Sheila had wanted.

During that time, something else happened—Logan became even more successful. Several years before, he had branched out from residential architecture to land development and commercial construction, but most of his money had always come from clever investments in other people's businesses. Suddenly, clients seemed to line up at his doors. He'd added six architects to the four he already employed so that they could do the routine work he didn't enjoy. He doubled and tripled his prices—and still his clients came back for more, with gigantic checks in hand. Logan said it was because he'd finally learned to stop pushing all the time and to let things come to him. That made sense to Leigh.

Although she didn't see Sheila professionally again, Leigh saw her often at social gatherings and charity committee meetings. After one particularly frustrating meeting, the two of them decided to have dinner together, and they ended up laughing and talking for hours. From that encounter a strong friendship had developed, one that included many shared confidences from Sheila as well as Leigh.

CHAPTER 18

Joe O'Hara had been right—Leigh felt better within minutes of Sheila's sitting down beside her. Dressed in a chic black wool suit with her blond hair caught up in a smart chignon, Sheila was a breath of fresh, bracing air.

Matter-of-fact, compassionate, and wise, Sheila listened intently while Leigh told her everything that had happened since early Sunday morning. Leigh managed to do that without breaking down, but when she came to the end—and it was time to go on to the next most obvious topic—she suddenly felt as if a fist were clamping her vocal cords and an ocean of tears were building up behind her eyes. The problem with having unburdened herself to Sheila was that it was now virtually impossible to avoid confronting reality. In agonized silence, Leigh stared helplessly at her friend's sympathetic expression; then she hastily turned her face away and tried to focus on something else.

The doorway into a spacious dark-paneled room lined with books stared back at her. Logan used it as his office. The lights were off inside it; it was dark and empty.

Her life was dark and empty. The light had gone out of it, too.

Logan was gone.

He wasn't coming back.

She swallowed convulsively, and the words came out like a whisper, wrenched from her soul. "He's gone, Sheila. He can't come back."

"Why do you say that?"

Leigh slowly turned her head and looked directly at her friend. "He's been gone a week. I know that if he were still alive, he'd have found a way to get word to someone by now. You know him."

"Yes, I do," Sheila said firmly. "I also know he is extremely resourceful and levelheaded. He was alive and well on Sunday, and this is Saturday morning. That means he's been gone five full days, not one week. A man can live a lot longer than five days under worse conditions than a snowstorm."

Hope flared like a skyrocket in Leigh. Sheila saw the change in her features and smiled reassuringly. "You'd be thinking the same way I am if it hadn't been for your accident. You've not only had a double mental trauma, you've had a severe physical trauma. We need to start building your strength back up. Let's start taking some short walks together. I don't see patients on Mondays. You'll be up to a little exercise by then, won't you?"

Leigh wasn't really interested in doing anything that didn't involve finding Logan, but she knew Sheila was right. She needed exercise to build up her strength and stamina. "A very short, very *slow* walk," she stipulated.

"Thank God," Sheila said with a laugh as she put her teacup down on its saucer. "The last time we exercised together, I couldn't cross my legs without whining for days afterward. My patients started giving *me* advice on exercise.

Besides being mortified, I was afraid they'd expect a discount on my fees!"

Leigh managed an actual smile, and Sheila glanced at her watch; then she hastily picked up her purse and stood up. "In fifteen minutes I'm seeing a patient who is chronically late for everything. I hope I haven't cured him of that yet." Leaning down, she pressed a kiss on Leigh's cheek. "I phoned in a prescription for antianxiety medication for you. Are you taking it?"

"I took one of the pills."

"Take them as I directed," Sheila said firmly. "They'll help you. They won't cloud your thinking; they will just enable you to think more normally."

"There is nothing 'normal' about the things that are happening," Leigh pointed out, and then she relented because it was easier. "Okay, I'll start taking them."

"Good—and please call Jason. He called me twice yesterday. He's beside himself because he hasn't seen you yet and doesn't know when you're going to resume your role."

That information made Leigh feel both guilty and unjustly harassed. "I haven't spoken to him since I left the hospital, but he leaves messages for me every day. He said Jane Sebring is doing an excellent job in my role."

At the mention of Leigh's gorgeous costar and understudy, Sheila grimaced with angry distaste. "She must be heartbroken that you didn't die in your accident. I hate that she's benefiting from your misfortune."

Leigh gaped at her. Sheila never made statements like that; she was a shrink and so she normally looked for explanations for people's attitudes rather than condemning them for their feelings.

"Don't get me started on that woman—" Sheila glanced

at her watch again. "I'm going to be late; I have to run. You know how to reach me, day or night."

THE PHONE HAD BEEN RINGING regularly while Sheila was there. When she left, Hilda brought in the phone messages she'd taken, and Leigh leafed through them. Among the calls were two that Leigh felt she needed to return: one was from Michael Valente; the other was from Jason.

The woman who answered Michael Valente's phone had an attitude that verged on abrasive. Besides being coldly formal, she was needlessly inquisitive and noticeably mistrustful of the answers Leigh gave to her questions. She not only insisted on knowing what Leigh's call was in regard to, she insisted that Leigh give her phone number and address, and then she abruptly put the call on hold and left it there. Since Leigh's name had been plastered all over the news for nearly a week, and linked with Valente's since yesterday, it seemed a little difficult to believe any of those questions were really necessary. If the woman was his housekeeper, then she was under an iron edict to screen all his calls thoroughly and without exception. If the woman was his live-in girlfriend, then she had a whole lot of jealous insecurities about any female who called him. Either way, Leigh realized that Michael Valente must be a very difficult man to reach.

She was left on hold for so long that she was growing weary and exasperated and was about to hang up when he finally picked up the phone. "Leigh?"

For some reason, Leigh's nervous system reacted with a jolt to the sound of his voice and his familiar use of her first name. There was something very . . . distracting . . . about it.

"Leigh?" he said again into the silence.

"Yes, I'm here. I'm sorry, I was—distracted."

"Thank you for putting up with the inquisition and waiting for me to answer your call," he said. "My secretary thought you were another reporter who'd dreamed up a fresh angle to bring me to the phone. When I called you earlier, I was preoccupied with something else or I'd have given you my private phone number, which is what I meant to do. Have you had any word about Logan?"

"No, nothing," she said, wondering if he was always under siege from the media or if—God forbid—his situation at the office was the result of his kindness to her. She had an awful feeling it was the latter.

"Leigh?"

She gave a shaky sigh. "I'm sorry. You must feel like you're talking to a dead phone. I was hoping you always got plagued by the press, and that I'm not the reason for what's happening today." As soon as she said it, she realized her hope was absurd, and—worse—she'd just rudely referred to his unsavory reputation with the law and the media. She put her forehead in her hand and closed her eyes. "I'm so sorry," she whispered bleakly. "I didn't mean that the way it sounded."

"You have nothing to apologize for," he said, but his tone turned brisk and chilly. "I was wondering if I could stop by tomorrow sometime and pick up the documents I need from Logan's office. In the rush yesterday, I forgot about them."

In "the rush yesterday," he'd canceled his own schedule, located his pilot, put up with O'Hara's argument, lent her his helicopter, stayed with her in the freezing cold, tolerated humiliation from the police, *and* carried her back and forth through the snow at the cabin. In her weakened emotional state, Leigh couldn't seem to get over her seeming lack of gratitude, or ignore his reaction. "I'm just . . . so sorry," she said again, tearfully.

"For what?" he said wryly. "For reading about me in the newspapers? Or for believing what you've read?"

Leigh lifted her head, her brows furrowing, something niggling at the back of her mind. Something troubling. "For everything," she said absently.

"What time would be convenient for me to stop by tomorrow?"

"It doesn't matter. I'll be here all day unless I hear something about Logan."

When she hung up, Leigh looked at the phone for a moment, trying to focus on the cause of her uneasiness. Something about his voice. Voices without faces . . . A man's voice, pleasant at the time, but associated in her mind with uneasiness later, with danger . . . *Excuse me, you dropped this* . . .

Leigh shook off the thought of the man outside Saks. That wasn't Valente. That couldn't have been Valente. That was an insane notion—proof that she was teetering on the brink of mental and physical overload.

She decided to return Jason's phone call, and found herself cheered by his familiar, frenetic energy and genuine concern. "You can keep telling me you're fine," he proclaimed at the end of their call, "but I want to see you with my own eyes, darling. What time shall I be there tomorrow?"

"Jason, I'm really not very good company."

"But I am always good company, and I am going to share it with you tomorrow. Shall we say noon?"

Leigh accepted that he was going to be on her doorstep whether he was wanted or not, but she also realized she'd actually be glad to see him. She was dying of solitude and loneliness. "Noon is fine," she said.

CHAPTER 19

Located on East Seventy-second Street, on the Upper East Side, the Eighteenth Precinct had the swankiest address of any of Manhattan's twenty-three precincts.

In an effort to keep the exterior from looking like a blight on the fancy neighborhood, the building had a pair of heavy, ornate front doors flanked on both sides by antique gas lanterns. Inside, however, the place was as unappealing and overcrowded as any other NYPD precinct.

Shrader was already waiting outside Captain Holland's office when Sam arrived at noon on Saturday. He looked tired, disheveled, and moody. "Damn," he said with a yawn, "I was hoping to get a day or two off while CSU went over the cabin. It felt good to sleep in my own bed last night. What time did Holland call you this morning and tell you to come in?"

"A little before eight," Sam replied.

"The man doesn't sleep. He's always here. He lives for his job," Shrader said.

In Sam's opinion, Thomas Holland was more likely living for his next job. Everyone knew there was going to be an opening for a deputy commissioner, and the rumor was that Thomas Holland was a top candidate.

"Steve Womack is coming back to work on Monday," Shrader added with another yawn. "He says his shoulder has healed up fine after the surgery, and he can't stand another day at home."

The news that Shrader's regular partner was returning meant that Sam would be assigned to someone else, and her heart sank at the thought of being pulled off the Manning investigation. "I guess that's why I'm here then—" she said aloud, "Captain Holland wants a verbal report from both of us and then he'll reassign me."

Shrader grinned. "You'd better put on a happy face, Littleton, or I'll get the impression you're gonna miss me."

Sam neither confirmed nor denied it. "I'm going to miss being on the Manning case," she told him instead, "—assuming there is a case."

The door to Holland's office opened suddenly, and he gestured them inside. "Thanks for coming in on your day off," he said, closing the door behind them. "I have to sign some papers, and then we'll talk. Have a seat," he added, nodding toward the two chairs in front of his desk as he walked behind it and picked up his pen.

As precinct captain, Holland had an office that was situated at the end of a long hallway, somewhat removed from the general chaos, and it was larger than the others scattered about the old building's four crowded floors. It also had some unusually nice personal touches, like the antique leather bookends on his desk and the centuries-old globe that stood on an ornate brass stand in the corner by the windows. The pieces weren't overtly valuable, but Sam knew they were, and they gave his office a subtle touch of elegance that was meant to be appreciated by those few visitors with enough taste to recognize their merit—and to be overlooked by everyone else. Just like the deliberately understated, but expensive, clothes he wore, Thomas Holland's office was as subtly distinctive as the handsome man who occupied it.

Like his uncles and his grandfather, he'd made law enforcement his career, but unlike them, he had a master's degree, a trust fund, and a feasible hope of becoming police commissioner. At forty-one years old, he not only had an outstanding record as a cop, and an even better one as an administrator, he also had the refined good looks and polished veneer that Mayor Edelman needed to enhance the NYPD's public image.

He signed the last paper, laid his pen aside, and looked at Shrader. "There's been a development in the Manning investigation," he said briskly, but there was an edge to his voice that made Sam think he didn't like the development. "Commissioner Trumanti wants a team of four investigators on the case, and he's handpicked the lead investigator. You and Womack will be on his team."

"Who's the lead?" Shrader said shortly.

"His name is McCord. Trumanti wanted to move the investigation to headquarters, but this is *our* case, and it's a potential bombshell. I persuaded Trumanti that we can keep a tighter control on leaks if the investigation stays right here. The Feds have never been able to make a case against Valente that sticks, but *we* are going to nail that bastard and send him away. Thanks to the press, the Feds already know he's involved in this case, and they're looking for a chance to get in on the investigation, but that's not going to happen. The one thing Trumanti and I agree on is that we want this case kept under tight wraps while we find out exactly how Valente is involved. Nobody—and I mean nobody," he emphasized, finally looking at Sam, "talks to the press, or to anyone else not directly involved in the investigation. Got it?"

Sam nodded.

"Got it," Shrader said.

"Whatever you need," Holland continued, "just ask for it and you'll have it—overtime, additional manpower, warrants, whatever. The DA's office will get us anything else we can't get for ourselves." He stood up, ending the meeting. "McCord will be using Lieutenant Unger's vacant office during the investigation. He's up there now, and he wants to meet with you at twelve-forty-five. Sam, I've recommended that McCord make you the fourth member of the team. If there's a case here, it's because of you; however, the final decision about you is up to him. Any questions?"

Shrader spoke before Sam could say thank you. "Mc-Cord?" he repeated. "You don't mean Mitchell McCord, do you, Captain?"

Holland nodded curtly. "The great man himself."

"Thank you, Captain Holland," Sam said formally.

Shrader headed out of the office, but Holland signaled Sam to stay behind for a moment. He waited until Shrader was out of hearing; then he lowered his voice and said with a smile, "Nice work finding that note Valente wrote to the Manning woman. Your father is going to be very proud of you."

"I haven't spoken to my stepfather about any of this," she said, subtly reminding him of her actual relationship to the man. "He and my mother are very busy this time of year, and I've been a little preoccupied."

"I understand," he said; then he dismissed her with a quick nod and another brief smile. "Close my office door behind you when you leave."

Sam closed his door as bidden.

Tom Holland decided to call her stepfather. He picked up his telephone and spoke to the clerk outside his office. "See if you can locate Senator Hollenbeck."

CHAPTER 20

Shrader was predictably irritated at not being the lead on the Manning investigation, but what amazed Sam was that he was also a little excited about working with Mitchell McCord. "The guy's a legend," he told her as he put another quarter into a vending machine in the canteen on the third floor.

"Why?"

"A lot of reasons; some of them no one knows."

"That's informative," Sam said with a grin.

Challenged to substantiate his claim that McCord qualified as a legend, Shrader came up with some details. "Ten years ago, when he was with the Major Case Squad, he worked the Silkman kidnapping. Joey Silkman was the little kid who was buried alive for four days in a wood box, remember?"

Sam nodded.

"McCord's team caught one of the kidnappers when he tried to pick up the ransom money, but the guy would not talk. Two days went by, then three days, and then McCord had him released into his custody, and took him out for a ride and a private chat. The next thing you know, the guy spilled his guts and took McCord to the burial site. The two of them dug the kid out together."

"Are you suggesting McCord beat the information out of him?"

"No. There wasn't a mark on the guy. He pleaded guilty, got a break from the judge for helping in the rescue, and went away for twenty-five years. His two pals got life." Shrader waited for Sam's reaction while he tore the top off his bag of M&M's.

"Sounds impressive," she said, depositing her coins into one of the soft drink machines, "but not enough to make him a legend."

"There's a lot more, but I have to think a little. Oh, yeah, McCord headed up the Hostage Negotiation Team when four psychos took over a boys' summer camp and threatened to kill one kid every hour."

"And he rescued them all without using his weapon or raising his voice?" Sam teased.

"No. The first kid was shot in the head while McCord's team was still arriving on the scene and getting into position."

Sam sobered. "Then what happened?"

"As I said, his people were still arriving, so no one saw everything exactly as it happened. There were a lot of conflicting reports from the eyewitnesses. Basically, McCord lost his cool. He walked right into the clearing where the kids were being held, stretched out his arms, and said something like, 'Why waste your time on twelve-year-olds when you can kill yourself a cop?' Then he told the captors that he'd instructed his men to open fire in sixty seconds. He told them that, since they were already killing the kids, there wasn't any room for negotiation."

In spite of her earlier skepticism, Sam was riveted. "Then what happened?"

"McCord told the kids to 'hit the ground so the shooting can begin.' That's one version. Another version is that McCord yelled to the kids, 'Hit the ground!'"

"And?"

"The psychos yelled at the kids to stay standing."

"And? And?"

"The kids obviously figured McCord was crazier and more dangerous than their captors, because they all landed in a heap on the ground, and the sharpshooters opened fire. When the smoke cleared, there were four dead captors. That's when he got promoted to sergeant. No—no, he got that promotion after he cracked a bribery-and-extortion case that involved some high-level city officials. A couple years ago, he moved over to the Organized Crime Control Bureau, and made a record for himself there, too; then he transferred back to Borough Command and made detective lieutenant.

"He's in his mid-forties, and everybody figured he'd make division captain in a couple more years, then maybe chief of detectives, but that's not what happened."

"What did happen?" Sam asked, glancing at her watch. They still had fifteen minutes to waste before they were supposed to report to McCord.

"Nothing. A year ago, he told people he'd decided to retire when his twenty years were up, which is anytime now. I heard last month that he'd already left, but maybe he had a lot of vacation time piled up and decided to use it." Shrader nodded toward the empty metal tables scattered around the canteen. "We might as well sit in here instead of hanging around outside McCord's door like a couple of peons waiting for an audience with the pope."

Normally the canteen was crowded at this time of day, but everyone on duty this Saturday had evidently eaten earlier, because the remnants of their meals were all over the tops of the round metal tables. Sam looked for the table with the fewest used paper plates, crumpled napkins, and sticky substances on it, but Shrader had no such compunctions. He sat down at the closest table and shook a few more M&M's into his palm. "What are you doing?"

"Looking for something to wipe off this chair with," she replied before she thought about it. Shrader guffawed.

"Littleton, how are you going to be able to stomach digging through garbage Dumpsters, looking for evidence?"

"I'm planning to wear gloves, like everyone else does," she informed him as she sat down on the chair.

Shrader generously held out his hand with a colorful supply of M&M's in his palm. "Here, have some."

They looked good. "Have you touched anything besides the back of your chair with that hand?"

"You do not want me to answer that."

Sam looked at him in disapproving silence while a slight smile touched the corner of her mouth. The silence was to discourage similar remarks in the future; the smile was a good-natured acknowledgment that, this time, she'd inadvertently given him an irresistible opening for a line exactly like that.

Shrader understood the subtlety behind both gestures and settled for regaling her with more glowing tales of McCord's feats in the area of law enforcement.

By the time they stood up, Sam was looking forward to meeting the man who evidently possessed the instincts of a clairvoyant, the intellect of a rocket scientist, and the persistence of a pit bull.

"Wait one second," Shrader said as they passed the rest rooms on the way to McCord's office. "I want to stop in here."

While she waited for Shrader, several men and women

walked past her down the hall, cops and clerks and detectives she'd seen around the precinct before, but instead of snubbing her as they'd done before, most of them nodded or mumbled a greeting. A shift was taking place in the general attitude toward her, and she realized it was because Shrader had gone out of his way to make certain that Holland—and several of the cops in the Catskills—knew she'd made some sort of an inroad on the Manning case herself.

Despite the stocky build and ferocious appearance that had reminded her of a rottweiler and caused her to think of him as "Shredder," she had a feeling there was a streak of kindness in Shrader that he carefully disguised with scowling brusqueness. When he finally emerged, Sam forgot about all that and bit back a wayward grin. He had carefully wet down his short black hair with a little water, tucked in his shirt, and straightened his tie. "You look very spiffy," she joked. "McCord is going to be dazzled when he sees you."

Sam had little expectation of actually liking Mitchell McCord herself, but she was now doubly eager to meet the man who could actually make Shrader self-conscious about his appearance. In the Catskills, Shrader had worn the same three shirts and trousers for a week. Although he'd spoken only of McCord's heroics and accomplishments, she wondered if Shrader had stopped to "primp" just now because he also knew McCord had a reputation for being appearance-conscious. Given McCord's rapid ascension up the ladder at division headquarters, Sam surmised he was not only talented, but also politically astute, probably arrogant, and possibly a good dresser.

CHAPTER 21

The main area of the third floor was the squad room, a vast bull pen of metal desks and filing cabinets used round the clock by three different shifts of detectives, including Shrader and Sam. The place was always busy, and this Saturday afternoon was no exception. Several detectives were filling out reports and making phone calls, two robbery detectives were interviewing a group of indignant tourists who'd witnessed a mugging, and a woman with a wailing child in her lap was filling out a complaint against her husband.

Lieutenant Unger's former office was on the far side of the floor, facing the bull pen.

McCord wasn't in the office when Sam and Shrader arrived, but the lights were on and the transformation that had taken place in there made it clear that the office was definitely under new management. Like any unoccupied space in an overcrowded building, Unger's old office had quickly been appropriated for a variety of unauthorized uses, including an auxiliary canteen, a meeting area, a storage closet, and a depository for broken furniture. All that had abruptly changed.

Gone were the pictures of the mayor, the governor, and the police commissioner that Sam had seen hanging on the wall behind the desk; gone were the plaques, citations, certificates, and commendations that had covered the rest of the wall. The old bulletin board on the left-hand side of the room had disappeared along with the notices, clippings, and ads pinned to it. The dusty chalkboard on the right-hand side of the room was the only surviving adornment on any of the walls, but now it was scrubbed perfectly clean. The wooden tray attached to the bottom of it was devoid of dusty erasers and bits of used chalk; instead, there was a single, fresh box of chalk and one new eraser positioned in the center of the spotless tray.

The only furniture in the room was a metal desk that faced the doorway, a credenza behind it, and two guest chairs in front of it, plus one narrow table with two chairs against the left-hand wall. "It looks like McCord likes to keep things a little more orderly than Unger," Shrader whispered as they settled onto the pair of chairs in front of McCord's desk.

Sam thought that was a wild understatement. The metal furniture had not only been scrubbed and repositioned, it was actually centered and aligned with the walls. The credenza behind McCord's desk was empty, except for two computer screens, one of them on a laptop unit that obviously belonged to him, the other a bulky monitor-type that belonged to the department. The laptop was positioned directly behind McCord's chair, its dark blue screen lit up by two flashing white words: "Enter password." The larger computer monitor had been shifted to the left and was turned off. Four neatly labeled stacks of files were arranged on his desk, one stack per corner, one color label per stack. In the center of the desk, directly in front of his vacant swivel chair, was one fresh yellow tablet and one newly sharpened yellow pencil. Beneath the yellow tablet were two file folders, covered up either by accident or design, the labels on them partially visible.

Sam wouldn't have been quite so fascinated with all this housekeeping if McCord had been trying to set up a more personalized environment for himself, one that might make it more pleasant for him during an investigation that could last for weeks or even months. But that didn't appear to be the case. There was not a single picture of a wife, a girlfriend, or a child in evidence; no personal coffee mug, nor paperweight, nor memento of any kind was in evidence anywhere. Not even the nameplate that every cop took with him and put on whatever desk was his at the moment.

Despite the tales she'd just heard of McCord's manly courage and exploits, Sam decided Shrader's hero had either a prissy, fastidious streak or an outright neurosis. She was leaning over to tell Shrader that when she caught the name on one of the file folders peeking out from beneath the tablet and realized that McCord had commandeered their personnel jackets. "Shrader, is your first name . . . *Malcolm?*"

"Do I look like a Malcolm?" he shot back indignantly, but Sam knew embarrassed denial when she saw it.

"That's a perfectly good name. Why deny it?—You're Malcolm Shrader."

"In that case," Mitchell McCord interrupted as he strode swiftly into the office, "you must be Samantha Littleton."

Shock, not protocol, drove Sam to her feet next to Shrader for an exchange of handshakes. "And if I'm right so far," McCord added dryly, "then my name must be McCord." In one swift motion, he nodded for them to sit down, sat down himself, and reached for his phone. "I have one quick call to make, and then we'll get down to business."

Glad to have a few moments to gather her wits, Sam looked at Mitchell McCord's scarred cheek and rough-hewn features, and instantly discarded the notion of prissi-ness, but she could not come up with words to classify him. Nothing about him seemed to fit exactly with the overall impression he gave. He was tall and he moved with the quickness of a man who was physically fit, but he was thinner than he should have been. He was in his middle for-ties, but his hair was gray and was cut in a style that re-minded her a bit of George Clooney. He was dressed well, particularly for a detective; his brown trousers were freshly pressed, his leather belt was just the right shade of brown, and his beige polo shirt was immaculate—but the brown tweed jacket he was wearing was too large for him, particularly in the shoulders.

None of that mattered, of course; Sam knew you couldn't tell much about a man from the way he dressed; but that face of his was another matter entirely, and in some ways, just as puzzling. He was sporting a deep win-ter tan, an indication that he possessed not only the money, but also the temperament, to spend weeks in the tropics, lying on a beach in the sun. Obviously he pos-sessed both those things, but there was absolutely noth-ing idle or self-indulgent about that harsh-featured face with its two-inch-long scar curving down his right cheek, or the thicker scar slashing across the eyebrow above it. In addition to his scars, he also had deep grooves at the sides of his mouth, creases in his forehead, and twin fur-rows between his eyebrows.

Mitchell McCord's face was not youthful or handsome. In fact, it was a long way from being handsome. But it was stamped with so much character and etched with so much hard-bitten experience that it was—beyond any doubt—the most charismatic, riveting face she had ever seen on a man.

When her next thought was one of passing regret that she hadn't washed her hair and worn something nicer than a sweatshirt and jeans, Sam frowned in surprised disgust and brought herself up short.

McCord hung up the phone a moment later and addressed his comments to Shrader, not Sam, which was appropriate given Shrader's superior rank and experience. "Okay, bring me up to speed. Give me a minute-to-minute, blow-by-blow of everything that's transpired so far." He glanced at Sam. "If he leaves anything out, speak up immediately, don't wait, and don't hold back any details, no matter how small."

Without another word, he picked up the yellow tablet and pencil from his desk, swiveled his chair to the side, propped his ankle on one knee, and propped the tablet on his lap. He began making notes as soon as Shrader began speaking.

Sam made several mental notes herself, but they concerned his face, his body language, and the fact that his brown loafers were polished and shiny. After that, she devoted her attention totally to the subject at hand and, in the process, she managed to forget how strangely attractive she thought McCord was. She did that so well that when he glanced sideways at her and fired his first question at her, she answered him calmly and concisely.

"In the hospital," he asked her, "did you believe Leigh Manning when she said she didn't know Valente, that she'd met him for the first time at a party the night before?"

"Yes."

"At that time, were you also convinced that her concern for her husband was genuine?"

"Yes," Sam said again, and nodded for emphasis.

"In retrospect, now that you know she was lying, can you think of any small thing she said or did that would have given her away—if you'd been watching for it?"

"No—"

He caught her hesitation and homed in on it. "'No,' what?"

"No," Sam said, and reluctantly added, "and I'm *not* certain she's been lying about her fear for her husband. The first night we saw her in the hospital, she was drugged and she was confused and disoriented, but she wanted to see her husband and she seemed to truly believe he could be somewhere in the hospital. The next morning, she was no longer disoriented, but she seemed frantic, and she also seemed to be struggling to keep her panic under control. She did not seem to be trying to put on a frenzied show for us, she seemed to be doing exactly the opposite."

"Really?" he said, but he was patronizing her, and she knew it.

After asking a great many more questions of Shrader, and not a single additional one of her, he finally came to the end and laid down his pad. He unlocked a drawer in his desk and extracted the tan evidence envelope that Harwell had signed for in the mountains and delivered to Captain Holland at Shrader's instructions. McCord removed the clear plastic bag inside it containing Valente's handwritten note. Smiling, he turned it in his fingers, and then he read what it said aloud: " *It was harder than I ever imagined it would be to pretend we didn't know each other Saturday night.*' "

Still smiling, he looked at Sam. "You thought her alleged stalker sent the basket of pears, and that's why you hunted this note down, is that right?"

"Yes."

"Why did the pears bother you?"

"Because Mrs. Manning mentioned that she always eats them for breakfast and that her husband teased her about it. The basket of pears was an elaborate, expensive gift, and I assumed whoever sent them had to have knowledge of her personal habits."

"Did it occur to you that her husband might have sent them himself? He'd vanished mysteriously, and suddenly the pears turned up without a card. It could have been a private communication between the two of them. Did you consider that?"

"Not then, no. If I hadn't found the note from Valente, I'd have started wondering about that if, and when, Logan Manning didn't turn up alive."

"He isn't going to turn up alive. Valente will make certain of that. Unfortunately, this note to Leigh Manning isn't incontrovertible proof of a murder conspiracy. He'll deny he wrote it; we'll get handwriting experts to testify he did; then his lawyers will find handwriting experts to refute our experts. Handwriting analysis isn't perceived by juries as a legitimate science, and handwriting experts generally make unconvincing witnesses. As far as this stationery goes, Valente's lawyers will argue that anyone with a two-hundred-dollar printer could have made it—including some enemy of Valente's who wanted to implicate him."

Glad for a chance to contribute something of value to the discussion, Sam said, "Valente's name isn't printed on that stationery, it's engraved. That means a professional printer somewhere did the work."

"How can you tell?"

"Turn it over and run your finger lightly over the back

of it; there's a slight indentation behind each letter of his name."

"You're right, there is." She couldn't tell if McCord was impressed at all by this information, which was fairly common knowledge to women who'd priced invitations or stationery in a good department or stationery store, but she didn't feel a need to mention that fact to him. She had the distinct feeling he was more than a little ambivalent about letting her remain on his team.

"All right, we know with a little effort we should be able to prove she's been having an affair with Valente, and we also know her accident occurred when she was driving back to the city, not into the mountains." He looked at her steadily, and Sam began to wish he weren't, particularly when he asked the next question. "What's your opinion of the way the case is shaping up at this point?"

Sam wondered if he was testing her by throwing her a trick question, because, at that point, there was no case. "What case?" she replied cautiously.

"Based on what you've seen and heard so far," he clarified impatiently, "what is your theory?"

"I don't have a theory. There are no facts to support any theory. We know that Mrs. Manning and Valente knew each before last week and that they wanted to keep it a secret. Beyond that, all we know is that Mrs. Manning wanted to get to the cabin as quickly as possible last week, and she was willing to be seen with Valente in order to do it. Are we trying to prosecute them for adultery? Because if we are, we couldn't do that with what we—"

The look McCord gave her made Sam feel as if she were flunking his test—a test he had hoped she'd pass—and she stopped in mid-sentence, completely confused. He picked up his tablet, turned in his chair again, and propped the tablet in his lap. "Are you telling me you haven't seen or heard anything in the last week that makes you suspicious?"

"Of course I'm suspicious."

"Then let's hear your opinion."

"I haven't formed an opinion worth giving," Sam said stubbornly.

"Americans have opinions about everything, Detective," he said impatiently. "No matter how ill-informed, one-sided, or self-serving that opinion may be, they have a compulsion to not only share it, but to try to inflict it on each other. It's a national pastime. It's a national obsession. Now," he said sharply, "you're supposed to be a detective. By definition, that means you're observant and intuitive. Prove it to me. Give me some observations, if you can't come up with opinions."

"About what?"

"About anything! About me."

Sam's six older brothers had spent most of their lives trying to goad her; she'd become supremely impervious to male goading a long time ago. But not completely—not right at this moment. At this moment her defense system was under unexpected siege and the only thing she could do was deny him the one satisfaction males wanted most at a time like this: the satisfaction of *knowing* she was riled. For that reason, she widened her eyes and smiled warmly at him when he snapped, "If you're at all aware that I'm here, Detective, let's hear your observations about me."

"Yes, sir, of course. You're approximately six feet one inches tall; weight about one hundred seventy pounds, age mid-forties."

She paused, hoping he would back off, knowing he wouldn't.

"That's the best you can do?" he mocked.

"No, sir. It isn't. You had every piece of furniture in this office scrubbed, not merely dusted, which means you're either unusually fastidious or you're just plain neurotic."

"Or it could mean I don't like cockroaches in my desk drawers."

"You didn't find cockroaches in your desk. The canteen is on the other side of this floor and if we were going to have roaches on the third floor, that's where they'd be. But they aren't there, possibly because this floor was fumigated less than two weeks ago. I know because I'm allergic to the chemical."

"Keep going."

"You can't stand clutter, and you have an obsession with orderliness. The furniture in here is centered exactly on the walls; the files on your desk are arranged in precise corners. If I had to guess, I would say you are probably a control freak, and that is usually symptomatic of a man who feels powerless to control his own life, so he tries to control every facet of his surroundings. Shall I stop?"

"No, please go on."

"You're wearing brown loafers, brown pants, and a brown belt. Your face is tanned, which makes you look healthy, but you've lost a lot of weight recently—possibly due to an illness that required you to take enough time off in the winter to get that tan."

"What makes you think I've lost weight?"

"Because the jacket you're wearing is too big for you, especially in the shoulders."

"Which could mean that I stayed at my sister's house last night and borrowed this jacket from my brother-in-law when I realized I had to come in here today."

"You wouldn't use someone else's clothes; you don't even like using someone else's office." She paused and asked with convincing meekness, "How am I doing so far?"

He looked down at his tablet, and the crease of his scar

deepened enough to give Sam the impression he might actually be smiling. "Not bad. Go on."

"Instead of facing people at your desk, you sit sideways in your chair. That could mean you're self-conscious about your scars, which I doubt. It could mean you have a hearing problem that is helped when you turn your good ear to whoever is speaking, which I also doubt. It's possible you sit that way because you have some sort of back problem, or because it enables you to concentrate better. People with ADD sometimes do that."

"And do you have an opinion as to which of those theories about the way I sit might be correct?"

"Not one worth giving," Sam said stubbornly, but with an innocent troubled expression.

"Give it anyway."

Graciously, she inclined her head, yielding to his rank and his right to command. "I think you sit that way so you can hold your tablet out of sight where no one can see what you're writing. I also think it may have been a necessity for some reason in the past, but that now you do it more out of habit."

"What color are my socks?"

"Brown."

"What color are my eyes?"

"I have no idea," Sam lied. "I'm sorry." He had steel blue eyes, but she had already won his tournament, game, set, and match. She was not going to let him score a point for his ego in overtime!

However, her confidence began to fade a little as she waited for him to write something on his damned yellow pad—an evaluation of her observations, an appraisal of her, a grade. She knew instinctively he intended to do exactly that; she knew it as surely as she knew that after he wrote down his evaluation and his decision about keeping her on the team, he would tear the yellow sheet off his pad and put it into the folder near his elbow that had her name on it. What she couldn't figure out was why he was still sitting there, pencil in hand, taking so long to make up his mind.

She stared at his inscrutable profile, willing him to write something down. She was watching him so closely that she actually saw the muscle at the corner of his mouth move before the movement became a hint of an actual smile, and he finally began to jot notes on his tablet.

She had qualified to stay on the team! She knew that much from his expression. Now she wished more than anything that she knew what he was writing.

"Curious?" he asked without looking up.

"Of course."

"Do you think you have a chance of seeing what I'm writing about you here?"

"About the same chance I have of winning the lottery."

His smile deepened. "You're right." He flipped the page over and wrote several other notes on the next sheet. Suddenly he tore both sheets off and swiveled his chair to the front. He put the first sheet into the folder with Sam's name on it; he slid the second sheet into his top desk drawer.

"All right, let's get started," he said abruptly. "There are four stacks of folders on my desk. The stack with the blue labels on the folders contains all the information we have right now on Logan Manning. The second stack with the green labels covers everything on Leigh Manning. The stack with the yellow labels pertains to their known friends and associates. The stack with the red labels is the tip of the iceberg on Valente. I'm having all his files copied and sent over here, but it will take a few days. By next week, that table over there will be covered with files on him.

"Each of us will take a stack, and we will read every sheet of paper in every single folder. The documents in the folders are all photocopies, so you can take them home with you. When you've finished going through all the files in your stack, start on a new one. By the end of next week, I want all of us to be completely familiar with every document in every folder in these stacks. Oh, and one more thing—these stacks are partials; we're still searching the archives on everyone except Valente. We already know all there is to know about him. Any questions?" he asked, looking from one to the other.

"I have a question," Sam said as she stood up and reached for the armload of files on Logan Manning. "There were two words scribbled on the bottom of Valente's note, written in what I assume is Italian. They don't make sense to Shrader or me. We wanted to check them out. Could I get a copy of the note?"

"No. Nobody gets a peek at that note or a hint of what it says until we're ready to show it. The last time the Feds went after Valente, there were so many leaks that his lawyers were filing motions to suppress while the Feds were still trying to figure out what evidence they had and what it could mean. Never underestimate Valente," McCord warned, "and don't underestimate his influence and connections. His connections go all the way to the top. And that," he said meaningfully, "is why *we* are keeping this case right down here, in the Eighteenth Precinct—right at the bottom of the ladder of justice. Valente won't be looking for it here, and we're hoping he won't be able to get at it so easily."

When he finished, he looked from Shrader to Sam. "What's bothering you?"

"Instead of making a copy of the note, could I write the two words down?"

Leaning across his desk, he jotted the two words on his yellow tablet, tore off the sheet, and handed it to her.

"We've already run them through the system. 'Falco' turned up as an alias he's used before. It's a common Italian surname. We're still checking the other one out for associations." He looked at Shrader. "Any comments or questions, Malcolm?"

"One," Shrader said, looking absolutely ferocious. "I would appreciate it if you would never call me that again, Lieutenant."

"I won't."

"I hate that name."

"My mother liked it. It was her maiden name."

"I hate it anyway," Shrader announced, picking up his stack of files.

As soon as they were out the door and out of hearing, Shrader looked at her and shook his big head. "You lead a charmed life, Littleton. So help me God, when you told him he was a neurotic control freak with a neatness compulsion, I broke out in a sweat."

Sam thought it was touching that Shrader had worried that much about her. Her next thought was that she should have thanked McCord for letting her stay on the team. Viewed from any direction, this was a chance of a lifetime and she was a neophyte who really shouldn't be getting such a chance. On the other hand, she reminded herself, if she hadn't found Valente's note, there wouldn't be a "team." She dumped the files on her desk, asked Shrader to keep an eye on them for a moment, and walked back to the lieutenant's office.

McCord was leaning back in his chair, reading a file with a red label, a tablet at his elbow, pencil in hand, ready to make notes. He even looked tough and fascinating when he read. She knocked politely on the doorframe, and when he glanced up, she said, "I just wanted to thank you for having enough faith in me to let me work this case."

He regarded her steadily, his expression amused. "Don't thank me, thank the cockroaches."

Sam hesitated, holding his gaze, trying not to laugh. "Is there any *particular* cockroach I should thank?"

McCord returned his attention to the file folder and turned a page. "The one I found in my desk drawer that's big enough to drive a Volvo. His cousins live in the canteen."

CHAPTER 22

"I can't believe you've kept your friends away for so long!" Jason chided Leigh as soon as Hilda let him in Sunday afternoon. The energy and animation he exuded made Leigh feel both enlivened and exhausted, but she could barely hide her displeasure when he turned aside to hand Hilda his coat and she realized he wasn't alone. Behind him stood Jane Sebring.

Ruddy-faced from the cold and boyishly eager to see her, Jason left Jane in the foyer and rushed across the room to plant a kiss on Leigh's cheek. "I couldn't stop Jane from coming," he whispered. "She insisted. She got right into the taxi with me. She won't stay long, though. She has to be back at the theater for the matinee, but I'm free all afternoon!" Straightening, he stood up and surveyed Leigh's face, his own face registering unconcealed horror. "How long will it be before you look like yourself?"

"Not long," Leigh said, wincing as he settled himself close beside her on the sofa, but her attention was on Jane, who had stopped at a mirror to inspect her flawless face.

In the tradition of the Barrymores, four successive generations of the Sebring family had become theater legends. Jane was the first member of her illustrious family ever to be regarded as extraordinarily beautiful; she was also the first member of her family to be savaged by theater critics in her first Broadway role. In reality, she'd simply debuted in a major role that was far too challenging for an inexperienced actress of twenty-one, but she'd been given that opportunity because she was a Sebring. And because she was a Sebring, the critics had held her to the impossibly high standards set by her more experienced, and far less gorgeous, famous ancestors.

Two weeks after the play opened, she left it in disgrace and went to Hollywood. There, her family's contacts opened doors for her, and her stunning face and figure mesmerized the cameras. With good direction and good editing, her performances improved along with her roles, culminating in an Academy Award for Best Supporting Actress last year.

Her Oscar gave Jane a stature in films that her forebears had never achieved in their motion picture careers, but that wasn't enough. Apparently still wounded by her long-ago humiliation on Broadway, she'd passed up two stellar film opportunities and a fortune in money in order to take a role in *Blind Spot.*

"You poor thing!" Jane said as she put her cheek near Leigh's and blew a kiss in the air; then she straightened and did her own inventory of the fading bruises and healing cuts on Leigh's face. "You've been through so much since opening night—"

Hoping to avoid probing questions about the details of what she'd been through, Leigh resorted to formalities by asking them if Hilda could bring them something to drink.

"I'll have my usual," Jason said, looking over his shoulder at Hilda, who he knew from experience would be hovering nearby, ready to bring refreshments. "A vodka martini," he clarified, "with two olives."

"Jane?" Leigh asked.

"I don't drink," Jane reminded her, her expression gently chiding Leigh for failing to remember that Jane did not drink alcohol. Although past generations of the Sebring family had all been as notorious for their vices as for their talent, Jane Sebring had none of their predilection for excesses. She did not drink or smoke, she abhorred drugs, and she was a physical-fitness fanatic. "I'll have some bottled water, if you have it."

"We do," Leigh said.

"I prefer Weltzenholder," Jane added. "It's bottled in the Alps. They only export a thousand cases a year to the U.S. I buy one hundred cases at a time."

"I'm sorry, but the other nine hundred cases went to someone other than us," Leigh said lightly. "What else would you like?"

"Pellegrino will be fine."

Leigh nodded and looked at Hilda. "I'd like tea, Hilda. Thank you."

Jason watched Hilda as if to make sure she was out of earshot before he asked a question, but Hilda was completely trustworthy. Jane was the fascinated outsider who would repeat and embellish everything she heard to friends, strangers, and reporters alike. Leigh could have strangled him for bringing her along.

"What news have you heard about Logan?" he asked Leigh as soon as Hilda disappeared beyond a doorway.

"Nothing. You know as much as I do."

He looked genuinely shocked. "Darling, this is unbelievable, impossible! What could have happened to him?"

He died. . . . I know it. . . . He died. . . . I know it. . . .

Leigh tensed her entire body in an effort to block out the terrible chant pounding in her brain. "I don't know."

"Is there anything I can do?"

Leigh shook her head. "The police are doing everything they possibly can. Commissioner Trumanti has sent helicopters, squad cars, and detectives into the mountains to search for him."

"What about you? How are you feeling? Really?"

"I'm stiff and sore, and I look like hell, but that's all that's wrong. Other than the fact that my husband is d— missing," she corrected, struggling to recover from another tidal wave of despondency and grief.

Jason fell silent, looking helpless and forlorn and completely empathetic, but only for a moment. His expression cleared almost immediately and he broached a topic that affected his own personal well-being and therefore was of maximum importance to him. "Do you think it would help you to come back to work soon?"

"Physically, I could probably manage it next week—"

"Fantastic! That's my girl! You're a trooper. I knew I could count on you to—!"

"But not mentally," Leigh interrupted emphatically. "I can't think of anything except Logan. I wouldn't even be able to remember my lines."

"They would come back to you the minute you stepped onstage."

"Maybe they would," Leigh said, letting her gaze shift to Jane, "but I don't have one bit of emotion left over to invest in them. You understand, don't you, Jane?"

"Perfectly," Jane said. "I even tried to explain to Jason how you'd be feeling right now, but you know how all-important the play is to him." To Leigh's surprise, the actress actually seemed disgusted as she added bluntly, "Jason wouldn't care if you were on life support, so long as they could unplug you and prop you up long enough to say your lines."

"That's not completely true," Jason said, looking stung. "I'd restage your scenes so you could say your lines lying down." He paused long enough to take his martini glass from the tray Hilda was holding out to him. "I'm a selfish bastard," he declared with an impenitent grin. "But you have to admit," he added with a wink at Leigh, "I'm a brilliant selfish bastard."

Leigh assumed he was making a lame attempt to amuse and distract her, and she managed to give him a wan smile.

With no verbal reply from Leigh to encourage further banter, Jason stopped talking about himself and regaled her with a discussion of his play's fabulous reviews, box office sales, and lighting problems, and followed that with an irate description of his latest quarrel with the play's director. Leigh let him talk, but his words never actually registered on her. Reclining against the arm of the sofa, she watched his mouth move, and she looked automatically toward Jane when the other woman spoke, but she had little idea of what they were saying and even less interest in it.

When Jane finally stood up to leave, Leigh realized that she was going to have to deal with Jason alone, and she almost regretted the actress's impending departure.

"Robert and Lincoln asked me to give you their love," Jane told her.

Leigh hadn't given a single thought to any of the actors in *Blind Spot* until that moment. "Please give them mine. Did Robert's wife have their baby yet?"

"Yes, a little girl."

In an effort to hasten Jane's departure, Jason headed for the closet in the foyer, where Hilda had hung their coats. Removing Jane's sable coat from its hanger, he held it up like a matador waving his cape. "Jane, you're going to be late for the matinee!" He jiggled the coat for emphasis. "Darling, get your famous ass into your coat so you can get going."

"Has he always been this obnoxious?" Jane asked Leigh as she gave her hand a farewell squeeze.

Startled by the undercurrent of genuine animosity in Jane's voice, Leigh said, "He's under a lot of stress right now. Don't take it personally. He has a play with two strong female roles and only one established actress to fill them."

Instead of replying to that, Jane hesitated, glanced at Jason, and then said awkwardly, "Actually, I came here today because there was something I wanted to say to you, face-to-face. I want you to know that I am deeply sorry about your accident. I won't pretend that I haven't been dying to play your role from the moment I read *Blind Spot*, but I wanted to win the role on my own merit, not by default and not by tragedy."

To Leigh's surprise, she believed her. Jane was notoriously ambitious and self-centered, but she was not exuding her usual glamorous self-confidence. She looked tense and a little tired, and she actually winced when she looked at Leigh's face. "At least you won't need surgery."

"No, and I'm sure you'll have many leading roles if you decide to stay in New York instead of going back to Hollywood."

It wasn't until after Jane left that Leigh realized Jane had used the word "tragedy" to describe Logan's disappearance.

"Now," Jason enthused as soon as he closed the door behind Jane, "we can talk and talk and talk!"

Leigh honestly didn't know how she was going to endure another two minutes of Jason's rapid-fire banter, let alone another hour or two of it. She didn't know how he could expect her to care about anything he was saying, and she didn't know how she was going to concentrate on whatever it was. Hilda's announcement offered her an unexpected solution: "Courtney Maitland wants to come up and see you," she said from the kitchen doorway. "She's very insistent. She says she's going to steal an elevator key to get up here and pitch a tent in the foyer if you won't let her come in for a few minutes."

Leigh actually smiled at the very real possibility of Courtney's doing exactly that. On the other hand, if Courtney was there, she would deflect some of Jason's conversation. "Tell her to come up, Hilda."

"Who is Courtney Maitland?" Jason demanded, looking less than pleased at the prospect of having to share Leigh's company with anyone else.

"She's a teenager who is staying with a family in my building while she takes a special course at school. I met her several weeks ago in the lobby."

"I detest children in general," Jason replied, "and adolescents in particular."

"This particular 'adolescent' has a genius IQ, and I think she's wonderful."

CHAPTER 23

Jason was in the kitchen, showing Hilda how to prepare what he wanted to eat for lunch, when Courtney Maitland arrived, so Joe O'Hara went to the front door to let her in. "I'll tell Courtney to keep it short," he told Leigh.

"No, don't do that. I'd like her to stay for a while."

"Just don't let her talk you into playing gin rummy with her," he said, opening the door, "because she cheats."

"I do not," Courtney retorted, stepping into the foyer.

Over her shoulder, Leigh smiled at the sixteen-year-old's latest fashion statement. Tall, slim, and flat-chested, she was wearing her permed dark hair pulled up into a thick ponytail over her left ear, a red woolen scarf around her neck, a sweatshirt that said Nirvana, a pair of jeans with huge holes in the knees and thighs, and a pair of combat boots, unlaced. For earrings, she'd chosen what appeared to be three-inch-long gold safety pins.

"I didn't realize you and Joe knew each other," Leigh said.

"I hung around up here while you were in the hospital," Courtney explained. "It was the only way I could find out anything."

In front of the sofa, Courtney gazed down at Leigh's face, and it was the first time Leigh had ever seen her look solemn, but her remark was typically and refreshingly ir-reverent. "Wow," she said. "When I saw the pictures of your car on TV being brought back here on a wrecker, I thought you'd look like you'd been in a really bad accident."

"How *do* I look?"

"Like you've been rollerblading," she said with an imp-ish grin. "On your face."

Leigh laughed, and the sound of it seemed foreign and unfamiliar to her.

"Do you have company?" Courtney asked as Jason's voice drifted in from the kitchen. "If you do, I can come back later."

"No, don't go. In fact, you'll be doing me a favor if you stay. The man who is here is a good friend who thinks that conversation is just what I need, but I'm having a lit-tle trouble concentrating on the subjects that interest him right now."

O'Hara had been standing close by, waiting to ask Courtney if she wanted something to drink. "Why don't you let Courtney play gin rummy with him," he said crossly. "He'll be flat broke in a half hour and need to borrow money for a taxi."

Courtney gave him a disgusted look. "I will be on my very best behavior," she promised Leigh. "I will listen to him very attentively and say all the right things."

"Just be yourself. I'm not worried about anything you may say. I'm worried about what Jason may say in front of you."

"Really? That's a switch. My father usually breaks into a cold sweat whenever I walk into a room with strangers in it." To O'Hara she said, "If you want to try to win your money back, I'll give you a chance later, in the kitchen."

"I'll go find an ATM machine in the meantime. You want your usual—Coke with a maraschino cherry and a shot of chocolate syrup?"

"My God, that sounds vile!" Jason said, walking in with a plate in his right hand and a martini in his left.

Leigh introduced them to each other. "Courtney is enrolled in a special writing program at Columbia for gifted high school students," she told Jason as he put his plate and drink on the coffee table. With one glance, he took in the teenager's tattered jeans and well-worn combat boots, and dismissed her with a shrug. "Good," he said without a trace of interest.

Leigh flinched at his rudeness. "Courtney, this is Jason Solomon, who wrote *Blind Spot.*"

"It got great reviews when Leigh was in it," she said, sitting down carefully on Leigh's sofa.

Jason frowned at her casual use of Leigh's first name and then addressed her in the superior tone of an adult lecturing a backward eight-year-old. *"Miss Kendall,"* he emphasized, "is a very fine actress, but it takes more than fine acting to make a Broadway play a critical success."

Instead of replying, Courtney snapped her fingers, jumped up, and headed for the kitchen. "I forgot to tell O'Hara to skip the ice in my Coke."

As soon as he thought she was out of earshot, Jason leaned forward. "Do you know the couple she's staying with in your building?"

"No."

"Well, you ought to warn them. I know another wealthy couple who let an impoverished student move in with them while she went to school. The girl seduced their son when he came home for Christmas, she got pregnant, and it cost them a fortune to pay her off. She wanted the boy to marry her! Girls like Courtney have big social ambitions. They attend school on scholarships while trying to ingratiate themselves with wealthy, unsuspecting families like the one she's staying with—" He glanced over his shoulder, saw Courtney coming toward them with a Coke in her hand, and broke off.

Leigh considered setting him straight, but she was so disappointed in his assumptions that she decided to either let Courtney handle it or let him go on thinking whatever he wanted. She smiled at Courtney as she sat down on the sofa. "Did you find out what your journalism class assignment is yet—the assignment that's going to account for half your final grade?"

Courtney nodded. "We have to interview the most famous or influential person we can possibly get access to, and the harder it normally is to get an interview with that person, the higher our grade will be. Grades will also be based on the quality of the interview, the uniqueness of the 'slant' we take for the interview, the quality of any new or unusual information we extract from that person, and the overall quality of our reporting. Only one *A* will be given. I have the highest average in the class right now, but not by a big margin, so the pressure is really on me."

"Do you have any idea who you want to interview?"

She shot Leigh a guilty smile. "You were the first person I thought of, but we're supposed to really dig around for . . . well . . . new information, buried secrets, things no one else has discovered in their interviews. Even if you had any deep, dark secrets, I wouldn't want to betray them to anyone."

"Thank you for that," Leigh said with a relieved sigh. "Who else do you have in mind?"

"No one yet. Camille Bingley is going to interview Archbishop Lindley—he's a friend of her dad's. She thinks she might be able to get him to reveal new things about the problems in the Catholic Church right now. Brent Gentner's father is a friend of Senator Kennedy's, and Brent is positive he can get an interview with the senator." She paused to sip her drink. "In order for me to outdo Camille and Brent, I'd have to get an interview with the pope or the president."

Jason's voice was amused. "Do you think you could pull that off?"

"If I wanted to. The problem is that the pope is really sick, and the president already gives lots of interviews—"

"Even if that weren't true, they might be a little difficult for you to reach," Jason pointed out condescendingly.

Courtney gaped at him as if she couldn't believe anyone was as obtuse as he. "I wouldn't telephone them myself. I would call Noah and ask him to do it."

"Noah—as in 'the ark'?" Jason joked.

"Noah—as in my brother."

"I see. Your brother, Noah, has a direct line to the pope and the president?"

"I'm not sure about the pope. We're not Catholic, but Noah donated the land where—"

Suddenly Jason tied her brother's first name to Courtney's last name, and came up with the name of a renowned Florida billionaire. "Your brother is Noah Maitland?" he exclaimed.

"Yes."

"*The* Noah Maitland?"

"I'm sure there are others. I don't think Noah has copyrighted his name yet. He's probably tried, though," she added with an irreverent grin.

Leigh knew what was coming next, and she braced herself. Jason was a brilliant wordsmith, but he'd made the mistake of openly patronizing a sixteen-year-old who had a genius IQ and absolutely no social inhibitions about saying whatever it took to shock her adversary into speechlessness. Leigh had seen Courtney in action on a few other occasions.

"*The* Noah Maitland from Palm Beach?" Jason persisted.

"Yes."

Jason gaped at her youthful, freckled face and undeveloped figure. "How could that happen?"

"The same way it always happens: Sperm meets egg, fertilization occurs—"

"I mean," Jason interrupted, "I was under the impression Noah Maitland was in his forties."

"He is. Noah and I have the same father, but different mothers."

"Ah," Jason said, his mind inevitably focusing on the possibility of obtaining yet another backer for a future play, a backer with bottomless pockets. Trying to atone for his former blatant disinterest in her, he began plying Courtney with the sort of questions he assumed other people must ask sixteen-year-olds. "And do you have any other brothers or sisters?"

"No, but my father has had four wives, so I'm sure he tried."

"It must have been terribly lonely for you growing up," he said sympathetically.

"Not at all. Two of my father's wives were nearly as young as I was. I played with them."

Jason gawked at her, his eyes wide, his mouth slightly open, and Leigh reached for Courtney's hand and gave it an affectionate squeeze. "Courtney, you don't realize it, but this is a momentous occasion. Normally, Jason is responsible for saying the sort of things that make people look exactly as he does right now."

Jason reached the same conclusion, and for a moment he stared at Courtney with what appeared to be disgruntled awe; then he leaned back and grinned at her. "I'll bet you are a first-class pain in the ass."

"No," she corrected him proudly, "I am a *world-class* pain in the ass."

Since Jason and Courtney seemed to have established a reasonably cordial truce, Leigh leaned back against the sofa and pulled a peach cashmere throw over her that she'd been using earlier.

Their voices ebbed and flowed around her.

Her eyes closed. . . .

She awoke with a start when Jason kissed her cheek. "I'm leaving. My ego cannot bear another affront. Not only did my hostess fall asleep while I was talking, but that irritating brat just relieved me of fifty dollars in two hands of gin rummy in the kitchen."

When he left, Leigh listened for a while to O'Hara and Courtney playing cards in the kitchen; then she forced herself to get up. Michael Valente would be arriving at any time, and she decided to splash cold water on her face and brush her hair. For nearly a week, she'd been wound tight with tension, unable to sleep, shaking inside and outside. Now she could barely put one foot in front of the other.

CHAPTER 24

The day after the cabin was located, it had taken Shrader and Littleton only an hour at the local county courthouse to obtain a copy of the property tax records with the owner's name and last known address.

It took the next two days to locate the deceased owner's heir, a grandson, who was sailing on his yacht in the Caribbean. On Sunday morning at seven, he finally returned Shrader's call from his ship-to-shore radio. He told Shrader everything he could remember about his grandfather's property in the Catskills, including the existence of a narrow garage built into the back of a hillside during the early 1950s. Originally intended as a bomb shelter, it was hollowed out of the rock, supported with timbers, and lined with shelves where canned goods and emergency supplies had once been stored.

After that, it took less than an hour for a county sheriff to locate the entry to the bomb shelter-garage. The doors opened outward, and the snow on the hillside had slid downward, creating a giant drift that had to be completely cleared away at the base before they could be opened. After an hour of hard shoveling, the sheriff was finally able to open one door wide enough to beam his flashlight into the blackness of the hillside cavity.

Four shiny chrome letters leapt out at him: **JEEP.**

CHAPTER 25

Shrader picked up Sam at her apartment an hour after the Jeep was discovered, but the medical examiner and CSU were already at the scene when he and Sam arrived. He pulled to a stop behind several other vehicles parked on the main road and, with Sam in the lead, they made their way down the slippery path trampled into the snow by the parade of heavy, booted feet since Friday.

The cabin was tucked close against a high tree-covered hill at the rear, a position that gave it shelter from behind while allowing a spectacular, unobstructed view of the mountain scenery from the front. The bomb shelter–garage was around the corner and on the back side of that same hill. "Who'd have thought there was a hole in the damned hill behind this place?" Shrader commented as they trudged past the cabin, following a fresh path of footprints around the hill to the back.

McCord was standing just outside the open garage doors watching an NYPD crime scene unit methodically going over the narrow interior, gathering samples and taking photographs. Two more members of the unit were standing outside with him, waiting to go inside when there was more room.

"What have we got?" Shrader asked McCord.

McCord started to answer, but the M.E., a heavyset man with red cheeks and blue earmuffs, walked past the doorway just then and assumed the question was directed at him. "We've got a corpse, Shrader," Herbert Niles said cheerfully. "A nice, perfectly preserved corpse, thanks to this underground freezer he's been sitting in. He's not as pretty now as he looked on his driver's license, but it's definitely Logan Manning."

As the M.E. spoke, he walked into the garage, leaned into the Jeep and carefully lifted first one wrist and then the other, swabbing each hand on the back, the fingers, and the palm with sticky pads used to pick up traces of nitrates found in gunpowder residue. "We've also got what appears to be a self-inflicted gunshot wound to the right temple—"

Sam moved to the side and got a full view of the male body slumped partway between the steering wheel and driver's door, the window beside his head heavily splattered with blood and brain matter, the passenger's window partway open and unharmed.

"Weapon?" Shrader prodded.

"There's a recently fired thirty-eight special, with two empty cartridges in the chamber, lying near the victim's foot—" Niles paused to deposit the last sticky pad into an evidence bag and write down the part of the hand where he'd taken the swab. "One slug penetrated his skull and exited on the left side, traveling through the driver's side window and lodging in the left wall."

"What about the second one?" Shrader asked.

"I think we can reasonably conclude that he didn't fire the second one *after* he blew his brains out. That could mean he missed his own head the first time he aimed at it, or—more likely—and this is the theory I like—he fired the first shot a year ago at an empty beer can on a fence."

Since transferring to homicide, Sam had worked with only two other M.E.'s, both of them as humorless as the work they did. Herbert Niles was in charge of the M.E.'s office, and despite his glib remarks, he was reported to be even more conscientious than the more serious-minded M.E.'s who reported to him. She glanced at McCord, but he was watching one of the CSU people who'd stopped taking photographs and was using a flashlight to inspect the old cans and containers on the steel shelves. He was looking for that second slug.

Niles backed himself out of the Jeep and stripped off his rubber gloves. "The light is lousy in this cave, and the battery's dead on the Jeep, so we can't use its headlights. CSU has more lights with them, but there's no room for them in there until we get the vehicle out." He looked at the men waiting outside with McCord. "I'm done. Go ahead and push the vehicle out; then we'll bag and tag Mr. Manning and I'll take him back home. After that, this place is all yours."

He looked at McCord. "I suppose you'll want to know what's on those swabs first thing in the morning, Mack?"

Instead of replying, McCord lifted his brows.

Niles sighed. "Right—I'll let you know in about four hours. That gives me three and a half hours to make the drive back and a half hour to study the swabs under the microscope. Assuming your dead guy didn't warm up in there during the last week, any powder residue on his hands will still be there, and the swabs should have picked it up. You'll have to wait until tomorrow for us to match up prints and start the rest of the process. Don't expect much from me on a T.O.D." he added. "Manning's body is perfectly preserved with no apparent signs of deterioration."

"Not a problem," McCord said. "Detective Littleton has already figured out when Manning died." It was the first time he'd actually looked at Sam since she arrived. "Haven't you?"

Sam slid her sunglasses low on her nose and eyed him reproachfully above the frames for subjecting her to another pop quiz. "I'd put his time of death at last Sunday, between three P.M. and three A.M. the next morning—probably closer to three P.M., Sunday."

"How did you arrive at that?" Niles asked.

"There were a couple inches of snow on the Jeep in the garage, which means Manning put the vehicle in there sometime after two P.M., when the snow really started falling. By three A.M., there was almost a foot and a half of snow on the ground, so the drifts down here would have barricaded the doors completely, preventing him from being able to move the vehicle in or out. The doors were still barricaded by snow this morning, which means he's been in there all this time."

"Sounds good to me," Niles said, jotting down notes about her timing.

McCord wanted to look around the inside of the house. "I've been over the photographs CSU took last week," he said to Littleton, "but I'd like you and Shrader to show me what you saw and point out where everything was."

They were standing in the main room a few minutes later, discussing the glasses in the kitchen sink and the presence of only one sleeping bag, when one of the CSU guys poked his head inside the open doorway. "We've got the second slug, Lieutenant."

All three of them turned at once. "Where was it?" McCord asked.

"Lodged in the timbers of the right-hand wall of the garage."

The Jeep had been pushed outdoors and was being

dusted for prints and checked for fibers, which left room inside for CSU's battery-operated high-wattage lights. "We'd have spotted it sooner if we'd been able to get our lights in here earlier." He walked over to the wall on the right and pointed to a fresh hole in the timbers about four and a half feet up from the floor. "Was there anything in front of it on the shelf?" Sam asked.

"Nope. No one tried to hide it. We just couldn't see it until we lit the place up."

Silently, Sam gauged the height of the newly discovered hole and turned, comparing it to the height of the open window on the passenger door of the Jeep.

"Interesting, isn't it?" Shrader said, arriving at the same possibility Sam had reached.

"I assume the window on the passenger side was down when you got here?" Shrader asked him.

"If it's down now, it was down when we got here."

"Was that a definite yes?" Shrader said impatiently. "Or was it 'I think so, it should have been, it probably was.' "

"The windows are electric and the battery is dead, so it had to have been down when they got here," Sam pointed out in a low voice.

"I know that," Shrader said irritably. "I just don't want to listen to any smart-ass answers on my day off."

"It was definitely down when we got here, Detective," came the more respectful reply.

"Thank you," Shrader retorted.

An hour after Niles left with Manning's body, Sam and Shrader hiked back up to the main road behind McCord. "It's two-thirty," McCord said. "By the time we get back to the city, Niles should know whether or not Manning was holding that thirty-eight when it fired. Once we know that, we can call on his widow in person and watch how she takes the news."

"I'm going to let the two of you handle that yourself," Shrader told him. "I had to miss my granddaughter's birthday party today, and I'd like to go by and see her before she's in bed asleep. Is it okay if Sam rides back with you?"

"It's fine," McCord said.

Her unexpected attraction to McCord yesterday had surprised and concerned Sam so much that she'd made a very deliberate, and successful, effort to rationalize it out of existence by the time she went to bed. As a result, she was able to spend three and a half hours in the car with him, talking about nothing in particular, without experiencing so much as a tiny, inappropriate tremor of sexual awareness. There was no more banter between them on the trip back to the city, no stimulating repartee or personal comments.

Only two things bothered Sam in that regard: One, she rather missed all that, and two, she didn't think McCord even noticed it was missing.

Shortly before six P.M., McCord stopped at a convenience store to buy a sandwich, and while Sam waited in the car, Herbert Niles phoned. He was still reexamining the last swab under a scanning electron microscope, but he was eager to impart his findings to Sam the instant she picked up McCord's cell phone from the seat and answered it. "There was no residue on Manning's right palm," Niles told her, "so he wasn't holding up his hand in a defensive pose when the shot was fired. I got residue off the fingers of his right hand, so there's no doubt his hand was on the weapon when it fired at least one of those shots. But you know where else I ought to find residue if he fired that weapon without any 'assistance'?"

Sam named the only other location he would have swabbed: "On the back of his hand."

"That's right. I'm looking at the swab of the back of his

right hand right now, and it's perfectly clean. You've got yourself a homicide, not a suicide, Detective."

Sam tried not to sound as surprised as she felt when she relayed Nile's findings to McCord a few minutes later: "Niles called. Someone else's hand was covering Manning's and holding it on the thirty-eight when it fired."

"There was no powder residue on the back of his hand?" McCord's smile was slow and satisfied.

Sam shook her head. "No. The only residue was on the fingers of his right hand."

"I knew it," McCord said softly. "I knew it was going to play out this way as soon as CSU dug the second slug out of the wall. It always amazes me . . ."

"What does?"

"The stupid mistakes murderers make."

CHAPTER 26

Courtney glanced at the clock in the kitchen. "It's almost six, and I've got a lot of work to do for class tomorrow."

"You're calling it quits?" O'Hara said with relief, tallying up the score. "Why stop now, when I've still got some money left in my pension fund?"

"Call me softhearted."

"You're a cardsharp. Do you fleece those people you're staying with out of their money, too?"

She grinned as she slid the cards back into their box. "The Donnellys are either out, or they're sleeping—" The telephone rang, and since Hilda had gone to a movie, O'Hara got up to answer it. When he hung up a moment later, he was frowning.

"Was that about Mr. Manning?" Courtney asked worriedly.

"No. It's Michael Valente. He's in the lobby. Mrs. Manning is expecting him."

"What's he like?"

"All I know is that he's big trouble for Mrs. Manning.

You saw what happened when the reporters found out she'd been with him on Friday in the mountains. You'd have thought she was sleepin' with the devil or something, just for being in his helicopter. I was with the two of them every second, and nothing happened. Nothing. Mrs. Manning doesn't even call him by his first name."

"I'd never heard of him until I saw all that stuff about him on the news this week," Courtney admitted. "I guess he's really famous, though."

"Yeah, for a whole lot of bad stuff. I owe you sixteen dollars." He dug the money out of his pocket and put it on the table.

"Did he seem like a bad guy the day you were with him?"

"Let me put it this way—I wouldn't like to be around if he ever loses his temper. The cops were needling him that day, especially a cop named Harwell, and Valente didn't like it. He got real, real quiet . . . And his eyes got *real, real* cold . . . Know what I mean?"

Courtney was intrigued. "He looked like . . . what . . . murderous?"

"Yeah, you could say that."

"Maybe I should stay while he's here, just to make sure Leigh is all right?"

The buzzer at the front door sounded, and O'Hara dismissed her suggestion. "I'll be close by while he's here, but I don't think there's anything to worry about. From what I've read over the years, he's involved in a lot of shady business deals, but he hasn't done anything violent in a long time."

"How reassuring," Courtney said sarcastically.

"Well, maybe this will be more reassuring . . ." he said with a confiding wink. "That day in the mountains, the cops told Mrs. Manning to wait up at the road while they checked out the cabin. When nobody came back up to tell us anything, Valente picked Mrs. Manning up and carried her in his arms through the snow, down to the cabin. Then he carried her all the way back up to the road. He turns into a real Sir Galahad when he's around her."

"Really?" Courtney breathed. "How . . . *interesting.*"

"I'll call you when we hear anything about Mr. Manning," O'Hara promised on his way toward the living room.

Instead of letting herself out the service door to the kitchen, Courtney strolled quietly over to the doorway into the dining room. Leaning her shoulder against the doorframe, she peered thoughtfully at the tall, broad-shouldered man walking down the foyer steps into the living room. According to what she'd read and heard about him this week, Michael Valente was as adept at eluding reporters as he was at eluding attempts to put him in prison.

He was certainly "high-profile," especially right now.

She already had access to some "new and unusual" facts about him.

As an interview subject, he could prove to be a lot more intriguing than the pope or the president.

She studied his solemn smile as he held out both hands to Leigh and said, "I've been worried about you."

His voice gave Courtney a jolt. He had an amazing voice, deep and distinctive. If he hadn't chosen to be a criminal, he could have used that voice to great advantage on the radio or television.

She stepped out of O'Hara's way, her gaze shifting to the large flat white box that Valente had handed him when he walked in. Tucked under O'Hara's arm was a brown bag, twisted at the top, which Courtney assumed contained a bottle of something with an alcohol content.

"You still here?" Joe asked her in surprise.

"I'm leaving, but I wanted to get a look at Valente in person," she replied, following him into the kitchen. "What's in the box?"

"I don't know," he said, putting it on the island. "But if I had to guess, I'd say it's a pizza."

"He brought her a *pizza?*" Courtney exclaimed with a muffled laugh. "A *pizza?* He owns a helicopter and entire blocks of buildings in New York City—I'd have figured him for a seven-course take-out meal from Le Cirque, with maybe a gaudy diamond bracelet as a napkin ring."

"Really? I guess you know more about him than I do."

"I don't know much of anything about him, but I'm going to do some research." She lifted the cover of the flat white box and shuddered with revulsion. "Oh, yuk!"

In the midst of trying to figure out how to turn one of the ovens on, O'Hara looked over his shoulder to see what her exclamation was about.

"It's an uncooked pizza," she said, pointing accusingly at the item, "covered with huge shrimp." She shuddered again. "How Italian is that?"

"I dunno. Me, I like pepperoni."

"I hate shrimp in all its disguises." She opened the brown paper bag, extracted the bottle of red wine inside it, and scrutinized the label. "This guy is really twisted. He drinks three-hundred-dollars-a-bottle red wine with shrimp pizza."

O'Hara's mind was on the task at hand. "Valente told me to put that in the oven. Normally, I'd tell him to mind his own business, but Mrs. Manning hasn't eaten a cup of food in days. Do you know how to turn this oven on?"

"How hard can it be?" Courtney replied, changing places with O'Hara, who began uncorking the wine at the center island. For a brief moment, she studied the array of dials and buttons above the four stainless steel ovens built into the brick wall, her agile mind quickly calculating probabilities. "This one," she said emphatically. And changed the time on the clock.

CHAPTER 27

"I don't know where Logan keeps anything in here," Leigh explained to Michael Valente as she switched on the lights in Logan's office. She walked over to his desk and sat down on his leather chair. Logan's office was so uniquely, poignantly, his that it felt all wrong for her to be sitting at his eighteenth-century carved desk.

Trying not to dwell on that, she reached for the handle on the center drawer. The drawer was locked. She tried the drawers on the right side. They were locked. So were the drawers on the left. Embarrassed, she looked up. "I—I'm sorry. I didn't know they'd be locked." Leigh nodded toward a wall of built-in, oak-fronted file cabinets and got up. "Maybe the file you're looking for is in one of these."

"Take your time; I'm in no hurry," he said politely, but she could feel him watching her as she crossed the room, and it made her distinctly uneasy. His *voice* made Leigh uneasy. Or maybe what made her uneasy was having him there when she realized, for the first time, that her husband had started keeping everything under lock and key, in his own home.

The file cabinets were all locked, too.

"I think Brenna—my secretary—may know where Logan keeps a key." She sat back down at Logan's desk and called Brenna from his phone. Brenna was home, and she knew Logan kept his desk and files locked, but she had no idea where Leigh might find a key.

"I'm very embarrassed that you have to leave here empty-handed a second time," Leigh said, pausing to turn off the office lights.

"Don't be. I can wait for the documents I need until you find the keys."

Leigh walked back into the living room and paused at the sofas, intending to either invite him to sit down for a few minutes or show him to the door if he was ready to leave. "I don't remember if I ever thanked you for letting me use your helicopter last week, and for carrying me back and forth through the snow."

Brushing back the sides of his sport jacket, he shoved his hands into his pants pockets. "Actually, there's a way you can thank me for all that. When is the last time you ate?"

"I haven't been very hungry."

"I had a feeling that might be the case. As a way of thanking me, I'd like you to have dinner with me tonight."

"No, I—"

"I haven't eaten since breakfast," he interrupted. "I brought dinner with me. Which way is the kitchen?"

Leigh gaped at him, amazed and annoyed at his high-handedness. His expensive haircut, tailor-made jacket, and three-hundred-dollar tie gave him a veneer of prosperous, well-bred elegance, but nothing could offset the granite strength in his features, the harsh defiance in his tough jaw, or the cold, predatory gleam she'd glimpsed in his amber eyes when Harwell insulted him. Logan had mistaken Michael Valente for a tame, predictable businessman, but he wasn't that. He wasn't that at all.

On the other hand, he had gone to a great deal of trouble for her last week, so she led the way into the kitchen.

The big room was empty, but all four of the ovens were glowing, and there were two glasses of wine on the island next to plates, napkins, and a large knife. Valente shrugged off his jacket and draped it over the back of a chair; then he handed her one of the wineglasses. "Drink some," he ordered when she shook her head and started to put it down. "It will help things."

Leigh wasn't certain what things he thought it would help, but she took a swallow because she was simply too worn down to put up much opposition to anything, particularly something inconsequential. She felt the effect of the potent wine within moments.

"Have a little more. Do it for me."

She took another sip. "Mr. Valente, this is very nice of you, but I'm not very hungry or thirsty."

He gazed at her in speculative silence, a glass of wine in his right hand, his left hand shoved deep into his trouser pocket. "Under the circumstances, I think it would be more suitable if you called me by my first name."

A knot of nervous tension tightened Leigh's stomach. His voice . . . his eyes . . . his attitude. "I'm actually a rather formal person."

Instead of responding, he turned and walked over to the ovens. Bending down slightly, he studied whatever was in there through the glass in one oven door. "I'm curious about something," he said with his back to her.

"What's that?"

"I sent you a basket of pears in the hospital. Did you get them?"

Shocked and embarrassed, Leigh stared at his back. "Yes, I did, only there was no card with them. I'm sorry. I didn't realize it was you who sent them."

"That explains it," he said.

"I love pears—" Leigh began, intending to thank him for them now.

"I know you do."

Her uneasiness began to escalate. "How do you know that?"

"I know a lot of things about you. Have some more wine, Leigh."

Alarm bells began screaming in Leigh's brain. That voice. She knew that voice! She replayed his clipped commands along with others like them: *Wear this for me . . . Drink this . . . Love Me . . . Have a little more . . . Do it for me . . .*

"I know you like pears, you love shrimp pizza, and you hate most vegetables," he continued, his back still to her. "I know you sunburn easily, and you dislike any soap with a strong scent. I also know you aren't 'a rather formal' person." He paused to pick up two pot holders lying beside the ovens.

Behind him, Leigh picked up the big knife lying on the island, her heart pounding with fear and rage. She could hear faint sounds of a television set—the stock car races—coming from O'Hara's room down the hall and around a corner. She didn't think Joe would hear her if she screamed.

"The truth is," Valente continued as he removed the pizza and juggled it onto the granite countertop, "you are innately kind and unaffected. You will take time to talk to anyone who you think is lonely or in need of cheering up, you can't stand to hurt anyone's feelings, and you will go out of your way to find something to like in almost anyone. Including me."

He turned around and saw the knife in her hand.

"Get out of here!" Leigh whispered savagely. "Get out of my house before I scream for help and call the police."

"Put that knife down! What the hell is wrong?"

"You've been stalking me! It was you! I know your voice. You're the one who sends the flowers, and the presents—"

"I am *not* your stalker—"

Leigh began backing toward the telephone on the wall near the hallway, and he moved forward, matching her step for step. "Pears," she ranted accusingly. "Pears and pizza and soap!"

"Groceries—I used to watch you buy them."

"You've watched me buy them while you stalk me!"

"Put the damn knife down!" he said just as she bumped into the wall.

"I'm calling the police." She whirled around and grabbed for the telephone.

"You're not doing anything of the kind!" He slammed the receiver back into place, covered it with his hand, and flattened his body against hers, imprisoning her, and her knife, between the wall and his own body. "Now drop the goddamned knife," he ordered in a low, awful voice against her ear. "Don't make me hurt you to get it away from you."

Instead of dropping it, Leigh clutched the handle harder. Fate had already done everything it could to torment her. She wasn't afraid of anything *he* could do to her. "Go to hell," she whimpered.

To her utter disbelief, that made him chuckle. "I'm glad to see you no longer freeze up when you're in danger, but I'm too old to show off my combat skills for you again, and besides that, I'm afraid if I let you go, you'll skewer me with that damned knife before I can tell you who I am."

"I know who you are, you bastard!"

"Will you just listen to me for a moment!"

Leigh was mashed against the wall, her right cheek flattened to it. "Do I have a choice?"

That question amused him thoroughly. "You're the one holding the knife. The guy with the knife always gets first choice about what happens next. That's the rule."

"Did you learn that in prison?" she snapped, but she was beginning to feel almost as foolish as she was angry.

"No, I knew it long before then," he replied blandly. "And I remembered it fourteen years ago when you left Angelini's Market late at night with some pears and a shrimp pizza. Two punks threatened you on the street. I walked you home afterward."

Her entire body stiffened. "Falco?" she uttered after a stunned moment. "You're Falco?"

He stepped back so she could turn around, and Leigh gazed in wide-eyed wonder at his face. He held out his hand. "Could I have the knife now—not the pointy end," he joked.

Leigh gave it to him, but she couldn't stop looking at him. He was a part of her past, and she felt a rush of sentimentality because he'd reentered her life at its lowest point and had been trying to "rescue" her again in whatever small way he could—and with very little appreciation from her. Unconsciously she held out her hands to him, feeling almost maternal when he took them in his. "I can't believe it's you! I can't believe you were hiding a face like this under that awful beard. And you changed your name. How is your mother?"

He smiled at her barrage of comments, a quick, startlingly glamorous smile that transformed his features and shocked Leigh into remembering they were holding hands. "You thought my beard was awful?"

She withdrew her hands quickly, but made no

attempt to withdraw from the warm sentimentality of the moment. "I assumed you were hiding something terrible behind it."

"A weak chin?" he suggested. He retrieved the pizza from the counter beside the ovens and transferred it to the island. There he began slicing it with the same knife she'd threatened him with moments before.

Leigh clung to this brief respite from her anguish over Logan and reached for the wineglass on the counter to help her sustain it. "The possibility of a weak chin never occurred to me. I thought it could be scars from . . ."

He looked up, waiting.

"From being in fights—from being in prison."

"That's good," he replied dryly. "Just so you didn't think I might have had a weak chin."

"How is your mother?"

"She's dead."

"I'm so sorry. I liked her very much. When did it happen?"

"When I was ten."

"What?"

"My mother and father died when I was ten."

"Then . . . who is Mrs. Angelini?"

"My mother's sister." He picked up their plates, and Leigh carried the wineglasses and napkins over to the table. "The Angelinis took me in after my parents died and raised me with their own sons."

"Oh, I see. Then how is your aunt?"

"She's very well. She made this pizza for you herself, and asked me to tell you hello for her."

"This is so thoughtful—of both of you," Leigh said.

He dismissed that without comment and reached for the light switch, dimming the bright overhead lights a little before he sat down across from her. "Eat," he ordered, but he picked up his wineglass, Leigh noted, not his pizza. He wasn't hungry as he'd claimed earlier. That had been a ruse to make sure she ate something. She was so touched that she tried to do it, and tried *not* to think of the reason all this seemed necessary to him.

"You changed your name from Falco Nipote to Michael Valente?"

He shook his head. "You have that backwards."

"You mean your name was Nipote Falco?"

"No, I mean I haven't changed my name, *you've* changed it."

"But those are the names Mrs. Angelini called you."

"*Nipote* is Italian for 'nephew.' *Falco* means 'hawk' in Italian. In the old neighborhood, we all had nicknames. My cousin Angelo was called 'Dante' because he hated being called Angel, and because he definitely wasn't one. Dominick was 'Sonny,' because he was—" He paused to think about that and wryly shook his head. "—because he was always called Sonny, even by my uncle." He looked around for the wine bottle, realized it was still on the island, and got up to get it.

"Why were you called Hawk?" Leigh asked him as he added more wine to their glasses.

"Angelo started calling me that when we were little kids. He was three years older than I was, but I wanted to tag along with him on his exploits. To keep me out of the way, he convinced me I had especially good eyes—eyes like a hawk—and that his pals needed me to be their 'lookout.' I functioned in that capacity until I realized they were having all the fun and I wasn't."

"What kind of fun were they having?"

"You don't want to know."

She sobered. He was right—she did not want to know that. "Thank you for all the kind things you've done—Friday and tonight. It's almost impossible to believe you've gone to so much trouble for me."

"Why is that?"

"Because, fourteen years ago, you barely bothered to answer me when I spoke to you."

"I was working up to it."

"What got in the way?"

Logan got in the way, Michael Valente thought, but he didn't say it. He didn't want to spoil her mood by mentioning the husband she was never going to see alive again. "Maybe I was shy."

She overruled that with a single, emphatic shake of her head. "I wondered about that back then, but shy people aren't deliberately rude. The nicer I was to you, the more curt and rude you became. After a while, it was perfectly obvious that you couldn't stand me."

"That was perfectly obvious?"

Leigh heard the amused irony in his tone, but she was preoccupied with more pressing questions. "Why didn't you tell me who you were last Saturday night at the party?" At the mention of the festive party, Leigh could no longer keep the gruesome reality of the present from crashing into her thoughts. She forgot the question she'd asked him and gazed out the window beside her, fighting back tears.

As if he sensed what had just happened to her, he skipped the discussion of the party. "I told you who I was in the note I sent with the pears."

Leigh tried to refocus on that issue only. "You must have thought I was incredibly rude not to mention it when you took me to the mountains, or when I phoned you yesterday, or even tonight, for that matter."

"I assumed you either hadn't read the note, or that you read it and preferred not to acknowledge any prior acquaintance with me, of any kind."

Leigh looked at him steadily. "I would never do that."

He held her gaze. "Unless, in the last fourteen years, you had become 'a rather formal person.' "

She acknowledged the gentle "gibe" with a slight smile; then she had to bite her lip to keep from crying. Tears were so close to the surface, every minute of every day, that anything—nice things, humorous things—could make her feel like crying without warning.

CHAPTER 28

Joe O'Hara strolled into the kitchen just as Michael poured the last of the wine into Leigh's glass. In one startled glance, he took in the dimmed lights and cozy scene, and tried to back out of the room. "Excuse me—"

"Wait, Joe—don't leave," Leigh said, anxious to correct his impression. "I want to introduce you properly to Mr. Valente—"

"We already met, Mrs. Manning. Remember? Last Friday?"

Despite all her very serious woes, Leigh laughed at his baffled expression. "Of course I remember. What I'm trying to say is that I didn't *remember* that I knew Mr. Valente when I saw him on Friday. Many years ago, when I was in college and living downtown, he worked in his family's grocery market on the corner, and I used to shop there. He had a beard and I didn't know his name, but his aunt—who I thought was his mother until tonight—made shrimp pizzas just for me!"

O'Hara's gaze bounced to the empty wine bottle, then

shifted accusingly to Michael Valente. "How much of that wine have you given Mrs. Manning?"

"I am not drunk, Joe. I'm trying to explain why I didn't recognize Michael until tonight. He saved me from being mugged—and probably much worse—one night."

"And I guess you probably forgot to ask his name afterwards?" Joe O'Hara suggested, but instead of sounding skeptical, the loyal chauffeur sounded as if he were trying to believe the unbelievable. He approached the table, ready to acknowledge the formal introduction that Leigh, in her present state of mind, felt was absolutely necessary.

"I knew his name at the time," Leigh explained, "but in those days, everyone in Michael's neighborhood had nicknames. He was called Hawk back then—Falco in Italian— and Falco is the only name I knew him by, until tonight."

O'Hara reached out to shake Michael Valente's hand, but his announcement carried an unmistakable warning to the other man: "We had nicknames in my neighborhood, too," he said bluntly. "My nickname was Bruiser."

Leigh swallowed a laugh at Michael's grave response. "I'll keep that in mind."

When Hilda returned from her afternoon out a short while later, Joe O'Hara imparted the same information to her about Valente while Leigh and Michael looked on. It was the only relief from anguish and suspense that Leigh had known in a week. It ended abruptly when the telephone rang.

Hilda answered it, spoke briefly to the caller; then she turned slowly to the table. "Detective Littleton and a Detective Lieutenant McCord are on their way up here."

Leigh jumped up from the table and rushed into the living room, filled with hope and fear.

In the kitchen, Hilda looked worriedly at O'Hara and lowered her voice. "Detective Littleton wanted to be sure

Mrs. Manning wasn't alone. She wanted to be certain someone would be here with her—"

"That doesn't sound good," O'Hara said, turning automatically to Michael Valente for his opinion. "Does it?"

"No," Valente said tightly. "It isn't good." He nodded toward the doorway. "Both of you need to go out there and stay with her."

O'Hara did not suggest that Valente step into view along with them. He had already seen how Leigh was treated by the police when she was with him. Instead, Joe took Hilda's arm and they went into the living room.

Michael Valente remained out of sight, listening to the voices in the living room, unable to protect her—or even stand at her side—while she heard news he knew was going to wound her more deeply that any assailant's knife. . . .

Leigh looked at both detectives' faces, her mind trying to reject what they were telling her. "You're wrong! He wasn't at the cabin. I was there. You found someone else!"

"I'm sorry, Mrs. Manning," Detective Littleton said. "There is no doubt. His body was discovered in his car, in a garage cut into the hillside behind the house."

Her tear-brightened eyes grew huge with anguished accusation. "He froze to death while you people wasted time—"

"He did not freeze to death," the man who called himself Detective McCord told her unemotionally. "Your husband died of a gunshot wound to the head. The weapon was on the floor of his automobile."

Wildly, Leigh shook her head. "Are you crazy? Are you telling me you found a man who shot himself in his car and you think it's my husband? Logan would never do that! He would never, never, *never* do that!"

Leigh believed none of it, none of it . . . except that

Logan was dead. No matter how much she stood there, try-ing to argue, she already knew he was dead. He would have come home to her days before if he'd been alive. He would have crawled or hitchhiked or dragged himself. She felt Hilda's arm slide around her shoulders, and she twisted the hem of her sweater like a frantic child trying to understand why the grown-ups were punishing her. "He—he did NOT kill himself, do you hear me?" she cried. "You're lying. Why are you lying?"

"We don't think your husband took his own life," Mc-Cord told her bluntly. "We'll know more tomorrow, but at this point, we have reason to believe someone else pulled the trigger on his revolver."

Leigh's vivid imagination chose that moment to display a horrific scene—Logan, with a gun held to his head by someone else. Someone else pulling the trigger, ending his life. Ending her life. The room began to sway and twist, and she clutched at Hilda's sleeve. Her eyes swimming with scalding tears, she looked at the kinder of the two detec-tives, and she nodded her head, as if by nodding at Sam Lit-tleton, she could force the other woman to nod, too, and agree with her. "He's wrong, isn't he? He is. Say he is." She held out her hand to her. "Please. Say he is."

Detective Littleton's soft voice was sympathetic but certain. "No, Mrs. Manning, he isn't wrong. I'm very sorry . . ."

HILDA PUT HER TO BED that night. O'Hara fixed two stiff drinks and made Hilda have one of them. He finished his, and escorted the heartbroken housekeeper to her room; then he went to his own room and had two more drinks, leaving Michael Valente to let himself out.

At eleven o'clock, Joe got up to make certain every-thing was locked up. He was partway across the silent living room when he realized Valente hadn't left. The man was sitting on an uncomfortable, straight-backed chair at the far end of the living room, next to the hallway leading to the master bedroom. His head was bent, his forearms propped on his thighs, hands clasped loosely in front of him. He was listening to the anguished weeping of the woman down the hall.

He had stationed himself there like a centurion.

As Joe silently moved closer, trying to decide what to say, Valente wearily rubbed his hands over his face.

"Are you plannin' to sit there all night?" Joe asked softly.

The other man jerked his hands away and looked up. "No," he said.

If Joe hadn't had those drinks, he would have kept his realization about the other man's motives to himself, but he had been drinking, so he didn't do that. Instead, he said, "You might as well go home and get some sleep, Hawk. You can't do anything to protect her from what she's going through tonight."

Valente neither confirmed nor denied Joe's interpretation of his motives for being there. Instead, he stood up and slowly put on the jacket he'd hung over the back of his chair. "In that case, Bruiser, I'll leave her to you."

CHAPTER 29

"I know this is a difficult time for you, Mrs. Manning," Sam Littleton said as she and McCord sat down in the living room the next morning. Shrader was in the kitchen, interviewing the housekeeper, the chauffeur, and the secretary. "We'll try to make this visit as brief as possible," Sam continued. "There are some questions we need to ask you, and some of them may seem offensive or even cruel, but I assure you they are just routine. They're the same questions we ask every spouse after a homicide."

Sam paused, waiting for some response from the pale, shattered woman across from her. "Mrs. Manning?" Sam prompted.

Leigh pulled her gaze from the large crystal starfish on the end table next to McCord's elbow. Logan had fallen in love with the beautiful crystal piece in Newport last summer, and she'd surprised him with it when they got home. "I'm sorry, I was thinking about something else. What do you want to ask me?"

"Now that you've had a few hours to adjust to the

tragic news of your husband's death, can you think of any reason why someone might have wanted to kill him?"

A few hours to adjust, Leigh thought in disbelief. She was going to need a few lifetimes to adjust. "I—I stayed awake all last night, thinking about that, and the only thing that makes any sense is that it was some sort of hideous, unplanned event. Maybe some lunatic vagrant has been living up there, and he felt—believed—the place belonged to him. Then, when he saw Logan bringing things into the house and putting his car away, he got out his gun and—he killed him."

"Unfortunately, that theory isn't supported by the facts," Sam told her. "The thirty-eight-caliber revolver found on the floor of your husband's vehicle was registered to your husband." When Leigh stared at her, Sam said, "Did you know your husband owned a handgun?"

"No. I had no idea." Leigh couldn't, *wouldn't* believe that anyone had actually planned in advance to murder her husband, so she tried to make the new facts fit her scenario. "If there was some psychopath living in the cabin, then it's possible he followed my husband to his car, and when Logan got out the gun, there was a struggle, and the gun went off accidentally."

Detective Littleton evidently thought Leigh's theory was too far-fetched to consider because she ignored it and asked another question. "Can you think of some reason why your husband might have felt he needed to carry a gun?"

Leigh tried to think of an explanation, no matter how outlandish. After a few moments, she said slowly, "In the last few years, Logan has branched into commercial construction. I know there are labor unions involved, and from what I've read, things can get—" Leigh stopped. "No, wait—I was being stalked. That must be why Logan bought a gun."

"When did you first become aware of this stalker?"

"A couple of months ago. We filed a police report. You have the records."

Sam made a note, but she already knew the police report had been filed in September, six months *after* Logan Manning purchased his handgun. "How would you describe your relationship with your husband? Were you happily married?"

"Yes. Very."

"Did he confide in you?"

"Of course."

"Think carefully. Did he mention being worried about anything—business problems, for example."

"Logan's business has been doing extremely well. Particularly for the last two or three years. He didn't have any business problems."

"Has he seemed preoccupied?"

"No more than usual."

"Would you mind if we spoke to the people at his office?" The question was purely rhetorical, since McCord had already compiled the employees' names and divided them between Sam, Shrader, and himself for later questioning.

"Please speak to anyone you like," Leigh said. "Do whatever you think you need to do."

"Who else did your husband confide in, besides you?"

"No one."

"He didn't have any close friends?"

"We were each other's closest friend."

"I see. Then you don't have any close friends, either? People you confide in?"

She said it in a way deliberately designed to make Leigh feel like an antisocial loner if she couldn't come up with a single friend either of them had, and the ploy worked. "I'm in show business, and my friends are mostly in the arts and entertainment world. They tend to be people who enjoy publicity more than privacy, so they aren't very good at keeping secrets—their own or mine. I've learned not to confide things that I don't want to appear in Liz Smith's column or the *Enquirer*."

Detective Littleton nodded as if she completely understood, but her words proved she was frustratingly single-minded. "According to an item I read in Page Six in the *Post* about your birthday party, there were over three hundred people here to celebrate with you. Didn't you or your husband know any of them well enough to confide something, sometime?"

Leigh realized that if she didn't give Sam Littleton some names, the detective was likely to keep pressing her on this pointless topic until nightfall, so she mentally replayed a few minutes of her party, and gave Sam Littleton the names of the first people who came to mind: "Jason Solomon is a friend of mine."

"Personal as well as business?"

"Yes. Sybil Haywood is another friend; so is Theta Berenson . . ."

"The artist?"

"Yes. Oh, and Sheila Winters. Dr. Winters is a friend of mine and also of my husband's."

Sam made a note. "Dr. Winters? Did your husband have any serious health problems?"

"No. Sheila is a psychiatrist."

McCord spoke for the first time. "Were you patients of hers?"

Leigh felt uneasy about the question, as if she'd laid a trap for herself. "We saw her briefly several years ago as patients. Now she is simply a close friend of ours."

"Who needed the psychiatrist?" McCord said bluntly. "You or your husband?"

Leigh was on the verge of telling him to mind his own business, and she would have if Sam Littleton hadn't quickly said, "You don't have to answer that question, Mrs. Manning, if it will make you feel at all uncomfortable. Lieutenant McCord and I haven't worked together before, but from the sound of his question, he's one of those men who prides himself on letting a cold turn into pneumonia rather than seeing a doctor. He probably changes the oil in his own car and pulls his own tooth, rather than going to a dentist." She smiled warmly at Leigh. "Unlike the lieutenant, I know that intelligent, busy people who can afford it usually prefer to save time and effort by consulting with specialists in every field, whether it's auto mechanics, computer technology, or"—she transferred her smile to the man beside her—"medicine."

Leigh was so much in agreement with Sam that she felt compelled to prove Detective Littleton's theory to the man who outranked her, and she explained the minor reason Logan and she had consulted with Sheila. "Logan didn't know how to slow down and enjoy life. Sheila helped him realize very quickly that he was missing out on some of the best things in life by driving himself so hard."

Detective Littleton leaned forward eagerly. "Is it possible that your husband might have confided in Dr. Winters—as his friend—that he'd bought a weapon, and why he bought it?"

"I don't know. I doubt it. Sheila and Logan had lunch now and then, but it was purely social. They came from the same background and knew a lot of the same people. I called Sheila this morning and told her about Logan. She would have told me this morning if he'd ever mentioned buying a gun."

"Maybe she didn't feel that she could or should. Do you mind if we talk to her?"

Leigh shook her head. "No, but I'm sure Logan bought the gun because of the stalker."

Detective Littleton's expression turned somber. "I had hoped to spare you this knowledge, Mrs. Manning, but your husband purchased that gun in March—six months before your stalker entered the picture." While Leigh was still reeling from that information, Detective Littleton said, "Now do you see why it's important we talk to Dr. Winters? If your husband was afraid for his life, he might have—even inadvertently—given her some idea of why he was afraid . . . or *who* he was afraid of."

"Then, by all means, talk to her."

"We'll need your written permission, and I'm sure Dr. Winters will require it also, before she feels entitled to breach doctor-patient privilege. Would you be willing to give us that permission?"

"Yes, if you promise to keep the information confidential."

"We will be very, very discreet," Detective Littleton promised as she tore a small sheet of paper out of her notebook and handed it to Leigh, along with her pen. "Just write something out that says you authorize her to give us information about your husband."

Leigh did it automatically, following wherever she was led . . . or pushed. When she handed the paper back to Sam Littleton, she said, "I keep thinking about the person who ran me off the road that night. Maybe that's who murdered my husband."

"We're looking for him, and we've redoubled our efforts since finding your husband yesterday. We'd like your permission to not only talk to your husband's employees, but also to remove and inspect any records we think might be pertinent to this case. We'll see that they aren't lost. Is that all right with you?"

"Yes."

Sam closed her notebook and looked at McCord. "Do you have any other questions, Lieutenant?"

McCord shook his head and stood up. "I'm sorry about my reaction to the mention of Dr. Winters. Detective Littleton has me pegged right—I still change the oil in my own vehicle, and my computer at home hasn't worked in two years because I won't let someone else fix it. The only dentist I know is the one I'm investigating right now."

Leigh accepted his apology, but she was startled by his humble tone because it seemed at odds with his cold gaze and perfunctory smile. "The medical examiner should be ready to release your husband's body tomorrow," he added. "Let us know about the funeral arrangements. With your permission, we'd like to have our people at the funeral services."

Leigh grasped the back of the sofa for support, shuddering at the casual, unfeeling way he referred to her "husband's body" and "funeral arrangements." Logan was dead. He would never smile at her again, never pull her close to his body in bed when he slept. His body was in a morgue. She hadn't given a thought to funeral arrangements yet, although Brenna had gently brought up the subject that morning when Trish Lefkowitz called to offer her help. "Why do you want your people there?" she asked when she could trust her voice.

"As a precaution, that's all. You had a stalker, and your husband's been murdered."

"Do whatever you think is necessary."

McCord looked over his shoulder toward the kitchen. "I'll see if Detective Shrader is finished."

Detective Shrader was not only finished, he was enjoying a cup of coffee and a homemade biscuit while the chauffeur chatted with him about football.

The three detectives rode down in the elevator in silence. For security purposes all visitors to the Mannings' building were required to register in a large book when they arrived and to sign out when they departed. The keeper of the visitors' register was an elderly uniformed doorman, whose name tag identified him as "Horace." He was seated at a curved, black marble desk in the center of the lobby. "Such a shame about Mr. Manning," Horace said, handing Shrader a pen so that he could sign all three of them out in the big leather-bound book he'd signed them in on earlier.

Instead of taking the pen, Shrader took the book and handed the doorman a folded subpoena. "This subpoena allows us to take this item into evidence," he told the startled doorman. "Do you have another book that you can use?"

"Well, yes—but we aren't supposed to start using it until January, and this is only December."

"Start using the new one right away," Shrader ordered. "And if anyone asks what happened to this one, just say someone spilled something on it. Can you do that?"

"Yes, but my boss—"

Shrader handed him his card. "Have your boss call me."

CHAPTER 30

Shrader was driving, so Sam took the visitors' book from him and slid into the backseat, letting McCord sit next to Shrader in the front. She had the book open before they pulled away from the curb, and she began looking through the names, beginning at November 1 and moving forward.

"What did you get from the housekeeper?" McCord asked Shrader.

"According to Hilda Brunner, the Mannings were a 'perfect' couple. No quarrels, not even an occasional spat. Mr. Manning came home late sometimes, but he always phoned, and he was always home by eleven or twelve at the latest. He's taken a few short business trips. Mrs. Manning hasn't spent a night away from home without him in the three years the Brunner woman has worked for them.

"She confirmed that Manning left the apartment on Sunday morning sometime around eight, and that he made two trips down to his car with items he was taking to the mountains. Among those items were two crystal glasses, a bottle of wine, a bottle of champagne, and . . ." He let the sentence hang for effect before he added with a grin of triumph, "*two* dark green sleeping bags. She's sure there were two sleeping bags because she had to help him find them in the back of a closet, and she saw him carry them out of the apartment."

"Anything else?" McCord asked, pleased.

"Yeah. She gave me a fantastic biscuit and a warning not to upset Mrs. Manning or get crumbs on the floor."

"What about the chauffeur?"

"His name is Joseph Xavier O'Hara, and he gave me nothing. Zero. Nada. He actually works for another couple—Matthew and Meredith Farrell from Chicago. They left a couple of weeks ago on a world cruise. When the Farrells found out about Leigh Manning's alleged stalker, they 'lent' O'Hara to the Mannings until they get back."

"That's it?"

"No. O'Hara knows something—something he doesn't want to talk about."

"Valente?"

"Could be. Probably is. You said not to mention Valente, so I didn't ask O'Hara about him, but he didn't volunteer anything either."

"That's all you got from him?"

"No, I got a warning from him, too." Shrader said wryly. "He told me not to upset Mrs. Manning and to forget it if we thought she had anything whatsoever to do with her husband's death. He's not naïve, and he's not just a chauffeur. He's a bodyguard, and he's licensed to carry a weapon."

"What about the secretary?" McCord asked.

"Brenna Quade," Shrader provided. "She actually works mostly for Mrs. Manning, and she backed up the housekeeper's story—she said the Mannings were a very happy couple. She gave me a copy of the guest list for the party a week ago." He reached into his jacket pocket and removed several sheets of paper with neatly typed names in alphabetical order. "Another copy was given to the doorman so he knew who the invited guests were. Guess whose name wasn't on the original list?"

"Valente," McCord said, unfolding the list and scanning the names.

"Right. His name was added in pencil the afternoon of the party—at Logan Manning's request."

"What about you?" Shrader asked McCord. "Did you find out anything interesting?"

McCord inclined his head toward the backseat, where Sam was poring over the visitors' register. "As a matter of fact," he said dryly, "I found out that Detective Littleton thinks I'm an elderly, toothless redneck with an oil rag hanging out of my pocket and an uneducated attitude toward doctors of all kinds, and shrinks in particular."

Sam didn't bother to defend or explain her actions, and she was a little surprised when McCord did it for her. "Littleton realized I'd spooked the Manning woman, so she teed me up and took a swing at me, right in front of her. In return, she got the woman to sign a release so that their shrink has to talk to us. I couldn't believe Littleton got her to do it, and so easily."

"It's always easy to persuade innocent, uninvolved people to do the right thing," Sam murmured, turning the page. "I'm not saying I definitely think she's innocent, but there's something about her that I just can't reconcile with being a coconspirator in the murder of her husband. Last night," she continued, directing her explanation to Shrader, "when we told her that her husband was found shot to death, Leigh Manning held her hand out to me and begged me to say McCord was wrong. My God, I was almost in tears, and—" Sam broke off, staring at a scrawled name entered in the visitors' register the night before; then she slammed the book closed. "Dammit! I cannot *believe* it!"

"What can't you believe?" Shrader asked, glancing at her in the rearview mirror.

McCord's voice was laced with cynical amusement. "I think Detective Littleton has just discovered that Valente was in Manning's apartment last night, staying out of sight, while the widow put on her performance for Littleton and almost made her cry."

Sam's anger with herself began to turn outward toward a new target—Mitchell McCord. "How did you know that?" she inquired with a calm she didn't feel.

"I saw Valente's name in the register last night when I signed us in and out."

That was exactly what Sam had suspected he was going to say. Furious and disappointed in him, she laid the heavy book on the seat beside her and looked out the window while she forced her features into a pleasant, noncommittal mask. When McCord asked her a few minutes later if she wanted to accompany him to Forensics to check on Manning's tests, she said very pleasantly, "Of course."

SHEILA WAS WITH A PATIENT when Leigh called, but she returned the call a few minutes later. "I just have a quick question," Leigh explained. "By any chance, did you know Logan bought a gun?"

"No."

"I didn't think so, but the police are going to ask you about it anyway. They think Logan may have confided in a friend."

CHAPTER 31

Ballistics confirmed that the slug that penetrated Logan Manning's brain and lodged in the left-hand wall of the garage was from the .38 special found in his vehicle. So was the slug recovered from the right-hand wall.

The medical examiner hadn't completed his written report yet, but Herbert Niles was perfectly willing to give Sam and McCord the highlights of the findings. "Logan Manning definitely went out with a buzz," he announced cheerfully.

"That's cute, Herb," McCord retorted impatiently.

"I wasn't being 'cute,' I was being literal—and cute. Cause of death was a gunshot wound to the right temple, which occurred less than an hour after he had imbibed the better part of a bottle of wine. White wine chardonnay, I'd guess."

CHAPTER 32

Logan Manning's funeral service was a media event, attended by five hundred business, political, and community leaders as well as prominent members of the arts and entertainment world. Two hundred of the mourners joined the funeral procession to the cemetery afterward and stood in the cold and mist to bid a final farewell to the slain socialite and to pay their respects to his famous widow.

Notably absent from those services was Michael Valente, and though the media was quick to remark on that in their news coverage that evening, they had focused all their attention on familiar faces and recognizable names among those present. The photographers who lined up at the chapel and followed the funeral procession to the cemetery did not waste any film on an elegantly attired, gray-haired woman in her early seventies who was last in line to speak to the widow at the graveside.

No one paid any attention when the woman took Leigh's hands in hers, and only Leigh heard what she said: "My nephew felt his presence here today would only distract from the solemn occasion. I have come instead to represent our family."

Although she looked like several of Logan's elderly, well-to-do relatives, her eyes were more compassionate, and her voice held the soft lilt of Italian that instantly reminded Leigh of the warm welcomes she had always received at Angelini's Market years before.

"Mrs. Angelini?" Leigh said, squeezing her gloved hands. "It's so kind of you to come!" Leigh thought she had wept herself dry of all tears, but the kindness in the woman's eyes, her thoughtfulness for standing out in the freezing cold, pushed Leigh to the brink of tears all over again. "It's much too cold and damp for you out here."

No other elderly people who had attended the funeral service had braved the elements at the cemetery. They'd either gone home afterward or gone to Leigh's apartment, where caterers were serving food. Leigh invited Mrs. Angelini to go there, but she refused. "May I drop you somewhere?" Leigh asked her as they walked past the sea of headstones toward the line of automobiles parked in the street.

"I have a car." Mrs. Angelini nodded toward a uniformed chauffeur who was holding open the rear door of a black Bentley. Leigh recognized the chauffeur at once.

"Please tell Michael I'll call him soon," Leigh added as Mrs. Angelini slid into the backseat.

"I will tell him." She hesitated as if weighing her words very carefully. "Leigh, if you need anything, you must tell him. He will not fail you as others have."

CHAPTER 33

Brenna had arranged for Payard, the French bistro and patisserie, to provide the food at the apartment after the funeral. By the time Leigh arrived, the guests had already formed into the same groups they'd formed at Leigh's party a little over a week before, except that now the primary topic of conversation was the identity of Logan's murderer.

Leigh moved mechanically from group to group, accepting condolences and listening to all the trite things people say in a helpless, futile effort to make the darkest occasion in human experience seem somehow less tragic. Logan's friends and family were the *"Chin up, Buck up, Stiff upper lip,"* crowd. Judge Maxwell patted her shoulder and solemnly said, "It may not seem like it now, but there are brighter days ahead. Life goes on, my dear."

Senator Hollenbeck said, "You're strong, you'll make it." His wife voiced her agreement, but in a more personal way: "I thought my life was over when my first husband died, but I made it and so will you."

Logan's ancient great-aunt, one of the few surviving

members of his immediate family, laid her blue-veined hand on Leigh's sleeve, peered long and solemnly at her, and said, "What was your name, dear?"

Leigh's friends tended to demonstrate their empathy and sympathy by describing the effect Logan's death was having on them. As a group, their attitude was, *"This is a tragedy for you and for everyone who knew Logan."* Theta Berenson had worn one of her most somber and conservative hats—a black one with a huge brim adorned with white silk fruit and black berries, but no feathers. "I'm just *devastated* for you," the artist told Leigh. "Positively *devastated.* I keep thinking about that weekend we all spent together in Maine, and I've decided to paint the harbor scene the way I remember it. I want you to have it when it's finished."

Claire Straight, who was embroiled in a bitter, ongoing divorce battle, hugged Leigh and indignantly said, "There's no justice in this world! Logan is dead, while Charles—that bastard—goes right on living. I'm so furious with fate that I can't get over it. I've started seeing Sheila Winters for help with anger management."

Jason was with Jane Sebring and Eric. He looked more distraught than Leigh had ever seen him. "Darling, what you're going through is tearing me to pieces. You need to come back to work soon. Logan would want you to go on with your life."

Jane Sebring had been crying. Her face was pale, her beautiful eyes were shadowed and without makeup, and she was upset enough not to care about her looks. "I just can't believe it's true," she told Leigh. "I have nightmares about it, and I wake up thinking this is all a bad dream, but it isn't."

Sybil Haywood, who had taken Michael Valente off Leigh's hands the night of the party, was stricken with grief and guilt. "I'm completely to blame for this," she told Leigh fiercely.

"Sybil, that's ridiculous—"

"It isn't! If I had been a true friend—the kind you deserve to have—I would have finished your chart in time for your birthday. I wouldn't have let business get in the way of friendship. Well, I've finished it now, and it was all there—tragedy and violence. I could have forewarned you—"

The astrologer was so filled with self-blame that Leigh offered her the one consolation she could give. "I'll tell you a little secret," Leigh confided, sliding her arm around Sybil's waist. "It wouldn't have made a bit of difference if you'd finished that chart and given it to me."

"What do you mean?"

"Logan thought astrology was a farce. I believe in *you*, and in your honesty and dedication to it, but I'm . . ." She paused to choose her words carefully. ". . . a little ambivalent about it."

Instead of being comforted by that, Sybil was hurt and very disappointed.

Sheila Winters was the one steady, shining light in the entire day. She was at Leigh's side often, sensing when she was needed. She arrived just as Leigh finished talking to Jane, and she stayed there through Sybil's comments. "You need a few minutes alone now," she said. "You've been giving more comfort than you're getting from a lot of these people."

"I'll rest later," Leigh said. She felt limp with exhaustion, but she didn't want to leave, even for a few minutes. The people who were there had come out of respect and affection for Logan, and she loved each and every one of them that day for going to the trouble to do it.

Exempted from her affection and goodwill were the half dozen plainclothes detectives, including Littleton, Mc-

Cord, and Shrader, who'd been at the funeral and were now stationed throughout the apartment. Detectives Littleton and Shrader had persuaded her that Logan's murderer might be among the mourners. Without saying so, they implied that Leigh's life might also be in danger from the killer. Leigh thought the notion absurd, but she didn't have the strength to argue with anyone about anything yet. Until yesterday, she'd convinced herself that Logan's murder had been a case of mistaken identity or, more likely, the act of someone who'd been living near the mountain property and felt it belonged to him.

Whenever she happened to notice one of the detectives, she nodded politely, but she let them fend for themselves. No one knew they were present, and no one took any notice of them—no one, except Courtney Maitland. To Leigh's astonishment, the teenager spotted all of them, including Sam Littleton, and she arrived at Leigh's side with a plate of food for Leigh and a side order of astute observations. "I count six cops," she whispered to Leigh. "Am I close, or have I missed some?"

Courtney had met Logan only once, for a few moments. She was not grief-stricken over his death, and she was too forthright and honest to put on a funeral face. Leigh hugged her tightly. "You're right on target. How did you know?"

"You're kidding, right?" Courtney said with a grin.

"No, I'm serious."

"Who else but cops would go to a gathering like this and not talk to anyone—or look for anyone to talk to? They're not eating, they're not sad, and they're not—" She broke off.

"Not what?"

"Let's just say they're not trying very hard to make a fashion statement. The tall guy with the gray hair is interesting." She nodded toward McCord, and Leigh followed her gaze, mostly because it was a relief to be talking about something else. "He's interesting because he's got those great scars and that lean, tough face. The brunette was the hardest one of all to pick out as a cop."

"Because she's a woman?"

"No, because she's wearing seven-hundred-dollar Bottega Veneta boots."

CHAPTER 34

Sheila stayed after everyone left, and while Hilda and the caterers cleaned up, the two women went into Leigh's bedroom. Leigh curled up on one of the chaise lounges near the window and wearily rested her head against the back of it. Sheila did the same thing on the other one.

"Jane Sebring was genuinely upset by all this," Leigh commented after a moment.

"I'm not surprised. She probably thinks she's the widow."

Leigh looked sharply at her. Although Sheila's chocolate wool suit was without a crease and her blond hair was swept up into a chignon without a hair out of place, there were dark blue smudges beneath her eyes, and her voice was taut with exhaustion and annoyance. "Why did you say that?"

"Because it's perfectly obvious to me that Jane Sebring wants to be you. She can't stand being second-best in anything. When she couldn't make it on Broadway, she went to Hollywood, took off her clothes for the camera, and won an Academy Award. But that wasn't enough. Now she's come back to Broadway to claim what she regards as her birthright, and you're in her way. In her mind, you've 'stolen' what is rightfully hers. She feels entitled to your enormous talent, your success in the legitimate theater and everything else you have."

"Unfortunately, that attitude is not all that unusual in my business, Sheila."

Sheila crossed her feet at the ankles, and sighed. "I know. She's just so damned greedy and competitive. I'll never understand what possessed Jason to put her in his play in the first place. She has a reputation for causing trouble with everyone she's ever worked with."

"Money was the reason," Leigh said wearily. "Jason's backers wanted her because she's a fantastic box-office draw."

"Not like you are."

"She draws movie fans into the theater, which is something I don't. She was a bonus—an insurance policy the backers wanted."

Sheila said nothing after that, and Leigh closed her eyes, trying not to wonder, to think, to place any particular significance on what Sheila had said. But she couldn't do it. She drew in a long, unsteady breath and kept her eyes closed, but her voice was determined. "Sheila?"

"Yes."

"Are you trying to tell me something you think I should know—"

"Like what?"

"Was Logan having an affair with Jane Sebring?"

Sheila was instantly apologetic. "I should have realized that we're both too exhausted to put coherent thoughts together. I wasn't trying to tell you anything of the kind. In fact, I watched her when she stopped by your party for a few minutes. She was hanging on Logan, but he did everything to cool her down, short of dousing her with the ice in his glass."

Leigh swallowed and forced words past the knot of emotion in her throat. "Let me put the question a different way: Do you think it's possible Logan was having an affair with her?"

"Anything is 'possible.' It's possible Logan might have taken up hang-gliding next week or joined the circus. Why are you pursuing this, Leigh?"

Leigh opened her eyes and looked directly at Sheila. "Because the last time you developed a severe personal dislike for a woman that we all knew socially, it turned out Logan was having an affair with her and you knew it."

Sheila returned her gaze unflinchingly. "That was a meaningless fling, and you understood why it happened. The two of you worked through that together."

Leigh pushed that painful memory to the back of her mind. Logan's fling had not been "meaningless" to her. "I've tried to convince myself that Logan's murder was a random act committed by some homeless, local madman who thought Logan was trespassing or something," Leigh said. "There's just one thing about that theory that doesn't work."

"What's that?"

"The gun they found in Logan's car was registered to him. He bought it in March. Why would Logan buy a gun and carry it? Is it possible he was in some sort of trouble?"

Instead of giving her an answer, Sheila studied her intently and asked a question of her own. "What sort of trouble could he have been in?"

Leigh lifted her hands, palms up. "I don't know. He was involved in dozens of business ventures, but he didn't seem to be particularly worried about any one of them. Even so, there were times lately when he seemed distinctly worried about something."

"Did you ask him about it?"

"Of course. He said he wasn't worried. Maybe 'worried' was the wrong word for me to use just now. He seemed very preoccupied."

Sheila smiled knowingly. "Would you call it 'unusual' for Logan to be preoccupied about business or money?"

She meant that to be a reassurance, Leigh knew, but in her present, conflicted state of mind, Leigh couldn't find much solace in anything. "No, of course not. You and I both know there isn't enough money in the world to make Logan feel absolutely secure."

"Because of his childhood," Sheila reminded her.

"I know. But has Logan *ever* said or done anything that might have made you think—"

"I'm a psychiatrist, not a psychic. Let the police solve this. You and I aren't equipped to do it."

"You're right," Leigh said, but long after Sheila left, Leigh sat alone in the dark, asking herself questions she couldn't answer, tortured by the fear that she might never have the answers.

For some reason, Logan had bought and carried a gun.

For some reason, someone had murdered him in cold blood.

Leigh wanted reasons. She wanted *answers.* She wanted *justice!*

But most of all—most of all—she wanted the same thing Jane Sebring wanted. She wanted to wake up and discover that this was all a nightmare.

CHAPTER 35

McCord slid a videotape of Logan Manning's funeral service into a VCR on the credenza behind his desk, pressed the fast-forward button, and turned on the monitor. "As we already know, Valente wasn't there yesterday, but it turns out he sent in an emissary who slipped right past us, unnoticed." As he spoke he handed out three copies of a composite photograph to Sam, Shrader, and Womack. "This is his cousin, Dominick Angelini," he said.

The composite contained several photographs of a male in his mid to late thirties, all of them shot from different angles and at different times. In one of the photographs, he was carrying a briefcase and walking up the steps of the federal court building. Sam didn't recognize him, and she'd not only attended all the funeral activities, she'd also watched the videotape before she went home for the night.

"The photograph of him in front of the federal court building was taken in August, and it's the latest one," McCord provided. "A federal grand jury had subpoenaed him to testify about Valente's accounting and business practices."

"I don't remember seeing this guy yesterday," Womack said. At fifty, Steve Womack was five feet ten with thinning gray hair, a wiry, slender build, and a face that was completely forgettable except for a pair of pale blue, keenly intelligent eyes that looked even more so behind the powerful lenses of his silver-rimmed glasses. Despite his insistence that he was ready to return to work after his recent surgery, Sam noticed that he rubbed his left shoulder frequently, as if it were hurting him. He was unassuming but sharp, and she was inclined to like him.

"I didn't see him either," she said.

"He wasn't there," Shrader stated emphatically.

"You're right, he wasn't," McCord said as he passed out three sets of pages containing nothing but signatures. "With the Widow Manning's kind permission," he explained, "I took the guest book yesterday and made copies of it last night. I thought it would make a handy list of Manning's friends and associates for us, but if you'll take a look at page fourteen, I think you'll spot what will now be an interesting name to you."

Sam spotted the signature at the same time Shrader did. "Mario Angelini?" he said.

"That's the way I read it, too, so this morning I watched the videotape of each person signing the guest book, while I ticked off their names, and this is what I discovered. . . ." He turned to the VCR on the credenza. The videotape had already stopped at the end, and he did a quick, brief rewind; then he pressed the play button as he said, "This is the best shot we have of Valente's emissary, Mrs. *Marie* Angelini." The tape showed a well-dressed, gray-haired woman with her hands in Leigh Manning's.

"What's the relationship?" Shrader asked.

"Marie Angelini is Valente's aunt. She raised him along with her sons, Angelo and Dominick. Angelo died in a fight twenty-five years ago, when he was in his early twenties. Dominick, whose picture you have, became a CPA and has a firm of his own. Guess who his biggest client is?"

"Valente," Womack said.

McCord nodded. "Right—Valente in all his many and varied corporate entities. One of those entities, a very minor one, is a large restaurant and market in the East Village called Angelini's. According to the records filed with the secretary of state in Albany, Marie Rosalie Angelini is the sole owner, but when the Feds were investigating Valente, they discovered that he put up all the capital for the new restaurant and the expansion of the original market next door. He also owns the buildings they're in."

"I've heard of Angelini's," Sam said, startled. "It's very popular. It takes weeks to get a reservation."

"The market and the restaurant are both cash businesses," Womack put in, "which makes them a very convenient place for Valente to launder some money."

"That's what the state prosecutors think, but they haven't been able to prove it." McCord paused to turn off the VCR; then he looked at the people gathered around his desk. "Now let's talk about what we know, and what we need to find out. Right now, all we know is that someone held Manning's thirty-eight to his right temple and blew his brains out. Then they wiped their prints off the gun, wrapped Manning's hand around it and fired it again, this time through the open window on the passenger side of the vehicle.

"The lab is still going over all the fibers, hairs, and particles that CSU collected from the vehicle and the house, but that's going to take time and I'm not counting on any great revelations from the lab. I think it's possible, even likely, that Valente and Leigh Manning were at the cabin together at some point, cleaning up. We know Manning drank wine with someone before he died, but *both* glasses had been rinsed—with snow, I presume—and then carefully wiped clean of all prints. The floor in the closet was coated in dust, but the rest of the floor was freshly swept to make certain we couldn't get any footprints."

He reached for a yellow tablet and glanced at his notes before he said, "That's all we know right now. In order to build our case against Valente, we need to establish that he's involved with Leigh Manning. We also need to find out if Logan Manning knew about it. If he suspected his wife was screwing Valente, then he probably told somebody else. We need to find out who he talked to, and what he said. I'd like to know why he suddenly invited Valente to his home for a party, and I'd like to know the real reason he bought that gun. I think it's possible he bought it because of Valente. It's even possible that he invited Valente to the cabin in the mountains and threatened him with it. Or tried to use it on him.

"Leigh Manning isn't going to talk to us about Valente, but you can bet she's confided some of the tender details of her affair to someone else, probably another woman. I've never met a woman yet who could keep an extramarital affair a total secret. We need to find out who she's talked to and what she's said.

"On the other hand, I can guarantee you that Valente hasn't talked to anyone about anything, so there's no point in looking for his confidants. I'm getting Valente's telephone records, but don't count on seeing any calls to Leigh Manning on them. He's too cagey for that. He'll have used a phone that can't be traced to him."

Womack rubbed his shoulder as he said, "I just want to be clear on what we're after, Lieutenant. Obviously, we want to hang Manning's murder on Valente. But when I talked to Captain Holland this morning, I got the impression that we're also trying to use the Manning murder investigation as a means to investigate Valente from other aspects, too."

"The answer to that question has three parts, so listen very closely, Womack: One, we want to hang Manning's murder on whoever killed him and whoever conspired with the killer. I have no doubt that Valente conspired with Leigh Manning in that murder. Two, we want to use this murder investigation as a means to investigate Valente from every possible angle. That should be easier for us to do than it was for the Feds because in the process of investigating a murder at the local level, we'll be able to get our local judges to sign wiretap authorizations, search warrants, and whatever else we need. Three—and this is just as important as number one and number two—Captain Holland isn't calling the shots in this investigation, I am. I report to Commissioner Trumanti, and for the duration of this investigation, you report to me, not Captain Holland. Is that clear?"

Womack looked fascinated and agreeable, but not particularly intimidated. "I hear you, Lieutenant."

"Good. In the future, if you have any further questions or comments, you take them to me, not Captain Holland. I'll keep him informed as I see necessary. Is that also clear?"

Womack nodded, and McCord looked satisfied. "We've already had one setback with Valente."

"What setback is that?" Shrader asked.

"Ever since the media found out Leigh Manning was with Valente in his helicopter last week, they've been speculating and investigating on their own, and stirring up a stink in the process. Valente knows it, and he'll be even more careful than usual. Our job is to get information about him from witnesses, without appearing to be too interested in him."

"Too bad we couldn't ask the media to back off," Shrader said.

McCord gave a short, mirthless laugh. "Don't even think about it. If you ask reporters to back off on an investigation like this one, they not only intensify it, they start investigating *you*, looking for a connection or complicity."

He walked over to the chalkboard and picked up a piece of yellow chalk. "Okay, let's start talking to people. Thanks to Mrs. Manning, we have carte blanche to question everyone she and Manning knew, including their shrink and Manning's business associates. Let's start with the names she mentioned, make out a preliminary list, and see where they lead us."

He wrote down four names in the top left-hand corner: *Jason Solomon, Sheila Winters, Theta Berenson, Sybil Haywood.* "Naturally, we'll want to talk to the people at Manning's office as well." As he said that he wrote *Manning Development* under Sybil Haywood's name. He paused and looked over his shoulder. "There's one more person we should talk to soon." He wrote Jane Sebring's name on the board, then turned and said, "I was watching that videotape last night, and it seemed to me that Miss Sebring seemed unusually sympathetic and distraught for an ambitious, self-centered sex goddess with a reputation for using everybody she knows to get whatever she wants."

"Where did you hear that about her?" Shrader asked, his forehead furrowed.

"It was in the *Enquirer* last week."

Shrader laughed out loud. "You read the *Enquirer*, Lieutenant?"

"Of course not. I happened to notice the article on the front page"—as he finished the sentence he looked at Sam and smiled as if sharing a private joke with her—"while I was standing in line at the grocery store."

Instead of sharing his little joke, Sam lifted her brows and looked at him with an expression of "And so?"

He actually looked a little rebuffed by her distant reaction. "Shrader," he continued, "you and Womack start interviewing the people at Manning's office today—" He broke off to answer the telephone. "McCord," he said irritably, but his expression cleared within moments. He hung up and looked at the three detectives. "The Good Samaritan who rescued Leigh Manning the night of her accident has just turned up."

"Where is he?" Shrader asked.

"Downstairs with his attorney. He wants to make a deal before he'll talk to us."

"What kind of deal?" Womack asked quickly.

"I don't know, but let's find out."

CHAPTER 36

Shrader and Womack watched through the two-way mirror as the man they'd dubbed the "Good Samaritan" sat down with his attorney in the interviewing room. McCord and Littleton sat down across the table from them.

"I'm Julie Cosgrove," the attorney said, "and this is Mr. Roswell." Roswell was in his mid-sixties, with a dissipated, weathered face, bad teeth, and a guilty, nervous smile. His jacket was torn at the right elbow, and the soiled cap that he politely removed as he sat down proclaimed him to be an aficionado of Coors.

"Mr. Roswell has answers to all your questions," the attorney continued. "However, we want your assurance that if he gives you a statement, nothing he tells you here will be used to prosecute him."

McCord leaned back in his chair, idly tapping his pencil on the yellow pad he'd carried into the interview room, until Roswell squirmed in his chair and looked uneasily at his attorney. "Just what does he think we would prosecute him for?" McCord said finally. "Other than withholding information and leaving the scene of an accident."

"He didn't leave the scene of the accident, he brought the victim to a safe location and asked someone to phone for help. As far as withholding information goes, his Fifth Amendment rights allow him to withhold information that might be self-incriminating. He's here now because Mr. Manning was found murdered, and it's been on the news that you thought there could be a connection between the murderer and whoever found Mrs. Manning that night and then disappeared."

"What is it that he's afraid we will prosecute him for?" McCord repeated implacably.

The attorney cleared her throat. "For operating a motor vehicle without a valid New York driver's license on the night of November twenty-ninth."

In comparison to the things Sam had been imagining, that was such a minor offense it was nonsensical, and she pressed her lips together to hide a wayward smile. Even McCord's voice lost its edge. "Since that offense was not committed within my jurisdiction, I can't guarantee that. However, I can guarantee that I will not feel inclined to report what I now know to the local authorities in the Catskills or to the state police. Will that suffice?"

The lawyer looked at her client and nodded reassuringly. "Go ahead, Wilbur, tell them what happened that night."

Roswell nervously twisted his cap in his callused fingers and switched his gaze from McCord's face to Sam's because he obviously found her less intimidating. "I was driving down the road that night at a little after eleven, but I hadn't been drinkin'—not a drop, I swear it." He raised his right hand, for emphasis. "It was snowing real hard, and I saw this big dark lump on the side of the road, kind of hanging partway over a snowdrift. I pulled over to drive around it, and I seen it was a body."

He looked down at the table. "I wasn't supposed to be driving because my license got suspended for driving under the influence, so I decided not to stop, but I—I couldn't just leave her there to freeze to death. So I pulled over and got her into my car; then I drove her down the mountain to a motel. I woke up the night manager, and he helped me get her into a room in the motel. He thought I should stay until the cops or an ambulance arrived, but I knowed—knew—if the cops came, they'd ask for my name and address and my driver's license. So I told the manager to stay with her in the room while I got her stuff out of my car, but I took off instead."

Since he'd spoken directly to her and avoided McCord, Sam took over. "You helped her, even though you knew you were taking a risk," she summarized with a smile. "That says a lot about the kind of man you are, Mr. Roswell."

After living with six brothers, Sam knew the difference between a male who was simply embarrassed by a compliment and one who felt guilty because he knew he didn't deserve it. The moment Roswell's gaze shifted away from hers, she knew he fell into the latter category and that her original hunch about his story was right. Without changing her mild, encouraging tone, she asked a question. "You said that the reason you stopped was because you couldn't leave her on the side of the road to freeze to death?"

"Yeah. I mean, yes, ma'am."

"It was dark, and it was snowing. How did you know that 'big, dark lump' was a woman's body, instead of a man's?"

"I—I didn't until I got up close."

"But when you pulled over to help, you did know that the person lying on the road was still alive, didn't you? That's why you had to stop to help, why you couldn't leave her there to freeze to death, isn't it? You have a drinking problem and you lost your driver's license because of it, but you're basically a decent man, even a brave man, aren't you?"

"I don't know as anyone's ever called me decent or brave," he said uneasily. "And I don't know as anybody's ever had call to say I was."

"I have a very good reason to say that, Mr. Roswell. When you stopped to help Mrs. Manning and drove her to that motel, you weren't just worried that the police might find out you were driving without a license. You were afraid they'd look at your car, realize that you were in that accident, and even blame you for it. You risked a great deal that night in order to help Mrs. Manning, didn't you?"

His face turned ashen. "I—" he began, but his attorney put her hand on his sleeve to stop him. "Don't say anything else, Wilbur, not another word."

To Sam she said, "Mr. Roswell has told you everything he knows about that night."

Sam ignored her and looked at Wilbur Roswell. With a gentle voice and soft smile she said, "Then let me tell him something that he *doesn't* know. Mrs. Manning admitted to us that she had slowed her vehicle almost to a stop that night—on a hazardous blind curve—in extremely dangerous weather conditions. I've seen the curve myself, and if I'd been driving Mr. Roswell's car that night, I wouldn't have been able to stop either. If anyone is responsible for that accident, I would say it was probably Mrs. Manning."

"Nevertheless," the attorney said sternly, "my client has nothing more to say. If he was driving the other car involved in that accident—and that is not my understanding—then your assurance that the accident was Mrs. Manning's fault doesn't mean a thing. She could disagree, she could try to sue him in civil court, and you could try to prosecute him for leaving the scene of an accident, at the very least."

Sam propped her elbows on the table and perched her chin on her folded hands. "Your attorney is right, Mr. Roswell. However, if you weren't drinking that night—"

"I wasn't and I can prove it!"

"I believe you. And if you can prove it, I will testify in your behalf in any civil suit Mrs. Manning might bring that the accident was unavoidable. Furthermore, I know Mrs. Manning, and I really don't think she's the sort of person to sue the man who saved her life and risked going to jail in order to do it. Also, she doesn't need money, so there's no point in suing you. If you can provide proof that you weren't drinking, I think I can extend Lieutenant McCord's earlier promise not to notify any other law enforcement agencies of what you've told us here or to prosecute you for leaving the scene, or anything else." Sam had been so intent until that moment that she'd virtually forgotten McCord was present or that she might need his cooperation. She looked at him then, her eyes begging him not to be a hard-ass. "Would you agree to that, Lieutenant?"

To her shock, McCord smiled a little and his smile became conspiratorial when he transferred it to Roswell. "I don't know about you, Wilbur, but I have a hard time saying no to any woman who looks at me like that, don't you?"

Wilbur hesitated; then he grinned at McCord. "She sure is pretty. And she's real nice, too."

The only one with reservations about all this was his attorney, which was appropriate. She frowned. "Was that a 'yes,' Lieutenant McCord? Are you agreeing to extend your promise not to prosecute Mr. Roswell if he admits to driving the other vehicle in that accident?"

"As long as he can prove he wasn't drinking that night. If he was, all bets are off."

"I wasn't! I was at Ben's Place all night drinking Cokes, and shooting a little pool. Ben will say so and so will everybody else I was with."

"Good for you!" Sam said. "Now, here's why it's important that we stop beating around the bush and you tell us straight out if you were driving the other car in the accident that night: We've all been thinking that the same person who killed Mr. Manning might have also tried to kill Mrs. Manning by running her off the road. If that was just an accident, then we need to drop that theory and start looking for other suspects right away, before we lose any more time."

Wilbur Roswell straightened in his chair and slapped his hat on the table. "It was just an accident," he proclaimed. "I was driving that night. You can look at my car and see how bad it got wrecked."

Sam nodded and stood up. "I'll find someone to come in here and take down your statement." She walked around the table and held out her hand to him. "I was right about you," she said with a smile. "You're a good and decent man. And a brave one."

She shook Julie Cosgrove's hand next. "Thank you for encouraging Mr. Roswell to come here today. It was the right thing to do."

Sam was wending her way across the squad room when McCord emerged and joined Shrader and Womack at the two-way window. Shrader looked at McCord and chuckled. "When's the last time you charmed a witness, then shook hands with him *and* his lawyer?"

"I don't believe I have that much charm," McCord said wryly.

"She's one smooth talker," Womack put in. "She had that lawyer eating out of her hand."

"Which isn't surprising," McCord replied, "since Littleton practically spelled out for her that Mrs. Manning was more to blame for the accident than her client. As we stand here, that lawyer in there is mentally drafting a letter to Leigh Manning's insurance company demanding money for damages to her client's vehicle, et cetera, et cetera."

Shrader came to Sam's defense. "Littleton's brand-new at the job. Give her time to learn that it's usually a mistake to volunteer any information in interviews. She slipped up a little, that's all."

McCord gave him a skeptical look. "Littleton didn't slip up. She did it on purpose."

CHAPTER 37

"**D**id you do it on purpose?" McCord asked her when they were in his car on the way to Jason Solomon's apartment on West Broadway in SoHo.

"Roswell and his attorney were entitled to know what information Mrs. Manning gave us in her first statement about the accident. You saw how he was dressed. I'll bet he can't afford to repair his car, and I'm sure it was badly damaged from the accident. Shrader and I saw where the accident happened, and I drove the route myself. It's a blind curve, and she was virtually stopped in the road. The miracle is that he didn't go over the embankment with her. Besides," Sam finished with a shrug, "I'm sure Mrs. Manning's insurance will cover whatever claims Roswell files."

McCord shot her a puzzled glance. "Did you think my question was some sort of criticism?"

That's exactly what Sam had thought. She looked at him in surprise. "No, not at all. Why?"

"I don't know. I just get the feeling you're . . ." McCord started to say "pissed off at me"; then he quickly squelched the absurd impulse. There was no way he was going to let her think it mattered a damn to him if she was pissed off at him. And the truth was, it *didn't* matter to him, because he would never *allow* it to matter.

Littleton's jaunty wit amused him, her mind fascinated him, and her elegant, fine-boned face and soft mouth were pleasing to his eye. Each of those assets interested him on an impersonal, almost intellectual level, but combined, they created a package that, on another level entirely, he found to be disconcertingly desirable. Even so, he was much too wise, too jaded, and too experienced to ever let a woman like that discover that she could get under his skin—most particularly at work.

She'd chosen a career in law enforcement; that meant she had to carry her own weight, deal with her own problems, work her own leads, and open her own doors. He knew how to do his job; she needed to learn how to do hers. She was his partner—temporarily—but she was *not* his equal.

He knew she'd taken his question about Roswell as a criticism, but that was her problem to deal with, not his. He was also certain she was upset with him about something, but even if he felt some inappropriate impulse to clear the air with her, he also knew it would be a total waste of time. Sam Littleton was a beautiful woman who would try to play women's games. That meant that if he asked her if she was upset with him about something, she would do what women all do at such times: She would deny that anything was wrong, then continue acting as if something was wrong, in hopes that he would do what men always do at such times—beg for an explanation, agonize over the answer, ask for hints, and then agonize a little more. Unfortunately for her, when it came to those kinds of games between the sexes, Sam Littleton wasn't his equal there, either. He'd already played them all, and they weren't a challenge anymore; they were predictable and boring. They were also dangerous and out of place at work.

There was a parking spot very close to Solomon's building, and he pulled into it, his attention on parking the car.

Beside him, Littleton had noticed that he hadn't finished the sentence he'd started and she courteously repeated it for him, making him feel as if she thought he was one hundred years old and forgetful. "You get the feeling I'm what?"

He glanced at her heavily lashed brown eyes and noticed for the first time the flecks of gold in them. "I get the feeling you're pissed off at me about something," he said, and then could not believe he'd said it! Disgusted with himself, he waited for the inevitable denial.

"I am," she said quietly.

"Really?" He was so shocked that she'd admitted it, and without any rancor, that he stared at her in silence.

After a moment, she smiled a little and gave him another helpful conversational nudge. "Would you like me to tell you why?"

A grin tugged at his mouth. "Let's hear it."

"I'm very aware that I'm a neophyte, and that I'm extremely lucky to be working on this case with you. I didn't really expect to be impressed with you that first day, but I was. Besides being highly organized," she said with a quick smile, "you struck me as a leader who actually deserves to be one. Not only that, but I honestly thought you were going to turn out to be one of those rare leaders who is also a team player."

McCord would have been more flattered by her remarks if he hadn't instantly realized that she was deliberately inflating his ego and pumping up his pride because she wanted to be sure he hit the ground really hard when she punctured them. She was really quite skilled at this game, he decided sardonically. "And now, for some reason, you realize I'm a complete jerk?"

"Not at all," she said, her gaze direct and disconcertingly honest. "But you're a guy who plays guy games, just like all the other guys try to play with me. And I'm just a woman who unfairly expected you to be bigger and better than that."

"Just what the hell did I do to drop so far in your estimation?"

"You knew Valente was with Leigh Manning the night we told her we'd found her husband dead, but you didn't tell me. That was an important piece of information, but you withheld it and let me stumble on it by accident the next day."

"I wanted you to discover it yourself."

"Why?" she said. "So you could be right and I could be misguided and naïve about Leigh Manning for an extra twenty-four hours?"

"I wanted you to discover for yourself that you had been misguided and naïve."

"Really?" she said flatly. "Does that strike you as an effective leadership technique on an important homicide investigation? Would you have done that to Shrader?"

"No," he said shortly.

"Would you have done it to Womack?"

He shook his head.

"Then I can only assume you did it to me because I'm a girl and you wanted to 'teach me a lesson' in order to 'keep me in my place.' "

He looked at her so long that Sam began to think he wasn't going to answer. When he did answer, she was speechless. "I did it to you because I've never seen a more promising detective than you are. You have more talent, raw intuition, and"—he hesitated, searching for the right word, and came up with one that seemed unsuited to the discussion—"and more *heart* than I've ever encountered. I wanted you to learn a hard, but painless lesson, about letting yourself get emotionally entrapped by anyone you're investigating."

He paused and then said, "However, that doesn't change the fact that you are right, and I was wrong, in the way I went about it. I would never have done that to another male detective. I would have told him when we left the building that night that he'd just witnessed a convincing act by a woman whose lover was hiding in the next room."

She looked at him in surprised admiration as if he were some kind of hero for admitting he was wrong, and to McCord's displeasure, he discovered he rather liked having her look at him that way. "I apologize," he said almost curtly. "It won't happen again."

"Thank you," she said simply; then she flashed him a sudden, embarrassed smile. "Actually, I think I may have made too much out of it. I didn't expect you to be so fair and reasonable."

He laughed as he reached for the handle on the car door. "Accept the apology, Sam, and don't backtrack. You won fair and square."

He got out of the car and so did she. He was so pleased with the outcome of the discussion that he didn't realize he'd called her Sam until they were walking down the sidewalk side by side. Even so, that didn't mean anything, he told himself. Everything was fine now; everything was exactly as it had been. Nothing had changed in those few minutes of honest conversation. They were detective partners, nothing more.

When they arrived at Solomon's building, he reached around her from behind and politely pushed the heavy door open for her.

CHAPTER 38

Jason Solomon greeted them with a towel draped around his shoulders and traces of shaving cream still clinging to his jaw and neck. "Come in, come in," he said, dabbing at the shaving cream with the end of his towel. "Give me two minutes to finish getting dressed, and then we'll talk."

He gestured them inside, and Sam looked around at a spectacular loft apartment that was as dramatic and interesting as the man who owned it. The floors were of mellow oak, punctuated with thick, biscuit-colored carpets and sleek, contemporary furnishings upholstered in butterscotch. A curving staircase with polished steel railings wound upward to a second story on the left side of the living room, while a fireplace of glittering white quartz soared two stories high on the far right. But all of that—the floors, walls, and furnishings in neutral, monochromatic colors—were simply a backdrop for what was one of the most breathtaking collections of vivid abstract art Sam had ever beheld.

Fabulous works by Paul Klee, Jackson Pollock, and

Wassily Kandinsky hung on one wall, while another held a series of four large portraits of Jason Solomon somewhat reminiscent of Andy Warhol's work. Sam walked over to them and looked at the artist's name. It seemed familiar, but not familiar enough to associate with any other pieces of modern art she'd seen. Whoever "Ingram" was, he was very good, but not very original. The psychedelic oil painting on the fireplace was also by Ingram, but this one was very original, and also depicted Solomon—this time with burning coals for eyes and fire coming out of his skull.

Above that hung a wildly exuberant oil in splashes of primary colors that Sam instantly identified as Theta Berenson's work.

McCord walked up behind her and stood so close that she could smell traces of Irish Spring, the same soap she used in the shower. He lowered his voice to a whisper. "Do you like all this stuff?"

"Very, very much."

"What's it supposed to be?"

Smiling, she turned her head. "Whatever you want it to be."

Jason Solomon's remark, as he strode into the living room, made her jump back in guilty surprise. "Am I interrupting anything?"

"Yes," McCord said calmly, "a lesson in modern art. Detective Littleton is in raptures over your collection. Where can we talk?" he added abruptly, putting an end to social chitchat.

"Let's go in the kitchen. Eric is fixing breakfast." Solomon led the way past the fireplace and into a large, sunny, ultramodern kitchen of oak and stainless steel. Eric was standing at the counter, a pitcher of orange juice in one hand and a bottle of white wine in the other, pouring some of each liquid into a stemmed glass. A good-looking man in his early thirties, he looked up as they entered and gave them a friendly nod.

"Would you like something to eat?" Solomon offered, sitting down at the table.

"No, it's a little too close to lunch," McCord replied.

"Then how about something to drink—one of Eric's specials?" Sam glanced at the bottle of wine and declined that offer herself. "No, it's a little too close to *breakfast* for that."

Satisfied that he'd done his duties as host, Solomon folded his arms on the table and looked at McCord. "What have you found out about Logan's death?"

"Actually, we were hoping you could answer some questions for us that might put us on the right track. Right now, we're just gathering background information, hoping that something someone says will point us in the right direction."

"I'll tell you anything I know."

"How long have you known Leigh and Logan Manning?"

Before he could answer, Eric arrived at the table with a plate of fluffy scrambled eggs, a wedge of cantaloupe, a slice of toast, and a glass of spiked orange juice. "This is Eric Ingram," Jason said. "Eric is a fabulous cook."

"Ingram?" Sam repeated. "Are you the artist who did the portraits of Mr. Solomon in the living room?"

Eric smiled self-consciously and nodded.

"Eric doesn't talk much, and never about himself," Solomon explained cheerfully. "That's why we get along so well—I do enough of that for both of us."

Eric had already retreated to the cooking area, but McCord looked over his shoulder at him. "Don't hesitate to chime in, Mr. Ingram, if anything you hear triggers some recollection. It's my experience that people who talk less, frequently notice more." To Solomon he said, "You were going to tell me how long you've known Leigh and Logan Manning."

Solomon thought about that while he chewed a bite of scrambled egg. "Let me think. The first time I met them, they came to an off-Broadway play I'd written called *Time and a Bottle*. It was one of my early efforts, and although the critics said I showed great promise, the play never quite caught on with the public. I still wonder if—"

"How long ago was that?"

"Thirteen, no, maybe fourteen years ago."

"Good. Let's focus on the last few months. Did you know that Mrs. Manning thought she was being stalked?"

"Yes, absolutely. Leigh was very frightened. Logan was even more so, but he didn't want her to know it."

"What did she tell you about this stalker?"

"Leigh said he'd sent her some gifts, and he'd called her a couple of times. Logan and she tried to trace the second call, but it was made from a pay phone in Manhattan."

"She may have known her stalker without realizing it. It's possible he hung around the theater on some pretense, or made it a point to be waiting outside when she left. Other than her husband and the members of your cast and crew, have you seen Mrs. Manning with any other men? Don't leave anyone out," McCord added, "no matter how above reproach he may seem to you."

McCord was hoping Valente's name would come up, Sam knew, and she listened while Jason Solomon came up with a few meaningless names, but in her heart she still wasn't convinced that Leigh Manning had knowingly collaborated in her husband's murder. Sam had seen Leigh Manning in the hospital, she'd seen her at the cabin when her husband wasn't there, and to Sam, she had exhibited every sign of a frantic, loving, terrified wife.

The day of Logan Manning's funeral, Sam had scarcely taken her eyes off the new widow, and what she saw was a courageous woman struggling to act with dignity even though she was emotionally shattered and physically wrecked. Sam was willing to believe that Valente wanted her badly enough to get rid of her husband, but she couldn't quite believe that Leigh Manning knew anything about Valente's intent.

On the other hand, Sam reminded herself sternly, she wouldn't have believed that Leigh Manning was having an affair with Valente in the first place, yet all the evidence clearly indicated that the actress had lied about her relationship with him and that she was trying to hide it from everyone. . . . But if Leigh Manning simply wanted to be free of her husband, why murder him? Sam wondered. Why not divorce him, instead? Spousal murder was normally motivated by rage or jealousy or revenge, yet as far as anyone knew, Leigh Manning had no reason to harbor any of those feelings toward her husband.

As absurd as Sam knew her attitude was, she could not accept that Logan Manning had been murdered by his wife or Valente simply because murdering him seemed expedient. They had to have had other reasons to commit such a heinous act.

Solomon had run out of names to mention, and McCord was taking another tack with his questions. "Would you describe the Mannings as a devoted, happily married couple?"

Solomon nodded. "Disgustingly devoted and revoltingly happy," he declared with an effort at humor.

At that moment, Sam happened to glance at Eric and she saw his face tighten. "Mr. Ingram?" she interrupted. "Is that how it looked to you? Was Mr. Manning devoted to his wife?"

"Yes, Detective, that's how it looked." Sam thought his answer left some room for interpretation, but McCord wasn't interested in Logan Manning, he was interested in his wife. "What about Leigh Manning?" he asked Eric. "Was she devoted to her husband?"

"Definitely."

He turned back to Solomon. "I imagine Mrs. Manning has been under a lot of stress these last few weeks—with a stalker following her and a new play opening. Did you notice anything unusual in her behavior that would indicate she was under stress?"

"My God, yes! We all were stressed to the breaking point! You would be astounded by the effort involved in launching a new play. The creative issues are only a part of it. The financial ones are nightmares—the backers want assurances, they want returns on their investments, and no matter how well you do for them, they get squeamish when it's time to ante up for the next play and you end up looking for new money all the time. I'm already doing that now—"

"So you don't finance your plays with your own money?" McCord asked idly.

"Oh, yes. I dump piles of my money into every play, but I don't shoulder the financial burden alone. Do you have any idea how much money actresses like Leigh Kendall and Jane Sebring get? Leigh's agent made impossible demands, as usual, but Logan persuaded him to be more reasonable, thank God. Even so, before the backers can break even, *Blind Spot* will have to play to sellout audiences for a long time."

McCord looked up at the ceiling, clearly trying to make some connection between what he was hearing and what he wanted to know. "Who are your backers in this play?" he asked absently.

"That's confidential."

His curiosity aroused by the other man's evasiveness, McCord lowered his gaze and focused it on the playwright, a slight smile tugging at the corner of his mouth. "When can I have a list?"

Instead of being in a snit over McCord's high-handedness, Solomon grinned and shrugged. "Will tomorrow be soon enough?"

McCord nodded. "Will there be any names on that list that I recognize?"

He was angling toward Valente again, Sam knew, and Jason Solomon's answer made her tense expectantly. "You'll definitely recognize one name."

"Which one?"

"Logan Manning."

"Logan Manning?" Sam repeated. "Isn't that a little odd?"

"In what way?"

He was playing cat and mouse with her, and Sam didn't like it. She made him pay for it by forcing *him* to prove her point. "You're the show business expert. You tell me."

"Well, on the surface it does seem to be a bit of a conflict of interest, I'll grant you that."

"Because?" Sam prompted him.

"Because, on the one hand, Logan was responsible for Leigh agreeing to take less money for appearing in the play. By doing that, there was more profit left for the backers."

"Including Logan Manning," Sam finished.

"Right."

"Did Leigh Manning know her husband was one of the backers?"

"Of course. The subject came up at a dinner party a week or so before opening night. She seemed a little surprised, but not upset." He held up his glass, and Eric appeared at his side with a refill from the pitcher.

As if belatedly realizing that both detectives might draw the wrong conclusion from what he'd said, he added an explanation. "Logan said his decision to take a profit as a backer rather than making all the profits from Leigh's salary was related to their income taxes. The income tax on Leigh's salary would be thirty-nine point six percent. The capital gains tax on profits from investments—including an investment in *Blind Spot*—is only twenty percent."

"How much money did he invest?"

Solomon shrugged. "Very little—two hundred thousand dollars."

"Just one more question," McCord said. "You're very creative, which tells me you're also highly intuitive, and you're also accustomed to working with actors. You just said that Leigh Manning seemed 'surprised' when she realized at a dinner party that her husband's financial advice had obviously been in his best financial interest, but not hers. You've also said that the Mannings were happily married. Is it possible that Mrs. Manning, who is an acclaimed actress, has simply been giving some very convincing performances offstage, as well as onstage?"

Solomon dusted crumbs of toast from his fingers and wiped his mouth with his napkin; then he leaned back in his chair, folded his arms over his chest, and gave McCord a long, measuring look. In a surprisingly chilly voice, he said, "Just exactly what are you getting at? Are you suggesting there is even a remote possibility that Leigh killed Logan?"

"I'm not suggesting anything right now, I'm merely hypothesizing."

Jason Solomon didn't buy that for a moment. "That is exactly what you're suggesting. In which case, I feel compelled to give you the benefit of my unabridged, highly intuitive opinion: You are full of shit. You are wasting your time, and you are wasting my time."

"Excellent," McCord replied smoothly. "Now that we've abandoned polite formalities, where were you on Sunday, November twenty-ninth, from three P.M. to three A.M. the following morning?"

Jason gaped at him. "Now you think *I* murdered Logan?"

"Did you?"

"What reason would I have to do that?"

"Let me think . . . For starters, I'm sure you have a large insurance policy on Leigh Manning. How much money would you receive if she were declared mentally unable to resume her role? Jane Sebring has taken over her role. How much money would you save if you didn't have to pay Leigh Manning and Jane Sebring remained in the role?"

"This is insane!" Jason said angrily. The doorbell rang and he glanced at Eric. "Answer that, dammit."

"If that sounds too far-fetched," McCord said when Eric was gone, "try this out: You're gay and you're sure as hell not interested in poor Eric, except as a cook and servant. Did Logan Manning appeal to you? Did he turn you down and wound your ego when you made your move?"

"You son of a bitch!" Solomon said softly.

McCord reacted to that slur on his mother's morals with tranquil amusement. "I'm always surprised by the number of people who knew my mother."

Solomon gaped at him; then he threw back his head and shouted with laughter. "I'm going to use that line in a play."

"If you do, I'll tell everyone you're a plagiarist."

"Sue me instead. I—" He broke off, turning in surprise

at the sound of a woman's voice raised in hysteria in the living room.

"Get out of my way, Eric!" she cried. "I don't care who he's with. It doesn't matter if they hear! By tonight, everyone is going to know—"

Jason jumped to his feet, nearly overturning his chair, just as Jane Sebring burst into the kitchen, her face devoid of makeup, tears streaming from her eyes. "A reporter called me a few minutes ago," she stormed. "He wanted a statement from me before they break the story on tonight's news."

"Calm down, darling," Solomon ordered, opening his arms to her and patting her back. "What are you talking about?"

"I'm talking about Logan!" she cried. "Some sleazebag reporter went through my trash and bribed my doorman."

Solomon moved her forward enough to look at her wet face. "And the sleazebag found out what?"

"He found out Logan and I were having an affair!" she cried.

His face white with shock, horror, and fury, Solomon dropped his arms and stepped back. Sam looked at McCord, who seemed fascinated; then she looked at Eric Ingram.

He looked disgusted. He did not look at all surprised.

"WELL, WHAT DO YOU THINK NOW?" McCord asked Sam as they walked along the sidewalk to his car. He was thoroughly pleased with Jane Sebring's tearful revelation. "Tell me, did Leigh Manning have a motive for murder, or what?"

Sam looked up at the bright strip of blue sky, thinking. Until a few minutes ago, she hadn't believed Leigh Kendall would have gone along with any plan of Valente's to murder her husband, but Logan Manning's affair with Jane Sebring changed things. . . . "I want the answers to two questions before I decide."

"What questions?"

"I want to know if Leigh Manning knew about her husband's affair with Sebring. I'd also like to check out the alibi Jane Sebring just gave us for Sunday night. We know that Leigh Manning had to stay after the matinee to work out some glitches with Solomon. But Jane Sebring says she left the theater right after the matinee and went directly home. She says she went to bed, but then she got up later, had dinner alone, and watched a movie on television. That's not much of an alibi," Sam pointed out.

"She told us what movie she watched, how much more proof do you need?"

"If she was smart enough to wrap Logan Manning's hand around his gun after she blew his brains out, I imagine she's smart enough to have looked at a *TV Guide* when she got home so that she could tell us what movies she watched. Oh—" Sam said, when she saw his smirk. "I thought you were serious."

"You don't want to believe Leigh Manning is guilty, do you?"

"I don't have a preference," Sam protested. "I just want to feel absolutely sure."

"Check out Sebring's alibi. She used a car service to take her home after the matinee, so they'll have a record. She said she spoke to her doorman when she came in after the matinee."

"The same doorman who took a bribe to rat on her about her affair with Manning? I'd be really impressed with his integrity."

"He doesn't work twenty-four hours a day. Maybe it was another doorman who saw her come in."

"She could have left again without him seeing her. If

she left right away, she would have made it to the mountains before it really started snowing."

"True," McCord said, glancing at his watch. "Let's go over to Manning's office and help Shrader and Womack question the employees."

CHAPTER 39

Manning Development's suite was on the fifteenth floor, directly off the elevator, behind a pair of imposing double doors that opened into a spacious, circular reception area with offices and conference rooms surrounding it. Groupings of curved sofas and rounded chairs in shades of plum and blue were situated between ornamental stainless steel columns.

When Sam and McCord arrived, the reception area was empty except for a receptionist at a semicircular desk to their far right. She directed them to an office on the opposite side, where Shrader and Womack were interviewing the staff.

"We've had a rather enlightening morning so far," Shrader said. "Womack just went to question Manning's secretary. Did you two get anything out of Solomon?"

McCord quickly filled him in on what they'd learned while they were at Solomon's place; then he asked for details on Shrader's morning.

"I think we're in luck," Shrader said. "One of the architects who works for Manning—George Sokoloff—told me he's in charge of a big project called Crescent Plaza that Manning wanted to design and construct. It had twin residential towers attached to a fancy shopping mall. Guess who Manning's 'secret investor' was likely to be?"

"Valente," McCord said with satisfaction.

"Right. Valente and Manning were doing a lot of talking. Here's what makes that especially interesting: Sokoloff told me the design for Crescent Plaza was really unique, really spectacular, and that Valente loved it when he saw it. Valente wanted to hire Manning as supervising architect, but build the plaza himself. Sokoloff said Manning refused and was adamant about being a major partner in the building-and-development phase and part owner of the finished project."

"Valente doesn't like partners. He's not a team player."

"Right," Shrader said. "But he really wanted Crescent Plaza, and Logan Manning not only owned the design, he also owned an option on the land it was designed to fit on. I figure Valente may have popped Manning so that he could do Manning's wife *and* the Crescent Plaza project. Now that Manning's dead, Valente will be able to buy the plans and the land, hire his own supervising architects, and build it himself. I'm sure Manning's widow will make that very easy for him."

"You know," McCord said thoughtfully, "I'm starting to wonder if Detective Littleton had it right from the very beginning. She's said all along that she didn't think Leigh Manning was sexually involved with Valente."

"I don't remember saying exactly that," Sam interjected.

"You didn't have to say it. You get this balky, stubborn look every time the suggestion comes up. My point is that Valente and Leigh Manning's alliance may have been a straightforward business arrangement. Valente wanted the

Crescent Plaza project for himself, and she wanted her husband out of the way because he was cheating on her."

Womack walked in and heard the end of that sentence. "How did you find out Manning was screwing around?" he asked.

"Jane Sebring—the costar—told us this morning," McCord replied.

"The costar knew Manning was fooling around with the secretary?"

"What are you talking about?"

Womack jerked his thumb toward the doorway. "Manning was screwing his secretary. Her name is Erin Gillroy. She burst into tears and confessed the whole thing just now. Who were you talking about?"

"Jane Sebring."

His eyes widened and he looked ready to laugh. "Manning was screwing her, too? Hell, if I had a chance at Jane Sebring, I'd take it. That woman has—" He lifted his hands as if cupping breasts the size of watermelons; then he stopped and looked at Sam. "Littleton, why don't you go talk to the secretary and see what you can get out of her, besides tears and snot? Take it easy on her, though; she cracks like a raw egg. All I asked her was how long she'd worked here and if she was familiar with Manning's personal habits. She started bawling on the first question and confessed before I finished asking the second one."

"I'd like to talk to Sokoloff," McCord said, standing up, but Womack stopped him with a question.

In no hurry to deal with a weeping secretary, Sam walked slowly past the offices, stopping when she came to an open doorway of a large conference room. In the center, on a table, stood a scale model of a beautiful crescent-shaped plaza with art deco touches adorning its two soaring circular towers. The model was about five feet square and complete to the tiniest detail, including miniature fountains, ornamental streetlamps, pathways, and lush landscaping.

A studious-looking man in his late thirties was gazing at it, his shoulders slightly stooped, his hands clasped behind his back. "Is that the model for Crescent Plaza?" Sam asked, walking into the conference room for a closer look.

The man turned and pushed his glasses up on his nose. "Yes, it is."

"I'm Detective Littleton with the NYPD," she explained.

"I'm George Sokoloff," he said.

Sam's attention reverted to the model in front of her. "This is breathtaking," she said. "The towers remind me just a little bit of the top of the Chrysler Building. Mr. Manning must have been incredibly talented and incredibly proud of this."

He opened his mouth to say something, then quickly closed it again.

"Am I wrong?"

"Partly," he said; then he squared his shoulders and said almost bitterly, "Logan was very proud of it; however, now that he's dead, I see no need to go on pretending that this was a collaborative effort between Logan and me. The concept and design are all mine. In the past, I've agreed that the firm would receive the credit, rather than myself. This time, Logan promised I would be supervising architect and receive a share of the credit."

McCord's voice bisected their conversation, and they both turned toward him. "How did you feel about letting Logan Manning take all the credit, or is that typical in architectural firms?"

Sam tried not to think about how good it felt to watch Mitchell McCord walk into a room. His sport coats were no longer too big at the shoulders; he'd remedied that a couple of days after they started working together. Now they fit him beautifully, but she liked him best in open-necked polo shirts and the scarred leather bomber jacket he wore sometimes. Sam backed out of the conference room and quietly left McCord with the architect.

Logan Manning's office was at one end of a curving hallway that originated at a decorative paneled wall behind the receptionist's desk. Erin Gillroy was standing in front of his desk, head bent, clutching a fistful of tissues. She looked up as Sam walked in. "Miss Gillroy, I'm Detective Littleton."

"Hello," she said hoarsely but calmly.

"Would you like to sit down?"

"Not particularly. I think I'll feel less vulnerable and foolish if I'm standing up."

Sam perched on the corner of Manning's desk and took a pen and notebook out of her shoulder bag. "Detective Womack thought you might have an easier time talking to a woman."

"Really? He didn't strike me as being a particularly sympathetic type."

In contrast to Womack's description of Erin Gillroy, Sam's impression of the young woman was that she wasn't weak or timid. "How long have you worked here?"

"Almost two years."

Sam made an issue of writing that down while she decided how to approach the next topic, but she needn't have bothered, because Erin Gillroy answered the question without being asked. "My relationship with Logan Manning started—and ended—six months ago."

Sam studied her in silence, wondering why she was so willing to confess everything and get it out in the open to two detectives who were strangers. "Who else knew about it?"

She clenched her hands into fists. "No one! The only

person I ever told was my roommate, Deborah, but last night a reporter called and told her that he knew I'd had an affair with Logan Manning. And my roommate, my *friend*," she emphasized bitterly, "did not feel it would be honest to *lie* to him about it, so she told him everything." She looked at Sam and said fiercely, "Will you explain to me how someone who reads the Bible and quotes from it all the time, like Deborah does, can betray a friend and break a promise without a qualm, and do all that in the name of *'righteousness.'* All Deborah had to do was hang up on the reporter, or take a message."

She gazed at Sam, waiting for an answer, insisting on one, and Sam said the only thing that came to mind: "Some of the most unkind, judgmental people I've ever known go to church every Sunday and read the Bible. I don't know how some people are able to disassociate their own cruelty and shortcomings from their religious obligations and convictions, but many are able to do that."

"Deborah is one of them."

"How do you think the reporter found out about the affair?"

"I don't think he knew *anything* at all—he was just fishing! Reporters have been calling every woman Mr. Manning knew saying things like that. One of them called Jacqueline Probst last night and told her the same thing. Jacqueline told the reporter she'd sue if her name was mentioned; then she hung up on him."

"Who is Jacqueline Probst?" Sam asked.

"One of the architects here. The detectives have already spoken to her. Jacqueline Probst is sixty-four years old. She's almost old enough to be Logan's grandmother."

Sam deliberately changed the topic for a moment. "Did you handle all of Mr. Manning's correspondence and phone calls, personal as well as business?"

"Yes."

"Do you keep a call log?"

She nodded.

"I'd like to have that and some other records as well. We have Mrs. Manning's permission."

"I'll get you whatever you want." Distracted, she ran her finger over a gold pyramid-shaped paperweight on his desk; then she carefully straightened his leather paper tray. "I just can't believe Logan is dead."

"Who ended your affair?" Sam asked. "You or Mr. Manning?"

"It really didn't deserve the importance of the word 'affair,' " Erin replied, shifting her gaze to Sam. "Last spring, I was engaged and expecting to be married in a big June wedding my family had been planning for a year. A month before our wedding my fiancé dumped me.

"I did everything to get past my wedding day as it came closer. I jogged, I meditated, and I tried to keep really busy by working extra hours here. On the night that would have been our rehearsal dinner, I volunteered to work late and Logan stayed, too. We had dinner delivered, I started to cry, and Logan tried to comfort me. He knew the significance of the day to me. He was funny like that—at times he could be completely inconsiderate, and yet he would remember little things that are important to people. Anyway, he told me I was too good for my fiancé, and he put his arm around me, and the next thing I knew, we ended up on the sofa over there. He was so incredibly good looking that my fiancé had been jealous of him, and I guess that had something to do with why I went along with it."

When she paused, Sam prodded gently. "And then what happened?"

"A month later, I missed a period and got a false positive on a home pregnancy test. I was frantic. Deborah had only moved in with me a few weeks before, but she seemed so nice and I was . . . hysterical. I don't believe in abortion, so that was out of the question. Anyway, I ended up telling Deborah the whole sordid tale that day."

"Which she repeated to a reporter on the phone last night?" Sam finished for her.

Erin nodded, looking physically ill. "Do you think they'll mention this—me—and Logan in the news?"

Sam hesitated and then nodded. "I think you'd better be prepared for it. But if it's any consolation, I don't think you're going to be the only woman they mention tonight."

Erin tipped her head back and closed her eyes, her face a mask of bitter knowledge and dread. "Poor Mrs. Manning. I'll bet I can guess what two of the other names will be."

Sam kept her expression carefully blank. "What two names are those?"

"Jane Sebring and Trish Lefkowitz."

"Trish Lefkowitz—Mrs. Manning's publicist?"

First, Erin nodded; then she shook her head. "I don't know. Trish Lefkowitz was almost a year ago. Maybe she won't come up; maybe she'll know how to bluff her way out of it. She knows how to deal with the press."

CHAPTER 40

McCord was sitting at his desk, going over the day's events with Sam, Shrader, and Womack. The three men were amused and fascinated by Logan Manning's sexual athletics. "Erin Gillroy, Jane Sebring, and Trish Lefkowitz," McCord said. "A perky blonde, a gorgeous redhead, and a raven-haired beauty. Manning was not only a man of eclectic tastes in women, he was a man of notable courage."

"I don't think infidelity is admirable," Sam said; then she wondered where on earth her outburst had come from. Boys were boys, and men were, too. She knew that. Multiple clandestine affairs constituted a badge of accomplishment to boys, and to most men, too, whether they admitted it or not.

McCord slanted her a laughing look. "You obviously don't know Trish Lefkowitz, but I've known her for years. I can see Manning offering sexual consolation to a pretty, lovelorn secretary on the eve of her wedding; that would make him feel powerful. I can see him seducing a Hollywood sex goddess; that would make him feel special. But going to bed with Trish Lefkowitz? That took courage. He's lucky she didn't turn him into a soprano. That woman is like a black widow spider. I'd be afraid to close my eyes in bed with her."

McCord broke off to answer his phone, and Sam got up and went over to the table containing stacks of color-coded files on Logan and Leigh Manning, Michael Valente, and the Mannings' friends and acquaintances. Now it also held several armloads of files and documents they'd brought back with them from Manning Development that day. Shrader, Womack, and she had been systematically going through the files on individuals as McCord had instructed. Shrader had just returned the files on Leigh Manning, so Sam picked that stack up to take home with her.

McCord hung up the phone, looking well pleased. "That was Holland," he said. "Holland has the subpoena I wanted for Manning's income tax records, personal and business. Shrader, you and Womack serve it on Manning's CPA tomorrow. Once you get the records, make copies of them. Keep one set for us to go over, but bring the other set over to our bean counters. I want a Special Frauds auditor to look them over. If there's anything in Manning's tax returns that reflects money going to or from any of Valente's companies, our guys will find it."

"Why did we need a subpoena?" Womack asked. "I thought we already had Mrs. Manning's verbal permission 'to do whatever we think we need to do.' "

"We do, and that's one reason it was so easy to get a subpoena. But to protect his own ass, Manning's CPA may want something in writing before he hands over any records. I don't want him calling Mrs. Manning for permission, because there's always a risk that he'll advise her against the carte blanche she's already given us. Sooner or later, she's going to wise up and revoke it.

"That's why I'm in such a hurry to visit with Dr. Sheila Winters," he continued. "We have Leigh Manning's written consent allowing Winters to breach the doctor-patient privilege regarding her treatment of Logan Manning. When Mrs. Manning wrote it out, she didn't limit the consent to her husband's treatment alone, so Dr. Winters should be willing to talk to us about anything Mrs. Manning divulged during her own sessions with the shrink."

Shrader shook his head in wonder. "I still can't believe she agreed to that."

"She specifically asked that we keep the information confidential," Sam reminded the three of them.

"Yes, she did," McCord replied, "but you, Detective Littleton, promised only that we would be very discreet. Anyway," he finished, "with the need for haste in mind. I grabbed the first appointment Dr. Winters could give us, which happened to be tomorrow." He glanced at Shrader and Womack, "You two hand Manning's CPA the subpoena tomorrow and bring back everything he gives you. Littleton and I will call on Dr. Winters. Somehow, I don't think she's going to be anxious to cooperate."

CHAPTER 41

McCord's prediction proved to be true. Sam and he waited for forty-five minutes in a small, elegant anteroom before they were finally admitted to Dr. Winters's office, which was furnished like a beautiful library, complete with Oriental carpets, dark plank flooring, and tuxedo-style sofas and wing chairs in jade green leather.

With her blond hair caught up in an elegant chignon and her rose-colored Chanel suit, Sheila Winters looked absolutely right for that richly elegant, timeless setting, Sam thought.

"I'm terribly sorry to have kept you waiting," the psychiatrist said after shaking hands with each of them. "I had an emergency this morning and it put me behind."

"We appreciate your giving us your time today," McCord said. "The Manning case is being turned into a tragic farce, thanks to the media."

"You're right," she replied. "I thought things were as bad as they could get for Leigh, until last night when the media started running all those stories about Logan's alleged affairs."

"How is Mrs. Manning handling it? I assume you've spoken to her, since you're close friends."

Very carefully and very clearly, Sheila Winters said, *"As her close friend,* I can tell you that she feels like any other woman would under these circumstances. Two weeks ago, Leigh had a wonderful career, a happy personal life, and a bright promising future. Since that time, her husband mysteriously disappeared, she was in a near-fatal accident, then her husband was found murdered and she became a widow. Two days ago, she buried him with dignity and began the grieving process for a man she loved and respected. Thanks to the media, the world witnessed that funeral, the world witnessed her grief and her dignity, and people sympathized and respected her."

Anger had welled in her voice, and she paused, twisting her gold pen in her long fingers. When she spoke again, her voice was well-modulated and calm. "As of yesterday, thanks to that same media, Leigh's dead husband is now being portrayed as a compulsive philanderer, and she, by inference, is being made to look like a blind, pathetic fool. Even her career is affected, because whether Jane Sebring is lying or not doesn't matter. How will Leigh ever be able to walk back onto the stage with that woman?"

As she finished she looked at Sam, and Sam shook her head. "I couldn't do it. I wouldn't. I would be so angry, so humiliated, and so crushed that I don't think I could hide it."

Sheila Winters smiled and held up her hands in complete agreement. "You've just described how Leigh feels. And how I would feel in her place, too."

"It's always good to know I'm normal in the eyes of a psychiatrist," Sam said.

That made Sheila Winters laugh. "What makes you think psychiatrists are 'normal,' Detective?" she joked.

Satisfied that she'd reached an accord with Sam, she looked at the lieutenant. "Have I answered your question adequately?"

"Yes, but that was just my 'get-acquainted' question," McCord told her. "I have many others."

"I'm afraid I can't answer them. I've already told you everything I legitimately can. Anything else falls under privileged doctor-patient communication."

McCord ignored that. "Logan Manning was your friend as well as your patient," he said.

The gold pen twisted slowly in Sheila Winters's fingers; her polite smile remained in place. She did not confirm or deny it.

"When did he and Mrs. Manning first consult with you, and about what?"

The gold pen continued to twist slowly in Sheila Winters's fingers; her smile became slightly less polite.

"Dr. Winters, I'm sorry—I forgot to give you this. I should have done so before I asked you anything." McCord hadn't forgotten, Sam knew. For some reason, he wanted to get a reading on Sheila Winters. He reached into his navy sport jacket and produced the piece of paper on which Leigh Manning had written her permission, and he passed it across the desk to the psychiatrist.

Sheila Winters slowly laid down her pen and took the paper from him. She glanced at it and handed it back to him. "I'm not going to comply," she said flatly. "For one thing, I don't know if this is actually Leigh's handwriting."

"You have my word as a law enforcement official that it is her handwriting, and that she gave it to us personally four days ago."

"Very well. I'll take your word for it," she said, leaning back in her chair.

"Then will you answer my question?"

She smiled apologetically. "No."

Sam watched the back-and-forth with concealed fascination because she had a hunch McCord had met his match in uncompromising strength of will and determination.

"Why not?"

"Because Leigh Manning was obviously in a precarious mental state four days ago. If she were not, she would never have agreed to this."

"Are you trying to tell me she isn't mentally competent?" McCord asked.

"Of course not, and don't throw phrases like 'mental competence' around with me, Lieutenant. I am simply telling you that four days ago, Leigh was under extreme mental duress for obvious, normal, and understandable reasons."

Sam knew McCord's fear was coming to reality—at any moment, Sheila Winters was going to pick up the phone, call Leigh Manning, and tell her to revoke her permission. "Let me acquaint you with another phrase, Dr. Winters, one I feel even more comfortable 'throwing around.' It's called 'obstruction of justice.' You are willfully interfering with a murder investigation. I haven't asked for your records, but I'm prepared to do that and to wait here while Detective Littleton takes this slip of paper to a judge and gets a subpoena."

Mentally, Sam declared the situation a standoff, but McCord went on the offensive. He handed the slip of paper to Sam. "I'll wait here and keep Dr. Winters company. Find a judge, explain the situation, and bring me a subpoena. In fact, bring me a search warrant, too, in case Dr. Winters wants to carry this battle to its inevitable, tiresome end.

And bring Detectives Womack and Shrader with you to help locate whatever it is we're looking for."

"I'll offer you a compromise," Dr. Winters said, smiling a little.

"I'm not interested in compromise."

"The compromise I'm about to suggest will save us all a lot of wasted time."

"I enjoy wasting time," McCord replied mildly.

She laughed aloud at that. "No, you don't, Lieutenant. You are impatient in the extreme under normal circumstances. However, that verges on free analysis," she joked, "and that violates my principles. Here's what I would like to suggest. Actually, you don't have a choice, because Leigh Manning is due here any moment. Doctor-patient communication is a sacrosanct privilege, a concept that has been repeatedly upheld and protected by courts all over the land."

"So has the concept of obstruction of justice."

"I won't obstruct your justice. When Leigh gets here, I will tell her in front of you that I strongly advise her against authorizing me to breach that privilege. If she listens to me, and revokes that piece of paper you're holding, then that is her right. Isn't it?"

It was, and they all knew it.

"If she still wants to authorize me to disclose information to you, then I'll do it. Deal?"

There was no choice, and McCord knew it. He smiled slowly, the scar in his face deepening. "How can I argue with such flawless logic and reasonable negotiating?" he said lazily. "I'm curious, though . . ."

"I'll bet you are—" she agreed, smiling, and Sam wondered if she was witnessing some sort of high-level flirtation taking place between two very complex and inscrutable intellects. She felt a little left out. She also felt certain that Leigh Manning would revoke her permission.

"I'm curious about why Leigh Manning is coming here today."

"Oh, that's a question I can answer. She's been hounded by the press. They're staked out at the front of her building, and she hasn't been out of her apartment in more than a week, except to attend her husband's funeral. I threatened to kidnap her if she wouldn't have lunch with me today. For understandable reasons, she couldn't face going to a restaurant, so I told her we'd order in."

"I'm sorry to be ruining your lunch plans, Doctor," McCord replied.

She smiled at his foolishness. "You won't be ruining our lunch, Lieutenant. It will only take two minutes for Leigh to revoke her permission."

She was wrong about that, Sam realized with surprise a few minutes later. Although Leigh Manning looked deathly pale and terribly fragile, she refused to take Winters's advice. Wearing camel slacks and a white silk shirt, she sat down on one of the leather sofas and curled her legs up beneath her, looking like a young, vulnerable girl, without makeup or pretense. Her auburn hair fell forward against her translucent cheeks, and her huge eyes were the color of a blue-green sea on a sunny day. "They need answers, Sheila. Tell them whatever you know."

"Leigh, I am adamantly opposed to this. You're not thinking clearly."

"I came here today because I need answers, too. Please tell the detectives whatever they want to know about my husband, and I'll listen, because I don't know who he was, either. Not really. I only thought I did."

"All right." Sheila Winters rubbed her forehead for a moment, then she looked at Leigh. "Let me try to phrase this in the best way I can."

"Don't worry about sparing my feelings. What you don't tell me, I'm sure to read in the newspapers tomorrow or the next day. I asked you at the apartment if you thought Logan was having an affair with Jane Sebring, and you said no."

McCord interrupted. "When did you ask Dr. Winters that?"

Sheila Winters glared at him, and she answered in unison with Leigh Kendall. "After the funeral."

"What made you ask it?"

Instead of resenting his tone or his interruption, she lifted her eyes to his and answered him with quiet humility—as if she no longer noticed or cared about such meaningless annoyances. "The papers were full of what I thought were malicious rumors about that."

"Lieutenant McCord!" the psychiatrist warned. "You can question Mrs. Manning at your leisure. I can't stop you, but I can stop you from doing it in my office. Now, you wanted this question-and-answer session, so let me give the answers and get this over with. This is just about the most difficult thing I've ever had to do."

Having said that, she looked at Leigh Manning and her expression softened. "Leigh, Logan was a much more complex man than I originally thought when the two of you first came to see me. He was more complex, more troubled, and at the same time, more . . . basic in his logic than I imagined. I'm trying to put this in the most simplistic terms instead of resorting to psychobabble."

Reluctantly, Sheila Winters switched her attention to Sam and McCord, and explained, "Logan Manning was from an old, wealthy, and aristocratic New York family. Unfortunately, by the time Logan came along, his grandfather had squandered a major fortune, and the Manning family was reduced to a state of genteel poverty. Nevertheless, because of his family's social connections—and some money contributed by a wealthy great-aunt—Logan was sent to the same prestigious private schools his forebears had attended. There was one major difference: Logan was impoverished in comparison to his peers, and they all knew it.

"As a youth, Logan couldn't vacation with his school friends; he couldn't even bring them home. He grew up feeling ashamed of who he was and what he had. His father died when he was little, and his mother never remarried, so he had no male figure to encourage him or straighten out his priorities. What he did have was an endless supply of tales told to him by relatives about the Manning family in its heyday, stories about fabulous mansions and priceless antiques, stories about handsome Manning men who were notorious for their global gambling, whoring, and business accomplishments.

"From the time he was a very young boy, Logan began daydreaming about becoming one of those legendary Manning men and restoring the family fortune and prestige. He certainly inherited their good looks, and he also inherited the brains and ambition to go with it. He achieved everything he set out to achieve. . . ."

She paused and looked long and sadly at Leigh. "But it was never enough to make him feel good about himself. His insecurities were so deep that he needed to prove himself over and over again in every arena. You said yourself there wasn't enough money in the world to make Logan feel secure, and you were right. And in an ironic twist of fate, Leigh, you were a large part of the reason he continued feeling terribly insecure."

"How did I do that?"

"By being who you are. By being talented and admired and famous. Logan helped put you in the limelight, but he ended up being cast into the shadows in comparison to you, and his ego was too fragile to deal with that at times. So he needed to reinforce that ego."

"With other women," Leigh acknowledged shakily.

"Yes. The only area where Logan felt truly superior to you and everyone else was in his looks and his sex appeal."

Leigh said exactly what Sam had been thinking. "You're a psychiatrist, you knew the problem, and he came to you for advice. Why couldn't you have helped him?"

"Good question—direct and simple. Here's the answer in the same vein you asked the question: I'm a psychiatrist; I can usually fix what's broken in a patient, but I cannot create qualities that are not there, and are not desired by the patient. To put it in plain, simple English, Logan had a weak character, Leigh. When high-minded concepts like integrity and loyalty were contrary to his own personal wishes, Logan was fully capable of ignoring the concepts. If it's any consolation, he felt terribly guilty afterward, and vowed never to repeat the deed. But when an opportunity came along, if it happened to coincide with some personal need of his, then his needs came first. Not always, but all too often."

Sam's heart ached when Leigh Kendall bowed her head in absolute, abject despair. Her voice broke as she said, "Did Logan ever tell you anything about anyone . . . or anything . . . that would give us a clue about why he was murdered?"

"No, Leigh, he didn't."

"Do you know why he might have felt a need to buy a gun?"

"No, I'm sorry, I don't."

Logan Manning's widow stood up then, her pride and self-esteem ravaged in front of two strangers, her trust betrayed, her dreams shattered, and as Sam watched, she made a visible effort to straighten her shoulders and lift her trembling chin. She was fighting so hard to hold on to her composure that Sam thought she would surely walk out of the office—or run out of it—but instead of doing that she stopped in front of both detectives and politely said, "I have to leave now. Do you have everything you need?"

"Pretty much, I think," Sam said, looking at her tear-brightened green eyes.

When she left, no one spoke for several minutes, and Sam had the feeling that Sheila Winters was fighting very hard to get her own emotions under control. "She'll be all right," the psychiatrist said, although Sam didn't know whether she was trying to convince them or herself.

"Do you think she knew he was cheating on her?" McCord asked.

"She knew Logan was capable of it, because he did it a few years ago and Leigh found out. She was devastated."

"What about recently? Do you think she suspected anything?"

Sheila lifted her face and looked at him in angry disgust. "You saw her? What do you think?"

THEY WERE BARELY out of the office when Sam said fiercely, "I think it's too bad that whoever shot Logan Manning didn't torture him first!"

A laugh rumbled in McCord's chest, but he was smart enough not to make some sort of joke.

"Do you know what else I think?" Sam said, raising her eyes to his.

"No," he said, and for a second, Sam thought his gaze dropped to her mouth. "What else do you think, Sam?"

"I think that Leigh Manning had absolutely nothing whatsoever to do with her husband's death. Nothing."

"It's interesting that you got that out of our interview

upstairs. Do you know what I heard up there? I heard motive. Lots of legitimate motive."

"Then go after it, Lieutenant. But while you're trying to make the puzzle fit your picture, I'm going to try to make it fit mine."

CHAPTER 42

Courtney Maitland glanced at the cards O'Hara had just dealt her and laid her first discard on the kitchen table. "Why do you keep looking at your watch?" she asked him.

O'Hara heaved a gusty sigh and stood up. "I guess I'm nervous. I did something I maybe shouldn't have done."

"That's how I live my life, O'Hara. On the edge. It's exciting."

"This isn't about my life. I butted into Mrs. Manning's life today. It's been two and a half weeks since Mr. Manning's funeral, and she won't go out, she won't see her friends or talk to them on the phone. She talks to Mr. Solomon once in a while, but except for Hilda, Brenna, you, and me, she doesn't see anyone else. A lot of people still call and want to talk to her. I think most of them just want something to gossip about."

Courtney sobered. "Leigh doesn't know who she can trust anymore."

"Yeah, and who can blame her?" He took a beer out of

the refrigerator for himself and a Coke for Courtney and returned to the table.

He glanced at his watch again. "Mrs. Manning had a late appointment with a doctor who wanted to check her over after the accident. It's after five, and I figured she'd be home about now."

"Why didn't you drive her?"

"I was picking up some things for Hilda when Mrs. Manning remembered she had the appointment, and she needed to leave before I could get back."

Courtney waited until he'd taken a swallow of beer before she said impatiently, "What does all that have to do with butting into her life?"

"Because a little while ago, I told somebody that Mrs. Manning was going to be home this evening. He's called a couple of times, but she wouldn't see him, and I thought it might do her good if she did. I told him to come over."

Courtney looked uneasy. "I don't know if you should have done that."

"Me neither, but it seemed like the right thing to do when I did it."

"Everything wrong I've ever done has always seemed like the right thing to do at the time." She picked up her cards again. "So, who did you invite up here?"

"Michael Valente."

She gaped at him. "Why did you do that? The last time he was here, nobody was happy about it. You said yourself that Leigh doesn't even know the guy."

"I did it because the last time Mrs. Manning smiled was the night Valente was here. I know he's got a bad reputation, but here's why I decided he could come over—"

"I can't believe you discarded that six of hearts when you saw me pick up the six of clubs a second ago." Without waiting for a reply, she picked up his discard and simultaneously said, "Why did you decide he could come over?"

"Because the night he came here with the pizza, Mrs. Manning realized that she'd known him a long time ago. When she was in college, Valente worked in a grocery store right near where she lived, and his aunt used to make shrimp pizzas for her. One night, he even saved her from a mugging."

"Why did it take her so long to recognize him, or at least his name?"

"He had a beard back then, and she only knew his nickname. I can't remember what it was, but it means 'hawk' in Italian."

"Really?" Courtney said, drawing a card and discarding it. "So that probably explains why he carried her down to the cabin in the snow that day, and why he came to her rescue right away with his helicopter. He's sort of like . . . what—an old boyfriend?"

"I'd have probably said they were just old friends, but Valente did something the night he was here that really made me wonder."

Fascinated, Courtney prodded him for an answer when he paused to study his cards. "What did he do?"

"A couple hours after the cops broke the news to Mrs. Manning about her husband, I got up to turn out the lights and lock up. I thought Valente had left long before, but he hadn't. He was sitting all alone on a chair near the hall by her bedroom, and he was kind of looking down at the floor like he was sad and real tired. It was sort of like he was on . . . I don't know . . . guard duty." He drew another card. "Gin!" he cried happily, and the telephone rang at the same time.

He rushed to answer it, and returned to the table. "Valente is on his way up here."

"Great!" she proclaimed.

"Yeah, well, I hope Mrs. Manning is half as happy about it as you are."

"I'll let him in while you—do whatever you need to do," she said, and was out of the kitchen, en route to the front door, before Joe could protest.

In her haste, Courtney yanked the apartment door open with enough extra force to turn the simple act into an exaggerated theatrical flourish—one that caused Valente to step back and momentarily look at the apartment door as if he had gotten off on the wrong floor.

"I'm Michael Valente," he explained.

"I know you are. I'm Courtney Maitland," she said, offering her hand.

For a moment, he looked as if he wasn't going to shake hands with her; then he changed his mind and did it. "How do you do," he said perfunctorily.

"I do very well," she replied, "although I have no idea what it is I do well. The other thing that always baffles me is why people ask each other that question. It always strikes me as corny and meaningless. How does it strike you?"

He eyed her for a long moment, standing in the foyer, his coat over his arm. "It strikes me as corny and meaningless."

"Why do you suppose that is?"

"Because," he said bluntly, "it *is* corny and meaningless."

Courtney had been prepared to either like him or dislike him, but she had not expected to find him . . . interesting. She rarely met anyone over thirty who was interesting, and according to her preliminary research, Michael Patrick Valente was not only over thirty, he was one year past forty. He was also one quarter Irish—on his grandmother's side—three inches over six feet in height, and he preferred custom-tailored suits from Savile Row. He had a hard jaw, thick dark hair, straight brows, and interesting eyes—eyes that were narrowed on her at the moment.

"Are you planning to invite me in?" he asked.

"Oh. Yes, of course. I'm sorry. I was thinking about something else. Do you play gin?"

"Is Mrs. Manning home?" he replied.

"Not yet, but O'Hara and I are in the kitchen. Why don't you join us there?"

He looked relieved at the mention of O'Hara's name, and after handing her his coat to hang up, he accompanied her to the kitchen. Courtney stopped in the doorway and let him precede her; then she leaned against the doorframe as she had the last time he'd been there and studied his profile at her leisure. She knew he'd served four years in prison for manslaughter and spent his free time there reading law books in the prison library. She also knew he'd spent the next six years working and earning an undergraduate degree with a dual major and a 3.9 average from the State University of New York at Stony Brook and the two years after that getting his MBA from Harvard.

O'Hara started forward as soon as he saw Valente walk into the kitchen, but Valente was blocking O'Hara's view of Courtney in the doorway. "I'm sorry," O'Hara said, "but Mrs. Manning isn't home yet, and so I never got a chance to tell her you were coming over."

"That's okay," Valente said. "I haven't any plans for the evening." He reached out and shook O'Hara's hand, a smile lurking at his mouth. "Are you playing governess, as well as bodyguard and chauffeur these days, Bruiser?"

"You're talking about Courtney," Joe guessed. "No, I'm playing gin rummy with her and for once I'm not getting my ass whipped. We may have a while to wait before Mrs. Manning gets back. You want some coffee or wine or something?"

"Coffee sounds good. Black."

Joe poured coffee into a cup and handed it to him. "You want to wait in the living room?"

"No, I like it better in here."

"It's real cozy," he agreed. He glanced uncertainly at the table where he'd been playing cards with Courtney, as if he couldn't decide whether it was more appropriate to clear the cards away for the guest in the kitchen, or to invite the guest—who was actually a coconspirator—to join Courtney and him at the table.

Courtney had absolutely no interest in being appropriate and had a very strong desire to capitalize on this golden opportunity to spend time with a notoriously illusive billionaire with a criminal record and a history of ongoing clashes with the legal system. "Why don't we all sit down at the table," she suggested.

Relieved that she'd made the decision for him, O'Hara picked up his beer from the counter and walked over to the table. Valente sat down next to him and casually propped his elbow on the back of his chair. Courtney sat down next to Valente and opposite O'Hara. In the awkward silence that briefly followed, she decided the best way to accomplish her immediate goal was probably to force both men into a state of relaxed congeniality, whether they wanted it or not. She picked up the deck of cards, split it, and let the cards cascade into place with a whoosh and a snap. She repeated the process twice more, and dealt O'Hara a hand.

"Go on with your game," Valente politely urged the chauffeur. "I didn't mean to interrupt it."

"You can play the winner," Courtney informed Valente, giving him no choice in the matter. She dealt out the cards to O'Hara, but all her conversation was aimed at Valente. "Joe was telling me that you and Leigh are old friends?"

When Valente didn't answer, she was forced to look up

inquiringly from her hand. Valente's only response was to quirk one eyebrow at her.

"If I remember correctly," she continued a moment later, "Joe said you knew each other when Leigh was in college." When he still didn't answer, she glanced sideways at him and drew a card. This time, he raised both brows and looked speculatively at her.

"I think Joe also mentioned that—at some point—you saved Leigh from a mugging?" Frustrated by his silence, she discarded the card she meant to keep. "Is that right?" she demanded a little testily, looking at him. The lights in the kitchen were slightly dimmed, but there was enough light for Courtney to catch the spark of amusement in his eyes. O'Hara drew his next card; then Courtney drew hers, started to discard it, rolled her eyes in frustration, and laid down her hand instead. "Gin!" she declared.

Valente's shoulders started to shake with laughter. Confusion and uncertainty were emotions Courtney was accustomed to evoking in others; she wasn't accustomed to experiencing them personally. The sensation was so novel that she rather admired Valente for putting her into that unaccustomed emotional state; however, she had no idea what he was finding so amusing, and she did not intend to let the status quo continue.

She picked up the deck and shuffled the cards. "Let's make it interesting," she said to Valente, dealing out both hands with the skill and speed of a professional gambler.

Forced into playing gin with her, he slowly removed his arm from the back of the chair, picked up his hand, and lazily inquired, "How interesting?" at the same time his discard hit the center of the table.

He was very quick, trying to rattle her and force her to play too fast. "Twenty dollars a point," she replied, ignoring Joe's horrified gasp, and making her own discard.

"Can you afford to lose that much?"

"Yes," she replied, making her next play. "Can you?"

"What do you think?"

Courtney drew a card, but paused so that she could look at him as she answered. "I think you don't like to lose," she told him. "Not money, not at cards, and not at anything else either." She laid down her discard and waited for him to take the bait and say something informative.

He glanced at her discard and said, "Gin."

"What! I don't believe you!" she exclaimed, leaning forward to look at the cards he'd fanned out for her inspection. She stared in disbelief at a hand that was nowhere near a winning one. "What is that supposed to be?" she demanded, scowling.

"At twenty dollars a point, I'd say that's either a used car or a fur coat for you."

Courtney gazed at him, caught somewhere between irritation and bafflement. "I don't want a car or a fur coat."

"You don't?" he said smoothly, shoving the cards toward her so that she could deal them again if she chose. "Then why are we playing for twenty dollars a point?"

Without taking her eyes from his face, Courtney slowly picked up the cards and began to shuffle them. She smiled because she couldn't help it. She smiled because she thought he was actually quite handsome. She smiled because she thought he was inscrutable, complicated, clever, and very possibly dangerous. She smiled because she thought he was awesome. But then a thought hit her and she suspended her good opinion, pending his answer. "By any chance," she said, watching him closely as she dealt the next hand, "did you do that because you thought I couldn't afford to pay twenty dollars a point if I lost?"

"No. I imagine your allowance is big enough to cover your gambling losses."

"Why, specifically, would you think that? It can't be the way I'm dressed."

"Aren't you Noah Maitland's sister?"

Courtney nodded. "How did you know?"

"I've met your brother."

A horrible thought struck Courtney, one that made her forget all about her cards. "Noah didn't—testify—against you, or anything, did he?"

He laughed, and it had a deep, rich sound, but a rusty one, too, as if he didn't laugh often. "No. He and I were involved in a deal together a few years ago, and I saw you when I was meeting with him at your house in Palm Beach."

A sigh of relief escaped her, and she settled down to play gin with a man who had turned out to be a challenge. A difficult challenge. A surprisingly difficult challenge.

CHAPTER 43

Leigh let herself into the apartment and heard Courtney's laughter coming from the kitchen as she hung her coat in the front closet. O'Hara was laughing, too, and the sound of their raised, cheerful voices sounded foreign and out of place. Laughter had been absent from her home in the month since Logan left for the cabin in the mountains.

Christmas had passed by two days ago with nothing to mark it, not even a Christmas tree or the garlands trimmed in ribbon that she usually draped across the mantel at Christmastime. The mantel was empty except for stacks of unread Christmas cards. She'd ordered gifts from the Neiman Marcus Christmas catalogue for Hilda, Brenna, Courtney, and O'Hara. She hadn't bothered with anyone else.

Somber silence had hung over her home like a giant pall, thick and heavy, but protective, too, insulating her from the need to talk, or express her feelings, or even acknowledge them. She no longer wept. She had no tears left, no feelings to burst to the surface and suddenly wound her. She was numb now, and safe. Quiet.

At this moment, however, that insulating buffer of quietude was being disrupted by laughing voices in the kitchen, and she followed the sound.

O'Hara saw her first and jumped up guiltily, almost overturning his chair. "Would you like some hot coffee?" he burst out. "We got company. Look who's here—"

Leigh stopped short, taken aback by the sight of Michael Valente, who'd evidently been playing cards with her chauffeur and her teenage neighbor. He stood up slowly, a solemn smile on his face—a man who knew he shouldn't be where he was, but who was determined to be there anyway. She read all of that, and more, in his expression as he walked toward her, but she felt unable to do anything except stand there when he stopped in front of her.

He lifted his hand, and she started to raise hers for what she thought would be a handclasp, but his hand bypassed hers and settled under her chin. With narrowed eyes, he turned her face slightly to the right, then slightly to the left, inspecting it, and she simply let him do it, her own eyes wide and unblinking.

He was an old friend, and by now she already knew the sort of murmured concerns that old friends—the true ones and the false ones—all said to her when they saw her. She waited for him to say "How are you feeling?" or "Are you doing all right?"

Instead, he dropped his hand and stood there, his broad shoulders blocking her view of the room, his deep voice tinged with a pretense of hurt feelings. "I haven't seen you in weeks. Aren't you going to ask me how I feel, Leigh?"

Her eyes widened in disbelief, and shock tore a forgotten response from her. Leigh laughed. She held out her hands to him, but her laughter dissolved as suddenly as it swelled to the surface, leaving behind a sudden, overwhelming impulse to cry. She clamped down on the impulse, and forced herself to keep smiling. "I'm sorry," she said. "How are you feeling?" It took her a moment to realize he was switching roles completely with her.

"I feel like hell," he said somberly, "I ache all over, but mostly inside. Everything I believed in turned out to be wrong, and the people I trusted betrayed me. . . ." To her horror, Leigh felt tears flood her eyes and spill over her cheeks as he continued quietly, "I can't sleep, because I'm afraid I'll start dreaming. . . ."

She reached up to brush the tears away, but he pulled her forcefully into his arms and pressed her face against his chest. "Cry, Leigh," he whispered. "Cry."

Moments before, he'd made her laugh; now she found herself sobbing helplessly, her shoulders shaking with the force of her pent-up anguish. She would have pulled away and run, but his arms tightened around her when she tried, and his hand cradled her face, his fingers tenderly stroking her cheek. "It's going to be all right," he whispered when the flood of tears finally began to recede. "I promise," he added, offering her a handkerchief with one hand.

She took it and leaned back in the circle of his arms, wiping her eyes, too embarrassed to look at him. "I don't think I'm going to be able to get over this," she admitted.

He put his hand beneath her chin and tipped it up, forcing her to meet his gaze. "You aren't suffering from terminal cancer or any other incurable disease, so you *can* get over it. You have the power to decide how long, and how badly, you're willing to go on suffering for your husband's betrayals and your misplaced love."

She sniffed and wiped her eyes. "I've gotten angry at times, but it doesn't help."

"Anger is nothing but self-inflicted torture."

"Then what am I supposed to do?"

"Well, for your own self-respect, I think you might feel better if you fought back and got even with him."

"Fine!" she said tearily. "Get a shovel and we'll dig him up!"

He laughed, and pulling her close, he laid his jaw against the top of her head. "I like your spirit," he said with tender amusement, "but let's start with something a little less strenuous."

Self-conscious about standing in his embrace, Leigh stepped back after a moment and managed a halfhearted smile. "What do you recommend?"

"I recommend that you have dinner with me tonight."

"All right. I'll ask Hilda to fix—"

"Not here."

"Oh, you mean a restaurant? I don't think— No, really—"

He looked as if he wanted to argue, but she shook her head, appalled at the thought of having to face the prying eyes of strangers and the inevitable pack of reporters who would surely turn up before they finished eating. "Not a restaurant. Not yet."

"Here, then," he agreed.

"I'd like to shower and change clothes," she said. "Would you mind waiting for me for a half hour?"

The question seemed to amuse him. "Not at all," he said with exaggerated formality. "Please take all the time you need."

Disconcerted by the hint of mocking humor in his reply, Leigh headed toward her bedroom on the opposite side of the apartment.

Michael watched her walk away. *Did he mind waiting a half hour for her?*

Not at all.

He'd been waiting years for her.

Belatedly recalling that he'd been playing cards with O'Hara and Courtney Maitland when Leigh walked into the kitchen, he turned abruptly. Courtney was staring at him, transfixed; O'Hara was standing beside his chair, frozen in the same position he'd been in when he first announced to Leigh that Michael was there.

Shoving his hands into his pockets, Michael lifted his brows and returned their stunned gazes in wordless acknowledgment of what he knew they were thinking.

Courtney finally reached for her purse and slowly stood up. "I have—" She paused to clear her throat. "I have to go now."

Her words seemed to release O'Hara from his own paralysis. "I'll tell Hilda to fix a nice dinner," he said, sidling along between the island and the kitchen counter, toward the rear hall.

Courtney started past Michael, then paused and looked searchingly at him.

"Yes?" he prompted her after a moment.

She shoved the strap of her purse onto her shoulder and shook her head at whatever she'd been thinking. "Good night," she said instead.

"Good night."

As she reached for the service door that opened from the kitchen into the elevator foyer, she glanced over her shoulder at him one more time, and when she spoke she no longer sounded like a flippant teenager. "Leigh told me once that she loves to sit in front of a roaring fire in the fireplace."

CHAPTER 44

Michael tossed another log onto the fire he'd built in the fireplace and used the poker to move it back farther on the grate. In the dining room, Hilda was setting the table for dinner. Straightening, he brushed off his hands and stood up just as Leigh walked into the living room wearing a long, belted cream wool dress with large covered buttons down the front, a wide collar, and full sleeves.

It reminded him of a dressy robe until he realized that was purely wishful thinking.

"You've built a fire," she said as he handed her a glass of champagne.

Her auburn hair was loose at her shoulders, shiny in the firelight, more red than brown in that light.

"Champagne?" she asked, lifting questioning eyes to his.

"It seemed appropriate for such a special occasion," Michael said.

"What occasion is that?"

In answer, he touched his glass to hers and made a toast. "To a new beginning. To fighting back—Phase One."

"To Phase One," she declared with a brave smile, and took a sip of champagne. "What was Phase Two again?"

"That's the getting-even phase."

She didn't ask for the details of Phase Two, and he was glad, because she wasn't ready to hear them, let alone put them into practice.

"I've been thinking," she said.

Michael looked at the luminous eyes that had mesmerized him fourteen years ago, and he watched her reach up and comb her heavy hair off her forehead with her fingers. He remembered the gesture as clearly as he remembered that in bright daylight her eyes were aquamarine, but in other light—like now—they turned the deep blue-green of zircons. He remembered the attentive way she listened, with her head tipped slightly to the side, as it was now. His gaze dropped to her lips, and he remembered the way she looked a month ago, coming toward him in that little red dress—leggy and sophisticated and gracious. "What is it that you've been thinking about?"

"I'd like to make a deal with you," she said as he raised his champagne glass to his mouth.

He paused warily. "What sort of deal?"

"I would like us to agree that tonight we will not talk about Logan. If I start to do it, I'd like you to stop me. Agreed?"

The night was looking better and better. "Agreed."

"Can I choose what we talk about instead?"

"Absolutely."

"And can we agree we'll talk completely openly and honestly?"

"Yes."

"Promise?"

Michael's guard went up again, but it was way too late. He'd already agreed. "When I said 'yes,' that constituted a promise."

She took a sip of champagne to hide her smile. "You look awfully uneasy."

"Because I *am* uneasy. What is it you want to talk about?"

"You."

"That's what I was afraid of."

"Are you going to back out?"

He looked at her and said firmly, "You know I'm not."

She glanced around him at the dining room table, where Hilda was lighting clusters of candles. "What are we having for dinner, Hilda?"

"Lasagna. It's in the oven. I've made a fresh Caesar salad to go with it."

"We'll serve ourselves," Leigh told her. "There's no need for you to do anything else when you're finished setting the table." To Michael she added, "Hilda's lasagna is divine. She must have made it in your honor because you're Italian."

"I made it for *you*, Mrs. Manning," Hilda said bluntly, "because it's the most fattening dish I could think of. Mr. Valente?"

Michael turned. "Yes?"

"Be sure that fire is out when you leave," she warned him. "And don't get any ashes on the carpet."

Michael was both startled and amused by her tone, and Leigh understood why. As soon as Hilda made another trip to the kitchen, Leigh lowered her voice and said, "Hilda does not abide dirt in any form, and she bosses us all around. She is also totally loyal to me."

She was worried about his feelings, Michael realized, and he wanted to pull her into his arms. Even with her life in shambles, she was thoughtful and kind and courageous. He wanted to tell her how proud he was of her. Instead he made small talk with her until Hilda announced that they could eat whenever they wished and that she was going to her room for the night.

"Shall we go into the kitchen?" Leigh suggested.

On the center island, Hilda had put out a bowl of cooked jumbo shrimp in an icy nest, surrounded with lemon wedges and parsley. Leigh pulled two wrought-iron stools out from beneath the island and perched on one. "Hilda is out of earshot, and your reprieve is officially over," she warned him, smiling. "Let's talk about you now."

The champagne he'd been pouring for her was having the effect he'd hoped it would. Her smile came more readily, and her eyes no longer had a wounded look. "Where do you want me to begin?"

"Begin when they started calling you Hawk."

"You already know how I got that nickname," Michael told her bluntly. "I was the lookout. Are you trying to find out about my early life of crime?"

She hesitated, and then nodded. "Yes," she said simply. "I guess I am."

He walked to the other side of the island and leaned his hip against the counter behind him. "In that case, I'm going to add an amendment to our bargain." Nodding toward the bowl of shrimp in front of her, he said, "I'll talk about all that, but you have to eat while I do it."

She picked up a shrimp and dipped it in cocktail sauce, and he kept his part of the bargain. . . .

"I was about eight and my parents were still alive when Angelo tagged me with the nickname. He was eleven and a born leader with a devoted group of followers, including me, and also my best friend, Bill, who lived next door. Bill and I started out with hubcaps, but within three or four years, we were helping Angelo and his guys heist anything on the street that was moveable and saleable. We spent the rest of our time helping them 'protect our turf,' with fistfights at first, but by the time we were in our teens, knives were the weapon of choice—among other things."

When he paused, Leigh leaned forward. "Go on with your story."

"Have another bite of shrimp."

She obeyed automatically, and Michael stifled a grin at how intent she was on hearing the tale. "When I was about sixteen, we made a little foray into the turf of another, much bigger gang, and in the fight that followed, I got cut up pretty badly. Angelo pulled two guys off me, and he nearly died from the wounds he got. We were the only ones there when the cops arrived, and of course, we both got busted."

"Was that the first time you were arrested?"

"No, but it was the first time I nearly got killed, and I didn't like it. I was supposed to be the 'idea man,' the brains behind Angelo's operation, but," Michael admitted, "I was not cut out to be an active participant."

"Why do you say that?"

"Because I hated the sight of blood, particularly my own, and I didn't see the point of wasting it."

Leigh giggled in spite of herself and took a sip of champagne and another bite of shrimp. "You were living with your aunt and uncle by then. What did they think about the trouble that you and Angelo were getting into?"

"My uncle died of a heart attack a year after my parents were killed, and my aunt couldn't control Angelo or me. She didn't even believe we were doing the things we were getting busted for doing. She thought the cops were persecuting us."

"What about Bill's parents? What did they do when he got busted?"

"They called Bill's uncle, who was a lieutenant with the NYPD, and he got Bill off, and also made sure there was no record of the bust. Bill was the only one of us without a police record, thanks to his uncle. What made that so ironic was that Bill was probably the meanest hothead in the neighborhood, but he was very small and slight, so neither his parents nor his doting uncle could believe he was as bad as the rest of us.

"As time went on, it began to infuriate Angelo that we all had rap sheets, except for Bill, and Angelo started cutting Bill out of everything we did; then he put the word out on the street that Bill was a snitch."

"How did you feel about Bill getting off?"

"I wasn't nearly as hostile about it as Angelo."

"Because you were—what?—more reasonable?"

"No, because in the early years, Bill's uncle also saved my ass along with Bill's several times. Remember, before my parents died, Bill's family and mine were friends. Bill's uncle still harbored sentimental memories of Bill and me in the same playpen while the two families had dinner together."

Leigh leaned her chin on her hand and came up with a heartfelt explanation to justify what he'd been in those days. "There were very good reasons for the way you were and the things you did."

"Really," he said, fascinated. "What were the reasons?"

"Well, you lost your parents at an early age, and you came from a disadvantaged neighborhood. There was poverty, bad schools, bad companions; you were disenfranchised—"

"Leigh—" he interrupted.

"Yes?"

"I was a thug. I was a thug because that's what I chose to be."

"Yes, but the point is, what made you choose that?"

"I chose it because I wanted things for myself, but I wanted to get them my way, not the system's way."

"Go on with your story."

"After my near fatal brush with death, I decided to limit my excursions with Angelo's gang to an occasional one that would be unlikely to get me killed or arrested. I also did a little research and discovered that the moronic teachers at my high school were actually telling the truth: Without an education, I didn't have a shot at the big bucks."

"Yes, but why did you still do some illegal things with Angelo and the gang after that? Why didn't you just give it up and—" Leigh faltered, trying to think of the right term.

"And stick to the straight and narrow?" he suggested.

"Exactly."

He feigned a look of horror. "I had a reputation to maintain! Anyway, it all ended one night in June when I was seventeen."

"How?"

He reached for the bottle of scotch on the liquor tray and poured some into a glass; then he took a long swallow as if to wash away the taste of what he was saying—or about to say. "Bill was pushing drugs by then, but he was using, too, and my cousin Angelo was just as high as he was that night. They got into a fight, and Bill killed him."

"My God."

"The cops came to tell my aunt, and she went crazy with grief."

"What did you do?"

"I went looking for Bill. I found him within an hour, still high. He hadn't washed his hands, and he held them up and showed them to me. They were covered with Angelo's blood."

"And?" she whispered.

He shrugged and took another swallow of his drink. "And I killed him."

Leigh gazed at him in stricken silence, unable to assimilate that he could have done that, that he could have told her this so unemotionally, and then shrugged and taken a drink. Except—she realized—he had taken the drink before he told her. He put down the empty glass and folded his arms over his chest, looking at her as if waiting to hear her conclusion and not particularly interested in it, one way or another. He was no longer the compassionate, civilized man he'd become in her imagination lately; he reminded her of someone else. . . .

He reminded her of the cold, hostile young man she'd known fourteen years ago—a rude, indifferent man who wouldn't give her the time of day. Except he'd evidently cared enough about her even then to remember now that she liked pears and shrimp pizza.

She stared at him, searching his inscrutable features and hard face, and a thought suddenly occurred to her. Hesitantly, she said, "Did you actually mean to kill him?"

Instead of answering, he asked her a question, but there was a barely perceptible softening of his jaw. "Why wouldn't I have meant to kill him?"

"You said he was your best friend. You shared a playpen. You said Angelo was high on drugs and so was Bill. You didn't sound like you thought Angelo was innocent."

"You're right," he said with an odd expression in his eyes. "I didn't intend to kill him. But I didn't intend to make nice with him either. I probably would have beaten him half to death if I'd have been able to get the gun away from him."

"But you couldn't?"

"I should have been able to do it. I was a hell of a lot bigger and stronger than he was, but he was high and I was in a blind rage. He waved the gun at me, and I went for him. The gun went off in the struggle. He died in my arms."

"And that's why you went to prison?"

He nodded and poured more scotch in his glass. "Angelo's funeral was the same day as Bill's. Unfortunately, I wasn't able to attend either one of them."

"But what I don't understand is why you went to prison for what you did. It was self-defense."

"Bill's uncle disagreed, and by then he was a precinct captain. He had a good point—I was a lot bigger than Bill and almost a year older. He held me completely responsible for the death of his namesake and his sister's only child. He told me he was going to spend the rest of his life making sure I never enjoyed mine, and he meant it. William Trumanti is a man of his word."

"William Trumanti!" Leigh exclaimed, leaning forward. "You killed Commissioner Trumanti's nephew?"

"That's right."

"My God . . ."

"I went to prison for four years for it, and I spent every minute of my free time in the library, studying."

"Studying what?"

"Law," he said. "I figured that since I kept running into the law, I needed to find out how to get around it. Later, I decided there were more interesting things to study. When I got out of prison I enrolled in college, and then I went to graduate school."

Leigh got up and uncovered the Caesar salad Hilda had made. "And then what?" she asked.

"I discovered I had a knack for making money—legitimately—particularly in construction at first. I'd grown up on the streets, and I could deal with construction workers on their level, but I also knew how to put together a profitable deal and keep it profitable.

"For the first few years, everything went fine; in fact, it went even better than that. And then my business started getting big, and Trumanti heard about it. The next thing I knew, I was being arrested for 'attempted bribery of a city inspector.' The rest is history. The bigger I became, the bigger and more damaging were the accusations."

He paused, and looked at her hands. She had scooped salad out of the bowl and was holding it in midair, riveted. "Are you planning to put that on a plate?"

"What? Oh. Yes. Go on—then what happened?"

"You know the rest. Trumanti has influential friends on the state and federal level, too, and with my history of arrests, he has no problem convincing a federal prosecutor or a district attorney to look into my affairs. I've spent millions of dollars in legal fees alone defending myself in various courts. It's become a game he and I play—an ugly one. He's dying of cancer now, but it hasn't softened his attitude one bit. *Vendetta* is an Italian word, and he believes in it. Now," he said finally, "have I kept my part of the bargain?"

Leigh gazed at him in silence and nodded, trying to assimilate what he'd said. She had no reason to believe he'd told her the whole truth, but she did believe it. For some reason, she believed it completely. Suddenly she remembered how eager Trumanti had been to help her, how willing to commit all of the NYPD's resources to hunt for Logan. At the time, she'd been too demented with fear to question her entitlement or his actions, but now she wondered if Trumanti had known that Logan had been meeting with Michael Valente, and if that had anything to do with his willingness to help her.

Wordlessly, she picked up the salad plates, and he

reached for the open bottle of red wine that Hilda had left on the counter. As Leigh put the plates on the dining room table, she belatedly realized that he hadn't asked her if she believed what he told her.

She watched him pouring wine into goblets, his proud, hard face an expressionless mask in the candlelight. He wasn't going to ask if she believed him, she realized. He would never stoop to that or try to persuade her to believe him. She remembered the incredible things he'd said to her when she first got home and walked into the kitchen. When she couldn't put her own feelings into words, he'd sensed it and done it for her. . . .

"I ache all over, but mostly inside. Everything I believed in turned out to be wrong, and the people I trusted betrayed me." He'd forced her to cry, because she needed to cry, and then he'd held her in his arms while she did, cradling her face against his chest, his hand drifting soothingly over her back. He'd held his best friend in his arms when he died, too, and she had a feeling he'd been as tender then as he'd been tonight, with her.

He stopped in front of her, waiting to pull out her chair for her, and Leigh gazed up at him, shaken by a myriad of emotions. "Leigh?" he said, his brows drawing together into a frown. "Are you crying?"

Dishonestly, she shook her head; then she said fiercely, "I hate Trumanti!"

He burst out laughing and snatched her into his arms.

CHAPTER 45

A week and a half later, Michael stood in the private elevator foyer outside her apartment with Leigh beside him, waiting for the elevator to take them to the main floor. "Are you sure you don't want me to have O'Hara bring my car around to the alley?" he asked.

"I'm sure," she said.

In the week and a half since he'd told her about his misspent youth, the police had subpoenaed all her husband's business papers from his office at home, and on New Year's Eve, a local television station broke the story that she was supposedly a suspect in her husband's murder. Michael had witnessed her reaction: She'd stood up slowly, her arms wrapped around her middle, her face turning deathly pale. He'd put his arm around her shoulders—and she'd leaned into him, closed her eyes, and turned her face into his jacket. She'd been devastated, but not angry enough to fight back or even make a phone call in her own behalf.

Since then the media speculation had gone completely wild. Depending upon which newspaper, magazine, or news program was doing the story, *everyone* was a suspect—and as of that morning, Michael was now one, too. Up until then, brief mentions of his comings and goings to her apartment had appeared in the press, but that morning the *Daily News* had run a headline that read:

VALENTE IMPLICATED IN MANNING MURDER

According to the story that accompanied it, the police had "new evidence" to support a theory that Michael had killed Logan Manning in order to free Leigh of her cheating husband, take over his business, and then claim Leigh for himself.

Before the *Daily News* article, Michael hadn't been able to convince her to leave the apartment and go out in public for her own sake, but when Leigh saw the *Daily News* headline that morning, she'd been so angry she'd phoned him and invited him out to dinner. She was absolutely certain William Trumanti was responsible for the leak to the press. "It sounds just like the things he's done to you in the past," she told him on the phone, "but he isn't going to get away with it this time. I think the worst thing we can do is hide from everyone as if you're guilty of something, don't you?"

She'd been too humiliated and crushed to stand up and fight for herself, but now she was determined to be his champion, and the realization filled Michael with tenderness. He didn't give a damn about Trumanti or the *Daily News* story, and he assured her of that, but she had a new cause—a distraction from her own woes—and he was willing to let her run with it. "Hiding could be a mistake."

"I think we should go out to dinner together tonight. That is, if you're not busy."

He assured her he was not too busy and told her he'd

pick her up at eight and that he wanted to choose the restaurant.

At a few minutes after eight, she'd walked out of her bedroom, dressed for battle in a long-sleeved black sheath and high heels that showed off her beautiful long legs. Her color was high, her neckline was low, and her eyes were bright. "Trumanti can't frame you for this. I won't let him," she added as she walked straight up to him and turned her back. Her zipper was stuck. She needed help with it, so she lifted up her heavy hair from her neck to show him the problem. The nape of her neck made his mouth go dry.

"Would you do something with that zipper? It's stuck."

To Michael's increasing amusement, William Trumanti was turning out to be quite an ally.

As soon as she stepped out of the elevator into the building lobby with him, a shout went up outside, and photographers and reporters flocked to the front windows. "Are you sure you want to do this?" he asked her worriedly.

She looked up at him, her porcelain skin and high cheekbones tinged with pink, her long-lashed green eyes uncertain, her lovely mouth soft and vulnerable; she looked too fragile to cross the lobby, let alone go near a pack of reporters. That was how she felt inside, he knew. Then she lifted her chin very slightly, gave her head an imperceptible toss, and before his eyes she became serenely calm. Regal. Distant and untouchable. Mesmerized by the unexpected privilege of watching an incomparable actress cloak herself for an important role she needed to play, he started to offer her his arm, but she smiled and shook her head. She was going to walk onstage unaided, unsupported, for this appearance in his behalf. Less than two months ago, she'd been Broadway's reigning queen; now she had abdicated, she was dethroned, but she was emerging from her self-imposed exile. For his sake.

He stayed one step behind her, his chest swelling with pride as she walked gracefully past a blinding barrage of camera flashes, past the same throng of shouting reporters she'd been hiding from for weeks. "Where are you going, Miss Kendall?" one of them called as Leigh started to step into the Bentley.

She'd ignored all the other questions they'd shouted at her, but she turned to answer that one. "Mr. Valente and I are going out to dinner."

"Do you have any comment about the story in the *Daily News* today?" the reporter from the *Daily News* demanded.

"Yes," she said with quiet disdain. "If Commissioner Trumanti, or anyone under him, approved of the slander you printed today, then he is as criminally irresponsible as your newspaper."

Having said that, she slid onto the backseat, and Michael followed her inside. He couldn't believe she'd dared to accuse a powerful newspaper of slander, the commissioner of police of criminal negligence, and the entire NYPD of implied misconduct. Michael knew she'd been shaken by the confrontation, but she hid it perfectly behind a happy face. "I think that went very well," she said, "don't you?"

He swallowed a laugh. "Not bad," he said, straight-faced.

He forgot about all that when O'Hara spoke from the front seat. "We've got a tail, Mr. Valente," he said. "A couple of reporters tried to follow us in a taxi, but I lost them in the second block."

Leigh leaned forward nervously. "The stalker?"

O'Hara shook his head. "This guy's in a dark sedan that makes every move we do. He drives like he's attached to my bumper with a chain, but he thinks he's invisible. That means he's a cop."

In the rearview mirror, O'Hara lifted his brows, waiting for instruction.

"Lose him," Michael ordered.

"Done."

Leigh gasped and grabbed Michael's knee as O'Hara floored the Bentley and sent it angling across three lanes of traffic and shooting into an alley. At the end of the alley he made a hard left turn, and Michael put his arm across the back of the seat, curving his hand around Leigh's upper arm to hold her against him. "Nice driving," he told O'Hara with a chuckle.

O'Hara glanced in the rearview mirror again and grinned. "You better hang on to Mrs. Manning."

He swung the Bentley down another alley, narrowly missing several Dumpsters, and Leigh looked at Michael in laughing terror. "What restaurant are we going to?"

"It's a surprise. You'll like it—trust me."

She nodded. "I do."

She did trust him, Michael knew. Despite all the betrayals she'd suffered, she trusted him completely, and she liked having him close by, not only because she trusted him, but because she was desperate for some sort of continuity in her life, and she'd known him longer than anyone else in New York. A few nights ago, she'd told him that she trusted him now because her instinct had been to trust him years before—back in the days when her instincts had been more reliable.

Michael had instincts, too, and they warned him not to wait much longer before he took her to bed—that it was a mistake to let her create a role of "dear and trusted friend" for him to play, because she would try to keep him locked in that role simply for the sake of safety and continuity.

He wanted to take her to bed before Logan's infidelities

and the public humiliation she was suffering because of them convinced her forever that she was somehow to blame, that she was inadequate as a woman and a wife. She'd already made remarks that indicated she was thinking exactly that.

Most of all, he wanted to take her to bed—because he wanted to take her to bed. He longed to take her to bed.

Her hand was resting on his knee, and he covered it with his own; then he twined his fingers with hers and held her hand on his thigh.

The gesture startled Leigh for a moment, and she looked down at the masculine hand engulfing hers. A treacherous feeling of safety came with that warm hand-clasp. He was her friend—she knew that beyond a doubt. In the past few weeks, she'd learned volumes about him. He had taken on the federal, state, and local law-enforcement authorities time after time and he'd not only beaten them, he'd prospered beyond imagining while doing it.

He had tolerated Trumanti's persecution for all these years, and yet she had a feeling that he wouldn't tolerate anything from anyone else. The unleashed violence she'd witnessed fourteen years ago, when he'd taken on two thugs with knives, had become a lethal, quiet strength, but it was still there, restrained, and just as potent.

The clothes he wore now were elegantly understated and beautifully tailored, but his shoulders were just as powerful and his hips just as lean as they'd looked in the snug jeans and faded T-shirts he'd worn long ago.

There were things about him that she'd never noticed before at all, like the startling glamour of his sudden white smile or the blatant sensuality in the mold of his mouth. Back then, his dark beard and unfriendly disposition had disguised those particular attributes, and his amber eyes had always been hard—except on the night of the fight when they'd taken on a chilling, feral gleam.

She thought back to the night of her party when she'd first seen him standing at the edge of the crowd in her living room, looking as coldly formidable and unapproachable in a dark suit and tie as he'd ever looked with a beard, wearing jeans and a T-shirt. What surprised her even now, though, was that she hadn't instantly recognized his voice the night of her party. That distinctive, rich baritone voice of his had sent an odd little thrill down her spine in the old days, and it still captivated her when he spoke.

When he was with her on New Year's Eve, he told her he'd been married once, briefly, a long time ago, but when she asked him about it, he immediately closed the door on the conversation.

Leigh sensed that he was a loner. She was a loner now, too. She wanted no more husbands, no more lovers or boyfriends.

And at the same time, she felt amazingly close to Michael Valente. He had walked into her life again, not to save it this time, but to help her save her sanity. If he'd given her a kidney, he could not have been more essential, and she could not have been more grateful, or felt closer to him, than she already did.

He hadn't spoken a word in many minutes, and Leigh pulled her gaze from their clasped hands and looked up at him. He was studying her very closely. "What are you thinking about?"

"Kidney donors," she joked; then she shook her head, negating the flippant answer, and quietly told him the truth. "I was thinking about you." His handclasp tightened.

In the East Village they turned onto Great Jones Street, and Leigh looked at him with unabashed delight. "I should have guessed you'd take us back home. I knew this place had changed, and I meant to see it for myself sometime when I was downtown, but I could never quite make myself do it. In my memory, it was so ugly and run-down, but just look at this—!" She leaned forward, gazing at a quaint neighborhood of beautifully restored, nineteenth-century buildings, some of them converted into fashionable boutiques, others into elegant loft apartments.

Angelini's Market was still on the corner, but it was no longer a dark, decrepit little store; expansion and a face-lift had turned it into an inviting gourmet deli and market. Next to it and extending partway down the block was a trendy restaurant/bistro with gaslights outside and the mellow glow of lanterns illuminating the windows from within. Above the door, a discreet brass sign said "Angelini's," and as Leigh stepped out onto the curb and saw it, she stopped short. "I knew a popular restaurant was called 'Angelini's,' but that's a fairly common name, and I thought the place was somewhere south of here."

She put her hand on his sleeve as he started past the market. "Wait, let's go inside for a minute. It's been such a long time."

A few people were waiting in line at the cash register to pay for their purchases, but no one looked their way. Relieved that they weren't going to be recognized, Leigh wandered down the first aisle, then the next one, and finally the one next to that, remembering her trips there when money had been so short, but life had been so uncomplicated. Somewhere behind her, she heard Michael remark with a smile in his voice, "You were right there the first time I saw you."

She turned, surprised that he would remember such a thing. "Really? You remember that?"

"Very clearly." He shoved his hands into the pockets of his cashmere overcoat. "You were wearing jeans and a sleeveless shirt, and you were juggling an armload of cans and fresh oranges. An orange fell off the top of the pile, and when you bent down to pick it up, the next one fell off, then the next one."

"Where were you?"

"Right here, behind you."

"Did you offer to help?"

He gave her a wicked grin. "And spoil that picture? You have to be kidding."

Blissfully unaware of the new, dangerous ground she was treading, Leigh laughed and rolled her eyes. "I should have known it wouldn't be my *face* that you admired. You were very perverse in those days."

"I wasn't completely perverse. I finally walked around in front of you when you spilled the whole pile onto the floor."

"How gallant."

"I wasn't being gallant. I wanted to see what you looked like from the front."

"What did you see?"

"Hair."

She choked, laughing. *"Hair?"*

He nodded. "You'd gotten down on your hands and knees to reach for some oranges that rolled under the shelf, and when you looked up at me, your hair had fallen forward, covering the side of your face. So all I saw was a curtain of shiny reddish brown hair—and two great big laughing eyes of Caribbean green." He shook his head, and said as if to himself, "I had the damndest reaction to those laughing eyes."

"What kind of reaction?"

"That would be a little difficult to explain," Michael said with veiled amusement; then he glanced at his watch. "Let's go next door." She joined him and strolled with him to the end of the aisle; then she faltered and stopped cold, staring at the newspaper and magazine rack directly in front of them.

VALENTE IMPLICATED IN MANNING MURDER

Beneath the *Daily News's* hideous headline were large pictures of Leigh and Michael shown in profile, as if they were looking at each other.

Mesmerized by the timing of the moment, Leigh glanced over her shoulder at the aisle where he'd first seen her picking up oranges. "Just think," she said somberly, "fourteen years ago we were back there. And now"—she nodded at their pictures splashed across the *News's* lurid front page—"and now we're there."

"Together at last," he joked, sliding his arm around her shoulders.

His outrageous quip wrenched a shriek of laughter from Leigh, and she buried her face against his chest, her shoulders shaking with guilty mirth, her hands clinging to his lapels.

Michael tightened his arm around her and smiled at her bent head. He'd finally seen those dazzling blue-green eyes light up with laughter again, and he was having the same old reaction.

CHAPTER 46

The interior of Angelini's restaurant was invitingly "hip," with exposed brick and mortar on parts of the walls and beautiful frescoes depicting the Tuscan countryside on others. The tables were dressed with fine linen, beautiful Italian pottery, tapered candles, and lavish bowls of fresh flowers. Trellises with flowering vines had been placed at strategic intervals to bring a cozier, more intimate atmosphere to what was actually a very large restaurant.

Business was definitely booming, with customers waiting at the maître d's desk and stacked three deep at a long, raised bar at the far left of the entrance. Michael handed their coats to an attendant; then he put his hand on the small of Leigh's back, guiding her through the crowd.

Near the rear of the restaurant, there were three empty tables in a row beside a frescoed wall. "This is perfect," Leigh told him as he sat down across from her at the table in the center of the three. As she reached for her napkin, she noticed the design on the colorful charger in front of her. There's a little village on a mountaintop in northern Italy where pottery like this is made," she said, recalling being there with Logan. By then, after two weeks in Italy, Logan had already run out of patience with everything, even the architecture of the medieval church in the center of the square. He'd hated to travel anywhere outside the U.S. because he felt too far removed from his business interests. "I've been there," she added.

"So have I."

"Really. How long were you in Italy?"

"A month, the last time," he said, pausing briefly while a young man filled their glasses with ice water. "I combined it with an extended business trip to France."

It was easy for Leigh to imagine him now as a world traveler. Leaning back in his chair, with his forearm resting on the table and a thirty-thousand-dollar Patek Philippe wristwatch peeking from beneath the monogrammed cuff of his shirt, he was the personification of relaxed masculine elegance, power, and wealth.

She started to ask him about his travels, but her concentration was derailed by the excited voices of four people at a table across the aisle who'd just recognized them and were discussing the article in the *News*. Leigh's spirits sank a little. "We've been spotted," she said, even though she knew perfectly well Michael could hear them.

"It was inevitable," he said, lifting his wide shoulders in a shrug that dismissed their audience as if they were mere specks of dust on the floor. His attitude amazed and dazzled her. She was an actress; she could pretend, but he wasn't pretending indifference. He *was* indifferent. He was accountable to no one but himself—the self-appointed master of his own destiny.

Their waiter, a jovial, heavyset man in his sixties, bustled up to them with a bottle of red wine that he put down on the table while he shook Michael's hand and was introduced to Leigh as Frank Morrissey.

"I'll tell Marie you're here," Frank told Michael. "She's in the kitchen arguing with the chef." He pressed the corkscrew to the bottle's cork and began expertly twisting it while he proudly explained to Leigh, "I knew Hawk before he was old enough to use a fork. In fact, I was there when he decided to have his very first glass of wine."

He glanced at Michael and chuckled as he drew out the cork. "Do you remember how old you were when I caught you and Billy with that bottle of wine?"

"No, not really."

"How old were they?" Leigh asked eagerly, noting Michael's pained look.

"I can't tell you exactly how old they were," Frank confided with a grin, "but they were too short to reach it without climbing on a stool."

Leigh laughed, reveling in the almost-forgotten feeling of being lighthearted.

"Leigh," Michael said with amused exasperation, "please don't encourage this."

Ignoring him, she looked hopefully at Frank and raised her brows. It was all the encouragement he needed. "I was also there when Hawk and Billy decided to take Billy's uncle's car out for a spin," he said, pouring some wine into Michael's glass for him to taste. "Billy snuck the keys outside, and Hawk got behind the steering wheel. He was only about five, so he had to stand up to see over it."

"What happened?" Leigh asked, looking from him to Michael.

"I started the engine," Michael said dryly, "and Billy turned on the siren."

"You were trying to steal a *squad* car?" She laughed.

"We weren't going to steal it; we were going to borrow it."

"Yeah," Frank interjected, "but a few years later—"

"—a few years later, we stole it," Michael provided with a sigh of frustration.

Leigh covered her laughing face with her hands, looking at him through her fingers. "My God."

Just then a man at the table across the aisle made an audible remark about Leigh being "a very merry widow," and she dropped her hands, sobering.

"I'll be taking care of you myself tonight, just like you wanted," Frank said. "I'll tell your aunt you're here." He turned to leave, but Michael said something to him in a low voice, and he nodded.

Leigh watched him walk away; then she looked at Michael. "The 'Billy' in those stories was Trumanti's nephew, wasn't it?"

"Yes."

"Doesn't Frank know how he died?"

"Of course."

"Then, I don't understand why Frank would bring Bill up, when he clearly has a deep affection for you."

"That's why he does it," Michael said, anxious to move to another subject before her mood was irreparably darkened. "It's his way of proving that he has no doubt that what happened between Bill and me was an accident. Put differently, Frank thinks that the act of hiding something implies guilt—or in his case, a belief in the guilt of another."

"That makes a kind of sense—" Leigh began; then she faltered as she noticed two waiters marching down the aisle carrying a large piece of lattice about four feet wide and eight feet high that was covered with silk ivy. They deposited it on the floor directly beside the table of diners across the aisle who'd been talking about Leigh moments before. It completely blocked the group's view of Leigh, but it also crowded the other table enough to make one of the men complain that he couldn't move in his chair.

"Is that better?" Michael asked.

Leigh tore her gaze from the ivy-covered barrier he'd just had installed, then she looked at the man who'd arranged for it without a qualm or concern for the paying customers' rights or comfort. It hit her then why there were still two empty tables on either side of theirs, even though at least fifty people were still waiting to be seated. She had no doubt that Michael had provided the money for the restaurant, and that if Logan had been in Michael's position, he, too, would have felt bad that she was uncomfortable. However, he would never have done anything that might have had negative financial repercussions, including offending four customers. She looked at her self-appointed protector and felt a surge of gratitude and poignant tenderness that she didn't attempt to hide. "Thank you," she said simply.

Michael looked into those candid, long-lashed eyes and marveled anew that fame and success hadn't changed or hardened her one bit. She could walk past a battalion of reporters with the poise and grace of a queen, but when he'd joked about their pictures on the front page of the *Daily News*, she'd hidden her laughing face against his chest and clung to his lapels. Seated across from him wearing a sophisticated black sheath and expensive gold choker, she was still as artlessly provocative as she'd been in blue jeans, chasing oranges. He smiled at the memory and said, "You're very welcome."

Leigh registered a new, subtle change in his voice, but instead of recognizing it as intimacy, she chose it as a topic. "I can understand why I didn't recognize your face when we met at the party, but I still can't believe I didn't recognize your voice. I should have begun to realize who you were while we were speaking. You had—have—a very distinctive quality to your voice."

"What kind of quality?"

She glanced away, trying to describe it for him, oblivious of any double meaning he might infer from her choice of words. "Very smooth. Very . . . sexy. Very, very deep."

Leaning back in his chair, Michael let his eyes drift over the elegant curve of her cheek and the soft swell of her breasts, his finger slowly stroking the curve of his wineglass.

NEARLY TWO HOURS LATER, Leigh declined dessert while Mrs. Angelini again urged her to have it. "I can't swallow another bite of food," Leigh told her. "I really can't." The meal had been wonderful and so had Michael. He didn't try to make her forget her problems, but he made her feel as if she were completely safe from them—as if nothing could wound her or touch her because he wouldn't let it. It was more than a feeling, it was a fact. Leigh knew it was, as surely as she knew she did not want to examine the reasons for any of it.

Mrs. Angelini leaned down and gave her an impulsive hug. "It is so good to see you smiling. Michael knows how to make you happy, and you know how to make him happy. Life is good."

During their meal, she had appeared at the table several times, hovering over them as if she could not tear herself away. She hesitated again, knowing they were leaving. "Long, long ago, when Michael went to see you in that play, I told him he should tell you how he felt."

With her senses delightfully dulled by fine wine, rich food, and cozy candlelight, Leigh's only reaction was one of surprise that Michael had seen her in a play "long, long ago." "What play did you see?" she asked.

"Constellations."

Stunned, Leigh burst out laughing, and looked from Mrs. Angelini's happy face to Michael's unreadable one. "I don't have to ask him how he felt about that play; it was awful! That was my first professional appearance as an actress."

"The play was bad," he said impassively. "You weren't."

The odd timing finally hit Leigh. "But—but that was back when you were working at the store. I didn't know you liked the theater. You never said you did. Of course," she added with an accusing smile, "you never said you didn't, either. In fact, you never said much of anything to me, period."

Mrs. Angelini looked up at a signal from a waiter and nodded. "I must go in a moment," she told Leigh. "You must stop in the store tonight before you leave."

"We already did. I should have bought pears there," Leigh added. "There's only one other place in New York that has pears as good as yours always were, but they're very expensive."

"Dean and DeLuca?" Mrs. Angelini asked.

"Yes, that's right—"

She nodded. "That is where your pears always came from."

"What do you mean?"

"Every week, Michael went to Dean and DeLuca to buy your pears." She shook her head, remembering. "He was going to school, and he had no money, so he stretched every penny like this—" She made a motion as if she were pulling on a rubber band. "But he wanted you to have the best pears. For you, only the best would do."

Leigh's gaze bounced to Michael, who was leaning back in his chair, an indescribable expression of resignation and amusement on his face, then she said good-bye to Mrs. Angelini and watched her leave.

When she looked at Michael again, he was still lounging back in his chair, but now his gaze was leveled on her, his fingers on the stem of his wineglass, slowly turning it in a circle.

"You went to Dean and DeLuca and bought pears for me?" she uttered.

He nodded imperceptibly, his inscrutable gaze unwavering.

Leigh could not believe the only explanation that came to mind: He'd bought her those pears, and gone to see her in *Constellations*. He remembered their first meeting in the store, right down to where it had occurred and what she had been wearing. Fourteen years ago, he'd rescued her from an attack on the street that he shouldn't have been able to see from inside the store—unless he'd gone to the door to watch her. Or watch out for her? She'd always wondered about her amazing good fortune that night. And now he'd come to her rescue again, at the worst time of her life.

Her heart gave a little lurch at the only possible explanation, but she tried to spare them both embarrassment by pretending confusion when she looked at him. She was, after all, an actress.

"I don't understand," she said.

His deep voice was quiet, but his reply forbade further pretense from either of them. "I think you do."

"No, I'm not sure—"

He didn't like her continued attempt to evade the issue, and he made it clear by putting his napkin on the table and saying, "Are you ready to leave?"

"Michael, please!" She felt admonished, ashamed, wrong. She leaned forward. "You can't expect me to believe you—you had some sort of crush on me?"

In answer, he lifted his brows and regarded her in silence.

Leigh still couldn't believe this was possible. She stared blindly at a tree in the fresco beside her, wondering how the man she'd married could have cared so little for her that he regarded adultery as a recreational sport. While the man she was with had—

Across from her Michael said quietly, "Haven't you had enough lies and deception in your life already?"

She nodded, but focused on a point just to the right of his shoulder because she couldn't quite meet his gaze.

"There's nothing to gain by arguing with me about something that you yourself already know to be true, is there?"

She shook her. "No."

"On the other hand," he said with a smile in his voice, "it was a long time ago."

Leigh suddenly felt silly for making so much out of ancient history. "Yes, it was." Drawing a shaky breath, she shoved her hair back off her forehead and smiled one of those breathtakingly warm smiles that always made Michael want to lean forward and cover her lips with his; then she added, "Thank you for insisting on honesty, and thank you for tonight. It's been a lovely, unforgettable evening in every way."

Michael's body, as well as his intellect, made the decision for him. "The night isn't over."

"What do you mean?" she asked as he got up and came around the table to pull back her chair.

"I'd like you to see where I live."

Leigh's heart slammed into her rib cage.

CHAPTER 47

Leigh slid into the backseat of the Bentley and sat next to Michael in the same place she'd occupied on the way there, but this time, he draped his arm across the back of her seat, a possessive gesture only if he touched her, but he wasn't touching her. For that she was as profoundly relieved as she was confused about his intentions later.

"How was dinner?" O'Hara asked.

"Very good," Michael replied after a pause that told Leigh he'd expected her to say something.

Leigh barely noticed. She couldn't seem to grasp all the implications of the last ten minutes in that restaurant. She hadn't been able to fully adjust to the things his aunt had told her, and she hadn't known how to cope with the way he acted after that. At first, he had looked at her in silence, steadily, neither apologizing nor making light of what he'd done. But when she tried to pretend she didn't understand the meaning of it, he'd made it clear he wouldn't tolerate evasions. On the one hand, he was perfectly willing to put up a wall in the middle of a restaurant to protect her and he was willing to show her the most amazing kindnesses, but he drew the line at a minor little deception.

She did not understand him at all. She honestly couldn't believe he intended to try to seduce her tonight; she couldn't even imagine why he would want to try. And yet . . . there was something about the decisive way he said, "The night isn't over," and "I'd like you to see where I live," that still alarmed her. He was such a magnificent man in so many ways, and she didn't want anything to spoil the amazing fledgling relationship she'd formed with him. She didn't know if it was strong enough yet to withstand a conflict over sex, and she didn't want to put it to the test.

Leigh gave an unsteady sigh and looked out the window. As if he sensed the tumult in her mind, his arm settled around her shoulders, drawing her close for a quick, reassuring hug. He released her almost instantly, but his hand stayed on her upper arm, drifting up and down, soothing.

O'Hara pulled to a stop in front of Michael's building on Central Park West. "Should I wait here?" he asked Michael as he helped Leigh out of the car. "Or should I come back in a while?"

"Don't you ever get a night off?" Michael joked.

Leigh's entire body seemed to lean in the direction of that conversation.

"Nope, never. I'm on duty twenty-four hours a day. It goes with the job."

"Then tonight's your lucky night," he said, closing the car door and the discussion. "I'll bring her home in a taxi and pick up my car then."

CHAPTER 48

He owned the penthouse, Leigh realized as he put his key into that slot inside the elevator. Too nervous to attempt idle conversation, she rode with him in silence to the twenty-eighth floor.

It was pitch black inside his apartment, but instead of turning on lights, he stopped close behind her and put his hands on her shoulders. "May I have your coat?"

His fingers brushed the bare skin of her shoulders when he started to draw it off, and Leigh shivered, pulling it back on. "I think I'll just keep it on. It's a little chilly in here."

"I'll turn up the thermostat," he replied firmly.

Leigh relinquished her coat, trying to adjust her eyes to the darkness as he opened a door next to them and hung up her coat, then his.

"Ready?" he asked her.

"For what?" she asked uneasily.

"For your first look." He stepped to one side, and a moment later a series of lights came on, illuminating what looked like an empty acre of gleaming black marble floors that were divided into two circular areas, each on a raised dais with graceful white columns and arches.

There was no furniture! No furniture . . . no bed. No bed . . . no danger to this extraordinary relationship that she treasured more every day.

"I haven't moved in yet."

Leigh's tension over his intentions evaporated in a rush of happy relief. "This is . . . glorious," she breathed, walking down the foyer steps. "You can see the Hudson from there." She pointed toward the huge dais on the left and looked questioningly over her shoulder at him.

"That's the dining room," he told her. "The dais on the right is the living room."

She turned back toward him, studying the wide curving staircase near the front door, her gaze moving along the intricate wrought-iron railing that had once adorned a palatial old New York mansion, tracing it across the balcony overhead. "It's exquisite."

From there, he guided her toward an arched hallway adjoining the dining room, their footsteps echoing hollowly in the high-ceilinged room.

"You dislike closed-in spaces," Leigh said, smiling. "So do I." A big, inviting kitchen was completely open to a family room whose two glass walls at either end had a view of the Hudson River to the west and overlooked Central Park to the east.

The south wall had a stunning alabaster fireplace surrounded by mellow wood panels and wide carved molding, all of it so distinctive that Leigh recognized it at once. "This came from the Sealy mansion." Clasping her hands behind her back, she slanted him a knowing look over her shoulder. "*You* were the 'unnamed bidder' who paid 'an undisclosed fortune' to get it." She walked over to the windows on the east. "Your views are all breathtaking. I can even see our—my—apartment over there across the park."

As she spoke, Michael walked over to the bar that was recessed in the wall, the family room shared with the dining area. He took off his suit coat and tie, tossing them over a barstool; then he loosened the top button of his shirt. She joined him at the bar, walking toward him with the same unconscious grace that he'd always admired in her. She'd relaxed the moment she realized his apartment wasn't furnished, so he intended to give her a glass of brandy to help her relax before she discovered that his bedroom suite *was* furnished.

She slid onto a barstool, folded her hands, and perched her chin on them. "I had such a lovely time tonight. I love your aunt. It must be nice to live where you grew up, and be able to see people like Frank Morrissey who've known you all your life."

"And whose personal lifetime goal is to assault your dignity every time he has the chance," Michael joked, locating the bottle of brandy. "The night I walked you home, you told me you were from Ohio. Is that where you were born?"

"No, I was born in Chicago. My mother was a nurse and I lived with her there until I was four."

"What about your father?"

"He left her as soon as she got pregnant with me. They weren't married."

"How did you end up in Ohio?" He bent down and located some brandy snifters in the moving boxes behind the bar, and then he straightened, but what she said next made him forget the snifters were in his hands.

"When I was four, my mother was told she had what was then an incurable form of fast-spreading cancer, so she sent me to live with my grandmother in Ohio. She thought it would be easier for me to make the adjustment to living permanently without her if she did it that way, in stages. She came to see us often at first, while she was undergoing an experimental treatment at her hospital, and she kept working as long as she possibly could."

"Then what happened?"

Leigh dropped her hands and spread them, palms down, on the bar as if bracing herself. "One day, when I was five, she hugged me and kissed me good-bye and said she'd see me soon. She didn't realize there wasn't going to be another chance for that."

Leigh's eyes, her face, her gestures—they were so expressive that they'd drawn him into the story with her, just as they mesmerized and drew in audiences that paid to see her perform. But she wasn't performing now, this wasn't a script, and he was a hell of a long way from being an impersonal observer. He had to look down and concentrate on pouring the brandy to break free of the spell. "Do you remember her well?"

"Yes, and no. I remember loving her and being excited to see her. I remember she read me stories at bedtime, and—as odd as this seems under the circumstances—I truly remember her as being happy and gay when we were together. And yet she knew she was dying, that her life was ending before it had a chance to begin."

This time, he met her gaze. "You must have inherited her gift."

"What gift?"

"Her gift for acting."

"I never thought of that. Thank you," she said softly. "I'll never forget it. The next time I walk onto a stage, I'll remind myself that a part of her is right there with me."

A minute ago, she'd made him ache for her; now she

smiled at him and made him feel like a king. Loving Leigh Kendall had always been an emotional roller-coaster ride for him. Long ago, he'd had to stay away from her, and that had been agonizingly hard. Now, he was with her, and he was growing so attuned to her that he could almost feel what she felt. "You grew up in Ohio, then?"

She nodded. "In a tiny little town you've never heard of."

"Were you lonely?"

"No, I really wasn't. Everyone in town knew my grandmother and they'd known my mother when she was a girl. I was 'a motherless waif,' so half the town just sort of— adopted me."

"A beautiful motherless waif," he clarified.

"I've never been close to beautiful, and especially not in those days. I had freckles and fire-engine red hair. There's a picture of me when I was about three, sitting on a sofa, holding my Raggedy Ann doll up to my face." Laughingly, she confided, "We looked like twins!"

Her smile was so contagious that he grinned at her. "How did you end up in New York?"

"My high school teacher decided I had a talent for drama and she made it her mission in life to get a scholarship for me to NYU. When I left for New York, half the town went to the bus station to see me off. They never doubted I'd succeed, and for a long time, I felt driven to do it more for their sake than mine. My grandmother died two years ago, and I stopped going back there."

Michael handed her a glass of brandy and picked up his. "Come with me," he said, "and I'll show you what architects refer to as 'the owner's retreat.' " He waited for her to stand up and take a sip of brandy; then he put his hand on the small of her back. He had waited long enough to taste those soft lips of hers.

She shivered and said, "The first sip of brandy always tastes like gasoline."

Leigh saw his mouth quirk in a half-smile. "Did I say something funny?"

The half-smile became a lazy grin. "No."

"Then—why are you smiling?"

"I'll tell you later."

CHAPTER 49

Anxious to see what he wanted to show her, Leigh walked with him to the far side of the foyer. Concealed from view of the living room by the curve of the staircase were a pair of doors that opened onto a beautiful, sunken sitting area with groupings of comfortable-looking sofas arranged in front of a fireplace.

Earlier, the absence of furniture had reassured her, but after the congenial time they'd spent talking in the family room, she realized her worries had been groundless. Michael hadn't made a single overture, and she wondered why she'd imagined he might be planning to. In the aftermath of Logan's death, her emotions weren't stable and neither, clearly, was her judgment at times.

As she walked down the steps into the sitting room, she looked around and said, "You own a piece of heaven, with the views to go with it."

"Do you like it?"

"I love it." On the right, through a wide arched opening, was what she assumed was the bedroom, but she had a clear view straight through the room to the wide windows beyond, overlooking Central Park, so she wasn't certain. However, on the left, a matching opening showed a glimpse of wood-and-glass-fronted cabinets with recessed lighting, so she assumed that room must be his study. "I thought you said you hadn't moved in?" she asked idly.

"I didn't mean to imply I wasn't living here yet. I had this suite furnished two weeks ago so that I could. The rest of my things will arrive next week, but there isn't much to bring here. I sold nearly everything with my other place," he explained as he walked into the study. Leigh put her brandy glass on an end table, and followed him. "The only significant things I kept are my desk, because I designed it, my books, and some art and sculptures I particularly value."

He touched a light switch and muted cove lighting glowed on the ceiling overheard. Everything in the study was paneled in rich wood the color of light mahogany, even the carved box molding on the ceiling overhead.

His desk was a beautiful piece, large without being massive, with rounded corners. It was positioned on the far left of the room, facing the glassed cases and art niches. Leigh walked over to admire it. "You have many talents," she said as she ran her finger over its smooth inlaid wood.

When he didn't answer, she looked over her shoulder and saw him still standing just inside the room, his left hand in his pocket, a glass of brandy in his hand . . . watching her, his expression solemn, yet amused. Puzzled, she turned away and looked at the books in the bookcases that lined the wall on the right, walking slowly along, scanning titles. "Is there anything you *aren't* interested in?" she asked with a quick smile.

"A few things."

An odd, brief answer, she noticed. Perhaps he was

tired. He seemed to have an inexhaustible supply of energy that enabled him to work all day and stay late at her apartment whenever they had dinner together. "Are you tired?"

"Not in the least."

She moved along the bookshelves until she came to where he was standing; then she turned and walked over to the wall of glass cases and niches facing his desk. "Now, let's see what art and sculptures you particularly value." His tastes were eclectic and refined, she thought—a fabulous Etruscan vase, a splendid marble bust, a magnificent carved lapis bowl inlaid with gold. She came to a small framed oil painting on a stand behind the backlit glass. "Please tell me you haven't had that Renoir here with workmen around the place."

"It's been in a vault until today, and the security system in this room is much more elaborate than it appears."

She looked in the next niche—a very small one—and stared in blank astonishment at what it held. In that niche was a small, inexpensive pewter figure of a knight in armor. Leigh turned halfway around, staring at him.

In response, he lifted his brows, waiting for her to discuss it with him. Inwardly, Leigh was reeling, but this time, she decided firmly, it was up to him to do the explaining voluntarily.

Michael knew she was genuinely shaken, but in a pulse beat, she turned into the actress she was and strolled nonchalantly to the next niche, clasping her hands loosely behind her back. "Is this glass sculpture a Bill Meek piece?"

"Yes," he said, trying not to laugh. She could not have made her attitude more eloquent unless she'd started humming, and she could not have looked sexier than she did in that long-sleeved black sheath that accented the same provocative curves it concealed from his view—temporarily. Very temporarily.

"I love Bill Meek's work. It's so uplifting it's almost spiritual."

He decided to call her bluff. "What did you think of the pewter knight before that?"

Politely she leaned back to reexamine it and said, as if truly looking for something about it to compliment, "It has excellent lighting."

Tenderness shook through him. "I've always admired the subtlety of its message."

"What do you think a piece like that is worth?" she inquired, feigning interest.

"That particular piece is priceless."

"I see." She moved away to another niche, and he watched the way her hair gleamed in the light when she leaned close to study its sculpture. "You know," she mused as if just recalling the incident, "a long time ago, I gave a man a little pewter knight like that one."

"Really? How did he react?"

"He didn't want it. In fact, he didn't want anything to do with me. He never spoke to me unless he had to, and when he did, he was either impolite or caustic."

"What a jerk."

She crouched a little to see into the niche below. "Yes, he was. But for reasons I couldn't understand, it always bothered me that he didn't like me. I kept trying to befriend him."

"He probably noticed that."

"Maybe so. But here's what's really peculiar: Years later, I discovered he'd spent his money to buy me special pears he wouldn't give to me in person . . . and he also went to see me in a play." She moved past the next case, stopping at the one after that, then she came to the end and began slowly retracing her steps. "One night, he risked his life to save mine. Don't you find all that a little odd?"

"On the surface, yes."

"What do you think I should do about it?"

"In your place," Michael said with solemn amusement, as he put his brandy glass on a shelf and started toward her, "I would insist on an explanation."

She sent him a sideways glance beneath her lashes. "Do you have one?"

"Yes." Putting his hand on her arm, he turned her around to face him while he told her the truth: "Fourteen years ago, I wanted you to have the most beautiful pears in the state of New York, and I wanted to be the one who got them for you. I wanted you to talk to me, and I wanted to talk to you. I wanted to keep the gift you gave me, and I wanted to give you gifts. In short," he finished, "I wanted *you.*"

She stared at him in a comic struggle to understand. "And you thought you could make *me* want *you* by being hateful?"

"No," he said, shaking his head firmly in the negative. "I already had a dark past and a gray future; I didn't want you to have anything to do with me. I wanted something much better for you, than me." In a tone of reprimand, he added, "I also wanted something a hell of a lot better for you than that phony, preppy asshole you fell for. I was furious when you told my aunt you were engaged to him. I could not believe I'd actually saved you from me, only to have you end up with Logan Manning."

For several moments, Leigh struggled against simultaneous urges to laugh, cry, and lean up and kiss his lean cheek. "That is the most *bizarre* story I've ever heard," she told him finally with a winsome smile. "And very possibly the sweetest."

Smiling back at her, he put his arm around her shoulders and started walking toward the doorway while he told her something so poignant that she leaned her head against his shoulder: "I've kept that knight somewhere in sight in every office I've had. It was my beacon. In the early years, if I faltered over a choice, I'd look at that little pewter knight and remember that I was 'gallant' in your eyes, and I would make whatever choice was ethical and right." Teasingly, he explained, "I didn't have a lot of opportunities to be 'gallant,' so I settled for ethical instead."

He stopped in the sitting room and perched his hip on the back of a sofa; then he drew her close against his legs and settled his hands on her waist.

Leigh sensed that whatever he wanted to say next was very important, because he seemed to be taking an unusual amount of time thinking about it. Either that, or he didn't know what he wanted to say. Reaching toward the table, she picked up her brandy and sipped it, waiting, noticing how attractive he looked in an open-collared white shirt. His was a sternly handsome face, more stern than handsome, at times, but infinitely more "male" than Logan's face. Michael had strength carved in his jaw and pride stamped on his rugged features. And he had wonderful eyes, eyes that could turn hard or be soft, but they were always knowing and wise. Logan's mind had usually been on something besides the person talking to him; his eyes had strayed along with his thoughts.

Michael didn't notice that she was taking stock of his face; he was trying to decide what to say next. He knew exactly what he wanted to say: *"I'm in love with you. Come to bed with me, and I'll make you forget how badly he hurt you."* The problem was that her husband's betrayal would stop her from believing him if he told her how he felt, just as it was going to stop her from wanting to go to bed with him now.

He was as sure of that as he was that her feelings for

him went much deeper than she wanted to realize right now. There had always been an inexplicable bond between them; some essential understanding that took over as soon as they were together. Years ago, she'd seen something good in him and instinctively forced it to the surface. Even now, when the world understandably believed the worst of him, when a newspaper could make a logical case for the theory that he'd murdered her husband, she—who should have been the most suspicious—was his staunchest supporter.

Unfortunately, those were all emotional issues, and he did not think she was ready to talk about them, because her emotions were already overburdened. But he decided to try that approach first. He slid his hands up her arms, and quietly asked, "Do you believe in fate?"

She laughed, and there was a catch in her voice. "Not anymore." After a pause she wrinkled her nose and said, "Do you?"

That catch in her voice made him hate Logan Manning twice as much as he already did. "I'm Italian and Irish," he joked. "My forebears invented superstition and folklore. Of course I believe in fate." She smiled at that, so he continued lightly, "I believe you were meant to give that knight to me. You were meant to be my beacon."

He watched uncertainty and disbelief darken her eyes, but he kept going anyway, testing her emotional boundaries. "I was meant to watch over you. I was meant to be there for you when two punks tried to attack you. I was also supposed to keep you," he added bluntly, "but I screwed up and let Logan Manning have you. Do you know what else I believe?"

"I'm almost afraid to ask."

Damn Logan Manning. "I believe fate is giving me another chance to do my job."

"And—what do you think your job is?" she asked with wary amusement.

"I told you," Michael said, trying not to sound as solemn as he felt, "my job is to watch over you. And part of that job right now is to help you get over Logan. It's time to get even with him for cheating on you and betraying your trust. You're not going to be able to feel like yourself until you get some of your pride back."

"And how would I get even?"

He looked at her with a slow, roguish grin. "An eye for an eye—" he said. "He cheated on you, so you have to cheat on him now—on his memory."

Her eyes were swimming with mirth and she bit her lip to stop from laughing, but there was unmistakable affection in her voice. "Have you ever considered an insanity plea, when the police hassle you?" she asked, "because I really think we could get you off with—"

" 'We'?" he repeated, interrupting her. "Notice how naturally you team up with me. You wouldn't fight for yourself, but when that newspaper said something evil about me, you came out swinging at everybody involved." He chuckled and shook his head. "We'd have made a hell of a team fourteen years ago."

With an effort, he put that poignant thought aside and braced himself for a brief skirmish. "But that was then, and this is now, and here I am—ready to do my job and help you get even with Logan tonight. Volunteering, in fact. Come to bed with me."

It hit Leigh for the first time that despite his teasing attitude, he was serious. Very, very serious. "No! Absolutely not! That's insane. It would change everything. We wouldn't be the same. I love the way we are. And besides that, it wouldn't be right, it wouldn't be fair."

"To whom?"

"To you! How could you think I would ever . . . use . . . you like that? I wouldn't dream of it!"

He chuckled. "I want to be used."

He was laughing, but he wasn't merely serious, he was resolute! She could hear it in his voice. The mere thought of going to bed with him, of exposing herself emotionally as well as physically, made her cringe with panic. She would lose him, along with what little self-respect she had left. "Please," she said achingly, "please don't do this to me. Let things stay the way they are. I don't want to . . . to do that. Not with anyone."

She pulled back enough to put her glass down, but his hands tightened and he stood up when she tried to back out of his reach.

"You're going to have to tell me why . . ." Rage at Logan Manning poured through Michael's veins like acid, but he kept his voice neutral. ". . . or I'm not going to take no for an answer."

Her voice broke. "Damn you, why are you doing this to me!" She leaned her forehead against his chest, her eyes flooding with tears of humiliation and despair. "Can't you leave me a little pride?"

He stared over her head blindly, his hands tightening protectively on her back while he purposely probed at her wounds. "I want you to tell me why you won't go to bed with me. I want you to tell me the truth."

"Fine!" she cried. "Here's your truth! The whole world knows 'the truth.' My husband didn't want me. I don't know what you think you'd get out of going to bed with me, but it wasn't enough for him, and it won't be enough for you. I loved him," she choked brokenly, "and he didn't even care enough about me to keep his hands off my friends, or my colleagues. Let go of me, I want to go home!" She struggled harder, and when his arms tightened even more, imprisoning her against his chest, she collapsed against him sobbing. "The names of his lovers are in all the newspapers. . . ."

"I know," he whispered. Holding her tighter, he rested his cheek against the top of her head, swallowing against the aching lump of emotion in his throat, his hands drifting over her sides and back while her slim shoulders shook with anguished weeping. He remembered the first time he saw those laughing green eyes looking up at him, framed by a curtain of auburn hair, and he squeezed his own eyes closed.

He waited until her crying finally started to subside; then he firmly shook off his own sorrow and resolved to make her laugh. "I don't blame you for crying. I mean, where will you ever find another man with so much integrity, loyalty, and *ego?*" With a joking sigh, he added, "You're going to have to tramp through a lot of manure-filled pastures before you can find a pile as big as the one you had."

Her body stiffened as if a jolt of electricity had shot through her, and after a moment of tense stillness, her shoulders began to shake again, only harder than before. Grinning, Michael lifted his head. He knew she was laughing even before she dragged her face away from his shirt and lifted her glorious eyes to his.

Leigh wiped her eyes with her fingertips and nodded. "You're right." She felt so lighthearted that it was almost a giddy experience.

He brushed his knuckles against her soft cheek, wiping a tear she'd missed. "I gave Logan my girl," he said with disgust, "and look what he did to her." He lifted his brows and added meaningfully, "I need to get even with him, too."

With an inner smile of surrender, Leigh realized that he was still adamantly determined to take her into that bedroom, and she also realized she wanted to go there with him. Very much. The suddenness of that yearning surprised her, but not as much as her wayward wish that Michael wouldn't make a joke out of it. On the other hand, she knew he cared about her, and that was what mattered. She decided to go along with it.

The instant Michael saw her eyes sparkle, he knew he'd won, and his entire body tensed with the urge to sweep her up into his arms, but he was afraid to make a single move until he knew where she was going to lead him. "You know," she pointed out to him very gently, as if trying to spare his feelings. "I was actually never *your girl*. I was Logan's girl."

He grinned because she was flirting with him, and he folded his arms across his chest. "I could have taken you away from him like that—" He snapped his fingers.

"You sound awfully sure of yourself."

He lifted his brows and arrogantly declared, "I am."

"And how would you have done that?"

His deep voice abruptly became husky, and Leigh felt it like a sensual caress. "I would have made love to you, exactly like I'm going to do tonight, and then you could have compared the two of us."

Unprepared for any mention of a comparison, Leigh felt her bravado crack for a split second, and reality nudged through the opening. Logan had been a wonderful lover— when he'd bothered to be her lover.

To her horror, Michael not only guessed what she'd been thinking, he decided to discuss it. Grinning, he studied her expression. "He was *that* good?"

She tried to make him drop the subject by giving him a quelling look and turning her head.

That didn't work. He leaned far to the side, studying the pink, embarrassed tint climbing up her cheeks. *"Really?"* he teased. "He was actually as good as that?"

"I cannot believe this conversation," she warned darkly.

Neither could Michael, but it had gotten her where he wanted her, so he stood up and put his arm around her, heading her firmly toward the bedroom. "Let the comparisons begin," he told her.

CHAPTER 50

In the bedroom, she moved away from him as soon as he dropped his arm from her waist, and she walked around to the far side of his bed. Turning her back to him, she unclipped an earring and put it on the nightstand.

Despite her smiling audacity a few minutes ago, she was evidently self-conscious about what they were doing, Michael realized, so he permitted her the illusion of privacy. However, since she hadn't asked him not to watch, he stationed himself at the foot of the bed—where he could stop her if she lost her nerve and tried to bolt—and then he indulged himself with the exquisite pleasure of watching the woman he loved getting ready to go to bed with him.

She took off her other earring, placing it on the nightstand; then she reached for her necklace as he unbuttoned his shirt.

She unfastened her bracelet and put it on the nightstand; he unfastened the buttons on his shirt cuffs.

She reached for her zipper; he reached for his belt.

She hesitated, her hands behind her back, near her zipper, he braced for a problem, but kept his tone friendly, offhand. "Need any help over there?"

"No."

She slid the zipper down; he unbuckled his belt.

Her dress went up over her head; his pulse rate climbed with it.

She reached for her bra; he slid down his zipper.

Black lace straps skimmed down her arms; his gaze skimmed down her back, boldly touching. Caressing. She sensed it and shivered. Michael saw it and smiled.

Sheer black panty hose were the last barrier between them, her last safe refuge. He finished undressing, holding his breath when she hesitated with her hands in the band at her waist—unable to breathe when she began to roll them down.

She sat down on the bed to finish, and one long, shapely leg emerged, glowing and bare. He was almost there. One more leg, and she was his. No more need to pretend to her that lovemaking was merely his idea of a casual, but enjoyable, diversion for them.

Bemused, Leigh slowly finished removing her panty hose and stood up to put them on a chair near the bed with her dress. She couldn't believe she was going to let this happen—couldn't believe the tug and pull Michael Valente had always exerted on her. He had treated this like a joke, and she'd actually gone along with it, but it didn't seem very funny anymore. It seemed lonely . . . impersonal.

She dropped her panty hose on the chair, then gasped as his hands grasped her arms and spun her around, pulling her almost roughly against his chest. Her mouth opened in shock; his mouth seized hers in a possessive, wildly erotic kiss that was stunningly . . . personal.

She landed forcefully on her back on the bed, and he

followed her down. He stretched her arms high overhead, laced his fingers tightly through hers, and held them there while he lowered his head, his mouth plundering hers, his tongue tormenting her. He made her melt; she made him hot.

He lifted his head and gazed into her eyes. His were heavy-lidded with desire; hers were wide with wonder. He bent his head again, and Leigh braced for another turbulent kiss like the last ones, but his mouth brushed hers softly. Unable to touch him, with her hands imprisoned in his, she followed his lead, rubbing her lips over his, and then asking for more. He gave, she took. She offered, he sampled. And then his mouth opened over hers, fiercely insistent and hungry again, his tongue caressing hers, his lips rough and tender. He made her soft and pliant; she made him . . . definitely not.

He lifted his mouth from hers and brushed it over her cheek, and trailed down farther, and touched it to one breast, then the other. He nuzzled, she gasped. He made them ache, and ache much more, until she whimpered. He made her desperate; she made him yearn.

He stopped, and tenderly laid his cheek against her thundering heart, while he slowly released their hands, and opened them. With his palms flattened and fingers splayed, he brushed his thumbs against her palms in an exploring touch she found strangely stirring; then he slid his fingers slowly down her wrists and forearms and back up again, then down lower in a shifting caress. Mesmerized, Leigh learned how it felt to be wanted in total.

She lifted her arms and kneaded his thick shoulders while his head moved lower. He brushed his lips on her waist, then her navel. It tickled, she giggled. Without warning, he moved even lower. She moaned in shock. And then pleasure.

She dug her nails into his back and shoved her fingers into his hair. Desperate, she pulled his mouth back up to hers and twisted him onto his back and kissed him until she was breathless.

She forgot all Logan had taught her and traded techniques for blazing desire. She crushed her mouth to Michael's lips and flattened her hands on his, following the corded muscles of his arms as he had done with hers. His arms were hard steel and rope, she learned with trembling delight, his mouth was hot velvet. She kissed his eyes, and made him smile. She nuzzled his chest and went lower. She made him gasp. He made her stop.

He rolled her onto her back, holding her mouth locked fiercely to his, and parted her thighs with his legs. With his hips pinning hers, and his rigid body poised to enter her . . . he stopped.

Leigh waited, breathing fast, her body feverish. She opened her eyes and looked into his. They were blazing. She lifted her hands and with a sense of awe, she touched his face, her fingertips skimming the hard planes of his jaw and cheeks. He entered her an inch. She yearned and lifted her hips. He bent his head and kissed her lips—and drove into her with a sudden force that made her body arch like a bow.

Her body was his violin; he played her steadily until her moans became his song. He changed her melody, the timing of her rhythm. She twisted and clung tightly, then she played her wild crescendo. And timed it perfectly with his.

Shattered, Leigh lay in his arms and buried her face against his chest. Her mind made no comparisons, but her heart already knew the answer: Logan could make her moan. But Michael made her weep.

He spoke, his deep voice like velvet, blanketing her

naked body. Quietly and solemnly, he said, "I'm in love with you."

Painfully poignant words. Too soon to hear them from another man; too soon to say them again herself. He wanted her to believe him, she knew, and then he wanted her to say them back. She felt the words, she couldn't say them. She gave him half of what he wanted instead. "I know," she whispered. And in the awful waiting silence that followed her woefully inadequate answer, she leaned up and looked at him with her heart in her eyes.

Michael saw the wonder and tenderness in them. He loved those eyes; he understood. They were telling him everything he wanted her to say—asking him to wait. Just a little while. And then those eyes lowered to his mouth and her lips touched his—brushing softly, slowly, back and forth. She was his.

His hands slid up her back to hold her lips to his. He was hers.

STANDING AT THE WINDOWS in the circle of Michael's arms, Leigh watched dawn lighten the sky over Central Park. Less than twelve hours ago, he had taken her hand and held it for the first time. Since then he had taken her to bed, made love to her twice, and stolen her heart. She leaned back against his solid length, and his hand slid over her breast in a possessive caress. It seemed wrong, foolish, to deny him the truth. "I love you," she said softly.

His arms tightened fiercely around her in response; then his left arm angled downward across her right hip, drawing her closer, as if he wanted to forge their bodies into one being. "I know you do," he whispered against her ear.

Leigh sighed contentedly; everything was resolved at last, serene. He allowed her a full minute to luxuriate in that thought before he said tenderly, and implacably, "Marry me."

Leigh could not possibly agree to that. In one half of one day, she simply would not go from holding hands to making a permanent commitment. He couldn't possibly expect such a thing, and not even Michael Valente could get her to do it. On the other hand, she didn't want to live without him, so she offered a compromise. "I think living together might be a good idea."

"Before or after we're married?"

"Before."

"After," he insisted.

Leigh looked over her shoulder at him in disbelief. "Are you saying we can't be together if we aren't married?"

He looked down at her, grinning. "Do you want to be together?"

She nodded emphatically.

"Do you want to be together very, very much?"

"Yes," she said unhesitatingly, "I do."

"Then those last two words are the ones you'll have to say."

Leigh dropped her head forward and hung it in laughing defeat.

"A nod isn't good enough," he said. "Was that supposed to be a yes?"

Leigh laughed harder and obstinately nodded.

"I can accept two nods," he said agreeably. "In business, two nods are equal to a handshake, and a handshake is contractually binding. Do you want to pick a date, or shall I?"

"I will," Leigh promised.

"That's fine," he said, smiling against her cheek. "What date have you picked?"

"Somehow," she said on a sighing laugh, "I knew you were going to say something like that."

"We've always had a psychic connection. Now, this is a test—what do you think I'm going to say next?"

"'When?'" She guessed with complete conviction.

"I was hoping you'd ask. I think—one month from today."

Leigh was horrified. She didn't want to begin their marriage while they were both tainted with suspicion regarding Logan's murder. Even without that, she was so sleepy at the moment that she could barely stand, let alone think about a wedding date. She closed her eyes and turned her face into his chest, and his hand slid upward from her breast, cradling her cheek against his heart. "I guess we could do it in six months," she whispered, loving the ways he touched her when they weren't making love.

His palm, which had been cradling her cheek, shifted slightly, leaving only the heel of his hand in contact with her chin. Leigh noticed the movement, but she was more intent on hearing his response. The more she thought about it, the more it seemed that six months was an awfully long time to wait, *particularly* if they weren't living together. She was surprised, and a little disappointed, that he was evidently willing to wait so long. She sighed.

"Too long?" he suggested, his voice tinged with knowing amusement.

Leigh giggled helplessly. "Yes."

"Want to change your mind?"

"Yes."

"Open your eyes."

She opened her eyes and saw the counteroffer he'd been making since his hand moved. In front of her eyes he was holding up two fingers. Two months.

With a smile of defeat, Leigh turned her face and kissed his palm.

He tipped her face up as he lowered his head. "A kiss on the hand," he warned tenderly against her mouth, "is equal to two nods. Very, very binding."

CHAPTER 51

Michael looked up from his desk as his secretary walked into his office at nine-fifteen that morning. He'd showered and shaved at the apartment; then he'd taken Leigh home and gone on to his company's offices for a nine-thirty meeting. "Mr. Buchanan is here," Linda told him. "He said he's a little early."

"Have him come in."

A moment later, Gordon Buchanan strode in carrying his briefcase. The senior partner at Buchanan, Powell, and Lynch, one of New York's most prestigious law firms, Buchanan was immaculately and expensively attired. He had silver-streaked hair, elegant manners, and a pleasant, aristocratic face. Socially, he was a gentleman; professionally, he was as smooth, and as dangerous, as a cobra.

"Good morning," Buchanan said. Although his firm had successfully represented Michael Valente in every legal action brought against him over the last decade, they were not friends—Valente wasn't a friendly man. But he had two rare qualities that made him a unique client in Buchanan's experience: He never lied to his attorneys, and he never wasted their time. In return, he required that they not waste his time.

For that reason, Gordon went straight to the matter at hand without indulging in any of the customary social preliminaries. "I set up a meeting at Interquest this morning," he said as he sat down in front of Valente's desk. "They have some information for us. Did you tell Mrs. Manning not to speak to the police again unless she checks with me first?"

"I told her several days ago," Michael told him. "They haven't made any attempt to talk to her since they subpoenaed her husband's personal files from the apartment—" He stopped and reached impatiently for the intercom buzzing on his desk phone.

"I'm sorry to interrupt you, but Leigh Kendall is on your private line—"

"Kendall?" Michael repeated, savoring the realization that Leigh had evidently switched to her maiden and stage name after last night.

"It's Mrs. Manning," Linda clarified, pretending in her irreproachably businesslike manner that she had no idea he was closely associated with the caller in any way. "But she specifically used 'Kendall,' so I thought I should, too."

"You were right," Michael said, already reaching for the button on his private line and swiveling his chair around for some privacy. When he answered the call, he used the voice he would use for any ordinary caller. "Miss Kendall, this is Michael Valente."

She expelled her breath in a startled laugh. "You sound terrifyingly cold and abrupt."

He switched to the voice he used with her. "I'm meeting with your new attorney. He thinks cold and abrupt are two of my warmest traits."

On the other side of the desk, Gordon Buchanan gaped

at the back of Valente's chair. He was surprised Valente indulged in any form of lighthearted banter with anyone, but he was completely astonished that Valente was indirectly including him in it.

"I don't want to keep you—" Leigh said quickly.

"Oh, yes, you do," Michael said with a smile in his voice. "Furthermore, you entered into a binding, nonnegotiable contract about that three hours ago. Why aren't you asleep?"

"Because Jason Solomon just phoned and insisted that Brenna wake me up."

"What did he want?"

"He wants to meet me for cocktails at the St. Regis tonight. He wouldn't take no for an answer. He's going to try to wear me down about coming back to work. I can't walk out onstage with Jane Sebring, knowing I look like a player in some sort of sordid freak show to the audience. Jason can't understand that. Anyway, you mentioned having dinner tonight, and I wanted to ask you to pick me up there instead of here."

"What time?"

"Could we make it seven? That will limit Jason to an hour of wrangling and harassment."

"Would you like me to join you at six instead, and be your reinforcement?"

He could hear the relief and wonder in her voice. "Is being my reinforcement part of your 'job,' too?"

"Absolutely. Check the contract you negotiated with me this morning—under Clause 1, Section C, headed 'Someone to Watch Over Me,' you'll see that you've been granted full rights to my diligent services in that regard."

"Michael," she said solemnly.

"Yes?"

"I love you."

Still smiling after they said good-bye, Michael hung up and swiveled his chair around. "Where were we?" he asked Buchanan abruptly.

Buchanan recovered his composure. "I was about to ask you if the police have made any attempt to question you yet about your whereabouts at the time of Manning's murder."

Michael shook his head. "They have no idea whether I can prove I couldn't have done it."

"Then the obvious answer is they don't *want* any proof that you couldn't have. They've probably persuaded a judge that you're a viable murder suspect and gotten him to authorize wiretaps, and whatever else they want, in order to look around for any other kind of wrongdoing they can find."

He was quiet for a moment, letting his client assimilate that; then he said, "Before I recommend a course of action, I need to know your priorities here."

"I want the police to find out who killed that son of a bitch. Instead of that, they're wasting time and resources on me."

"I can force them to cease and desist." Gordon drew a breath and braced himself for a spectacularly unpleasant reaction to what he was about to say next. "However, in order for me to do that, you would first have to voluntarily offer the police a schedule of your whereabouts at the time of the murder. Since they clearly don't want any proof of innocence from you, they'll resist a request from me for an informal meeting, but I can threaten them with a deluge of legal action if they decline. Once they have proof of your whereabouts in their hands, if they don't back off you, we can make things very unpleasant for them in court."

The negative reaction Gordon anticipated was not vocal—as he'd expected it would be—but Valente's jaw clenched in taut fury at the suggestion of volunteering any information whatsoever to the police. To Valente, voluntarily offering information to the police or prosecutors was tantamount to trying to appease his enemy, and that he wouldn't do under any circumstances. Time after time, he'd chosen to wage a costly battle in court, rather than attempt to avoid the battle by offering explanations and proof to the prosecutors in advance.

In every other respect, Michael Valente was the most coldly rational man Gordon had ever represented—but not when it came to appeasing the justice system. For that reason, Gordon was somewhat taken aback when Valente nodded and said in a low, savage voice, "Set up a meeting." He tipped his head toward the door of his office and added, "Use the conference room to make the call, and have my secretary type up the schedule I gave you of my activities that Sunday."

Gordon got up, and gave him another piece of news he was sure would further enrage him. "I'll try to get the detectives to come over here, but they'll make you go down to the precinct. It gives them a home-court advantage. And," he added, "undoubtedly some petty satisfaction."

"Undoubtedly," Michael said icily, reaching for a document lying on his desk and picking up a fountain pen.

"There's one more thing. . . ."

A pair of frigid amber eyes lifted from the documents to his.

"If we can't persuade them in this meeting that it's completely pointless and indefensible to keep after you, then I'll have to go to court to force them to cease and desist. That will take time, and time is what you don't want to waste. Then there's one other issue you need to be mindful of—"

"Which is?" Michael snapped.

"Mrs. Manning is undoubtedly a primary suspect. Her husband was cheating on her, so she had a motive, she had means—the gun—and she had a window of opportunity. I have no doubt the police have some sort of theory that you and she were involved and plotted together to get rid of her husband. If they ask you any questions about your relationship with her, now or in the past, I recommend that you answer them. Don't volunteer, but don't refuse to answer. I have a gut feeling the police are unduly suspicious of your relationship with her, even though it's been out in the open since you flew her to the accident site."

"Why do you think that?"

"Because you said they've never officially questioned her about her relationship with you. When the police refrain from asking the obvious, it's because they think they already know something and they don't want to tip their hand."

After Buchanan left, Michael waited a few minutes while he came to grips with what he'd agreed to do; then he reached for his phone and called Leigh's phone number, but not her private line. When Brenna answered, Michael asked her for Jason Solomon's phone numbers, and he asked her not to mention his call to Leigh.

It took Michael less than thirty seconds to persuade Solomon to meet him at five-thirty at the St. Regis that night for a private conversation before Leigh arrived. The first twenty-five seconds of that time were spent avoiding Solomon's excited inquiries as to Michael's relationship with Leigh.

CHAPTER 52

With her elbows on her desk and her neck between her palms, Sam idly massaged her nape with her fingers while she read the last report in Leigh Manning's file—a boring printout listing the names, addresses, and phone numbers of every single neighbor Leigh Manning had ever had, at every address she'd ever lived at in New York.

Sam had been through all the files once already, but in her spare moments, she was going through the files on Leigh Manning and Michael Valente again, looking for something to connect the two of them prior to Logan Manning's murder. The handwritten note Valente had enclosed with the basket of fruit was some proof of that, but the district attorney wanted to build a case against Valente for either first-degree murder or conspiracy to commit first-degree murder. After five weeks' investigation, however, they still didn't have a scrap of evidence to indicate the alleged conspirators had so much as spoken on the telephone prior to the weekend of Manning's death.

Shrader strolled past Sam's desk carrying his daily morning snack—two doughnuts and a cup of coffee. "Hey, Littleton," he gloated as he sat down next to her at his own desk, "did you happen to see your grieving widow on the news last night? She was all dressed up and going out to dinner with her boyfriend."

"I saw her," Sam said. She'd already been through this same routine with Womack this morning, and she was ready to concede that Leigh Manning's behavior at Dr. Winters's office may merely have been a fantastically convincing performance.

"She's brazen as hell now, isn't she?" Shrader barked cheerfully.

"They're not keeping their relationship any secret," Sam murmured, glancing at him.

Shrader took a bite of doughnut and a swallow of coffee; then he picked up a piece of paper propped on his telephone. "I got a note here from McCord that says he wants us in his office at nine-forty-five. You know what that's about?"

Sam nodded and turned the last page at the back of the earliest file on Leigh Manning. "The Special Frauds guy is coming over to tell us what they found when they audited Manning's books and records. Forensics sent up their final written report on everything collected at the cabin, but there's evidently nothing we didn't already know from the preliminaries. McCord wants a full review and update of the case with us after that."

Finished with Leigh Manning's "life history," Sam dragged the thick summary file on Michael Valente across her desk and opened it. It was hard to imagine two more opposite people than Valente and Leigh Manning seemed to be. Leigh Manning had never had so much as a traffic ticket, and she was a member of the mayor's commission on fighting crime. Michael Valente had been charged with a series of crimes and he was on the police commissioner's personal "Hit List" of known criminals whose activities he wanted closely monitored.

Beside her, Shrader made a phone call to an assistant DA who wanted to prep him for trial on an upcoming homicide case that Shrader had handled. Sam picked up a pen and began making a list containing the date of each case brought against Valente, the principal charges filed, and the ultimate outcome each time—one case per line.

She worked backward, starting with the most recent case, occasionally referring to the additional data on the summary sheets to clarify the details of the crimes he'd allegedly committed against city, state, and federal laws. One of the things she noticed was that the prosecutors had frequently gone to the grand jury to get an indictment, which usually meant they didn't have a strong enough case to get a judge to sign an arrest warrant.

When she was finished, she had an impressive list of arrests and grand jury indictments over the last ten years for nonviolent crimes including attempted bribery, fraud, intent to defraud, grand larceny, insider trading, and income tax evasion, along with many variations on those same themes.

The right-hand column, listing the outcome of each case filed, had only three results: "Case Dismissed," "Charges Dropped," "Not Guilty."

In every one of those cases, Valente had been represented by arguably the best criminal defense law firm in New York, but it was difficult to believe that even Buchanan, Powell could have gotten a patently guilty man completely off on every single case.

There were also occasional charges brought against him for minor offenses, including possession of a controlled substance, careless and reckless driving, and disturbing the peace. Sam had already read the individual files on each case; and, in her opinion, the controlled substance case had been particularly ludicrous. According to what she'd read, that arrest had evidently been based on Valente's having had a prescription for a painkiller on him when he was busted for speeding—at six miles over the limit.

Once again the right-hand column had only three results for these lesser cases: "Case Dismissed," "Charges Dropped," "Not Guilty."

The single exception to all that was the item at the bottom of her list—a charge of manslaughter in the first degree, brought against Valente when he was seventeen, for the shooting death of William T. Holmes. Unlike the other crimes, that one had been violent and Valente had pleaded guilty to it—his first and only time to plead guilty, rather than fight the charges and beat them. He'd been sentenced to eight years in prison, with eligibility for parole after four.

Sam flipped through the folders on her desk, looking for the case file on the manslaughter conviction, interested in the reason he'd done the crime, wondering if perhaps—that time—a female had been in any way responsible for his single violent act.

Unable to find the file, she leaned toward Shrader's desk, but none of his folders had red labels. Womack's desk was directly behind Shrader's, and she swiveled around in her chair.

"What are you after?" Womack asked, returning from McCord's office with a pile of folders in his hands.

"The file on Valente's manslaughter conviction," Sam told him.

"Haven't got it," Womack told her.

Sam got up and headed for McCord's office. He wasn't in there, so she started toward the table where the rest of

Valente's files were all neatly stacked, but as she passed McCord's desk, she noticed a red-labeled file folder on it that was glaringly out of geometric order. Instead of being neatly placed on a corner or in the center of McCord's desktop, it looked as if it had been thrown down. In fact, it was not only off center, it had papers spilling out of it. On a hunch, Sam checked the label on the folder and saw that it was the file on Valente's manslaughter conviction. She wrote a note on McCord's yellow pad to tell him she'd borrowed the file and returned to her desk.

Inside the file, she found the arresting officer's report, but all it said was that Valente had quarreled with Holmes and shot him with an unregistered forty-five semiautomatic belonging to Valente. There were no witnesses to the actual shooting, but the arresting officer had been driving by, heard the shot, and had reached the scene before Valente could flee. McCord had drawn a broad circle around the arresting officer's name and then written an address inside it.

Based on the information in the file, William Holmes had been a good kid with a clean record. Valente, however, had previously committed some other juvenile offenses, prior bad acts that the judge had taken into account, along with Valente's age, when handing down his sentence.

Sam closed the file, thinking. . . . At the age of seventeen, Valente had taken a life, which meant he was capable of the act, but based on the details in that file, he'd done it in the heat of anger. Premeditated murder was a different kind of crime.

Lost in thought, she doodled on the tablet, trying to get a fix on who Valente really was, what made him tick, what made him turn violent—and why Leigh Manning would prefer him to a cheating, but otherwise respectable, husband.

She was still pondering all that when Shrader stood up. "It's nine-forty," he said, and then half seriously added, "Let's not be tardy and give the lieutenant a reason to start the day pissed-off again."

"God forbid," Sam said flippantly, but she lost no time grabbing the borrowed file on Valente, a pad and pencil, and then getting up. McCord's grim mood yesterday had coincided with a trip he'd made to Captain Holland's office. When he walked in, he'd reportedly closed the door behind him in a clerk's face. When he walked out, he'd supposedly slammed it.

"Usually this place is an icebox. Today it's hot," Shrader complained, stripping off his jacket and tossing it next to a crumb-covered napkin. Sam, wearing a light-rust-colored shirt, suede belt, and matching wool pants, left her blazer on the back of her chair and headed for McCord's office.

She thought McCord's tense mood yesterday might have been the result of having caught hell from someone because the investigation wasn't moving fast enough, but five weeks wasn't a long time for a homicide investigation—particularly an investigation meeting McCord's incredibly meticulous demands for documentation and research. To McCord, everyone they interviewed was either an important potential witness who could help them or a very damaging potential witness who could help the defense—and he wanted to know everything there was to know, either way.

A few weeks ago when Womack had shown Valente's doorman a picture of Leigh Manning and asked him if he'd ever seen the woman at his building, the doorman had firmly denied it. When Womack reported that in a meeting several days later, McCord had reamed him out for not asking the doorman how much Valente tipped him.

Womack went back to the doorman, got that information, and reported the figure to McCord. McCord then ordered Womack to run a background and financial check of the doorman to ascertain his living style—just in case several thousand dollars, instead of several hundred dollars, had changed hands between Valente and the seventy-two-year-old man.

CHAPTER 53

When McCord strode into his office at precisely nine-forty-five, his mood did not appear to be much improved. He nodded curtly at the three detectives seated in front of his desk. "We're going to have some uninvited guests," he began; then he stopped as the Special Frauds Squad auditor—a balding, sweating man in his forties—walked into the office, juggling a tall stack of large manila envelopes.

"What did you find out?" McCord asked as the man looked around for a place to unload the items. He unwisely chose to dump them on McCord's desk, but McCord was too intent on hearing what he had to say to notice.

"Several things," the auditor replied. "First, your dead guy was spending more than he was making. Second, he either had an incompetent CPA, or else he was scared shitless of being audited because there's a lot of deductions he really should have tried to claim and didn't. Third, his spending habits changed a couple of years ago. Fourth," the auditor finished, his eyebrows levitating with irrepressible glee, "he's got a platinum credit card from an offshore bank!"

"Could you amplify the first item a little," McCord snapped impatiently.

"Sorry, Lieutenant," the startled man said. "I mean that, until a couple years ago, Manning was doing extremely well—several of his commercial projects paid off big time for him, and he was also making a shitload of money in the stock market. The market started to slide at about the same time his business turned stagnant, but he went ahead and moved his offices to a new location anyway. The rent on the space he moved his offices into is staggering, but Manning didn't seem to care. He then plowed over a million bucks into gutting, redesigning, and redecorating the place."

He paused to open a manila envelope on the top of the pile; then he extracted a written report and glanced at it as if to confirm what he was about to say. "At that point, Manning began running his architectural firm as if it were some sort of 'hobby' that didn't need to make a profit. It was costing him a lot to keep the doors open, and he was definitely spending more than he was taking in. Now, here's what makes all that so interesting. . . ."

He peered silently at his audience to emphasize the magnitude of his next announcement. "Until a couple years ago, Manning was a big earner and a conservative spender. Suddenly, the reverse was true. He started spending money like he had an unlimited supply of it. His spending habits changed, and *that's* what I look for!"

Sam was about to ask why having a credit card from an offshore bank was significant, but Womack spared her the need and the auditor answered the question.

"Let's say you've got a couple hundred thousand dollars in cash that you obtained illegally," the auditor proposed. "If you go to any U.S. bank and deposit more than ten thousand dollars in cash, the bank is obligated to report your name and social security number to the IRS. But you can't risk any inquiries from the IRS about how you came by the cash money, which leaves you very few choices: You can bury it in the backyard and spend it a hundred dollars at a time, or you can take it to a legitimate bank in any country with laws that don't require their banks to report to our tax authorities. Banks in Nassau, the Caymans, and Belize have been very popular for that purpose."

He looked around at his audience, realized he wasn't yet telling them anything they didn't already know, but he forged ahead, his enthusiasm mounting. "Now you've got the money in a nice safe offshore bank earning interest, but you can't spend it here, because you can't write a check on a foreign bank to buy much of anything in the U.S. *But*," he said significantly, "if your offshore bank issues you a platinum credit card with a high limit, or no limit, you can use it to buy virtually anything you want here. Logan Manning," he finished triumphantly, "bought two luxury cars in two years on his credit card, and then he sold them a couple weeks later, took the check he was given, and deposited *that* into a regular bank account.

"It's money laundering with a 'cute' twist. The only problem is the IRS just announced they're going to start auditing taxpayers with credit cards from offshore banks, so Manning will show up on their radar screen."

"Did you find any irregularities in Leigh Manning's finances?"

"No, but Broadway stars don't make nearly as much as I thought. Under her contract with Solomon, she gets twelve thousand dollars a week or five percent of whatever the box office takes in, whichever is greater. Based on my calculations, *Blind Spot* is taking in about five hundred thousand dollars a week at the box office, which means

Leigh Manning should actually earn about twenty-five thousand a week, or one point three million per year. I checked with an agent over at William Morris, and he said those figures are about average for a Broadway star in a nonmusical role, although he thought the five percent was a little low for someone like Leigh Manning. Now, if she had an established Hollywood name, then her percentage of the box office would be bigger."

Everyone was silent for several moments, processing the unexpected discovery that a socially prominent, "upright citizen" like Manning had evidently been getting his hands on illegal cash somewhere. How he had been doing this was a whole new question, and whom he had been doing it with was just as interesting. Valente, with his unsavory history of money-related indictments and charges, was the first known associate of Manning's to come to Sam's mind. McCord was clearly thinking along those lines, because the next question he asked the auditor was, "Did you turn up any business connection anywhere between Manning and Valente?"

"Not a one," he declared. "But I turned up something else that may be of even more interest to you. In fact, I may have saved the best discovery for last. You gave me some miscellaneous documents and correspondence of Manning's that you wanted me to look into, along with your notes on each subject."

"Right," McCord said when the auditor paused.

"Everything checked out, except one thing: According to your notes, Manning invested two hundred thousand dollars in Solomon's play. The file you gave me contains duly executed agreements between Manning and Solomon that indicate two hundred thousand dollars did, in fact, change hands. But you know what I can't find?"

McCord nodded slowly and emphatically, his lips

drawing into a hard line. "You can't find a *check* for two hundred thousand."

"You guessed it. Manning must have given Solomon cash in exchange for a share in the play's profits."

"And," McCord finished for him, "Solomon undoubtedly takes in plenty of cash at the box office during the run of a play, so Solomon would be able to take Manning's cash and deposit it into his own bank without raising an eyebrow at the IRS."

The auditor nodded. "My guess is that, knowingly or unknowingly, Solomon laundered two hundred thousand dollars for Manning."

McCord looked at Sam, his brows raised in a silent question. *You were there when we interviewed Solomon. What do you think?*

After a moment's contemplation, Sam answered him aloud. "I suppose it's possible. On the surface, Solomon is a brilliant, talented . . . flake, but there's more to him than that. He got pretty tough with you when he realized we were thinking of Leigh Manning as a suspect."

"He's no flake. He has enough business acumen to produce the plays he writes, line up his own backers, and maintain control over the production. According to what I've heard, that's not the norm."

Absently, Sam ran her hand around her nape, thinking; then she shook her head. "Solomon fancies himself a renegade, and I doubt he'd have a moral dilemma about laundering a little money for a friend, but at the same time, I don't know if he'd do anything for anyone that would put him in jeopardy of going to prison."

Instead of agreeing or disagreeing, McCord looked at Shrader and Womack. "You've already run a background check on Solomon, but now I want all three of you to start compiling complete files on him and his lover. Don't stop until you can tell me their life stories with all the details, right down to which one of them wears the pajama bottoms, and which one wears the top."

A prolonged silence followed the auditor's departure while all four of them automatically focused on the new, pressing question about the source of Manning's cash.

McCord walked around his desk and sat down across from her. Sam lost her concentration on the money issue, and her unruly mind focused instead on him. He looked preoccupied and distant—his brows drawn together, his hard jaw set with iron determination as he contemplated the game of human chess they were playing.

He'd invited Sam out to dinner a week ago, and somehow she'd gathered enough strength to decline. By then, her attraction to him had grown so powerful that she actually had to concentrate on breathing evenly when he was nearby. If she looked at his mouth, she wondered how it would feel to have those sculpted male lips on hers. If he was within arm's reach, she had an insane impulse to trace her fingertip over the scar on his tanned cheek—and then lean forward and press her lips to it. If he wasn't within reach—she wanted him to be.

The day he asked her to have dinner with him, they'd been in his office, combing through boxes of files and records subpoenaed from Manning's apartment. Before Sam had finished quietly saying, "I think that would be a mistake for both of us," she was already wishing she could take the words back. She felt much better when he said with a slight smile. "I'm sure it would have been." And then—inexplicably—she felt much worse.

He had a wary, sardonic charm that captivated and disarmed her, and to make everything more complicated, she genuinely liked and admired every single thing about him. He wasn't like any male she'd ever known before; he was smarter than she was, and she was very smart. He was wiser than she was, and she was pretty wise. He was stronger, tougher, and more astute than she was—and she loved the fact that he was those things. And she particularly loved that, unlike her brothers, McCord never felt a need to demonstrate that he was stronger, tougher, and more astute.

The telephone on his desk rang, and Sam watched his long fingers grasp the receiver and pick it up. He had beautiful, strong hands with well-shaped fingers—hands that would unerringly seek out every vulnerable spot on her body if she gave him a chance. But she wasn't going to give him one.

He hadn't repeated the dinner invitation or referred to it again. In fact, it was as if he'd never made the suggestion at all. He treated Sam exactly as he had before he'd asked and she'd refused him. No displays of wounded masculine ego. No subtle retaliations in any form. He still smiled at her when the occasion warranted, and he still frowned impatiently from time to time.

He was a splendid male in every way, Sam thought wistfully—a male who actually lived up to the fullest meaning of the word "manly." He was what men were supposed to be and rarely were. He had principles and ethics. He dominated without ever being domineering; he taught without lecturing; he guided but never shoved—although he nudged sometimes.

He was a born leader—a natural, gifted leader. But she was not a follower. She could never let herself be that.

He was tough as granite and soft as a whisper—or he would be, she was certain, if he were properly matched with the right woman.

But she was not that woman.

To allow a relationship to blossom between them would have been pure folly for them both.

She jumped when she realized he'd hung up the phone and was talking to them. "As I started to explain a few minutes ago—" he said with his gaze leveled on Sam, silently prodding her to snap out of it and pay attention, "we're going to be entertaining an uninvited guest this morning. Actually, this is an historic occasion, because this particular guest has made it a lifelong habit to throw our invitations into his lawyer's trash can whenever we've urged him to drop by for a chat."

"What?" Sam said with a chuckle at McCord's unprecedented lapse into lengthy metaphor when he was usually so crisp and frank.

"This morning, Valente's lawyer called and invited us to a tête-à-tête at his client's office," McCord clarified, and Sam realized it was helpless frustration that was making McCord avoid stating the simple truth. "I, of course, declined. Buchanan then suggested we meet here, instead. I declined again. However, after he warned me of the tiresome legal papers he'd file if I didn't invite him over here, I graciously agreed." He glanced at his watch and said abruptly and with distaste, "They'll be here soon."

"Did Buchanan say what the hell he wants?" Womack put in suddenly, wiping off the lenses of his bifocals. He was so quiet at times that Sam would almost forget he was there, but when he spoke, he was surprisingly forceful and frequently caustic.

"He said," McCord sardonically replied, "that he believes his client is the subject of our murder investigation and he wishes to spare all of us here the needless inconvenience and expense of pursuing a senseless theory."

"I wonder what brought that on," Womack said, his brows drawn together.

"For one thing, Valente knows he's being tailed. He shook off the tail last night as soon as Mrs. Manning fin-

ished 'chatting' with the reporters and got into his car.
However," he continued with grim amusement, "one of our
cruisers happened to spot Valente's Bentley down at a
restaurant on Great Jones Street. Guess which restaurant
he took her to?"

"His aunt's place," Shrader put in.

"Angelini's," McCord confirmed with a nod. "She also
spent the night with him last night." Leaning back in his
chair, he picked up a pencil, and flipped back through the
pages of his tablet. "I can't believe we haven't been able to
connect Valente and Leigh Manning prior to that opening
night party."

He read from his notes, ticking off each item as he covered it with them: "We've checked all of Valente's phone
records and the Mannings' phone records as well. The only
calls made to Valente were a few from Logan Manning's office placed during the month before he died. The only call
made to Valente from the Manning residence was on the
day before he disappeared, when Mrs. Manning was at the
theater getting ready for opening night."

He glanced up briefly to see if anyone had anything to
add. "We've checked with the doormen at both their resi-
dences, and we've checked with waiters at every restaurant
and bar where Valente's used a credit card in the last year.
Nobody has ever seen them together, except at that party on
the night before Manning disappeared. Now, of course,
they're inseparable and they phone each other regularly."

Tossing his pencil on his desk, he leaned back in his
chair. "We know from Valente's note to her that they were
pretending they didn't know each other that night, but
how in the hell have they been keeping in touch? How can
two people carry on an affair, let alone plan a murder, without leaving a trace of their association? When did they first
get together, how long has this been going on?"

Sam suddenly stiffened. "What street did you say Angelini's is on?"

"Great Jones Street. You were the one who knew all about that restaurant," he reminded her, frowning in puzzlement at her question and her sudden, avid interest.

"Yes, but I've never been there. What's the address on Great Jones Street?"

"The street is only a few blocks long. What difference does it make?"

Sam burst out laughing and stood up. "They've known each other forever!" Without another word, she turned and headed for her desk, where she'd left Leigh Manning's file.

CHAPTER 54

Several minutes later, Sam triumphantly placed Leigh Manning's open file in front of McCord and pointed to an old New York City address. For Shrader and Womack's benefit, she said aloud, "Leigh Manning moved to Great Jones Street while she was still attending NYU."

McCord glanced at the address in the file as he reached into his desk drawer and yanked out a phone book.

"I already checked," Sam said, returning to her chair. "There's an Angelini's Restaurant and an Angelini's Market listed, and I called there a moment ago. The market has been at that same address for forty-five years, and it's just down the block from Leigh Manning's old address. I also checked the early employment records in Valente's file—he worked there on and off during the same period Leigh Manning lived down the street."

Shrader sent Sam an approving, paternal nod for her discovery; then he turned businesslike. "Exactly how long ago did she live near the market?"

When Sam told him, he tipped his head back and

stared up at the ceiling, his eyes narrowed in thought. "So by the time she met Valente, he'd already done time for manslaughter . . ." In the pause that followed, no one attempted to confirm his statement, because they were all so familiar with Valente's life history by then that any one of them could have written his biography.

"Let's consider a different scenario for Valente and Leigh Manning and see if this one plays," Shrader said. "Valente meets Leigh Kendall when she lives down the street from the market where he works, and they have a fling. Naturally, he tells her the story of his life, and since Valente's a tough bastard and proud of it, he includes his stint in prison for manslaughter. After the fling is over, she goes her way and marries Manning, and Valente goes his way. Valente and Leigh Manning don't see each other after that. I mean, they never really had anything in common in the first place, right?"

"Right," Womack said. "Go on, I'm with you."

"Fourteen years go by," Shrader continued; "then one day, Leigh Manning finds out her husband is cheating on her, or laundering illegal money—or whatever—and she decides she wants to get rid of him, permanently. Now, who would she call to advise her about doing something like that? Who does she know who has firsthand experience with murder?"

"She'd call her old friend from Great Jones Street," Womack agreed aloud.

"Exactly. She calls him from a pay phone, and he picks her up in his car, and they talk there. They meet the same way another time or two to make their plans, but that's *all* they do. That would explain why we can't dig up any evidence they were having an affair—because they *weren't* having one."

He paused, his brow furrowing again. "When I think

about it, it's just as likely that she didn't call Valente out of the blue with her problem. Manning's secretary said Manning had been making some business overtures to Valente in the weeks before he died. Maybe Manning brought up Valente to his wife, and that's when she realized how helpful her old pal could be in disposing of her husband. Doesn't matter," he said, giving his big head a shake. "Anyway, on the night before they plan to off old Logan, he suddenly decides he could make some points with his potential business investor by inviting him to Leigh's fancy party. Mrs. Manning's secretary—Brenna something—specifically told me Manning added Valente to the guest list himself, at the last minute."

Womack looked impressed. "So Valente goes to the party, but for obvious reasons, he and Mrs. Manning carefully pretend not to know each other." He looked at Sam, who was frowning in thought. "You got problems with this theory?"

"I was thinking about the pears he sent her in the hospital," Sam replied. "I've always assumed he knew she liked pears for breakfast because they'd had a lot of cozy breakfasts together, but it's perfectly possible that Valente simply remembered her shopping habits at his aunt's market, and in a nostalgic moment, he sent her the pears in the hospital."

Satisfied, Shrader turned to McCord. "How does this sound to you, Lieutenant?"

The phone on McCord's desk had started ringing before Shrader finished the question. McCord answered it, listened for a moment, and then said curtly. "Put them in an interview room and tell them to wait there."

When he hung up, he said, "Valente and Buchanan are here"; then he unhurriedly considered Shrader's question. "I have one major problem with your theory, and it's this: The Feds call Valente the Ice Man because he's the most cal-

culating, cold-blooded son of a bitch they've ever encountered. Based on what I've heard, he wouldn't help out an old
girlfriend—or anyone else—unless there's something in it
for him. In order for him to agree to pop Logan Manning,
and risk getting a lethal injection for his trouble, Leigh Manning had to have something to offer him that he wanted very
badly."

Womack immediately came up with a viable possibility:
"Maybe she offered him her husband's dirty money. She
doesn't strike me as the type to try to launder it herself."

"That's an inducement that would appeal to Valente, as
long as there's a truckload of money involved," McCord
agreed. "Evidently Mrs. Manning also sweetened the deal
by offering him herself, because there is definitely something sexual going on between them now."

In the silence that followed, Sam reluctantly shook her
head. "I'm sorry, but I can't buy any of this."

"What do you mean you can't buy *any* of it?" McCord
said sharply, frowning at her. "It explains things that have
bothered me for weeks about their relationship. It makes
perfect sense."

"But only up to a point. It explains why and how two
guilty conspirators kept their acquaintance a complete secret while they planned to murder Manning. But what it
doesn't explain is why they abandoned all caution, even
before his body was discovered. Why would Valente be stupid enough to fly her in his helicopter to a place he knew
would be crawling with cops? Why are they flaunting their
relationship now, when they need to look innocent?"

Sam had been speaking to all three men, but she directed her last question specifically to McCord. "You said
Valente was 'calculating,' yet he's been visiting her openly at
her apartment. Last night, he took her out to dinner—very
publicly—and then he spent the night with her, even

though he obviously knows he's under surveillance." She lifted her hands, palms up. "Why would a cold, calculating man do such reckless things?"

"Based on my firsthand knowledge of man's basest nature," McCord said with a mocking smile, "I would have to assume that Leigh Manning offered herself to Valente as part of the bargain, and he's *extremely* eager to start collecting payment."

"You mean," Sam paraphrased with a smile, "he has the hots for her?"

"Obviously."

"I see," Sam said wryly. "So—apparently the 'Ice Man' is actually so 'hot' that he's willing to risk a death sentence to be with her?"

McCord sighed, but he didn't argue. He couldn't.

"I'm not saying Valente didn't murder Logan Manning," Sam added, "but I've met him, and I *don't* think he's as inhumanly cold and emotionless as you've been told. I was watching him when he got his first look at Mrs. Manning's Mercedes as it was being winched up to the road. He looked completely shaken and almost ill when he saw it. I also saw him carry her in his arms—up a steep hill, through deep snow—from the cabin to the main road. I'll be interested in hearing what *you* think of him," Sam finished.

McCord glanced at his watch. "Then let's go have a talk with him, so I can decide for myself." He phoned Holland's clerk and told him the interview was about to begin; then he pushed back his chair.

"If you ask me," Womack said as they all stood up to head toward the interview rooms, "Detective Littleton thinks the Ice Man is hot stuff."

Sam made a joke of it as she picked up her pad and pencil, though what she said was what she thought. "I think he's very attractive—in a dangerous, unfriendly sort of way."

As she finished speaking, she happened to glance at McCord, who was walking around his desk toward her, and she found herself momentarily impaled by a pair of blue eyes as sharp as daggers. "Is that right?" he inquired in a deliberately offhand tone that completely belied the expression in his eyes.

"Nope, not really," Sam said unhesitatingly . . . untruthfully . . . and completely unintentionally. Stunned by her involuntary reply, she started across the squad room toward the interview rooms, with Shrader and Womack in the lead, while she tried to understand what had just happened. That look on McCord's face had been there either because he thought she was biased in favor of a suspect—and a criminal, to boot. Or because he had been jealous. No, it couldn't have been jealousy, Sam decided. No way. Not McCord. Not possible.

After momentarily examining the reasons for her own reaction, Sam concluded that she'd denied her stated opinion of Valente either because she didn't want McCord to think her professional opinions could be influenced by any man, no matter how attractive he might be. Or—and she didn't like this possibility—because jealousy was an uncomfortable, unpleasant feeling and she didn't want to do anything, ever, to make that amazing man feel an unnecessary moment of unpleasantness. If so, that would indicate her feelings for him were very tender, and that he already meant a great deal more to her than she realized. But he didn't. She would never be foolish enough to let that happen.

Beside her, McCord sent her a slanted little smile and lowered his voice. "I think we got through our first lovers' quarrel pretty well, don't you?"

Sam turned the corner too sharply, and nearly hit the wall.

He spared her the need to reply by abruptly switching to the matter ahead as they neared the interview rooms at the end of the next hallway. "Shrader, do you want to sit in, or do you want to watch it from the other side of the mirror?"

"Since I'm not going to participate, I'd rather watch from outside. The view's broader from further away."

When Womack said virtually the same thing, McCord looked at Sam.

"I'd like to sit in on it," she said instantly. "I wish you'd ask him about his relationship with Mrs. Manning while he's here."

"If he's come here to hand me a solid alibi, there's no point in asking him about her, or anything else, because he'll tell me to fuck off. Mr. Valente," McCord continued snidely, "doesn't like us to 'pry' into his affairs. He once made the State's prosecutors spend months trying to force him to hand over some records they wanted to see in connection with their fraud case against him. First his lawyers stalled, then they argued, then they fought against it all the way to the New York Supreme Court. Do you know what happened when the Supreme Court finally made him turn over the files the prosecutors wanted?"

"No, what?"

"The records completely exonerated him. Valente knew they would. If he's actually got an ironclad alibi today, he's not going to give me one molecule of additional information. In fact, I still can't believe he's planning to volunteer anything. It's a real first for him."

CHAPTER 55

Formerly called "interrogation rooms," the interview rooms were located on the far side of the third floor, diagonally opposite McCord's office, between two short, busy hallways at the rear of the building. The front hallway had entrance doors into the rooms and large glass windows where passersby could see, and be seen. The rear hallway had one-way mirrors where detectives and police officers could gather to observe and hear what was taking place in each room without being observed themselves.

Instead of waiting inside the interview room as they'd been instructed to do, Michael Valente and his attorney were standing outside it in the hall, drinking coffee. It was, Sam decided, a small but deliberate defiance designed to subtly wrest control from McCord.

McCord took it as such and retaliated by stalking past both men without a glance. He opened the door to the interview room, and with a rude jerk of his head, he snapped an order at them. "Inside!"

Shrader and Womack were already making the turn to

the back hall as Captain Holland strode past Sam with four other men, all headed in the same direction. Valente's voluntary appearance at the precinct was evidently drawing a crowd, Sam realized, wondering how many people were already gathered back there to watch the proceedings through the one-way mirror.

She waited for Buchanan and Valente to precede her into the room; then she followed them inside and closed the door.

McCord went to the right side of the oblong table in the center of the room. "Sit down," he ordered his adversaries, nodding toward the chairs on the left of the table.

Valente unhurriedly sat down; then he opened his topcoat, leaned back in his chair, and casually propped his right ankle atop his opposite knee—a deliberately indolent posture that conveyed his utter lack of respect for the occasion, and for the detectives present.

McCord angled his chair sideways, put his yellow tablet in his lap, and looked over his right shoulder at Valente, impatiently tapping the end of his pencil on the table. Waiting.

Sam made a mental snapshot of the two silent men and subtitled it: *"If I can't win, I won't play."*

Buchanan sat down, opened his briefcase, and broke the electrified silence by saying, "It's our belief that Mr. Valente is a suspect in the murder of Logan Manning."

McCord's gaze shifted to Buchanan, and he shrugged. "No one has accused him of that."

"That's true. In fact, no one's even questioned him. Why is that, Lieutenant?"

"I'm the one who asks the questions," McCord explained as if he were reprimanding a rude fourth grader on a field trip at the precinct, "and you're the one who gives the answers. Now, you asked for this meeting. If you have something to say, say it. Otherwise," McCord added acidly, "there's the door. Use it."

Gordon Buchanan's aristocratic face remained perfectly composed, but Sam saw a muscle begin to tick in the side of Valente's clamped jaw. "For the record," Buchanan said smoothly and unemotionally, "Mr. Valente could not possibly be your murderer. Here is a schedule of his whereabouts on that Sunday, along with names and phone numbers of witnesses who can verify his presence. As you will discover when you read this, my client was at lunch and then a Knicks game with three business associates. After the game, the men went to the Century Club, where they discussed business until six. At nine P.M., he had dinner in a public restaurant where he is known and recognized, with a woman whose name is on that list. At one A.M., he returned home, where he made several lengthy telephone calls to business associates in Asia. His chauffeur, his doorman, and his telephone records will all verify the last part of that."

McCord reached for the paper and then deliberately ignored it once it was in his hand. "I'm told Mr. Valente doesn't like to volunteer information. One might even say that he always goes out of his way to be uncooperative. I'm curious about his motives for coming here today and offering information to assist us in this *particular* case."

Buchanan closed his briefcase. "My client's motives are none of your business. *Your* business is—presumably—to find Logan Manning's real murderer."

"Suppose I were to tell you that Mrs. Manning is our primary suspect," McCord drawled. "What would you say to that?"

Valente's savage voice was like the crack of a whiplash. "I would say you're out of your fucking mind."

McCord's head snapped toward Valente, and Sam

watched the two foes finally confront each other eye to
eye—a cunning hunter, a dangerous predator. They were
silent for a moment, mentally circling each other; then
the hunter smiled. "I was under the impression you and
Mrs. Manning were complete strangers until the night you
met at her party. Do you have more than a casual interest
in her?"

"Cut the bullshit!" Valente snapped, rolling to his feet
with the sudden, deadly grace of the panther he reminded
Sam of at that moment. "You've had us both under surveillance for weeks. You know damned well she spent the
night with me last night."

Buchanan hurriedly stood up, too, giving Sam the impression the attorney was worried about what his client
might do next, but McCord was moving in for another attack. "You knew her a long time ago, didn't you? Fourteen
years ago, to be exact."

"You just figured that out?" Valente shook his head as if
he couldn't believe the stupidity he had to deal with: then
he walked out with Buchanan on his heels.

For several moments, McCord stared after them, his
jaw clenched with inexplicable anger; then he said softly,
as if to himself, "*Son of a bitch! He was ready to talk. . . .*"

He glanced over at Sam and said in furious self-disgust,
"I should have gauged him myself, but I thought I knew
everything there was to know about him from his files, so I
shoved him into a wall right from the start. I showed him
how tough I was, so he had to show me he didn't give a
shit. You were right, Sam. The Ice Man has a hot spot—no,
he's got a *soft* spot for Leigh Manning. If I hadn't strong-
armed him, if I'd have played straighter with him, I think
he'd have told me something I needed to know. He'll never
give us another shot—"

Jumping to her feet, Sam ran for the door.

"Where are you going?"

"To try to play straight with him!" she called over her shoulder, racing toward the back hall and the stairwell there. She shoved past a startled Captain Holland and his group, who were still standing by the one-way mirror, talking about Valente's visit. Praying the elevators would be as crowded and slow as they usually were, she slammed against the heavy stairwell door and sprinted down two flights of stairs, her footsteps ringing loudly, her heartbeat almost matching them.

CHAPTER 56

The first floor was crowded with the usual mix of uniformed police officers, ordinary citizens, and attorneys heading in different directions, but Valente and Buchanan were nowhere in sight. Sam sprinted to the main doors, shoved one open, and saw the two men walking swiftly down the steps toward a black Mercedes limousine gliding up to the curb. "Mr. Valente!" she shouted.

Both men turned and watched her run toward them, Buchanan with a frown of surprise, Valente with an expression of scathing disbelief.

Specks of snow were swirling in the wind as Sam wrapped her arms around herself and tried to take control of a situation for which she was neither prepared, nor even dressed. "Mr. Valente," Sam began, "there are some questions, I'd—"

Buchanan interrupted her, his tone as frigid as the wind flattening her thin shirt against her skin. "You had your chance to ask your questions upstairs, Detective. This is an inappropriate place for whatever you have in mind."

Sam ignored the irate lawyer and focused the full force of her appeal on his cynical client. Trying to "play it straight," she said sincerely, "Mr. Valente, I'm a minority of one, but I've never been convinced that either you or Mrs. Manning murdered her husband."

"If this is a good-cop, bad-cop routine," Valente said contemptuously, "you're lousy at it."

"Give me time, I'm still new at my job," Sam quipped, shivering, and she thought she witnessed a slight, momentary crack in his glacial expression. Resorting to a tone of innocent sincerity that bordered embarrassingly on naïveté, Sam tried to sidle through that crack in his resistance. "I've only been a detective for a few weeks, so maybe I'm doing this all wrong, but if you could just explain something to me, then maybe I could help—"

"I repeat, Detective—this sidewalk is not the place for you to question my client," Buchanan warned angrily. To Valente he added, "We're going to be late." The chauffeur was standing at the rear of the limousine, and he opened the door as soon as Buchanan turned toward him.

The lawyer got into the car and Valente turned to follow him, but Sam stayed on his heels. "Mr. Valente, why did you and Mrs. Manning pretend not to know each other?"

"I've never pretended anything of the kind," Valente said curtly, sliding onto the backseat of his car.

That was true, Sam realized, recalling his behavior with Leigh Manning when Sam had seen them together. She leaned into the car so the chauffeur couldn't close the door, and, shivering convulsively, she tried to reason with Valente one last time. "That's right, you didn't—but Mrs. Manning *did* pretend, and that's what's creating our doubts and suspicion. If you really want us to look elsewhere for suspects, then you need to answer my question. Do you want us to look elsewhere—" She started to say "other than you and Mrs. Manning"; then she pressed his button with Leigh Manning: "—elsewhere, other than Mrs. Manning?"

He hesitated, and then to Sam's joyous surprise, he snapped, "Get into the car."

Sam climbed in, and the chauffeur closed the door. "Thank you," she said, rubbing her arms and trying to stop her teeth from chattering. She opened her mouth to ask a question, then stopped in shock as the limo pulled away from the curb.

"I'm late for an appointment in midtown," Valente said, his words clipped. "Do you want to get out?" he challenged. "Or do you want to go along for the ride?"

Sam caught the veiled irony in that last question, and she discarded several glib replies that came to mind. Her instincts warned her against sparring with him on any level, because she had the feeling Michael Valente was a far more formidable opponent than even his reputation allowed. She hesitated, wondering if she dared reveal anything about the note he wrote Leigh Manning to accompany the pears: then she decided to risk it. If he had an alibi, that note wasn't going to do McCord a bit of good. Even if his alibi didn't hold up, Buchanan would learn of the note under the rules of discovery.

"I'm waiting, Detective," Valente said impatiently.

Sam decided to opt for absolute sincerity if he'd let her—and for a new career if she'd already made the wrong decisions. "When Mrs. Manning was still in the hospital," she explained, "Detective Shrader came across a phone message from you, and he asked her if she knew you. She lied and said she'd met you for the first time at her party, a few nights before. Do you know why she lied?"

"She wasn't lying," he retorted.

Sam began to lose faith in McCord's judgment about Valente being "ready to talk." She looked at him, searching his forbidding features. "How long have you known Mrs. Manning?"

"Fourteen years."

Sam breathed an imperceptible sigh of relief. That at least was an honest answer, but she wasn't pleased with how she had to go about getting it. Carefully banishing all confrontational undertones from her voice, she said quietly, "If you will try to overcome your understandable resentment of having to answer my very personal questions—and answer them fully—I will try to ask as few of them as I can. And I'll even answer yours. Deal?"

Although he refused to make any such "deal" with her, he at least clarified his last answer. "She didn't recognize me when she met me at her party, because we hadn't seen each other in fourteen years. I had a beard when she knew me before."

"Are you saying she didn't even recognize your name?" Sam asked skeptically.

"She knew me by another name."

"Would that be 'Falco' or would it be 'Nipote'?" she prodded, watching for his reaction.

His reaction was a short, sardonic laugh. "You took the note I sent her with the pears," he said, shaking his head in disgust. "You people are unbelievable."

Reluctant to admit she had the note if she didn't need to, Sam said, "How would you reach a conclusion about a note from what I asked you?"

"You figure it out, Detective."

"No, that won't work," Sam said resignedly, but firmly. "Let's trade explanations instead?" She waited for him to agree in advance. Instead he lifted his brows and regarded her in noncommittal silence, so Sam took a major gamble and offered her explanation anyway. She explained why the basket of pears had originally concerned her and she told him exactly how she'd ended up finding and reading his note. When she finished, Sam paused deliberately, in order to lend greater significance to her next comment. "Mr. Valente, do you remember what you wrote in that note?"

He nodded impassively, but the implications of his written words—and what the police would naturally infer from them—registered on him, because his expression became fractionally less guarded and distant than she'd ever seen it.

Sam smiled a little without realizing it. "How did you conclude I'd found the note when I mentioned those two names?"

He hesitated a moment; then he reluctantly answered her. "I specifically wrote those names on my note because they were the only names Leigh knew me by in the old days. Now ask yourself a question," he instructed shortly. "Do you think I would have needed to further identify myself on my own letterhead if she already knew who Michael Valente was?"

Sam shook her head. "No," she said, and then she probed a little deeper. "When did Mrs. Manning finally realize you were her old friend 'Falco Nipote'?"

A sudden, fleeting smile flickered in his golden eyes and touched the corners of his mouth, momentarily softening his features in a way that made Sam catch her breath at the transformation. "I evidently said something very funny just now?" she ventured, trying to maintain her calm, businesslike approach.

He inclined his head in a slow nod, traces of the smile still lingering in his eyes, but he remained frustratingly silent.

"Give me a break—" she joked before she could stop herself.

He thawed another degree at her joking plea and actually gave her that break. *"Falco* is Italian for 'hawk,' which was my nickname in the old days. That's the name that Leigh heard me called."

"And *Nipote?"* Sam pressed. "That's Italian for—?"

"Nephew."

Sam's eyes widened in puzzlement. "That's what we were told when we checked with people who are fluent in Italian, but we thought it must have some other meaning between you and Mrs. Manning. Why would she know you as 'nephew'?" Sam realized the answer before she finished the question, but waited for him to confirm it.

"Leigh used to hear my aunt call me that, and she assumed it was my name."

"You didn't know each other well at all then?"

"We rarely spoke."

"I see." Sam remembered the important question that had started her down this surprising path, but which still remained unanswered. "When did Mrs. Manning realize that you were her old friend from Great Jones Street?" she asked as the car pulled over to the curb just past the corner at Park Avenue and Forty-eighth Street.

"The same night she learned her husband was dead. I had gone to see her specifically to tell her who I was, and to see how she was doing."

"Were you still with her when we talked to her that night?" Sam asked as the chauffeur got out and opened the back door of the limo. Her fragile truce with him collapsed the instant she asked that question, because he realized she was no longer playing completely straight with him.

"You know damned well I was," he retorted, then he nodded curtly to the open car door and said brusquely, "This is where we get out."

With no choice except to get out, too, Sam did so, and both men followed her onto the sidewalk, leaving her there. Valente paused to say something to his driver and then strode off with Buchanan, both of them with brief-cases in hand. Sam walked to the rear of the limo, her arms clasped around her, craning her neck for a cab; then she turned around to see where Valente and Buchanan were headed. She had no coat and no purse, ergo, no money for a taxi, but she could pay for one when she got back to the precinct.

Valente and Buchanan walked into the huge building that took up the whole block, and, on an impulse, Sam decided to follow them. "Where are you going, miss?" Valente's chauffeur called out as she ran past him. "Mr. Valente told me to take you back to the precinct—"

"Wait here or circle the block," Sam called to him. "I forgot to ask him something," she lied.

She dashed into the building just as the elevator doors closed behind Valente and his attorney. Backing up, Sam watched the lights above the elevator flash as it passed the floors, then glow a steady green on the sixteenth floor.

The building's directory was located between the elevators, and she scanned the names listed on it with suites on the sixteenth floor. There were only four names shown, which indicated they were very large suites. "Knightsbridge Obstetrics and Gynecology"; "Truman and Horn, Certified Public Accountants"; "Aldenberry, Smith, and Cromwell," a very well known law firm. Sam ruled out the obstetricians with an inner laugh. When Valente and McCord had been together in the interviewing room earlier, the atmosphere had been positively crackling with macho, killer-instinct, maleness. Definitely not the obstetricians. Valente's cousin handled his financial matters, and Valente was already represented by one of the most prestigious law firms in New York, so she ruled the other two firms out. The fourth suite of offices

on the sixteenth floor belonged to a company called
Interquest Inc.

Sam went to the reception desk, pointed to the ID
badge hanging from a chain around her neck, and spoke to
the guard. "What can you tell me about Interquest?"

"Not a whole lot, Detective. About all I know is they're
a private investigation firm on the sixteenth floor, and they
must be expensive as hell, because they've got a suite of offices up there you wouldn't believe."

"Thank you very much," she replied, glancing at his
name tag, "Leon."

LOST IN THOUGHT, Sam gazed out the window of Valente's
limousine at the tide of pedestrians hurrying past on the
sidewalk, their heads bent into the wind as they outpaced
the snarl of lunchtime traffic.

Since Valente and Buchanan had requested a meeting at
the precinct to discuss Manning's murder, and then gone directly to a private investigation firm, Sam had a strong
hunch that Valente had hired his own investigators to try to
find Logan Manning's murderer. A very odd thing for a man
to do if he thought the woman he was in love with had done
the deed. Either that, or Valente's lawyer was looking for viable, alternative suspects to throw at McCord like decoys
now—or to bring up in court later in order to confuse a jury
into believing there were other people besides Mrs. Manning with a motive and opportunity to kill Logan Manning.

That, of course, assumed that Valente's alibis checked
out and removed him from the list of suspects. Even if they
did check out, there was also the possibility that Valente
had paid someone else to murder Manning.

Sam sighed. That was all perfectly possible and even believable. What wasn't believable was that Valente had actually bothered to send her back in his nice, warm limousine.

On the sixteenth floor, Michael stood at the window, idly watching his car inching through traffic with Sam Littleton in it. "Littleton followed us into the building," he remarked to Buchanan.

The founder of Interquest, Stephen Wallbrecht, walked into his office and heard Michael's remark. "Samantha K. Littleton—" he provided, "the youngest and most inexperienced member of the team investigating Manning's murder."

CHAPTER 57

Asubtly dynamic man, Wallbrecht was tall and slender, with thinning hair, keenly intelligent light gray eyes, and an aura of absolute competence and relentless energy.

"Sorry to keep you waiting, Michael," he said, shaking hands with him and then Buchanan. He sat down behind his desk and removed some files from his bottom right-hand drawer. "As usual, I'd like to start by quickly evaluating our adversaries." While he spoke he handed both men a set of dossiers and laid the third set on his desk for reference if necessary. "You probably know already that the investigative team on the Manning case is made up of four members."

To Michael he said, "You mentioned Samantha Littleton, so we'll start with her first. She's thirty-three, and she only got her gold shield a little over a month ago. From what I can gather, whatever she lacks in experience, she evidently makes up for in raw intelligence and gut instinct. If you decide to piss her off," he added humorously, "be sure you're under cover. She's a crack shot, and she got her black belt in karate when she was still a teenager. Her father," he added meaningfully, "was Ethan Littleton."

"The football coach?" Buchanan asked. When Wallbrecht nodded, Buchanan said, "So that would make her Brian and Tom Littleton's sister?"

"Right again—two Heisman Trophy winners and a legendary coach in one family. Of the four remaining brothers, two are high school football coaches, one still plays minor league baseball, and the last one owns a gym here in New York. Samantha was the youngest of the seven kids, and according to some friends of the family, the boys got all the muscles, but she got most of the brains. After her father died, her mother remarried."

He paused again for effect, and then dropped a small verbal bomb. "Detective Littleton's stepdaddy is Senator Hollenbeck."

"I wish I'd known that a little earlier," Buchanan said ruefully. "I might have been slightly less offensive. Hollenbeck and I sit on a committee together, and we have friends in common."

Wallbrecht's phone rang, and he reached across his desk and pressed a button to silence it. Without commenting on Buchanan's remarks, he said, "When Samantha made detective and said she wanted Homicide, the senator pulled strings to get her into the safest precinct in Manhattan, which is the Eighteenth. I'm told that particular little 'sweetheart deal' was made between the senator and Captain Holland and that Detective Littleton doesn't know about it. She's not particularly close to her stepfather, possibly because he's as domineering as her father and brothers were. That last is unconfirmed gossip I collected for you, by the way, not necessarily fact."

Buchanan had opened her dossier, and Wallbrecht waited politely until the attorney was finished perusing it;

then he moved on to the next member of the investigative team. "Malcolm Shrader is an experienced detective with one of the best arrest-to-conviction ratios in the entire department. He's a hell of a lot smarter than he looks, so don't ever underestimate him. Word has it that he was mad as hell when he got stuck with Littleton as a temporary partner, but he's quite a supporter of hers now, so my advice to you both is—don't underestimate Littleton either."

Since neither man had opened Shrader's dossier, Wallbrecht moved on to Womack. "Detective Womack isn't as smart as Shrader, but he's good at his job. He's a plodder, but he's thorough. That's about all you need to know of him for now."

He paused, waiting for questions, and when none were forthcoming, he said, "Now we've come to Mitchell McCord, and therein, gentlemen, lies our most interesting challenge." Leaning back in his chair, he shifted his gaze to Michael and said bluntly, "According to my sources, Commissioner Trumanti handpicked McCord and gave him a single assignment: That assignment was to nail *you* on the Manning murder, or on anything else that might come to light during McCord's investigation of it."

"Trumanti should have chosen somebody who understood his assignment better," Michael said angrily, "because the son of a bitch he picked isn't sticking with me; he's trying to go after Leigh Manning."

Wallbrecht rolled his pen between his fingers, studying Michael Valente's face curiously; then he gave his own assessment of McCord. "Mitchell McCord is a human Sidewinder missile with a high-functioning intellect and a Ph.D. in criminal psychology," he argued. "If Mack decides you're guilty, he will lock on to you, and he will stay with you, and nothing you can do will shake him off or sidetrack him. He will keep closing the distance—*and he will bring you down.*"

Wallbrecht waited for some sort of reaction to that, but

there was none. Smiling slightly, he admitted, "You're right about what you said, though—Trumanti did pick the wrong man for this job. You can't send Mack after the *wrong* target and order him to stay on it for some self-serving reason of your own. If you try to do that, what you'll get is a shitload of embarrassing fallout, because Mack will not only go after the right target on his own, he'll bring him down and *then* he'll go after *you.* And that," he finished with a chuckle at Buchanan, "is why Mitchell McCord isn't next in line for Trumanti's job. He's the best detective the NYPD has ever had, but he won't play politics, and he won't kiss anybody's ass.

"I've been trying to lure Mack over here with an offer of a full partnership and a gigantic salary, but every time he's ready to turn in his resignation, somebody over at the department hands him a case he just can't resist." Wallbrecht tipped his chin and looked at Michael. "This time, the irresistible case was . . . yours."

Finished with his review of the major players in the case, Wallbrecht said, "Beyond that, all I can tell you right now is that your telephones are tapped and you have a tail, which you already knew. Mrs. Manning has a tail but no wiretaps yet. Now, tell me what you want me to do next."

"I want you to find out who killed Logan Manning. Whoever did it is walking around free, while his widow can't even eat in a restaurant without having people talking about her. Also, she had a stalker. Gordon will give you all the details. Whether he's involved with Manning's murder or not, I want him found and taken off the street so she doesn't have to worry about him anymore."

Wallbrecht leaned back in his chair and gazed at him in amazement. "So that's the way it is?" he said softly. "You're not interested in protecting yourself—it's Mrs. Manning you want to protect?"

"That's exactly the way it is," Michael said flatly. Opening his briefcase, he tossed the dossiers into it; then he snapped it and the locks closed.

Wallbrecht pulled a sheet of paper from a tray on his desk and held his pen poised to make notes. "Okay, what can you give us on Manning that might be helpful?"

"Very little, but you've got a file on him already. He wanted to do business with me, and in the course of normal operations, I not only asked him for a financial statement, I had one of your people check him out. Go over the report you gave me and look for anything irregular in his finances."

Wallbrecht's pen stilled. "I would have started looking for an irate husband or boyfriend of one of his bed partners. Why his finances instead?"

"Several reasons," Michael replied, standing up. "I threw my copies of his financial statements out, but I remember thinking he wasn't as solvent as I'd expected him to be, considering what I knew of his overall lifestyle."

Wallbrecht jotted a note. "What else?"

"The night before he disappeared he gave his wife a two-hundred-and-fifty-thousand-dollar ruby-and-diamond pendant in a Tiffany's box. For obvious reasons, she later decided she didn't want it, but when her secretary tried to return it to Tiffany's, she was informed it hadn't come from there. When the two women looked for a record of who he did buy it from, there was nothing—no record of a check being written for it, no credit card receipt, no bill—nothing."

Wallbrecht's expression turned suspicious. "He paid cash?"

"Evidently. There's one more thing—during one of our few dinner meetings, he bragged about a clever way he knew to spend offshore money in the U.S. without attracting the notice of the IRS. He didn't actually say he was doing it, but he may have been. If he was laundering dirty money, then whoever killed him may have wanted some of it." He shook his head in disgust as he shrugged into his top-coat. "I knew when Manning didn't turn up after a few days, he was never going to be found alive. Besides what he told me about the offshore money, he also mentioned he'd bought a gun."

Wallbrecht laid his pen down and looked at Michael in bewilderment. "Why would he tell you, a virtual stranger, that he owned a gun and knew of a scam to spend offshore money?"

"Because he thought I'd be interested and impressed," Michael said, picking up his briefcase from his chair. "After all, I'm the tough ex-con who keeps beating the system in court." Ready to leave, he nodded at Buchanan, who was going to take a cab back to his own office; then he looked at Wallbrecht and said, "I don't care how many people you have to put on this or how much it costs; find out who killed that worthless son of a bitch."

He strode to the door; then he stopped and turned, with his hand on the knob. "There's one more thing," he informed Wallbrecht. "I want you to tell McCord that if he ever uses Leigh Manning's name in front of me again in connection with that murder, I will take *him* down, and there aren't enough cops in the city of New York to stop me."

When he walked out, Wallbrecht and Buchanan looked at each other in stunned, wary silence. "I can't believe this," Wallbrecht finally said. "That's the same man who shrugged when the state of New York filed six counts of fraud against him."

Buchanan didn't smile. "Do us all a favor—find us a lead on the real murderer, and do it fast. Because if your friend McCord tries to implicate Leigh Manning, I guarantee you that Michael Valente will not be controllable."

CHAPTER 58

Shrader and Womack were walking down
the precinct steps when Sam got out of
Valente's limousine, his chauffeur holding
open her door. Ignoring their derisive grins, she ran past
them, her arms clutched around herself for warmth. "Why
didn't you tell Valente you wanted a fur coat instead of a
car?" Womack joked, following her inside, with Shrader
right beside him.

"Did you get anything from Valente?" Shrader asked.

Sam nodded, but gestured to the elevators. "Let's go upstairs where it's warmer, and I'll tell McCord at the same time
I tell you two."

"McCord already left," Shrader told her. "He had appointments."

"With who?" Sam said, too disappointed to hide it.

"I don't know, but his schedule's on his desk, where it
always is. He left a note on your phone. What did you get
from Valente?"

Sam told them what she'd learned, but the information lost much of its significance in the middle of the

noisy, bustling first floor, where the facts and timing couldn't be put into proper context, analyzed, and fully evaluated.

Shrader's reaction was understandably noncommittal. "I don't know what to think. Maybe he paid somebody to do the deed?" Distracted, he looked at his watch. "Womack and I are going to start checking out Solomon and his boyfriend. See you in the morning."

Frustrated at having to wait to talk to McCord, Sam jogged up the stairs to the third floor and went to her desk. He'd been so upset about mishandling Valente's interview himself that she couldn't believe he hadn't waited around to hear what she might have learned. On the other hand, McCord always kept his appointments and he expected everyone else to keep theirs.

Propped against her telephone was a folded note with her name written on it in his now-familiar handwriting. He had a remarkably legible handwriting for a man, Sam thought fondly—and *then* she remembered the astonishing thing he'd said to her on the way to the interview room this morning. In the uproar, she'd completely forgotten he'd been jealous of Valente and she'd been unable to bear that. She remembered the scene now though, in every poignant detail, right down to the knowing half-smile on his handsome lips as he said,

"I think we got through our first lovers' quarrel pretty well, don't you?"

Sam's heart did a swift little quickstep at the memory, so she firmly set the memory aside. She was not going down that path with Mitchell McCord—at least no *farther* down that path.

Calmly, she opened his note.

Sam—
In my center desk drawer is the file with notes
from my interview with Valente this morning.
Since you aren't back yet, I assume you talked to
him. Add your own notes to mine, while they're
fresh in your mind. I'll be back by 5:30. We'll talk
then if I haven't already reached you by phone.
                                                    Mack

He'd signed his note with his nickname for the first
time, and Sam's entire nervous system suffered a momentary meltdown. As far as she knew, very few people felt entitled to use that nickname. The mayor had called him
"Mack" one day when he stopped by during a strategy
meeting; Dr. Niles, the chief medical examiner, called him
"Mack"; and so had his sister when she gave Sam a message
for him one day. Everyone else called him "Lieutenant,"
which was respectful and appropriate.

Sam was not a relative of his, or a friend of long-
standing, or a political leader. If she were to use his nickname, she would be assuming a relaxed, easy familiarity
with him that she did not have. Sam wasn't certain if he, by
signing his nickname, was subtly telling her she *could* have
that familiarity with him. Or . . . *should* have it? Or . . . *already* had it?

Sam shook her head, trying to clear it, and headed for
his office. The man was driving her crazy. He was assuming
a relationship that did not exist, and then he was making
her react as if it *did*. This morning, he'd looked at her with
irate, narrowed blue eyes because he was jealous, but he
had no right to be jealous, and *she* had no reason to melt
with regret for making him jealous.

The problem, as she saw it, was that McCord was so

beguilingly *subtle,* so brilliantly nonchalant, and so smoothly indomitable, that she never quite realized he was leading her onto very shaky ground until she was already there.

Sam had been having a recurring vision of herself being led docilely along a path through the woods, attached to McCord by a gossamer thread she couldn't see or feel, and while she was looking around, admiring the flowers—and his muscular back and narrow hips—she was going to step off a cliff into thin air.

Inside his office, Sam studied his "desk calendar," which was actually an eight-and-a-half-by-eleven spiral-bound daily planner with a full page allocated for each day. Thinking he might be able to return sooner than he'd written in his note, she looked at the crowded afternoon he'd scheduled.

His mornings were usually blocked out for whatever work he could accomplish in his office, by phone or computer, and for the intensive meetings he held with Sam, Womack, and Shrader.

Afternoons were set aside for appointments, interviews, and whatever legwork he wanted to do. McCord handled departmental and administrative business by telephone, but he did almost everything else face-to-face, which required an astonishing amount of legwork.

He'd mentioned yesterday that he'd made arrangements to meet with every law enforcement official he could find who'd ever dealt with Valente on a personal basis, and as Sam ran her finger down his list of appointments, she could see that he'd started that process. Four consecutive afternoons were covered with them, starting at noon today with Duane Kraits, the arresting officer who'd successfully busted Valente on the manslaughter charge.

McCord was particularly interested in that case for the same reason Sam had been: It involved Valente's only violent crime, and it was the single instance where the charges against him had stuck. As Sam looked at McCord's busy afternoon schedule, she realized there was no way he would finish up and be back before five-thirty.

Disappointed, she sat down on the swivel chair behind his desk, opened his center drawer, and took out Valente's file. She made a few appropriate notes in it, but when she finished and slid the file back into McCord's desk, she felt curiously deflated.

Standing up, she looked around at his clean, neat office while she trailed her fingertips over the desk where he sat and wrote his copious notes. She'd joked about his compulsion for order in the beginning, but the truth was, she really liked his neat office and organized habits.

She'd grown up with six brothers, and until she was a teenager, she hadn't been able to walk through the family room without being hit by a throw pillow—usually a barrage of throw pillows, coming at her from different directions.

Her brothers had contests to see which one of them could be the most disgusting. If Sam's parents weren't there, they had belching contests at dinner. And—oh, God—the farting contests!

They kicked off their raunchy sneakers in the utility room when they came home, and no gymnasium on earth could smell as bad as that room did. And their gym socks were not to be believed. When they sat around watching television in their stocking feet, the odor made Sam's eyes sting and water. She complained about it only once, when she was eight years old. The next morning, when she woke up, her pillows were covered in smelly gym socks.

She learned early to pretend she didn't notice things,

because if the boys knew something grossed her out, they would find a way to torture her with it.

When she was little, they seemed to regard her as an animated, talking toy with multiple uses. If they played baseball in the vacant lot next door, they stood her in the outfield—holding her doll—and she was their designated "home run line." During backyard football practice, Brian and Tom had her hold up her arms like a goalpost while they kicked field goals at her.

They would have killed anyone who tried to hurt her, but at the same time, they teased her constantly and played endless jokes on her that weren't always funny.

Sam's father thought boys who were jocks should be allowed to be incredibly sloppy and unruly, but then what else would you expect from a man whose children called him "Coach," instead of "Dad"? The family house-keepers, of which there had been an army, never lasted more than a year.

Sam's mother disagreed with her husband about many of the things the boys were allowed to do, but she was out-numbered, and besides—she doted on him and on all her children.

McCord's neatness suited Sam just fine, she realized, walking out of his office and then turning in the doorway for one last, unconsciously tender look around. The truth was, everything about Mitchell McCord suited her. Even his nickname had a pleasing ring to it.

By the time she reached her own desk, she realized she was hungry and restless, and she really needed to get away for a little while.

Regular working hours for detectives on the day tour were from eight A.M. to four P.M., but Shrader, Womack, and she had been working late nearly every night and coming in on the weekends. Sam already knew she'd be working late tonight again, since McCord wasn't due back until five-thirty. She'd more than earned the right to take a few hours off now as "lost time."

Picking up her purse, she pulled on her jacket, and decided to go to Bergdorf's after-Christmas sale.

She checked her cell phone to be sure it was on and slipped it back in her shoulder bag. McCord was predictable and adhered to his schedule, so she didn't have to worry about being back here until five-thirty.

AT THREE O'CLOCK, Sam was on her way into a dressing room to try on a fabulous little cranberry knit dress and jacket, when her cell phone rang. She dug it out of her purse and was surprised to see Mack's office phone number flashing on her caller identification screen. She was even more surprised by the terse, ominous sound of his voice. "Where the hell are you?"

"I decided to take a few hours of lost time. I'm in midtown—at Fifty-seventh Street and Fifth Avenue," she said.

"You just went back on duty. Get over here."

"What's wrong?" Sam said, thrusting the cranberry knit dress into the arms of a startled clerk who happened to walk past her.

"I'll tell you when you get here. Where's the recap you were putting together this morning of all the charges ever filed against Valente?"

"It's in my desk." Sam was already at a near run. "I'll be right there."

CHAPTER 59

Sam paused at her desk just long enough to dump her purse in a drawer, lock it, and strip off her winter jacket; then she headed swiftly toward McCord's office, stopping uncertainly just inside the doorway.

He was standing behind his desk, facing the wall, with his hands shoved into his hip pockets and his head bent, as if he were looking at the computer on his credenza—except the screen was dark and his torso was so taut that the brown leather strap of his shoulder holster had tightened across his back, wrinkling the broadcloth of his shirt.

The file with her recap of Valente's arrest records was lying open on his desk, and his leather bomber jacket was flung over a chair—another sign that something was alarmingly out of the ordinary.

Sam decided to interrupt him and quietly said, "What's up?"

"Close the door," he said flatly.

Sam closed the door, her unease escalating. McCord never closed the door to his office when they were alone in it. Everyone on the third floor could see into his office because the upper half of the walls facing the squad room were glass, and Sam had sensed from the beginning that McCord was a good enough administrator to realize that frequent closed-door meetings between Sam and him would be noted and widely misconstrued—to the detriment of her future relationships with coworkers.

With his back still to her, McCord said, "Does the name William Holmes mean anything to you?"

"Of course. He was the victim in Valente's manslaughter conviction."

"What do you remember about that manslaughter case, based on the official information in our file?"

Sam's foreboding began to increase when he didn't turn around while she answered him. "The victim, William Holmes, was an unarmed sixteen-year-old male with a clean record who quarreled with Michael Valente in an alley over an unknown subject," Sam responded. "During the quarrel, Michael Valente—seventeen-year-old male with a long juvenile record—shot Holmes with a forty-five semiautomatic belonging to Valente. A patrol officer, Duane Kraits, heard the shot and was on the scene within moments, but Holmes died before the paramedics arrived. Officer Kraits arrested Valente on the scene."

"Go on," he said sarcastically when she stopped. "I want to be sure you read the same things in that file that I did."

"The M.E.'s report listed cause of death as a forty-five-caliber slug that ruptured the victim's aorta. Ballistics confirmed the slug came from Valente's unregistered forty-five semiautomatic. Valente's prints were on the weapon. The tox reports showed no sign of drugs or alcohol in Holmes or Valente."

Sam paused, trying to imagine what other salient

points he wanted her to recount, and she mentioned the only items that came to mind. "Valente was represented by a court-appointed attorney and he pled guilty. The judge in the case took Valente's age into consideration, but nailed him because of his priors and the unprovoked viciousness of Valente's act."

McCord turned around then, and Sam mentally recoiled from the menacing glitter in his steel blue eyes. "Would you like to know what really happened?"

"What do you mean—'what really happened'?"

"I spent a half hour with Kraits today. He's retired and he lives alone with a bottle of Jack Daniel's and his memories of 'the good old days on the force.' He was already half-tanked when I got there, and he was especially happy to talk to me about his true part in the Valente manslaughter bust because—in his words—he's 'a real big fan' of mine. It seems the report he filed about Holmes's death was a little skewed because his captain needed it that way, and in 'the good old days' cops stuck together and did favors for each other. Can you guess who his captain was?"

Sam shook her head.

"William Trumanti," he bit out. "Now, guess who the victim was."

"William Holmes," Sam said unhesitatingly.

"William *Trumanti* Holmes," McCord corrected acidly. Too restless to sit, he ran his hand around the back of his neck and leaned against the credenza. "Holmes was Captain Trumanti's sister's only child. Since Trumanti had no other siblings, young William was the last possible branch on their little family tree. Are you starting to get the picture here?"

"Not yet."

"No, of course not," he said, his jaw clenched so tightly that the thin scar on his cheek stood out. "You weren't around in his fucking 'good old days.' Let me fill in the blanks for you. I've already verified the important points by phone with another retired cop from Trumanti's old precinct. Here's what the file didn't include: William Holmes was a punk—who used to get hauled in along with his pal, Michael Valente. When that happened, his uncle had him turned loose and kept his record clean. From time to time, Captain Trumanti—who was Lieutenant Trumanti back then—also saved young Mr. Valente's butt."

Sam leaned forward in her chair. "Michael Valente and Holmes were friends?"

"They were *best* friends. In fact, they were childhood chums. Unfortunately, Holmes was not pals with Valente's older cousin, Angelo. The night Valente 'quarreled' with his pal and killed him—it was because William had just carved Angelo to pieces. Valente went looking for him, and young William was waiting for him—stoned out of his mind, still covered with Angelo's blood, and armed with a forty-five semiautomatic. That piece didn't belong to Valente, it was Holmes's, and Valente's prints were on the barrel, not the grip. Now do you have the whole picture?"

Sam sensed he needed to vent some of his fury. "I'd rather hear it from you."

"Trumanti wanted vengeance for his sister, and he fixed it so a seventeen-year-old kid got railroaded right through the system and shipped off to prison. Valente was no angel, but he wasn't a pusher, he wasn't a user, and he hadn't been in any trouble for quite a while. And," McCord added emphatically, "he sure as hell wasn't guilty of first-degree manslaughter."

He ran his hand around his nape again and flexed his broad shoulders, as if trying to loosen the tension in his body. "If he'd had a decent lawyer, he'd have gotten off with self-defense, and if the judge wouldn't completely buy that argument, he'd have gotten second-degree manslaughter with probation. Instead, Trumanti, Kraits, and the good old boys at the local precinct set Valente up; then they sent him away for four years. But that was just the beginning," he added scathingly.

"What do you mean?" Sam asked, but she already had an ugly premonition of where he might be heading.

"What do you remember about Valente's next few busts?" Leaning forward, he shoved the recap file across the desk to her. "Here, refresh your memory."

Sam automatically reached for it because he'd ordered her to; then she drew her hand back because she didn't need to look at the file. "For the first few years after Valente was released, his record stayed clean. There was a flurry of arrests for really minor stuff—speeding a few miles over the limit—possession of a controlled substance which turned out to be a prescription for a painkiller."

"And after that?" McCord prodded.

"About ten years ago, the charges became serious ones. The first one was attempted bribery of a city official—Valente attempted to bribe a building inspector who was going to write him up for some building code violations. There were several other, similar attempted bribery charges brought against him after that, and then the scope and number of the charges became much larger as time went on."

McCord dismissed that information with a look of withering scorn. "My second appointment today was with that building inspector Valente allegedly tried to bribe. Mr. Franz is in a nursing home now, and he's a little worried about what God is going to think of some of the things he's done in his life. He unburdened himself in five minutes."

"What did he say?"

"Valente *never* tried to bribe him, nor did he try to

bribe the two other guys who claimed he did in later cases that were filed. Trumanti put them up to it."

Straightening, he walked over to the table piled high with thick folders of information on the other court cases filed against Valente. He picked up a file and dropped it in disgust. "I can already tell you why all these cases ended with either 'Charges Dropped,' 'Case Dismissed for Insufficient Evidence,' or 'Not Guilty,' according to your recap. It's because they're a pile of crap. Fortunately, by the time they were being filed, Valente could afford his own attorneys to defend him instead of having to rely on the kind of public defender who let him plead guilty to first-degree manslaughter. I would also bet you that Trumanti was either directly or indirectly responsible for at least half of these accusations."

"What do you mean 'indirectly' responsible for them?"

"Trumanti built a few little fires with those early fraudulent charges, but he also created plenty of smoke, and prosecutors tend to believe the old adage 'where there's smoke there's fire.' They'll start hunting on their own for the blaze that escaped them the last time." He picked up another file and tossed it aside in contempt. "After a few years, Valente actually made himself into a bigger and bigger prosecutorial target."

Sam lifted her hands in confusion. "How did he do that?"

"By making a habit of annihilating his opposition in court, not just beating them. When I read the pleadings and transcripts in these files, it was obvious that Valente's battalion of attorneys have two assignments from him when they go into court. Their first assignment is to beat the charges, but their *second* is to beat the shit out of whoever is running and prosecuting the case. When I read the files, I could not believe some of the remarks Valente's attorneys made on the record. In every case, his attorneys started out by spanking the prosecutors—belittling them for things like spelling errors, grammatical errors, typos, being two minutes late—minor mistakes that, in their hands, begin to take on the taint of incompetence. In several of the transcripts the judges actually started going along with them and reprimanding the prosecutors.

"Once Valente's attorneys have embarrassed their opponents and made them look foolish, they get nastier and nastier, until they're on a tirade using terms like 'incurable stupidity' and 'inexcusable negligence' and 'gross incompetence.'"

He stalked back to his desk and sat down. "Attorneys like Valente's that cost two thousand dollars an hour or more do whatever they need to do to win a case. Period. They do not waste their time or their clients' money exacting revenge, but Valente's attorneys do it every time, and they obviously do it on his orders. Valente doesn't call them off until he's got the prosecutors' faces in the mud and his foot is planted on their heads. Then, and only then, does he let them up."

"I really can't blame him for wanting a little petty revenge."

"There's nothing 'petty' about his revenge. Prosecutors who are made to look like fools in big cases like Valente's can pretty much kiss their career ambitions good-bye. But prosecutors also have long memories and they can carry very big grudges. Moreover, every time Valente sends a few of them running for cover with their tails between their legs, there are a dozen more who are dying to step up to the plate and prove their own mettle by being the first and only one to successfully take Valente down."

He picked up a pencil lying on his desk and then tossed it aside with the same impatience he'd tossed aside the file folders. "When I took over this case, I thought Valente was nothing but a big shark who'd been chewing through our legal nets for years. *I* wanted to harpoon him for the same reason the prosecutors did. I'm no different from them."

"That is completely untrue!" Sam said so forcefully that surprise erased some of the anger on his face.

"How am I different?"

"You *believed* he was guilty of everything he'd been accused of when you took this assignment. Some of those prosecutors had to know they were making a mountain out of nothing."

Instead of replying, he shook his head at something else he was remembering: "The day Trumanti summoned me to One Police Plaza and told me he wanted me to head this investigation as 'a personal favor,' I *sensed* there was something almost obsessively vindictive about his attitude toward Valente. Besides cursing him out in every breath, Trumanti kept telling me that nailing Valente was his dying wish. I think the old man has actually convinced himself Valente is guilty of everything, beginning with Holmes's 'manslaughter.'" He glared at the top of his desk. "When I told him I was about to hand in my retirement notice, he told me if I nailed Valente on first-degree murder, I'd retire as a captain."

"Did that have anything to do with why you took the case?"

"If I had any real desire to make captain," he said with a disdainful smile, "I'd have simply managed my career a little differently." Nodding toward the table again, he added, "When I started going through that pile of crap over there, I noticed that the prosecutors were out of control with some of those charges. Even I could tell they couldn't make them stick. Valente's no Mafia kingpin with a network of minions doing his dirty work so it can't be traced to him.

He runs a legitimate multinational corporation. With the kind of intense scrutiny he's always under, his corporation must be squeaky clean, or else some prosecutor somewhere would stick him with something. The most they've ever found were some minor internal accounting irregularities like you'd find at any big corporation."

He was quiet for a moment, looking to his left at the chalkboard where they'd kept track of the circumstantial evidence they had been compiling against Valente: then he shook his head and gave a short, grim laugh. "I think it's safe to conclude that Valente didn't kill Logan Manning, nor did he hire someone to do it for him."

"What makes you so certain?" Sam asked, suppressing a pleased smile.

"Because, if Valente was willing to commit murder, he'd have targeted *Trumanti* a long time ago." He stood up then, still looking at the chalkboard, and he said of Valente, "Now there is a man who lives by the saying 'Never Complain, Never Explain.' No wonder you liked him."

Sam stood up, too. "What are you going to do now?"

"Among other things, I'm going to find out who really killed Manning. We'll start all over tomorrow morning, looking at alternative suspects and theories." Walking around his desk, he picked up his jacket and shrugged into it. "Get your coat," he told her. "I'll take you home."

He'd never offered to do that before. McCord had a car, but in decent weather Sam walked home; otherwise she took the subway. She started to decline, but she didn't do it. She told herself it was because he'd had a difficult enough day without her adding rejection of a nice offer to it. The truth was that he looked so weary and disheartened that she ached for him.

CHAPTER 60

A small crowd was waiting for the elevators, so McCord turned toward the stairwell and Sam followed him. He was two steps in front of her, which gave her time to dwell on the short hairs at his nape that touched his collar.

His mind was still on his unwitting part in trying to hang a crime on the wrong man. "I'm so damned glad I gave Valente the benefit of the doubt when I questioned him this morning," he told her sarcastically. "They've been trying to lock him up for years, but I was going to help them stick a needle in his arm for something he didn't do. How much worse can abuse of power and authority get?"

"I think he's actually a very lucky man," Sam replied behind him.

"How do you figure that?" McCord said derisively as they neared the landing on the second floor.

Sam's right hand actually lifted toward his shoulder, but she pulled it back. She'd been able to withstand his magnetic appeal when he was strong and sure of himself, but she was evidently not proof against Mitchell McCord when he was troubled. "Because you'd never have let that happen. You're nobody's henchman. That's what makes you so incredible—"

He stopped walking and turned so sharply that Sam couldn't stop her descent to the next step or her hand from colliding with his on the railing. Her heart began to beat frantically when she found her face only an inch from his, and her fingers seemed to have fused themselves to his on the railing.

Swallowing, she struggled free of the momentary spell and stepped upward a step. He stepped up onto the one she'd vacated, giving her a close-up view of the tanned column of his throat at the V of his open collar. Fear of their discovery by anyone walking into the stairwell made her chest rise and fall rapidly, and his gaze dropped to her breasts, noting it. What he said, however, was exactly the opposite of anything she would have imagined:

"No," he said on a harsh laugh, as if he couldn't believe he'd walked up that last step. "No." Turning, he moved down the stairs rapidly with Sam right behind him, completely mortified and adamantly determined not to show it. The outer door opened onto a tiny, badly lit parking area behind the building. "It's a nice night," she lied with a cheerful voice, stepping into the freezing air. "I'd really like to take the subway and stop for some—shopping on the way home."

She turned with a bright smile and then frowned when his hand locked around her elbow. "Get in my car," he ordered.

Sam pulled her elbow free, but not roughly—not in a way that would show she was upset. Showing a male that you were upset made him leap to a variety of conclusions, none of which were ever what you wanted him to conclude. However, *laughing* at a man in that same situation thoroughly threw him off guard. Sam laughed good-naturedly. "I appreciate your offer, but I would really rather take the subway and go shopping."

"Get in the car," he commanded, putting his hand in the small of her back to ensure she did that.

The next big mistake you could make with a male in McCord's inexplicably domineering mood, Sam knew, was to appear to make a big issue over nothing. Which of course made them conclude that the "nothing" was a big "something" to you.

Sam got into his car, and he closed the door behind her, then locked it with his key.

She almost got the giggles over that. "We're both armed, you know," she told him when he slid behind the steering wheel.

"One of us is better armed than the other," he replied brusquely.

Sam sent him a speculative smile. "Which one of us is that?"

He turned slowly and put his arm across the back of the seat, and for a split second, she almost thought he was going to curve his hand around her shoulder and pull her close. Instead he moved his arm and started the car. "You," he answered belatedly.

After Sam told him what little she'd learned from Valente in his limo, they made the rest of the ride in complete silence, a silence that had never been present in the past, because they'd always had things to talk about. Sam did not feel good about any of this. He was not behaving predictably at all. Of course, she hadn't behaved predictably in that stairwell either. She shouldn't have said the things she did, she shouldn't have let her voice go soft, shouldn't have stayed on that step with her hand touching his those extra seconds.

"Thanks for the ride," she said as they were pulling up to her building. She half expected him to remark on the fact that she lived at a very fancy address for a lowly NYPD detective, but he didn't. She reached for the door handle, and to her surprise he cut the engine. "There's no need for you to get out," she said, stepping onto the street.

He ignored her and got out anyway.

Nervousness was taking the place of Sam's usual rational calm with members of the male sex. "What are you doing?" she asked when he met her on the curb and started walking her into her building.

"Walking you to your door."

"You can't be serious!" she sputtered, laughing.

"I am *very* serious," he said curtly, escorting her past the doorman.

Sam pressed the elevator button and decided it was best to tackle the actual problem head-on. "I hope you aren't upset about that silly moment on the stairway."

He gave her a look so quelling that her heart dropped. "We'll discuss that upstairs."

Sam gave him another sidelong, amused smile—the kind that used to drive her brothers crazy and *always* discomfited even the most self-confident adult males. "Are—you under the impression I'm going to invite you in?"

"I am not only under that impression, I am certain of it."

Based on his tone and his attitude, Sam concluded the only thing she could conclude: He was evidently going to reprimand her for her inappropriate behavior. Telling a male colleague—and especially an immediate superior—that he was "incredible" and touching his hand showed bad judgment, probably verging on inappropriate behavior, in the strictest interpretation of the rules, but really—this was going too far!

Sam unlocked her apartment door, walked inside, and turned on the light switch beside the door. He followed her in but stopped there. Folding his arms over his chest, he stood with his shoulders against the door.

Out of some apprehensive need to at least look tidy while she caught hell, Sam nervously reached up and tightened the band that was holding her hair into a chignon at the crown. He stood there, watching her in silence as she did that; then he said, "There aren't going to be any stolen kisses in dirty stairwells or groping each other in parked cars in dark alleys."

He paused to let that sink in, and Sam's lips parted in disbelief that he would dare to exaggerate a few moments in a stairwell and a car, where *nothing* actually happened, into an attempt on her part to seduce him! McCord not only had a gigantic ego, but, she suddenly realized, he also had a clever little "approach" of his own to use on women he worked with—first a dinner invitation, then a mention of a "lovers' quarrel," then signing his nickname on a note. And it worked! It even worked on her, and she had never been reduced to a state of mushy hero-worship in her entire life. Everything she'd liked about him paled to nothing in comparison with this discovery.

"We not only work together, I'm your superior," he reminded her needlessly. "So I want you to understand that this will never have any effect on our working relationship or on your career. Are you clear on that?"

"That's very kind of you," Sam lied, maintaining her perfect, cool little smile as she, too, folded her arms over her chest. "I understand. Thank you, Lieutenant."

His eyes narrowed. "I am trying to assure you that you don't have to fear any repercussions from what I'm going to do."

Sam was losing her grip on her temper, and she *never*

did that! "Would you care to tell me what it is you're going to do?"

"That was my plan," he said, looking a little amused by her tone.

"Then what is it you plan to do?"

"First, I'm going to pull that band out of your hair and let it loose so that I can shove my fingers into it and find out whether it actually feels like satin or like silk. I've been dying to do that for weeks."

Sam's arms uncrossed and fell limply to her sides as she gaped at him.

"Soon after I do that," he continued in a husky voice she hadn't heard before. "I'm going to start kissing you, and at some point before I leave, I'm going to turn you into this wall—" He tipped his head to the wall right next to the door. "And then I am going to do everything I possibly can to imprint my body on yours."

Blood was beginning to race through Sam's veins, but her brain seemed to be deprived of oxygen, because she couldn't quite match the last part of this with his opening remarks. *"Why?"* she blurted, furrowing her brow.

He obviously didn't understand the scope of her question, but the answer he gave made her melt: "Because tomorrow, we're going to pretend this never happened, and we're going to go on pretending until the Manning case is over, or one of us is reassigned. If we don't wait—if we let this get started before then—we'll end up in that dirty stairwell and others just like it, trying to steal a few moments together and worrying about your getting caught. This isn't going to be a sordid little backstairs fling, and I don't want to treat it—or you—like it is one."

Sam looked at his ruggedly virile, implacable features while she tried to adjust to the new reality that Mitchell Mc-Cord did want her, and had wanted her all along, and at the same time he was also trying to safeguard her career and re-assure her about his feelings for her. He had been something of a hero to her before, but now everything she had imagined him to be seemed so much less than he actually was.

"While we're pretending," he continued after allotting her just enough time to catch up with his reasoning so far, "you'll have time to decide whether or not you want to be with me when this case is over. If, during this time, you decide the answer is no, I'll know it, and we won't discuss it. We'll part on the best of terms when this case is over, and you can simply go on pretending that the things I'm about to do to you, and with you, never happened." He paused again to gauge her reaction. "How does this sound so far?"

It was so like him—optimum planning and organizational skills in full use right to the end. Unable to control the trembling smile in her heart or the one lighting her eyes, Sam whispered, "It sounds ... *exactly* like you, Mack."

He rejected that reply as inconclusive and raised his brows, waiting for an answer, his blue gaze pinning hers.

In reply, Sam reached up and pulled the band and pins out of her hair; then she gave the heavy mass a hard shake that sent it tumbling down in a chestnut waterfall over her shoulders.

He took her face in his hands and slowly threaded his fingers through the sides of her hair, turning her mouth up to his. "Sam," he whispered softly, as if he held some special reverence for her name. Lowering his head, he touched his lips to hers. "Sam," he said again in an aching whisper.

When he left, Sam closed the door, secured the locks; then she turned and leaned against the same wall he had backed her against. Smiling, she slid slowly down it to the floor; then she drew her legs against her chest and wrapped her arms around them. Resting her cheek on her knee, Sam closed her eyes, savoring the lingering sensations of his hands and mouth against her skin, the hardness of his aroused body against hers. Her long hair, neat and orderly an hour before, spilled over her other cheek and across her leg in a tangled mass, crushed and combed by his hands.

She had followed Mitchell McCord right along that imaginary path, just as she'd known she was doing.

And she had walked off that cliff into thin air.

Oh, but what a fall!

CHAPTER 61

The King Cole Room at the St. Regis on Fifty-fifth Street was not Michael's idea of a good place for the sort of discussion with Solomon that he had in mind. Wide, shallow, and dimly lit, it was paneled in dark wood. Stretching its length was a long bar lined with barstools, all of them already occupied with the room's usual Manhattan crowd stopping for drinks after work.

The only other seating in the room was a few feet from the bar at a parallel row of tiny cocktail tables lined up along the wall with chairs jammed around them. It was not only dark as pitch in there, it was noisy, which, Michael thought with a knowing smile, was probably why Leigh had chosen it for her obligatory meeting with Jason. In the bad light, she wouldn't be recognized, and Jason would have to raise his voice to "badger" her about coming back to work.

Next to that room was a discreet little "salon" with cocktail tables, better lighting, and only a few customers. Michael chose a table that would at least enable him to see

Leigh if she used the side entrance, which was across the room and down a long, wide ramp; then he ordered a drink and impatiently watched the time.

Solomon arrived fifteen minutes late, exuding regret and bursting with nervous ire over the reason he'd been delayed.

"I can't apologize enough!" he said, shaking hands with Michael and sitting down. Since they'd never met, Michael expected him to start talking about Leigh right away, since she was the only thing they had in common. However, as Michael immediately realized, Solomon now felt he had something else—something very significant—in common with Michael.

"I'm late because of the cops!" Solomon exclaimed irately. "Two detectives showed up at the theater—without an appointment—asking me a lot of questions about my relationship with Logan Manning. I couldn't get rid of them! They're tenacious bastards, aren't they?"

"You won't get an argument from me on that," Michael replied.

"You have to deal with those people all the time," he reminded Michael. "How do you handle cops when they show up and start prying into your business?"

"I usually bribe them to go away."

"Does that work?"

"If it doesn't, I shoot them."

Belatedly realizing that he was being politely informed his comments were in bad taste, Jason leaned back in his chair and briefly closed his eyes. "Would you mind very much," he said bluntly, "if we started all over again?"

Michael glanced at his watch. "Let's just go on as we were."

"Are you interested in what the cops were asking me about?"

"Should I be?"

"They wanted to know how Logan paid me for his share in the play."

That interested Michael very much, so he lifted his brows inquiringly, and the nervous playwright gave him the details. "I told them Logan had two hundred thousand dollars in cash he wanted to use as payment for his share in the play, so I took it. We signed a contract, I gave him a receipt, and I deposited the money into the play's main bank account. What's the big damned deal? We deposit five or six hundred thousand dollars a week from box office receipts into that account."

Michael casually raised his glass to his lips in order to seem less intrigued than he was. "How much of your box office receipts are cash?"

"A big chunk, usually."

"But Manning's two hundred thousand dollars wasn't box office receipts. Why didn't you deposit Manning's money into a general account instead of calling it box office receipts and depositing it into your box office account?"

Solomon lifted his hands. "That's what the cops asked."

"What did you tell them?"

"I told them the truth. I'm not a bookkeeper and I'm not an accountant. Logan gave me cash and suggested I deposit it into the box office receipts account, and I did. I told the bookkeeper it was a shareholder payment, and she made the appropriate internal adjustments, whatever the hell they are. I hate accountants."

Jason looked up to signal a waitress and order a drink. He was very fussy about the way his martinis were made, Michael noted impatiently, so that took another two minutes of time that Michael didn't have to spare.

"Did Manning give you any idea where he got the money?" Michael asked when Jason had finished ordering.

"Logan said," Jason explained, "that somebody paid him in cash and he'd been hanging on to the money because he didn't want to deposit it into his own account."

"Did he say why he didn't?"

"The cops asked me the same question."

"What answer did you give them?"

Before replying, Solomon paused to search for a particular kind of nut in the bowl on their table. "Logan said he didn't want to deposit it into his bank account because he'd have to make twenty different trips to his bank. Did you know that if you deposit *or withdraw* one dollar more than ten thousand dollars in cash, your bank notifies the IRS? I mean," he asked Michael seriously, "who the hell wants the IRS crawling all over them?"

"Not I," Michael said gravely.

"They're the American gestapo."

"I couldn't agree more."

"In my case, though," Jason explained, hunting for another nut in the bowl, "we're a legitimate cash business, because of our box office receipts, so the IRS doesn't look at us in the same way." He watched the waitress carrying his drink to him, and while she waited, he tasted it to make certain it was "stirred, not shaken," and that "one drop, not two drops," of vermouth was in it. "This is fine," he told her; then he took a fortifying swallow, relaxed in his chair, and seemed to suddenly remember that Michael had specifically requested this private meeting with him before Leigh arrived. "Now then," he said cordially, "what can I do for you, Mr. Valente? Or—shall I call you Michael, since Leigh says you're actually an old friend of hers?"

Michael felt, absurdly, a pang of nonsensical hurt that Leigh hadn't told Solomon he was a little more than an old friend. On the other hand, he reasoned fairly, it was one thing to love him in private, but it was going to be difficult for her to explain to friends how she could possibly consider allying herself with the name *Valente*—whether she actually ever used it or not. Neither Michael, nor his name, would ever be an asset to her publicly. Just the opposite, in fact. "Call me whatever you'd like," Michael said. "There's nothing you can do for me, but there's something I may be able to do for you."

If there was one way to get Solomon's attention, Michael noted, it was to offer him something he wanted—even if he didn't know what it was. "Leigh tells me you want her to come back to work," he said.

"God, yes!"

"She won't do it as long as she has to share a stage with Jane Sebring."

"Leigh has no choice! She's a professional—"

"She does have a choice, and she's made it," Michael told him coolly. "She feels, understandably, that she'd be turning herself—her *private* self—into a public spectacle."

At his implacable tone, Jason stopped arguing, and for several seconds he appeared to lose himself in contemplation of the olives in the bottom of his glass. "I'm going to tell you the blunt truth," he said finally, lifting his gaze to Michael. "Jane Sebring is a little insane. I do not say that lightly. She has a sick obsession with becoming Leigh. Leigh is going to have something Jane wants more than anything in life."

"Which is?"

"Theatrical immortality."

"Excuse me?"

"The Barrymores and the Sebrings, except for Jane, have been immortalized for their work on Broadway. Only three actresses have ever reached that pinnacle—Ethel Barrymore, Marianna Sebring, and Delores Sebring. Leigh Kendall will be the fourth, but if she willfully banishes herself from the theater at this stage in her career—and over nothing but a cheating husband—she will lose her place in the clouds. Actors act!" Jason said fiercely, and Michael suddenly had the feeling he was hearing the speech Solomon had prepared to give Leigh. "They act when they're sick, when their father is dying, when they're so drunk they can't see straight, and when they're almost catatonic with clinical depression. When the curtain goes up, they get on stage, and *they act!*"

Michael was about to interrupt Solomon's lecture on theatrical customs, but the playwright's next words instantly captivated him. "Do you have any idea how incredibly, richly multitalented Leigh really is?" He held up a hand without waiting for a reply. "Don't try to answer because you *don't* know. No one knows. At NYU, they called her a prodigy because they didn't know how else to describe what she can do. The critics call her 'magical' because they can't explain it either." Folding his arms on the table, he leaned forward and said, "During opening night for *Blind Spot*, in the second act, when Leigh leans toward the audience and says she knows a secret, I watched the whole damned audience lean forward in their chairs to hear it."

Michael looked up and saw several people coming from the lobby toward the bar, and reluctantly ended stories that he would happily have listened to for hours. "Let's talk about Jane Sebring."

Jason shuddered and flopped back in his chair. "She's moved into Leigh's dressing room. The day after Jane's affair with Logan hit the papers, she told me Leigh would never come back to the play, and she told me she wanted Leigh's dressing room. I told her absolutely not. I mean, for god sakes, both dressing rooms are identical, but she wants to be where Leigh is. Literally and figuratively. Logan's death has turned out to be a complete boon to her.

Leigh can't come back to work, and Jane's got the leading role. I don't know what to do."

"Fire her."

"My God, there's nothing I would like more, but her agents drew up a contract that has me by the throat."

"Pay her off."

"I wish I could, but I don't have that kind of money lying around. I've already committed a large chunk of the profits from *Blind Spot* to my next play. If I weren't worried about financing that play, I'd pay Sebring off, believe me. Her understudy can play Sebring's part, and she'd cost me a fraction of what Sebring is getting."

"How much are you looking for to finance your next play?"

Solomon told him.

Michael reached into his jacket pocket. And took out a checkbook.

"You're serious?" Solomon breathed, looking from the amount written on the check to Michael's face.

"The proof that I am is in your hand," Michael said mildly, tipping his head toward the check. "Send the appropriate documents to my office by messenger tomorrow. Draw them up in Leigh's name."

"Leigh's name?"

Michael nodded.

"I could use another drink!" Solomon declared with a confused laugh. "How about you?" Without waiting for an answer, he signaled the waitress for another round. When he glanced back, he saw his companion looking at something outside the windows.

Michael was watching Leigh get out of the Farrell limo in a bright sapphire blue coat and dress. She was smiling up at O'Hara, who was holding the door.

A man was getting out of a taxi right behind her. He

hung back, then followed her slowly down the sidewalk toward the side entrance. Michael didn't notice; he was concentrating on Leigh.

"Is something going on out there?" Jason asked, turning around.

"Yes," Michael said, flicking a smiling glance at him. "Your new partner is just arriving."

Lost in the thrilling poignancy of the moment, Michael watched the woman he loved, knowing she was finally his. She was glamour and grace, coming to meet him at the St. Regis in an outfit of sapphire blue . . .

She was a laughing girl in jeans with an armload of oranges.

She was a solemn girl, trying to give a gift to a rude cynic who was crazy about her. *"I wanted to thank you properly . . . for being so gallant,"* she'd explained.

"Gallant? Is that what you think I am?"

"Yes, I do."

"When did they let you out of your playpen?"

"My mind is made up. Don't try to change it, because you can't. Here . . . this is for you."

She was the naïve girl he had rescued and walked home while she lectured him about civic duty. *"How do you expect the police to protect us if citizens won't cooperate? Among other things, it's every citizen's duty . . ."*

She was the entrancing young woman who had walked through a line of shouting reporters, armed with only her courage and loyalty to him, and launched a simultaneous attack on the entire NYPD and the *Daily News*. *"If Commissioner Trumanti, or anyone under him, approved of the slander you printed today, then he is as criminally irresponsible as your newspaper."*

She was the intoxicating angel who'd laughed in his arms the night before in a grocery market, where their pictures were plastered across the *Daily News*'s hideous front page. *"Together at last,"* he'd joked with her.

Michael watched her push through the entrance doors and begin walking up the long marble ramp. Smiling with possessive pleasure, he stood up to wait for her. *Together at last,* he thought.

Leigh felt excited, eager, and strangely nervous about seeing Michael after the night they'd spent together and the promises they'd made. It had all happened so fast. If someone else had been telling her this story, she would have sent the woman for extensive therapy!

She'd spotted him as soon as she walked into the side entrance, and she'd watched him come to his feet—a man who was six feet three inches of formidable masculinity, bold strength, and unbelievable gentleness. He was watching her cross the lobby, and the tender things he'd said the night before began to flash through her mind. *"I wanted something much better for you, than me . . . I believe you were meant to be my beacon. . . . I was meant to watch over you."*

She thought of him that morning, smiling into her eyes when she silently agreed to marry him. *"A kiss on the hand is equal to two nods. Very, very binding."*

And then she remembered what his aunt had said at dinner the night before: *"Every week, Michael went to Dean and DeLuca to buy your pears. . . . He was going to school, and he had no money, so he stretched every penny . . . but for you, only the best would do.*

"Michael knows how to make you happy, and you know how to make him happy . . ."

He was standing only a few yards away, his eyes smiling into hers, pulling her forward. Leigh started walking faster, and suddenly she was rushing straight into his arms. He caught her in a fierce hug, and laughing, she twined her arms around his neck, her cheek pressed to his chest. Pulling back, she looked up at him and said cheerfully, "Hi."

"Hi," Michael replied with a grin.

Ignoring Jason Solomon completely, she kept her arms around his neck and teasingly asked the question wives routinely ask husbands: "How was your day?"

Michael thought about that before answering. His day had started with lovemaking and a marriage proposal; then he'd met with his attorney, voluntarily gone to a police precinct, and been interrogated by an obnoxious asshole lieutenant. He'd been chased down by another detective who hitched a ride in his car and then followed him into a building where he was meeting with private investigators. He'd hired the investigators, had them relay a verbal threat to the lieutenant; now he'd just arranged to have Leigh's costar ejected from the play and Leigh made a partner in Solomon's next one.

"The usual," he said with a grin. "But it's improving fast."

"Jason," Leigh said without looking at the gaping playwright. "Can you keep a secret?"

He looked stung by the question. "No!" he unhesitatingly replied.

"Good. I just wanted to be sure you hadn't turned over a new leaf." Satisfied, Leigh told him the "secret" she didn't want him to keep: Looking into Michael Valente's eyes, she said, "I love you."

At a table nearby, a new customer sat down and watched the tender scene with shock. And then with fury. He stayed until the couple started to leave; then he threw a crumpled bill on his table and followed slowly behind them.

O'HARA WAS WAITING at the curb with the car. "Where to next?" he asked as he barged into traffic, cutting off another limo driver, who blasted him with his horn. "Do you want to get something for dinner?" he said, looking at Michael in the rearview mirror.

Instead of answering, Michael put his arm around Leigh, his fingers drifting over the side of her neck and her soft cheek, his gaze fixed on her lips. "Do you know what I really want?" he whispered.

Leigh looked into those heavy-lidded, smoldering amber eyes, and chuckled. "I'll bet I can guess."

"You've guessed the first half of it. The second half is directly related to the first half, but it's a slightly longer-term 'want.' Have you figured it out?"

Leigh considered the fact that he'd raced from platonic friendship to marriage in the space of twelve hours. After twenty-four hours, it seemed obvious where his thoughts would be by now. With absolute confidence, she smiled and said, "Grandchildren."

He threw back his head and gave a shout of laughter; then he said with a boyish grin, "I like the way you think."

Chapter 62

Sam pressed the *up* button again and looked at her watch while she waited nervously for the Eighteenth's old elevator to make its creaking journey to the first floor. She'd taken a taxi instead of walking to the subway because it was sleeting, and the cab had gotten hopelessly snarled in traffic. She was already five minutes late for work, and she hated being late for work—particularly today, when Mack might understandably think she was trying to take advantage of their new situation.

On top of that, she was supposed to meet her mother and stepfather for a little cocktail party fund-raiser at the Four Seasons immediately after work. As a result, she was dressed for the occasion in a pale gray suede skirt and belted jacket with matching heels. She was about to head for the stairwell and jog up two flights in high heels and a narrow skirt, when the elevator finally arrived.

MACK WAS STANDING at the chalkboard holding a clipboard in his left hand, writing a new list of possible suspects on the board, when Sam hurried into his office at 8:08.

The meeting hadn't begun yet, and Shrader and Womack were standing near the chairs in front of Mack's desk, drinking coffee. Shrader trumpeted the news of Sam's arrival in a way that made her long to strangle him. "My God, Littleton!" he exclaimed, "is that really you? Jeez!" He elbowed Womack. "Have you ever seen a better pair of legs than Littleton's got?"

"I'd have to see a little more of them before I could be sure," Womack said with an exaggerated leer. "How 'bout it, Littleton?"

Sam rolled her eyes at him and walked over to her usual chair, the one closest to the chalkboard on the end. Unfortunately, Shrader was truly fascinated by the "new her."

"So what's the occasion?" he demanded. "You got a hot date for lunch?"

"No, for cocktails after work," Sam replied distractedly. She hated feeling awkward, and she wished Mack would say something.

He did, and it was in a very cool, brusque tone. "You're late, Littleton," he said, as he continued to write on the board.

"Yes, I know. I'm sorry."

"Don't do it again."

That was unjust and pushing it too far. Sam had been coming in early, leaving late, and working weekends for weeks. She felt warm color rush up her cheeks, and unfortunately, Shrader not only saw it, he thought it was attractive, and remarked upon it, too. "It's not just the way you're dressed, Littleton. There's something different about you this morning. You got a . . . I dunno . . . a glow."

Too embarrassed and frustrated to think ahead, Sam retaliated against Mack's second warning about being late. "I'm just more relaxed today than usual," she told Shrader lightly. "Last night, I had an all-over body massage."

Mack's chalk snapped.

Sam bit back a satisfied grin as she bent down to pick up the broken piece that had rolled across the floor near her feet. At that moment, Mack turned around and walked toward her. Holding the piece of chalk in her fingers, Sam looked up at him from beneath her lashes and slowly stood up.

He held out his hand, his expression impassive, but she saw the warning in his eyes, and something else . . . something like accusation. She dropped the chalk on his palm—the same palm that had shoved beneath her bra last night and caressed her breasts. His long fingers closed on the chalk—the same fingers that had . . .

Sam cast that thought aside and watched him return to writing on the board. He was wearing a black knit shirt that outlined his broad shoulders and tapered waist, and Sam's thoughts promptly drifted to the way his bunched muscles felt beneath her fingertips. He was so beautiful . . .

She sat down again and made herself chat with Shrader and Womack, who were leaning against McCord's desk.

Dusting chalk from his hands, McCord turned abruptly and said, "Valente is off the suspect list permanently."

"What?" Womack exclaimed, straightening.

"Why?" Shrader demanded.

"I can't tell you the reason because it involves some departmental issues that I need to deal with separately, later. For now, I want you to accept my word that I have sufficient reason to disqualify him completely as a suspect. If either of you have a problem with that, say it now."

Shrader and Womack hesitated only a second; then Womack shook his head and Shrader said, "No problem. It's okay by me, if it's okay by you." Sam had known they wouldn't hesitate to take McCord's word: they were both as impressed by him as she was.

"Next," McCord said implacably, "I want it understood that *no one* outside this room is to know we're disqualifying Valente. No one," he repeated.

Shrader and Womack both nodded.

He glanced at Sam then, but it was merely a formality, and she nodded, too.

"Can I just ask one question—?" Shrader said. "Does the decision to take Valente off the list have anything to do with what Littleton learned when she chased him down yesterday?"

McCord shook his head. "No, but she can fill you in later on what she discovered. Right now, we've got a killer on the loose." He glanced toward the names on the chalkboard. "Littleton has said all along that she thinks a woman is the one who washed those wineglasses out—obviously in the snow, since the cabin had no running water—and then put them carefully in the sink, where they'd be less likely to get broken.

"Given Manning's love of the ladies, that theory fits. If so, then the missing sleeping bag could indicate he had sexual intercourse with someone who knew enough about police forensics to know we'd check that sleeping bag for traces of hair and fluids."

"Anybody who's ever watched a couple episodes of *Law and Order* knows that," Shrader pointed out.

"Exactly. And from any similar movie or television program, the killer would have learned that we'd check Manning's hands for powder residue, so she—or he—fired one of the shots with Manning's hand wrapped around the butt of the weapon."

Pausing, McCord tipped his head to the list of names on the board. "Let's start with the women we know of who Manning came into contact with through his wife, since he had a partiality for screwing her friends and acquaintances.

You've checked out their alibis but not as thoroughly as we would have if we hadn't been so sure Valente was our man."

Shrader and Womack settled into their usual chairs, and Sam slid hers back a little so they could see past her to the board. Normally these meetings in Mack's office were intense and fast-paced, but disqualifying Valente as a suspect left everyone without a focus, and the atmosphere in the room became noticeably desultory. Not only were they now without a suspect, they also had to come to terms with the unexpected reality of having dedicated enormous energy and time to a "sure thing" that wasn't one.

"What about Leigh Manning?" Shrader said finally. "She's not on the board."

For the first time, McCord's gaze shifted specifically to Sam, but the smile twisting the corner of his mouth was one of impersonal amusement. "I think Littleton has been right all along about Leigh Manning's innocence. I want to talk to Mrs. Manning myself today, but based on what Littleton learned from Valente in the limo yesterday, it's reasonable to believe Mrs. Manning had no idea that her old friend 'Falco Nipote' was actually Michael Valente until *after* her husband died."

"I find that hard to believe," Womack said bluntly.

Instead of impatiently telling Womack to take his word on it, McCord reversed his earlier decision and asked Sam to relate to them what she'd learned from Valente yesterday. Sam admired him for that. Mack was not only an extraordinary team leader, he was an all-out, full-fledged team member who understood when his teammates couldn't go forward without more background.

"That makes a lot of sense," Shrader said when Sam finished her tale about the note they'd confiscated. "I mean, why *would* a guy sign 'nephew' and 'Falco' on a note that already had his name printed on the top of the paper?"

"It also explains why we couldn't connect him with Leigh Manning before the murder, no matter how hard we tried," McCord said. "They *weren't* connected. If you have any doubts about why she didn't recognize him at her party, have a look at his mug shot when he was busted on the manslaughter charge. He had a dark beard. Hell, I wouldn't have recognized him."

Sam thought of Valente's voice in the limo, the smooth rich timbre of his baritone and McCord noticed her frown. "Are you disagreeing?" he asked her dubiously.

"No," Sam said emphatically as she reached behind her nape to tighten the wide silver clip holding her hair back. "I saw that old photograph in Valente's file. The only thing Leigh Manning could have recognized when she met him at her party was his voice. Valente has the most amazing voice. It's very deep and very mellow—"

Womack slapped his knee. "I knew it! I told you—Littleton has a thing for Valente. C'mon, Littleton, come clean—is your heavy date tonight with Valente? We won't tell a soul," he lied. "You can trust us," he lied again, oblivious to McCord's clenching jaw.

Sam was losing patience. She looked at Womack in bewildered disgust and said, "My 'date' is with my stepfather and mother! Now, knock it off, will you?"

"What's your stepfather do, anyway?" Shrader asked suddenly.

Unaware of the almost imperceptible softening in McCord's gaze when she mentioned the identity of her "date," Sam reached for a spare tablet lying on McCord's desk and took a pencil out of her purse. "He works for the government and lives off the taxpayers just like we do."

"Can we get back to business?" McCord said, but he sounded less curt than he had before, and several seconds later, Sam belatedly realized that he might have assumed she was all dressed up to go out with another man. Mack was a detective who would instinctively look for other, subtler, reasons for the things people did—which could have meant he wondered if she'd gotten dressed up and mentioned a drinks date just to tease him, keep him off balance, and make the waiting harder.

Shoving those thoughts aside, she looked up at the chalkboard as McCord pointed to the first name on it and said, "What about Jane Sebring, the costar? She said she went home and went to bed, then she got up later, and watched a movie on television. How thoroughly did you check out her alibi?" he asked Shrader and Womack.

"Her doorman confirmed that she returned to the building late in the afternoon, after the matinee," Womack said. "Her car service confirmed her ride from the theater to her apartment building at that time. That's not saying, however, that she didn't sneak out the back way later, rent a car or something, and drive herself to the mountains."

"Start checking out the car rental companies, and also check her credit card receipts and her LUDS."

Shrader nodded. "I'll check the other car services, too—"

Womack guffawed. "What—like she had a chauffeur drive her into the mountains, and wait for her, while she trotted down to the cabin and blew Manning away?"

Shrader actually blushed. His big, ferocious-looking face took on a hangdog expression, and he stared at his lap, shaking his head in disbelief. "I realized before I finished the sentence that couldn't have happened."

"Let's move on," McCord said, but a smile was tugging at his lips at Shrader's rare lapse into bad logic. "What about Trish Lefkowitz, the publicist?"

"Her alibi holds water," Womack said.

"Too bad," McCord said dryly, drawing a line through

her name. "Trish has the balls to shoot a guy in the head and remember to clean up the dishes in the kitchen afterward."

"You talking from *personal* knowledge, Lieutenant?" Shrader asked.

Sam was glad he asked that question, but she kept her expression perfectly bland as she waited for McCord to reply. His reply was a short laugh and an eloquent shudder. "No."

Sam believed him. She just wished she hadn't made that suggestive wisecrack about having had a massage last night. She was not only new at being in love, she was completely unprepared to handle that earthshaking experience with someone she worked for and with.

She'd made an agreement with Mack about how they were going to go on until the Manning case was over, and she'd broken it within minutes after walking into his office. And what made that much worse was that she was truly touched by his reasons for wanting the agreement. Unfortunately, she didn't think Mack would let her default pass without comment, which was why she had every intention of making a beeline out of his office the moment this meeting concluded.

"What about Sybil Haywood, the astrologer?" Mack asked. "She's attractive enough to interest Manning."

"What a kook!" Shrader said, slapping his knee for emphasis. "Before she'd talk to me when I got there, I had to give her my 'birth data'; then she ran some sort of computer program on my planets or some damned thing. She called it my 'astrological chart.' "

"What about it?" McCord asked, referring to her alibi.

Shrader misunderstood and thought he was asking about the astrological chart. "She said a young female who is close to me, but not a family member, is in grave danger, but could not be saved. She said I should remember that this life is only a stopping place to the next one, and we'll be together again."

"Did she have an alibi and was it solid?" McCord asked derisively.

"Yes to both questions. I just remembered something the Haywood woman told me," Shrader added as McCord turned to draw a line through Haywood's name. "I blew it off before, but she said that on the night of the party, Leigh Manning recruited her to entertain Valente. Haywood said Mrs. Manning was upset that he'd been invited—you know, because of his lousy reputation."

McCord nodded. "Which further substantiates the idea that Leigh Manning didn't know who Valente really was that night." He glanced at the next name on the chalkboard. "What about Theta Berenson? She's the artist."

"She's got an alibi and it checks out," Shrader said. "Anyway, Manning wouldn't have laid a hockey stick on her, let alone a hand. If being ugly was a crime, they'd be hunting that woman down with helicopters and bloodhounds."

"Shrader," McCord said with a reluctant smile, turning to mark off her name, too, "I hate to be the first to tell you this, but you're not exactly a Chippendales dancer, yourself."

Sam looked at her tablet to hide her smile. She looked up again as McCord folded his arms across his chest and turned back to the chalkboard, looking at the names left there.

"What about Claire Straight?" he asked.

"She's got a sound alibi," Womack said. "And she hates men. Her husband dumped her for a sweet, young thing half his age, and the woman is obsessed. If you ask me, she's turning into a lesbian over this divorce."

"Can that happen?" Shrader asked, looking to Sam for

an answer. "Do you think a formerly heterosexual woman can turn into a lesbian because a man cheated on her?"

Unaware that McCord had glanced over his shoulder, Sam leaned forward, smiled widely at Shrader, and said, "Yes, definitely. That's how it happened to me."

She leaned back suddenly, turned her head, and caught McCord looking at her. He had a look of pained laughter on his face; then he shook his head slightly and turned back to the chalkboard. Sam was a detective, too—she noticed that odd little shake of his head, and she identified it. It was the same thing she'd done a few moments before, trying to concentrate on work at hand instead of him.

"Erin Gillroy, Manning's secretary," Mack said, tapping the chalk next to that name.

"Didn't ask her for an alibi," Womack admitted. "Did you, Littleton?"

"No. I should have, though. At the time, I didn't think she was a candidate. I still don't, but you never know."

"Handle that, Womack," McCord said, then he pointed to the new name on the chalkboard. "Okay, here's the last woman on today's list: Sheila Winters."

"The shrink?" Shrader wrinkled his nose. "Jeez, can you imagine making love to a shrink while she analyzes the underlying meaning of your every groan?"

"Can we knock off the suggestive commentary and sexual references," Mack said testily. "What the hell is going on in here this morning?"

Shrader and Womack exchanged a startled look. McCord had made a comment himself about Trish Lefkowitz. Law enforcement was a tough, male-dominated domain, and nothing was taboo among the "boys." As long as they didn't aim it at Sam, they were pretty much free to carry on even under the department's regulations.

"Littleton and I interviewed Dr. Winters," Mack continued, "but not as a potential suspect, so we didn't ask for an alibi. She's blond and attractive, and Manning liked attractive blondes. She's a long shot, in my opinion, but we'll pay her another visit. That brings us to the three males on the list," he concluded. "The first name is George Sokoloff, the architect. Littleton checked out his alibi, and it's believable but not one we can completely substantiate."

"Motive?" Womack questioned.

McCord was quiet, thinking. "We'll have to check out his claims, but if he's telling the truth, he was the real talent behind several of Manning's successful projects. Manning had promised him full credit and major responsibility for the Crescent Plaza project. Maybe Manning told him he wasn't going to deliver on those promises."

Pointing to the last two names, Mack said, "That brings us to Jason Solomon, and his boyfriend, Eric Ingram."

"They're each other's alibi," Womack said; then he belatedly recounted what they'd learned about the two hundred thousand dollars cash Manning had used to buy a share in Solomon's play.

"Let's keep digging there," Mack said. "I think the path to our killer is probably going to be paved with greenbacks. We need to find out where the hell Manning was getting his hands on enough illegal cash to not only cover his additional office and living expenses, but buy cars for himself, and a share in a Broadway play, to name just the few items we already know of. Based on the way he was spending it, he seemed to be confident there was plenty more coming."

Womack took a sip of his cold coffee, then put the cup back on the desk. "Maybe he was peddling drugs?"

Mack shrugged. "Anything's possible, but I don't see him risking his own skin on anything that's dangerous and hands-on. I'd associate him with something a little more stealthy."

"Theft? Receiving stolen goods?" Womack proposed.

Mack shook his head. "Same answer as drugs."

"Blackmail?" Shrader suggested. "Extortion?"

"That would be my bet, but I'm going to have our profilers take a look at him and see what they say. Leigh Manning probably has the answer, whether she knows it or not," he finished, walking away from the chalkboard. "I want to question her today, but I'm going to try to be polite and do it with Valente's approval. That's all for this morning," he said.

Sam had been waiting for those words. Grabbing her purse off the floor, she stood up and shoved her chair back into place.

"Let's start working the leads we have—" McCord added, and Sam headed for the door, keeping Womack and Shrader between McCord and her, hoping they'd block his view. She made it almost to the doorway before McCord's implacable order checked her in midstride: "Detective Littleton. I'd like a word with you."

CHAPTER 63

Sam swore silently and turned, stepping aside to let Shrader and Womack pass her. With her handbag over her right arm, and her tablet against her chest, Sam reluctantly approached the man who had seated himself behind his desk and was looking at her in speculative silence.

"Why?" he demanded bluntly.

Several possible reactions flashed through Sam's mind, all of them excellent diversionary tactics and highly effective methods of revoking the power of a male who had it, and who intended to demonstrate it. She decided against all of them and opted for honesty. "Are you referring to the 'massage' remark?"

He nodded silently.

"I wish I could tell you why," she admitted, "but I'm not completely sure. I was a little off balance. You've probably been in situations like ours before, but it's a little new to me."

"Did your remark about the massage happen to relate to my hammering you twice about being a few minutes late?"

She thought about it, and nodded. "Yes. I'm sorry. I won't overreact again."

She saw it then—a glimmer of warm amusement in his eyes. "Neither will I," he promised. In thoughtful silence, Sam considered his confusing answer and his amused expression. "By any chance," she said, "did you do that because you thought I was all dressed up for a big date?"

He gave her a look of utter disbelief—as if the question she'd asked was laughable. "Of course."

Sam bit back a smile and momentarily lost herself in his eyes, then she turned to leave.

Behind her, Mack picked up a pencil and said, "I haven't pulled surveillance off Valente. When I know he's at his office, I want to go and see him. I want to persuade him to let Leigh Manning talk to us—openly, without a lawyer obstructing every question I ask her. If I have to, I'll have her brought in here for questioning, but I'd like to do this in a more civilized fashion for a change. You're my best hope for getting in to see Valente."

"Don't pin much hope on me," Sam said. "I crossed the line with him the moment I asked if he was there the night we told Mrs. Manning her husband was dead. He knew we would already know that, so when I asked him the question, he downgraded me to just another devious, conniving cop."

"Just out of curiosity, why did you ask him that?" Mack asked, doodling on the yellow tablet.

"I wanted to see if he'd try to lie."

Leaning back in his chair, Mack gazed thoughtfully across the room. "It's in his best interest to let us talk to Leigh Manning. If I can just get in to see him, I think I can convince him of it. If I have him brought in here, he'll come with a lawyer and we'll have an audience of eavesdroppers. What I have to say to him I can't say in front of anyone else."

Thinking, Sam shifted her tablet to her right hand and held it against her purse. "In order to persuade him to see you—particularly without his lawyer present—you'd need to convince him that you've had a huge change of heart after yesterday, and that it's final and authentic."

McCord's lips twisted in a sardonic smile. "He sent me a very clear warning yesterday through a friend of mine at Interquest. My friend says Mr. Valente is 'deadly serious.' "

Sam rolled her eyes. "Great." She brightened suddenly. "I know a way that might work, but you aren't going to like it."

"Try me."

"Give him back the best and only piece of incriminating evidence we have on him. Give him his note back."

"You're right, I don't like it. It's in complete violation of evidentiary procedure."

Tipping her head to the side, Sam said, "That's your position. His position would be that I confiscated something that didn't belong to us, and that we're keeping it in hopes of hanging yet another criminal charge on him and/or Leigh Manning. He knows that note is very valuable to us if we're going to continue trying to hassle the two of them. He would also know all about our 'evidentiary procedure,' because he's undoubtedly had to wait many times before we released his property back to him. Give him back the note," Sam said, "and you'll be making a very serious point with him."

For a moment, Mack hesitated; then he capitulated. "All right, but make a half-dozen copies and have them authenticated. Then call the senator," he added, "and tell him you may be late for cocktails."

He knew! Sam realized. But then, of course, he would have made it a point to investigate her very thoroughly before letting her on the team. Mack was extremely thorough about everything he did. Including kissing. "Very well, Lieutenant," she joked. "I'll do that."

Behind her, he spoke again, his voice solemn and husky. "Sam—"

She turned. "Yes?"

"You are very beautiful."

Sam's heart slammed into her rib cage. "Isn't that funny—" she said in a breathless little laugh. "I was thinking that same thing about you."

McCord watched her walk away; then he reached for his phone and noticed his doodling on the yellow pad. The page contained only one word, written several times in different scripts. *Mine.*

CHAPTER 64

At three o'clock, the police surveillance car following Michael Valente reported he'd returned to his company headquarters on Sixth Avenue, in midtown Manhattan.

At three-thirty-five, McCord and Sam opened the tall doors marked "Alliance-Crossing Corporation, Executive Offices," on the forty-eighth floor.

The receptionist's desk was made of thick glass and situated in the center of a vast, carpeted area surrounded with seating groups arranged at discreet distances from each other. Beautiful glass sculptures, some of them large and abstract, gleamed beneath spotlights at positions throughout the room.

Several office doors, all of them closed at the moment, opened onto the reception area. Two men and a woman were seated near one of them, talking quietly; another man was leafing through a magazine near the windows, his briefcase on the floor near his feet.

McCord presented his card to the receptionist and asked to see Mr. Valente. As a rule, when presented with an official "calling card" from an NYPD detective, a white-collar employee responded with either alarm, curiosity, shock, or, occasionally, wariness. They did not respond with derision. The receptionist at Valente's headquarters was a notable exception. An attractive young woman in her early thirties, she looked at McCord's card, and then at McCord, and literally rolled her eyes in disgust before she got up and disappeared down a long hallway.

"I don't think she was very impressed," Sam joked.

"I noticed that," McCord said, then he lowered his voice almost to a whisper. "If we get in to see Valente, he'll try to record the meeting for his own protection, in case this is some sort of trap. He's no novice with the games cops play. Don't say anything significant until I've persuaded him not to record it. If he doesn't believe what I tell him, or if he chooses revenge over caution, I don't want him to have a tape recording to give to his attorneys."

The receptionist returned promptly, followed by an impeccably groomed middle-aged woman in a pale pink wool suit. She had short dark hair and the erect bearing of a queen—or a headmistress. Her voice was beautifully modulated but businesslike. "I'm Mrs. Evanston, Mr. Valente's assistant," she enunciated. "Please follow me."

McCord and Sam followed her down a long hallway, through a passage door, then down another hall to an unmarked door at the end. As she pushed the door open and stepped behind them, she gave McCord a brief, businesslike smile and said in her very proper diction, "Mr. Valente suggests that you attempt to impregnate yourself."

The open door was directly across from the main elevators.

"I knew that was going too well." McCord said shortly as they again headed down the corridor toward the main doors into Alliance-Crossing's executive suite. "You try it this time."

"I'll have to give him back his note to Mrs. Manning, or it's a waste of time."

McCord hesitated, then nodded.

The receptionist glared as they approached her desk again, but Sam smiled briefly at her. From her handbag, she removed a pen and Valente's note, which was still in an NYPD evidence envelope. Across the evidence envelope she wrote, "Enclosed is our ticket of admission. It's yours to keep whether you agree to see us or not. Please give us a few minutes. It's about LM, and it's urgent."

She handed the envelope to the receptionist with one of her own business cards, and said, "Please take this to Mr. Valente's assistant and hold it in front of her eyes if necessary so that she reads it at once."

The receptionist obviously knew Valente's assistant had ejected them out the back door, and she took her cue from that. With a dismissive shrug, she pushed the envelope and card toward a corner of her desk and started to turn to her computer screen.

"No problem," Sam said pleasantly, reaching for the discarded items. "I'll just assume you're busy and you'd rather I take these to Mrs. Evanston myself."

The receptionist swung around, picked up the envelope and card, gave Sam a scalding look, and marched off in the same direction she'd gone before. "Valente seems to inspire a lot of loyalty in his staff," Sam remarked as they sat down to wait.

McCord said nothing; he was analyzing the note Sam had written on the envelope, and he was smiling a little. She'd written four short sentences, but each one delivered a significant psychological payload:

"Enclosed is our ticket of admission" . . . *If you're a*

reasonable man, you'll realize that our returning this note to you is an enormous gesture of good faith.

"It's yours to keep whether you agree to see us or not" . . . *There are no strings attached. We're not trying to coerce you, and we acknowledge in advance that we could not coerce you even if we tried.*

"Please give us a few minutes" . . . *"Please." There's a word you haven't heard from the NYPD, but we realize now that you're entitled to it.*

"It's about LM, and it's urgent" . . . *We are using Leigh Manning's initials because we, too, want to protect her privacy from whoever may see this note.*

MICHAEL HUNG UP THE TELEPHONE and glanced at Mrs. Evanston as she handed him an envelope and a business card with Detective Littleton's name on it. "They're back," she said, scowling.

Impatiently, Michael reached for the NYPD evidence envelope; then he glanced at Littleton's handwritten message. He opened the envelope, removed the white envelope inside it, and unfolded the note he'd written to Leigh with the pears he'd sent her in the hospital.

It was harder than I ever imagined it would be to pretend we didn't know each other Saturday night.

If he'd been trying to frame himself and Leigh for Logan's murder, he could not have chosen better phrasing, Michael thought with disgust.

He looked again at Littleton's words, and the underlying messages in her phrasing did not escape him, but the phrase that truly swayed him was the reference to Leigh and the word "urgent." If Littleton was smart enough to play on his feelings for Leigh, she was also smart enough to have kept copies of the note. On the other hand, copies were never as effective with a jury as an original, so she was taking a gamble by returning it—evidently with McCord's consent.

Michael hesitated, tapping the end of the envelope on his desk. The idea of letting McCord into his office made him grind his teeth. Wallbrecht's summation of McCord ran through his mind. . . . *Trumanti picked the wrong man for this job. You can't send Mack after the wrong target and order him to stay on it for some self-serving reason . . . because Mack will not only go after the right target on his own, he'll bring him down and then he'll go after you. . . . He's the best detective the NYPD has ever had, but he won't play politics, and he won't kiss anybody's ass.*

Personally, Michael couldn't stand the arrogant bastard, but Wallbrecht held him in the highest esteem, and Wallbrecht was the best in his business.

"Shall I call Bill Kovack in security and have him come down here and remind the detectives of the legalities involved in being on these premises without a warrant?"

"No," Michael said curtly. "Bring them in, but first bring a tape recorder in here."

She nodded. "I understand."

CHAPTER 65

Although Valente had consented to see them, Sam didn't expect a warm welcome from him and they didn't get one. He was standing behind his desk, his expression cold and forbidding.

Sam smiled a greeting anyway. "Thank you for seeing us," she said, and then she tried—without success—to inject a little humor into the taut moment by gesturing to McCord, who was on her left, and saying, "Unfortunately, you two have already met."

Valente's gaze sliced over McCord like a razor. "Your 'ticket of admission' buys you three minutes of my time," he warned him; then he added, "You realize, of course, that you're breaking the law by attempting to question me without my attorney present?"

McCord's primary interest at the moment was the tape recorder he spotted on Valente's desk. "I'm going to turn this off for a moment," he said calmly. "If you want to turn it back on after I start talking, you can, and then we'll leave."

Valente shrugged. "As long as *you're* going to do the talking, be my guest."

McCord pressed the *off* button and stepped back. "Now, the situation is this: We are not breaking any law by being here, because I have eliminated you as a suspect in Manning's murder. At the moment, you're under surveillance, which you already know, and your phones are tapped, but I'm going to let all that stay as it is—"

Valente laughed, a harsh contemptuous laugh. "Of course you are, you son of a bitch."

"You know," McCord said, "there's a part of me that would like to walk around that desk and beat the shit out of you for making this so hard."

Valente glanced at the floor near him and said in a soft, deadly voice, "Consider yourself invited."

Sam actually tensed during that opening exchange, but once McCord had fired his warning shot, he turned and strolled over to the windows. Looking out at the skyline, he said evenly. "But then there's another part of me that has to answer for how I would feel if I were in your position. How would I feel if I'd spent four years in prison paying for a crime the cops knew I didn't commit, all because the *doped-up* punk I killed in *self-defense*, with *his* gun, not mine—happened to be named William *Trumanti* Holmes."

Shoving his hands into his pockets, McCord studied Valente's reflection in the glass as he continued. "How would I feel if, after I got out of prison and started building an honest business, Trumanti sent three minions after me, each one swearing a false oath in consecutive cases that I tried to bribe him?"

From the corner of her eye, Sam saw Valente lean his right hip on the credenza behind his desk and fold his arms over his chest, his expression coolly speculative, rather than ominous.

"The attempted bribery cases were only the beginning," McCord said, switching to his own point of view, rather than continuing to speak from Valente's. "As the years passed, the bigger you got, the bigger the arsenal Trumanti hauled in to bring you down. The city got the state involved, then the Feds got into the act. You've become the target of every law enforcement agency around, and you haven't broken one goddamned law that I know of."

With a grim laugh, he added, "You're no martyr, though. The prosecutors who've gone after you end up lying bloodied on your battlefield, their careers and reputations destroyed. That's your revenge. Of course, it costs you millions in legal fees, and you still can't buy back the reputation they stole from you."

McCord turned slowly from the windows and faced him, his hands still shoved into his pockets. "Did I get the story right?"

"You had me in tears," Valente mocked.

McCord said nothing to that, and Sam studied the male tableau before her with fascination. They were still hunter and predator, still instinctive foes—cunning, wary, and aggressive—but for the moment, each man was maintaining a deliberately casual, noncombative stance: Mack with his hands in his pockets, Valente with his arms crossed over his chest and his hip perched on the credenza.

Separated by some silently agreed upon neutral zone of about eight feet, Valente wasn't on the offensive anymore, but he was refusing to engage. McCord was calculating the best way to make him engage—but not attack.

Switching to an offhand, almost friendly tone, McCord said, "I have a very clear picture of what happened in all

those other cases, but now we come to the Manning case—
my case—and my picture is a little hazy in places. Here's
the way I think you got involved, but I'd like you to correct
me if I'm wrong."

In reply to that request, Valente noncommittally raised
his eyebrows, but at least he was listening, and the three
minutes he'd allotted them was over.

"I think you got involved on November twenty-eighth,"
McCord began, "when you attended a party at the home of
a girl you used to know. I think the last time you spoke to
her, she was still an ordinary college kid and you were a guy
with a beard and no money, who was working in your
aunt's grocery market and going to school. But by the night
of the party, things were a lot different for both of you.
She's a Broadway star now, and you're a very rich man—a
tycoon, in fact, but one with a bad history. I also think—
and this is where I'm guessing—that you had a real 'thing'
for her in the old days. Am I right?"

Sam held her breath, waiting for Valente to answer—to
agree to engage.

"Big time," Valente finally confirmed.

While Sam gave a mental cheer, McCord continued
with his scenario: "Now, at the party, she doesn't recognize you. She takes you at face value—a notorious billionaire with an unsavory reputation, and she's *not* very
friendly. Even so, you're anxious to spend a little time with
her. Unfortunately, she won't give you much time. While
you're still trying to decide if, and when, to tell her who
you really are, she hands you over to a friend—an astrologer—and your opportunity vanishes. And here's the
real kicker to that," Mack speculated wryly, "although you
only spent a few minutes with her at the party—you got
hooked on her again, didn't you?"

Sam saw a slight smile deepen the corner of Valente's

mouth, and she assumed Valente was dismissing McCord's statement as ludicrous—until Valente slowly nodded, and Sam drew the only other possible conclusion: Valente was unwillingly impressed that a "tough guy" like McCord could have made such a leap of logic about another man—particularly one with Valente's reputation.

"A couple of days later," Mack continued, "you hear she's been in a car wreck, and she's in the hospital. You know she loves pears, because she used to buy them at your aunt's market. So you send her a basket of them with a note on your letterhead, and you sign it with the only names she ever knew you by. But she doesn't get the note because we have it. A few days later, when she gets home from the hospital, you go over to her apartment to see how she's doing—"

McCord stopped there and asked another question. "How did you get her to agree to let you come up to her apartment if she still didn't know who you were?"

"I told her that her husband had some documents that belonged to me and I needed them."

McCord nodded, assimilating that. "Was that true?"

"No."

"But the ploy worked," McCord continued. "As a result, you were there when we called to tell her we'd found her car, and you volunteered to fly her to the site in your helicopter. Hell, why wouldn't you volunteer to do that?" Mack asked with a shrug. It was a rhetorical question, one he answered himself on Valente's behalf. "You cared about her—you didn't know her husband was dead, and you have nothing to hide. In fact, you landed your helicopter, with her in it, on the road right in front of a row of police vehicles.

"Even after you found out that Manning was dead, you kept right on going to see her—and you did it knowing damned well the NYPD would try to make a case against you on any flimsy excuse you gave them. But you weren't worried about that, because you didn't know we had an excuse—and it wasn't flimsy. We had the note you sent Leigh Manning—a note that is so damning that *anyone* who wrote it would become Suspect Number One in a murder-conspiracy case."

As McCord came to his role in the scenario, he walked over to Valente's desk and restlessly picked up a paperweight, studying it as he spoke. "But you aren't just 'anyone,'" he said. "You're the object of Trumanti's vendetta, and from the moment he heard about that note you wrote Leigh Manning, his one goal has been to live long enough to sit in front of the window when you're given a lethal injection. That's where I come in," McCord added bluntly, putting the paperweight down and looking straight at Valente. "I'm Trumanti's handpicked 'assistant executioner,' whose job it is to help him stick the needle in your arm."

Sam couldn't see McCord's face because his back was to her, but she could see Valente's face, and he was scrutinizing McCord very closely, as McCord finished, "I'm not going to cancel the surveillance on you and Mrs. Manning or the wire taps on you. I can't risk giving Trumanti any reason to replace me with someone else who'll do his bidding. The best I can do right now is return that note you wrote to Leigh Manning as a gesture of truce—of goodwill."

"How many copies of it did you keep?" Valente inquired blandly.

"Six," McCord replied bluntly. "However, they're in my custody and they'll stay there unless I find out I'm all wrong and you did kill Manning. That's the best I can do right now. I'm sorry, but you'll have to live with it."

In reply, Valente pressed a button on his credenza, and

a dark glass panel slid open. Behind it glowed tiny red lights on an elaborate sound system. "I can live with that," he said, removing a cassette tape from the recorder, "as long as you can live with this."

McCord's eyes narrowed on the tape and then lifted to Valente's face. "Just out of curiosity, what do you intend to do with that?"

"It will remain in my custody," Valente replied, repeating McCord's earlier words, "unless you change your mind and decide either Leigh Manning or I killed her husband."

The day before, McCord wouldn't have believed a word that came out Michael Valente's mouth. Now he took his word about a very damaging tape and eyed his former foe with reluctant admiration. "Nice trick," he commented.

Sam bit down on her lower lip to keep from laughing and made a show of searching for something in her handbag.

"We need to talk to Mrs. Manning now," McCord explained, "because I think the murder may have been related to her husband's financial dealings. Naturally, you can be present while we talk to her."

"Naturally," Valente agreed dryly, reaching into his desk drawer and removing a cell phone. He glanced at it for a moment as if it were unfamiliar to him, then he turned it on.

"New phone?" McCord speculated with a twinge of a smile.

Valente looked at him as if the answer was obvious. "One of several," he averred, pressing the numbers on the keypad.

"I imagine they're probably the newest digital models, too—the ones that are very hard for us to monitor? And I imagine they're registered to someone besides you?"

"I'm beginning to see how you got to be a lieutenant," Valente told him with mocking amusement; then he broke off as his call was answered. "O'Hara," he said, "can Leigh take a phone call right now?"

While he waited for O'Hara to bring the phone to her, Valente explained, "Leigh's at the theater, rehearsing, but she should be finishing up about now. She's going on tonight—"

Sam heard the unmistakable pride in his voice as he made that announcement, but a moment later when Leigh Manning took his phone call, Valente's deep baritone gentled and his features softened so much that Sam was transfixed by the change. "McCord and Littleton are in my office," Valente told Leigh. He chuckled at her reply; then he looked straight at Sam and McCord as he said, "I made that same suggestion to them when they arrived, but they were very persistent." Teasingly, he added, "Aren't you the one who once told me it was every citizen's civic duty to cooperate with the police?"

When he hung up, his attitude reverted to brisk and businesslike. "She'll be here in a half hour. I've already asked her about Logan's finances, but she doesn't know of anything unusual—other than the fact that he seems to have paid cash for an expensive piece of jewelry he gave her the night of the party."

"Maybe she'll think of something when we talk to her," McCord replied, standing up. "We'll wait in the reception room until she gets here."

Valente looked at McCord for a long moment. "Why is it you're not trying to hang the murder on Leigh?"

"There's always a chance she killed him," McCord said, playing it absolutely straight, "but the only suspicious thing she's ever done was appear to be having an extramarital clandestine relationship with you—with a man who has a criminal record for a violent crime. Once I take all that out of the equation, she looks to me like any other widow."

WHILE THEY WAITED for Leigh Manning to arrive, McCord asked Sam to arrange for them to see Sheila Winters later that same day if possible. Sam phoned the psychiatrist and after some wrangling, Dr. Winters agreed to see them at four-forty-five, after her last appointment.

CHAPTER 66

Sheila Winters's receptionist had already gone home, and the elegant little anteroom was empty when Sam and McCord arrived a few minutes ahead of their allotted time.

Since the door to Dr. Winters's office was closed, they sat down on a pair of tufted, green leather wing chairs to wait until Winters finished with whoever was with her. McCord picked up a magazine from the stack on the lamp table between their chairs, propped his ankle on his knee, and began leafing through it.

Sam picked up a copy of *Vanity Fair* and opened it, but her mind was on the interview they'd just concluded with Leigh Manning. The actress had been so badly disillusioned by the police in recent weeks that she'd stood beside, and slightly behind, Valente's chair with her hand on his shoulder the entire time she answered McCord's opening questions.

At first, Sam had thought she was subtly seeking Valente's protection. It was fully ten minutes before Sam realized the opposite was true—Leigh Manning was afraid *for* Valente, and standing *with* him against McCord and Sam.

McCord thought so, too, and remarked on it when they were in the car on the way to Winters's office. "Did you notice Leigh Manning didn't leave Valente's side until she realized all our questions were going to be solely for her?"

"She reminded me of a lovely Irish setter trying to protect a dangerous panther," Sam confided, and McCord chuckled at her analogy. "I match up people with their animal counterparts," Sam admitted. "For example, Shrader reminds me of a rottweiler. I've nicknamed him Shredder—"

McCord's laughter cracked like a pistol shot.

The phone on Dr. Winters's receptionist's desk rang and the answering machine clicked on. McCord got up and restlessly studied a picture on the wall behind his chair.

"I'm surprised Dr. Winters doesn't use an answering service," Sam remarked quietly.

"She probably switches her calls over to one when she leaves," McCord replied, his voice lowered, too. "That's what my brothers-in-law do."

"Are they doctors?"

"Two of them are."

"Two of them? How many sisters do you have?"

He slanted her an amused sideways glance and silently held up one hand, the thumb folded back against the palm.

"You have *four* sisters?"

He nodded and shoved his hands into his pockets, his face toward the picture, his gaze slanted downward to her. "Until I was ten, I thought shower curtains always looked like legs with feet."

Sam grinned. "Panty hose," she concluded; then she said, "Did that brown tweed jacket you were wearing the first day really belong to your brother-in-law?"

Nodding again, he said, "The apartment above mine caught fire while I was on vacation. When I got home, everything in my place reeked of smoke and had to be cleaned and treated. The clothes in my suitcases were the only things of my own I could wear."

The phone rang again, and McCord turned, glancing impatiently at his watch and then the answering machine. "Dr. Winters is running almost ten minutes late. Shrinks are very clock conscious . . .". As he spoke he walked toward the door of her office.

He knocked.

No answer.

He reached for the knob and turned it as Sam put down her magazine. "There's nobody—" he began, standing in the center of the office; then he turned right and disappeared from Sam's line of vision. "*Shit!* Call for EMS!" he shouted.

Grabbing for her cell phone, Sam raced into the office, but all she saw at first glance was McCord's back as he crouched down near the back corner of the psychiatrist's desk.

"Never mind the ambulance," he told Sam grimly over his shoulder, "call Dispatch and tell them to get CSU over here."

Leaning over him with her cell phone to her ear, Sam did as he instructed, her gaze riveted on the corpse of the woman she had spoken to only hours before. Sheila Winters was sprawled facedown on the floor, her body behind her desk, her face peeking out around it, her eyes wide and staring, as if she were looking at the doorway. Her bright yellow dress was stained vermilion across the back where blood had poured from a gaping wound.

Careful not to alter the position of the body, McCord lifted Winters's left shoulder so that he could see the wound from the front; then he released his grip and stood up. "That's an exit wound in her back," he told Sam; then he gestured toward the blood spattered on the wall behind the desk. "She was probably standing near her chair when she was shot, and the impact slammed her against that wall; then she fell forward on her face."

Sam was about to answer him when McCord's cell phone rang. He grabbed it and opened it, and then listened for a moment, an odd expression crossing his face. "What's her home address?" he asked; then he said, "I'm at Sheila Winters's office, and she's a corpse. Get over here and sit on this crime scene until CSU arrives. I don't want any uniforms tramping through the place, destroying evidence."

He snapped his phone shut, and looked at Sam, his blue eyes restless and intent. "Shrader got a hit on Jane Sebring. She rented a car on Sunday and returned it Monday. Guess how many miles she put on it?"

"Enough to get her to the Catskills and back?" Sam speculated, her heart beginning to pound.

He nodded, glanced impatiently at Sheila Winters's body, and reversed his decision to wait there until Shrader arrived. Opening his phone, he ordered the closest patrol car sent to their address.

Two officers came running into the anteroom a few minutes later, and McCord backed them out of it into the hallway. "Stand outside this door," he ordered them, "and don't open it for anyone except Detective Shrader or CSU. You got that?"

"Yes, Lieutenant."

"And don't touch the damned doorknob!" he warned over his shoulder.

Sam kept pace with him, but even with her long-legged strides it wasn't easy in high heels, and she cursed herself for wearing them today, of all days.

In the car, McCord put his emergency light on the dashboard and slammed the car into gear.

CHAPTER 67

Once Leigh had publicly announced two nights ago that she was having dinner with Michael, the number of reporters hanging around outside her building, hoping for something inflammatory to print, dropped abruptly. She'd handed them their inflammatory story and they were running with it.

There were only two reporters huddling in their coats outside the lobby windows when Joe O'Hara pulled the limo to a stop at five P.M., but he escorted her inside anyway.

"Hey, Leigh!" Courtney Maitland called, rushing inside right behind her. When Leigh turned to talk to her, O'Hara touched Leigh's elbow and said, "Hilda has some things she needs me to pick up. I'll go on upstairs, get her list, and run her errands so I can get back in time to take you to the theater at six-thirty. Is Mr. Valente going to ride with us?"

"No, he's going to come later from his place. I have to be at the theater at seven, and there's no point in him waiting around there before the show starts. Jason Solomon will only make both of us crazy. He's in rare form today. Oh, and, Joe—" Leigh called a moment later as he headed around the potted trees in the lobby toward the elevators. "I have a ticket for you tonight, too."

He grinned at her and saluted, and Leigh turned to talk to Courtney, who was wearing an oversize coat that looked as if it came from a thrift store and a long red wool scarf that dropped below her hem.

"I'm absolutely going to use Michael Valente as the subject of my interview," Courtney explained in a rush. "Do you think you could get him to talk to me about really important things? I mean, I've already got some good personal stuff about him, but it's mostly from eavesdropping and playing cards with him that one night. I'd like to write about the man he is instead of the way other people see him. . . ."

Upstairs, Joe turned his key in the lock of the apartment's side door and walked into the kitchen. "Hilda?" he called, surprised that the apartment was dark. "Hilda?" he said, walking down the hallway that led to her room. He tapped on her door. "If you want me to do your errands, you'd better give me your list."

When she didn't answer his knock, O'Hara headed back into the kitchen, then through it, turning on lights as he went. He flipped on the dining room chandelier and saw the housekeeper's prone form near the table, blood seeping from her head into the carpet. "Hilda. Oh, no!—" Bending down, he felt for a pulse; then he straightened and ran into the kitchen. He picked up the phone and pressed nine-one—

His entire body seemed to explode with a pain radiating from his chest. With a groan, Joe O'Hara slid down the wall, clutching the receiver while the world turned black.

LEIGH PUT HER KEY in the front door, opened it, and walked into the living room, pausing to hang her coat in the closet. Anxious to lie down for a few minutes before she showered and got ready to leave for the theater, she headed directly to her bedroom.

The bed was already turned down, Leigh noticed as she walked into the bedroom from the hallway. Hilda never forgot anything, she thought with a smile, including Leigh's habit of grabbing a late afternoon catnap when she was performing. Intending to undress and put on a robe, she walked past the bed and glanced ahead of her at the large mirror above her dressing table. A woman was coming toward her in the mirror, a woman who was wearing the same red dress and ruby pendant Leigh had worn to her party. Except the woman was standing behind her, raising a heavy stone vase. . . .

CHAPTER 68

McCord badged the doorman at Jane Sebring's apartment building. "Have you seen Miss Sebring today?" he asked.

"Yes, sir. She left a few hours ago."

"Could she have returned without you seeing her?"

"It's not likely."

" 'Likely' isn't good enough," McCord said, stalking into the building.

A security guard in a maroon uniform like the doorman's was sitting at a desk in the lobby. McCord showed him his badge. "I need to get up to Miss Sebring's apartment."

"Apartment Twenty-four-A," the security guard said, standing up quickly and walking over to the elevator with them. He put his key in the lock and the doors opened. "Get somebody with a key to Twenty-four-A up there right away," McCord added as the elevator doors opened.

Sam walked inside with him, and her adrenaline level began to climb along with the elevator's ascent, but her features were perfectly composed. She knew this drill: she'd done it before. She recognized the fear coiling in her stomach; she acknowledged it, and drew on it to keep herself focused. Reaching into her handbag, she unsnapped the holster on her nine-millimeter Glock and let her hand rest lightly on its grip.

No one answered McCord's repeated knocks on the door of apartment 24A. He was pressing the buzzer yet again when the super got off the elevator carrying a key.

"Are you sure this is okay—for me to let you in, I mean?" the heavyset man asked.

"Would I lie to you?" McCord said, taking the man's elbow and moving his arm toward the door's lock.

The lock clicked open, and McCord pushed the man back and away from the door. "You stay over there," he warned. Reaching inside his jacket, McCord unsnapped his shoulder holster and pulled out a Glock forty-caliber.

"Holy God!" the man mumbled. "What are you doing?" His gaze flew to Sam, as if he expected a well-dressed young woman in an expensive suede suit to bring sanity to the situation. Silently, she stepped out of her heels, pulled her Glock from her handbag, and raised it high, clamped between her hands.

"Ready?" McCord said softly, standing to one side of the door and reaching for the knob with his left hand. He looked at her without a trace of hesitation, as if he knew his life was safe in her hands.

Sam nodded a firm *yes,* and pressed back against the wall, bracing herself as McCord shoved hard on the door and sent it crashing against the opposite wall.

Pitch blackness and silence greeted them.

Keeping his body out of the line of fire, McCord reached inside, feeling the wall for a light switch.

Overhead lights came on, revealing a living room di-

ctly ahead and a dining room on the left. Nobody—alive
dead—was in evidence.

Silently, he signaled Sam to follow him to the right.

Room by room, they searched the apartment from one
d to the other. "She must be at the theater," McCord said,
olstering his weapon. "Let's go."

"Take a look at this first," Sam said, leading him to one
the closets she'd checked while he was checking an-
her. With her foot, she nudged a long dressing robe aside
d exposed a dark green bundle, rolled and tied. "The
issing sleeping bag," he said tightly.

He was already issuing instructions to the super while
m hastily stepped into the suede high heels. "Stay in the
bby for fifteen minutes and if Miss Sebring shows up,
n't mention that we were here, but call me immediately.
l have a car out in front after that, and you can go on
out your business."

"Sure. Okay, Lieutenant," the super said eagerly, taking
cCord's card. Like most civilians in similar circumstances,
e super had reacted first with horror at the sight of drawn
eapons, and then with fascination when the danger was
er. "Listen, I don't want to tell you how to do your jobs,"
said as they waited for the elevator, "but didn't you two
rget a little something when you took your guns out?"

"Like what?" McCord asked dryly, but Sam and he both
ew exactly what the super was getting at.

"You know—like this—" He made a motion like some-
e grabbing the slide on the top of a semiautomatic
eapon and racking a round into the chamber.

"That's only in the movies," McCord told him as the el-
ator arrived and they stepped into it.

"It sure looks good," the super said.

"That's why they do it," replied Sam.

He looked disbelievingly at her, and she told hi
with a smile, "That motion you made sends a bullet in
the chamber." As if she were imparting a secret, she lo
ered her voice a little and told him, "In real life, we sort
like to have a bullet *already* in there when we take o
weapons out."

"No fooling!" he exclaimed.

At the front desk, McCord paused long enough to pa
along the same instructions to the security guard that he
given the super.

He was on his phone before they walked through t
front doors, arranging to have the building entrance p
under surveillance immediately.

CHAPTER 69

Jason Solomon was berating a stagehand when he saw Sam and McCord heading swiftly down the aisle toward him, and he turned his ire on them. "What the hell is the matter with you people?" he burst out, stalking toward the front of the stage. "Haven't you ever heard of making an appointment? It's polite, it's—"

"Where is Jane Sebring?" McCord interrupted sharply.

"How the hell would I know? She's probably at home."

"She's not at home. We just came from there. What time does she usually get here?"

"About now, usually, but I fired her this morning. God, what a day this is turning out to be! I've got sound problems and a curtain going up in an hour and a half."

"Shut up and listen," McCord snapped. "Where's Sebring's dressing room?"

"This way—" Solomon said, startled and resentful.

Sebring's things were still in her dressing room, but she wasn't there. "Was she upset when you fired her?" Sam asked. "I mean, did she expect it or did it surprise her?"

" 'Upset'?" Jason repeated sarcastically. "She was de mented. That is one lunatic woman," he added, walking to ward a tiny office at the end of the hall with Sam and McCord right beside him.

"Why did you fire her?" Sam persisted. "She had good reviews."

"I fired her because Leigh Kendall wouldn't appear on the same stage with her, and who can blame Leigh for that?

"Did Jane Sebring *know* that was why you were firing her?" McCord asked impatiently.

"Yes, of course. I explained the situation to her agent on the phone this morning when I started negotiating the buyout on her contract. The guy's a vulture; he—"

"If you fired her through her agent," Sam interrupted, "how do you know she was 'demented' about it?"

"Because she showed up here today, right after Leigh left to go to Valente's office and then home for a rest. Solomon stopped in front of his desk and turned to face them as he added, "I told Jane to clear her stuff out of Leigh's dressing room, but she left everything and ran out of here. The woman's crazy."

"What time was that?" McCord asked.

"What the hell difference does—" Solomon broke off and backed around his desk as McCord took one long step toward him. "Between three and four, I think."

"Get Leigh Kendall on the phone," McCord snapped. "Call her at whatever number you use to reach her."

"Can't you people just wait here until—"

McCord leaned across his desk, grabbed the tele phone, and shoved it toward him. "Call her!"

There was no answer at the first number Solomon called, so he tried two others. "That's odd," he said wor riedly as he hung up. "No one is answering Leigh's home phones, and she didn't answer her cell phone either."

"Did she happen to give you a cell phone number for Valente today?"

"Yes. How did you—"

"What is it?"

Solomon searched through papers scattered on the top of his desk, and found what he was looking for. "Leigh said I wasn't to give this number to anyone—" he began; then he looked at McCord's ominous expression and rattled off the number so Sam could write it down. "Where are you going?" he called, following both detectives as they ran down the hall. "Leigh is probably with Valente. They're in love, you know—"

CHAPTER 70

Outside on the street, McCord tossed the car keys to Sam and slid into the passenger seat. He was on the radio, calling the surveillance car assigned to Leigh Manning, when Sam started the engine and turned on their emergency light and siren.

"Where are you?" McCord asked when the surveillance officer answered his radio call.

"Outside Manning's apartment building, Lieutenant. She got home a little before five, hung around in the lobby talking to a teenage girl for a little while; then she went up stairs."

"Do you know who Jane Sebring is?"

"The movie star who did the nude scene in that—"

"Yes, right," McCord interrupted. "Has she gone into Manning's building since Mrs. Manning went upstairs?"

"No, and I'd have seen her. I've got a good line of vision right to the front doors."

"If you see Sebring, pick her up. She's A and D."

The surveillance officer took the warning seriously but was also delighted. "I'll have to frisk her twice, then—you know, once to see if she's armed, and once to see if she's dangerous."

"Just keep your eyes open," McCord warned shortly.

"Speaking of that, there's a guy who keeps showing up in a cab wherever Mrs. Manning goes. He's hanging around the building right now with a bouquet of flowers."

"Pick him up. She had a stalker; maybe this is the guy. More importantly, stay close to Leigh Manning if she goes anywhere."

"Yes, sir. But she's not going anywhere tonight—at least, not with her maniac chauffeur at the wheel."

"Why is that?"

"Because they towed her limo away a little while ago."

Sam felt the same tremor of alarm that tightened McCord's jaw at the news of the limo being towed away, however, she couldn't spare him more than a glance when he put the radio down. Traffic was thick and vehicles were moving aside to let hers through, but she was squeezing swiftly through tight spaces with scarcely an inch to spare on either side.

"I'm going to have Shrader and Womack meet us there," McCord said, reaching for his cell phone.

It rang in his hand as he pulled it out of his jacket pocket, and he turned up the volume so he could hear above the wailing siren. Michael Valente's deep, tense voice vibrated with enough angry force to carry to Sam's ears. "Solomon just called me and said you were at the theater looking for Sebring and trying to phone Leigh. She's not answering my calls, either. What's happening?"

McCord drew in a long breath, hesitating. "Where are you?"

"Answer my fucking question. What's happening?"

"We're on our way to Mrs. Manning's apartment right now," McCord explained in a calm, matter-of-fact voice.

"Sheila Winters was shot this afternoon in her office. We think Jane Sebring killed her and Manning, too. We're trying to find her. She knows Solomon fired her because Mrs. Manning wouldn't work with her, and Sebring was—very overwrought."

"Jesus Christ!" Valente exploded, correctly translating "overwrought" to *crazed and probably violent.* "I'm on my way to Leigh's right now. Where are you?"

McCord told him, and Valente said, "I'm closer, I'll be there before you are."

"You can't move through traffic as quickly as we're doing, but if you get there first, wait for us in the lobby!" McCord warned him.

Valente didn't bother to reply. "O'Hara is with her and he's armed—" he said, grasping at hope.

"The limo was towed away a little while ago," McCord said tightly. "I repeat—do not go up to that apartment until we get there." He took the phone away from his ear after a moment and began punching in Shrader's number. "Valente hung up on me," he told Sam.

Sam nodded, slammed down on the accelerator, and then hit the brake, cutting diagonally across an intersection and skidding around the corner in a perfectly executed maneuver that drew a grim laugh from McCord, who was waiting for Shrader to answer his call.

"Where are you?" he asked Shrader, and then he filled him in on what was happening. When McCord disconnected the call, he said, "Shrader and Womack will be about ten minutes behind us."

CHAPTER 71

At the edge of Leigh's consciousness, an odd humming sound blended with a hammering in her skull, the ringing of telephones, and the sensation of being paralyzed. Nausea rolled in her stomach, rising to her throat, and she swallowed hard, forcing her eyelids open, automatically searching for something to focus on to steady her reeling senses.

Her eyelids seemed to work, but what Leigh saw in front of her open eyes had no meaning to her. Her entire field of vision was obstructed by two similar hues of cream; one of them seemed to be flat and horizontal, the other vertical and wavy.

She blinked repeatedly, trying to refocus, and in the process she became aware of the different textures of the two shades. The horizontal cream color against her cheek was rough . . . carpet. The vertical, wavy cream color was . . . fabric . . . like . . . the dust ruffle on her bed? She was evidently lying on the floor beside her bed with her hands behind her back. She tried to move her hands, but they seemed to be bound at the wrists, and her legs seemed to be stuck together at the ankles.

Lifting her head with an effort, Leigh turned her face in the opposite direction, and the sight she beheld made her senses swim. Jane Sebring was sitting at the dressing table, wearing the red dress Leigh had worn to her opening-night party. The actress was humming and putting on Leigh's lipstick, but it was smeared grotesquely around her mouth and partially over her cheeks. Strewn across the floor near her feet were the slashed remains of several of Leigh's other dresses.

Lying on the table, near her left elbow, was a gun.

Sebring glanced down and saw Leigh's face reflected in the wide, lighted mirror above the dressing table. "You're awake!" she exclaimed. "You're awake. My audience is awake. . . ."

Leigh snapped her eyes shut.

"No, no, no, don't pretend you're sleeping. . . ."

Leigh kept her eyes closed, and heard the upholstered stool at the dressing table squeak a little as Sebring whirled it around and stood up. "Wake up, you bitch!" she snarled close to Leigh's ear; then she grabbed a fistful of Leigh's hair and nearly jerked it out by the roots. "That's much better," she exclaimed, her garish red mouth parted into a smile in front of Leigh's terrified eyes. In her other hand Sebring was holding a pair of long, sharp scissors.

"Let me help you sit on the bed. I don't like my audiences to fall asleep," she said, jerking hard on Leigh's hair to "help" Leigh slide awkwardly onto the bed. In the process, Sebring's scissors cut a searing path across Leigh's upper arm, but Leigh scarcely felt it. Fear, the greatest natural anesthetic, was pumping wildly through her veins. Her feet were bound with one of her silk scarves; the binding at her wrists seemed to be another scarf, but very tight.

"Your blood matches my dress," Sebring said, looking at the blood oozing from Leigh's cut. She rubbed her fingers on Leigh's wound and smeared some of Leigh's blood onto her own arm.

Every nerve ending in Leigh's body was screaming in terror, but her mind was snapping into focus, searching wildly for explanations and solutions. Somehow, she had to stall until Joe or Hilda or someone came looking for her. Trying to keep her voice steady, she said, "What are you doing, Jane?"

"I'm getting ready to go to the theater, of course," Sebring said, studying Leigh's face. "You look pale. You need lipstick." She sauntered over to the dressing table, picked up a lipstick tube, and carried it over to Leigh. Leigh jerked her face away, and Sebring didn't seem to mind. With the barrel of the lipstick clenched in her fist, she rammed it at the side of Leigh's face, rubbing it hard while she promised between her teeth, "Before too long, I am going to cut you into little pieces. I'm just marking my starting place."

She stepped back and surveyed her work; then she sauntered back to the dressing table and sat down. Holding the scissors in her right hand, she studied Leigh intently in the mirror; then she lifted up a fistful of her long red hair and chopped it off at shoulder length—like Leigh's. "Logan loved me," she informed Leigh. "We found that mountain cabin together one day. He wanted to leave you, but that bitch shrink talked him out of it." Tipping her head to one side, then the other, she studied the effect of her garish, one-sided hairstyle while she asked Leigh conversationally, "Would you like to know what your husband was doing just before he died?"

Her question sent a shudder through Leigh's entire body. Swallowing a surge of bile, she forced the word out. "Yes."

"He was making love to me on your sleeping bag in front of the fireplace. I surprised him at the cabin with a bottle of wine, and we drank it together and made love. And then—" She picked up the scissors and made another vicious assault on her hair. "—that spineless bastard told me he was finished with me for good. He told me I had to leave because *she* was coming to the cabin."

"Who was coming?" Leigh asked in a shaking whisper.

Sebring put down the scissors and opened a small compact with eye shadow. Dabbing a small brush on the eye shadow, she leaned a little closer to the mirror and put a slash of jade green across one eyelid. "Sheila Winters," she said as if Leigh should have been able to figure that out. "And after telling me that, he thought he could just drive me up to the road in his car and send me off in mine." Laughing softly, she put another slash of green on her other eyelid. "You should have seen his face when I pulled his gun out from under my seat and pointed it at him."

Leigh's body shifted as she began working frantically at the tight knot on the scarf binding her hands together. "How—how did you know it was there?"

"He showed it to me once," she said, putting the eye shadow down and studying the other colors she'd scattered on the table. "He didn't think I'd know how to use it. If he'd really been a big fan of my films, like he said he was, he'd have seen me using guns in them. He was such a liar," she hissed furiously.

The knot in the scarf wouldn't budge, and Leigh was losing control of her terror. When she'd first seen the gun on the dressing table, she hadn't completely believed Jane Sebring was capable of using it . . . hadn't wanted to believe it, but now she knew better. She darted a glance over her shoulder to the doorway on her right. Soon, Joe or Hilda would come looking for her, but if either one of them walked more than two steps into the bedroom, Sebring would see them in the dressing table mirror.

"Are you hoping to be rescued?" Sebring purred, watching her in the mirror.

Leigh snapped her gaze forward.

"No one will come," she said with another grotesque smile. "They're dead. Your fat maid is dead, and so is your driver."

Tears sprang to Leigh's eyes, and she blinked hard, her fingernails shoving against the knot at her wrists.

"So is your friend Sheila."

"Sheila is dead?" Leigh repeated hoarsely, trying to keep Sebring talking.

"Logan and she were blackmailing her patients," Sebring confided with absolute certainty.

"Logan told you that?"

"No, Sheila did, just before I shot her. People will tell you anything you want to know when you're pointing a gun at them," she sneered. "Though she did say she hadn't been having an affair with Logan, but she was lying, trying to save her own skin."

"How d-do you know she was lying?"

Sebring heard the heightened terror in Leigh's voice, and she smiled as she leaned forward to add some blue eye shadow above the green. "Are you getting scared now? You should be scared, you know. I'm going to kill you, too. And then," she added with a smile as she picked up the scissors and hacked another inch off the right side of her hair, "I'm going to go to the theater and take your place."

"How do you know Sheila was lying—about having an affair with Logan?" Leigh persisted desperately.

"Because," she enunciated silkily, "Logan admitted they *were* having one. And then," she finished, "I blew his brains out!"

CHAPTER 72

Three blocks from Leigh Manning's apartment, McCord radioed the officers in the surveillance car to meet him inside the main entrance and to have an elevator waiting. Sam found a slot in traffic, cut the siren, and screeched to a stop in front of the building.

As they raced across the sidewalk, a dark Bentley screamed to a stop and Valente got out of it, running.

He was closing the distance when they charged into the building. McCord shouted to the security guard to call EMS and have them standing by in the lobby, and Valente made it to the elevator as the doors were starting to close, his face white and taut. "Wait down here," McCord ordered him.

"In your dreams," Valente snapped, shoving between the doors and digging a key out of his pocket.

Instead of arguing, McCord gave instructions to the two surveillance officers as he unsnapped his holster and pulled the Glock out. "There's a private elevator lobby on the Manning floor. Don't let anybody on or off the floor. There are two employees, a man and a woman, who aren't answering the phone in the apartment. Once we've had a look inside and know what we're up against, you can start looking for the employees, but stay out of our way."

He looked at Valente then. "You know the apartment layout. What is it?"

"Living room and dining room open to view from the front door," Valente answered grimly. "Kitchen and servants' quarters to the far left. Master bedroom on the far right, down a long hallway."

"Give me the apartment key," McCord said firmly as the elevator slowed to a stop.

Valente ransomed the key, holding it above McCord's open palm: "I'm coming in right behind you."

Sam expected McCord to argue, but he evidently realized it was pointless. He nodded curtly. "Stay back out of our way."

Valente dropped the key into his hand.

At the apartment door, McCord silently slipped the key into the lock and put his ear to the door, listening for voices, while Sam pressed against the wall, her shoes off, her gun high. "Ready?" he asked softly.

Sam nodded.

The door opened noiselessly into the foyer. Beyond it, the living room spread out in darkness except for the light coming from the chandelier in the dining room on the left and from the kitchen beyond it.

They moved into the foyer, using the wall on the right for cover while they listened for any sound to tell them what direction to go. Sam spotted the maid's body lying near the dining room table, and nudged McCord, drawing his attention to it; then she lifted her arm, signaling to the surveillance officer standing in the doorway to check there as soon as they'd cleared the area.

McCord moved silently down the foyer stairs and

started to the left, toward the dining room and kitchen, but Valente grabbed Sam's arm in a vise grip and pointed to the right. He knew the apartment's sounds and shadows better than they did, and the almost imperceptible light on the far right was significant to him. Sam didn't argue with his knowledge. She moved close to McCord and gestured over her shoulder.

Valente was already halfway to the hallway at the far end of the living room when they caught him and moved in front of him. By then, Sam could also make out a woman's voice, very muted and soft, coming from an open doorway on the left, at the end of the hall.

McCord slid along the wall, flattened to it, until he was close enough to the open doorway to peer around it; then he moved swiftly to the other side of it. He signaled Sam and Michael that Leigh had seen him, and Sam moved into position at the center of the doorway, but far enough back to cover McCord when he swung around the doorframe and into the room. She sensed, rather than saw Valente's presence on her left and slightly forward, but she was concentrating on keeping her hands steady and listening for Sebring's voice so she could judge the target's location and gauge the angle of her shot if she needed to take one.

McCord held up three fingers, indicating a rush into the bedroom on the count of three; then he started the countdown. One finger up—Two fingers up—

"It's time for me to leave for the theater now," Sebring said to Leigh as she walked out of the bedroom closet wearing one of Leigh's coats. She stopped at the dressing table, picked up the gun, and pointed it straight at Leigh.

McCord stopped the countdown, thinking their target was going to walk out into range.

Leigh had caught a glimpse of McCord, but she didn't know if he'd be able to save her, so she tried desperately to save Michael while she still could. "Jane, please," she begged shakily, "tell me again that *you* killed Logan. That's all I ask. I want to die hearing you tell me that!"

It hit Michael exactly what Leigh was doing—and what was about to happen in that bedroom. As Littleton moved toward the open doorway, Michael let out a bellow of rage and hurtled forward, making himself a target as he launched himself horizontally at the bed, knocking Leigh over onto her back, covering her with his body while shots, and shouts, and a scream exploded in his ears.

He stayed there until he heard McCord call out to the other cops. "Clear! We're clear in here!"; then he eased up onto his elbows while one of the cops shouted back. "We've got vital signs on the man and woman out here, and EMS is on their way up right now."

Leigh's head was turned to the side, and her pale cheek was smeared with red. Her eyes were closed and she wasn't moving! Fear choked Michael's voice to a ragged whisper. "Leigh?"

Her eyes flickered open and focused on his face—eyes like wet zircons, shimmering with tears. Michael was so relieved, so utterly, overwhelmingly relieved, that he couldn't think of anything to say, so he moved her onto her side and unbound her wrists; then he eased her onto her back again and gazed down into the eyes he had loved from the first moment he saw them.

Leigh looked at his ravaged face and slid her arms round his neck, her fingers stroking the short hair at his nape. "Hi," she whispered with a teary smile. "How was our day, today?"

Michael dropped his forehead onto hers, his shoulders shaking with laughter, his eyes blurred with tears of relief. "The usual," he managed to mumble after a few moments. "But it's looking better."

Near the doorway, Sam slumped against the wall, her gun hanging loosely from her hand, her face averted from Jane Sebring's body. Looking at corpses and then hunting down the killers was her job. It was a service she performed . . . but, oh, God, it was another thing entirely to know she'd done the killing. McCord had needed to enter the room at an angle from around the doorframe, but Sam had had a straight shot, and she'd taken it the instant Sebring fired.

Around the corner on her right, McCord finished checking Sebring's body for vital signs; then he stood up and walked over to Sam. "Miss Sebring won't be making any more appearances anywhere," he told her quietly. "Nice shot, Sam."

"It would have been hard to miss her," Sam said grimly, lifting her eyes to his. "She was only ten feet away."

He understood the bruised look in them and slid his hand around her nape, pulling her face to his chest and sliding his arm around her waist. "I can only think of one heartfelt, reassuring thing to say at a moment like this," he whispered.

"What?"

"Better her than me."

Sam smiled a little.

"Everyone feels this way the first time," he added somberly. "With a little luck, it will be your last time."

It was at that moment that Shrader trotted into the room and stopped cold, taking in the scene with a puzzled grin. "You guys having a shootout in here or an orgy?" he asked, looking from Leigh's tied ankles to McCord's arm around Littleton's back. "I see bondage and some evidence of S and M. What I don't see is a victim. Anybody seen a victim lying around?"

"Over there," McCord said mildly.

Shrader caught his tone and correctly assumed Sam had fired the fatal shot. He strolled around the corner, walked over to Sebring's body, and gave a low whistle as he looked at the victim's face. "Wow! Talk about your bad hair days!"

He walked back over to Sam, who was standing on her own now, and patted her shoulder, offering his own kind of comfort for what he knew she was feeling. "Listen, Littleton, you did her a favor. She wouldn't have wanted to go on living with that haircut she's got."

When Sam smiled, he turned to the bed, where Michael Valente was untying Leigh's ankles. "Good evening, Mr. Valente," he said politely. "Good evening, Mrs. Manning."

Valente ignored him, but Leigh was anxious to foster good relations with the police for Michael in the future. "Good evening, Detective Shrader," she said. "How are you?"

"I'm pretty good. You'll be happy to hear that the boys downstairs picked up your stalker. He's volunteered to go for treatment, but we're going to check him out before we release him."

Satisfied with his visit to the crime scene, Shrader sauntered through the doorway with his hands in his pockets; then he leaned back inside and said, "By the way, the chauffeur had a flesh wound and a heart attack, but the paramedics said he's in pretty decent shape. The housekeeper's got a concussion for sure, and she's a little short on blood, but they're giving her a fill-up on the way to the hospital."

Leigh slid off the bed and stood up unsteadily, keeping her face turned away from Jane Sebring's body. "I'll go with them to the hospital," she told Michael.

"Yes, you will," Michael said emphatically, putting his arm around her as they started down the hall, "and while you're there, you'll have some X rays, too."

"Women who are probably pregnant have to be very careful about X rays," Leigh told him.

Michael grinned, but shook his head. "Isn't it a little too soon for you to know that?"

"It would be a little too soon for other women, but not for me."

"Why?"

She shook her head and smiled. "Because you're—you."

"In that case," he said after a split second's thought, "we need to move the wedding date closer."

She laughed softly. "I should have known you'd go straight to the heart of the matter."

Michael stopped her and pulled her tightly into his arms, his jaw resting atop her head, his mind on the way she'd tried to get Sebring to admit she'd killed Logan when she expected to be shot herself. His voice gruff with tenderness, he said, "*You* go straight to my heart."

CHAPTER 73

Standing in the living room, waiting for CSU to arrive, McCord updated Womack and Shrader on the events of the last hour. The apartment door was open and uniformed officers were standing around in the foyer, so he kept his voice low, but Sam could still hear him as she sat on a sofa nearby, making notes for the report she would have to file.

In the middle of a sentence, McCord suddenly stopped talking, and Sam glanced up in time to see him pull his cell phone out of his jacket pocket. It was vibrating, and he glanced impatiently at the caller's name; then he swore under his breath and reached for the television's remote control lying on the coffee table near Sam's knee. As he flipped through the channels, he jerked his head toward the living room windows and said to Shrader, "What's the street look like down there?"

Shrader walked over to the windows and looked down. "It's a zoo," he replied. "Ambulances, cruisers, and dozens of—"

"—news vans," McCord concluded in disgust. "They

must be running the story already, and Trumanti's calling me about it." As he said that, the television station he'd just tuned to interrupted its regular programming and an announcer said, *"We have a late-breaking development in the Logan Manning murder. Our reporter, Jeff Corbitt, is at the scene now, where ambulances have just left the Fifth Avenue apartment building where Logan Manning once resided with his wife, actress Leigh Kendall. Jeff, what's going on over there?"*

"It's pandemonium right now," the reporter on the scene replied, standing in front of the building, holding a microphone. *"The police have the lobby and sidewalk roped off. Three ambulances just left a minute ago, and the street is full of emergency vehicles. Michael Valente was here, and he left in one of the ambulances."*

"Was he in police custody?" the newscaster asked eagerly.

"No, he got into an ambulance with Mrs. Manning. It looks like Valente may have slipped through NYPD's net again, this time with Mitchell McCord in charge of the case. McCord is reportedly upstairs right now."

The news anchorman looked stunned and disgusted by the news that Valente had evidently been turned loose. *"We've just heard from Police Commissioner Trumanti's office,"* he said, *"and they assure us that Commissioner Trumanti will have an official statement for us shortly."*

Sam's cell phone went off before the end of that news announcement, and so did Shrader's and Womack's.

"Don't answer those calls," McCord said sharply when Shrader started to answer his phone.

Shrader complied instantly, but looked worried. "My call's from Captain Holland."

"So's mine," Womack agreed.

Sam's phone was vibrating for the second time. "Mine, too," she said.

"Who's your other call from?" McCord asked her.

"My stepfather," Sam said wryly after glancing at her phone again.

"I'll return his call for you in a minute," McCord said. "He has a phone number I need." He held out his hand for her cell phone, and Sam got up and gave it to him; then he spoke to all three of them in a clipped, imperative voice. "I don't want any of you to return any phone calls about this case to anyone tonight. In a minute, I'm going to phone Mayor Edelman and try to persuade him to handle the press conference himself tonight and keep Trumanti out of it. Regardless of what Edelman says he's going to do, I'll make a brief statement to the press downstairs exonerating Valente from all involvement in Manning's murder. That should temporarily discourage Trumanti from addressing the media on his own tonight and trying to incriminate Valente anyway."

Sam realized at once that Edelman's phone number was the one Mack needed from her stepfather, and she would have been happy to call him for it in front of Shrader and Womack, but Mack was obviously intent on protecting his team right then. He shoved his hands into his pants pockets and told them, "I'm going to fly solo on this case from now on. I want the three of you to stay clear of it. Tomorrow, write up your reports but stick to the bare facts and avoid any mention of the logic or reasoning you may have followed during the investigation. I directed your activities, so when you're questioned about why you did something, blame me."

"Why the hell should we worry about blaming anybody?" Shrader demanded. "We went by the book, we solved the case, and Sam saved the state a fortune in prosecuting and housing that crazy woman in the bedroom who killed Manning."

On the television set, the station broke again for the same news bulletin, and McCord picked up the remote control and pressed the *off* button. He tipped his head back, and Sam watched him carefully choose his phrasing. "In the course of the Manning murder investigation, I personally turned up a wealth of incontrovertible evidence that incriminates members of the NYPD in a long-standing, highly effective vendetta waged against Michael Valente using a variety of illegal measures." He looked down at them then and said bluntly, "I intend to take this evidence to the mayor, and if he doesn't act on it—publicly—then I will take it public, myself."

Shrader and Womack exchanged unhappy glances, and then Shrader spoke for both of them. "I don't like to see the department's dirty laundry hung out in public, Lieutenant. Why can't you let the department clean this up privately? Hand it over to Internal Affairs, or—"

"That's not an option," McCord informed him curtly. "Valente has been publicly victimized for decades by a high-ranking member of the NYPD and some of his cronies. When a private citizen becomes an intended victim of the department, then that's not an 'internal department affair' anymore—not to me. I want a little public justice here, and then I want a little public revenge. Valente's entitled to both."

"Who's the official?" Womack asked uneasily.

"Trumanti," McCord said flatly, after a pause.

"Oh, shit," Womack breathed. "I was afraid you were going to say that."

If anything, Womack's alarm only made Mack look more coldly resolute to Sam. He shrugged and said, "Mayor Edelman inherited Trumanti as commissioner, so he's not politi-

lly tied to him, but after I tell him what I know on the
hone, our new mayor may still want to avoid a public scan-
al involving the NYPD. He may prefer to treat Trumanti's ac-
ons as internal police department business that should be
ealt with privately. I'm fairly sure he'll demand Trumanti's
mediate resignation, but I want more than that."

When he stopped there, Womack said, "Exactly, what
it you want?"

Mack looked at him as if the answer should have been
ovious. "I want Trumanti's bare ass hung in public along
th everyone who knowingly collaborated with that
azy, vindictive bastard."

"What, exactly, did Trumanti do?"

"You don't need to know that." He broke off because
U was arriving, and he left Sam with Womack and
rader while he went to talk to the head of the team.

"Okay, Littleton, let's hear it," Shrader demanded.
Vomack and I have a right to know whatever you do. We
ve a right to know what we're up against."

Hesitating, Sam glanced out the window at the twin-
ng lights of the city's majestic skyline. She understood
ay Mack wanted to shield Womack and Shrader from the
tails, and she also understood why they felt they had a
ht to know them. The only thing she wasn't certain of
s whether her decision to tell them sprang mostly from
r conviction that Shrader and Womack were right—or
ether she couldn't bear for them to think Mack's deci-
n to go public was disloyal, unethical, or capricious.
ce Mack hadn't specifically ordered her not to reveal the
tails, she told Womack and Shrader very quickly about
ente's unjust manslaughter conviction and everything
t Trumanti engineered afterward. When she was fin-
ed, they both looked dazed and angry.

Unfortunately, when Mack returned to the group, he

took one look at Shrader's and Womack's faces; then h
looked straight at her. "You told them," he said, looking di:
gusted and disappointed in her.

Inwardly Sam flinched at his condemning expression
but she nodded. "They needed to understand where you'r
coming from."

Instead of replying, he looked harshly at all three c
them, "Now that you all know the details, it doesn't chang
a goddamned thing. What I said before still goes. I don
need or want your loyalty; what I need is to know that you'r
out of the way when the battle begins. I want you to go abou
your business tomorrow, and I want you to keep your opin
ions about me, this case, and everything associated with
entirely to yourselves. Got that?" he demanded.

Shrader nodded reluctantly and so did Womack; the
Mack's stabbing gaze swung to her. "That was an order
just gave you. Don't mistake it for a request!" he warne
her, his jaw hardening.

Sam had absolutely no intention of following that orde
if she ever came to a point where she had to choose b
tween loyalty to Mack and her job. Her career, she su
denly realized, was much less important than the ethi
involved—and vastly less important than the ethical ma
she was in love with who was willing to stake everythi
on what he believed in.

"I won't mistake it," Sam replied quietly.

He nodded coolly, erroneously believing that havi
understood his order, Sam would follow it; then he sai
"I'm going to phone the mayor. When the three of yo
leave here, you make no comment to the press."

He went into the kitchen and all three of them linger
for ten minutes, but Mack remained there, out of sight a
hearing. Finally, Shrader said, "I had the distinct impre
sion he wanted us to leave."

Sam had the same impression, but she would have ked to have stayed to hear what Edelman told him.

"C'mon, Littleton, it may take him an hour just to lo- ate the mayor," Womack said when she hesitated in the yer and cast an anxious look in the direction of the tchen's empty doorway. "He's already royally pissed off at ou. Let's get you out of here before he decides to bust you ack to Patrol."

"I didn't think he was *royally* pissed off," Sam mur- ured uneasily as she paused outside the apartment door d stepped into her gray suede shoes. She sent a quelling ance at a fresh-faced young officer in the elevator foyer ho was elbowing another officer, gesturing to her legs.

Womack watched her, but his thoughts were still on cCord's temper. "I'd say he was. In fact, I'd say the only ing that saved your ass was that you saved *his* ass in a ootout tonight."

"Nah," Shrader argued as they got into the elevator. "He asn't as mad as all that; he's just *focused*. McCord's like a ight train right now, roaring down a mountain with no akes, and Littleton just stepped a little too close to his cks for a moment."

With Womack to one side of her and Shrader on the her, they shouldered their way through the throng of outing reporters and blinding camera lights aimed at m outside the building.

Whether Mack was furious with her or not, Sam would ve liked to find a way to wait there and watch him talk to press. Most of all, she would have liked to have stood in shadows somewhere, silently lending him her support. t whether Mack was simply "focused" or "royally pissed ," she decided it was probably wisest to do as he'd in- ucted this time, and go home. Whatever happened, 'd be able to watch it unfold on television.

CHAPTER 74

Curled up on the sofa in a soft pale blue rob
with a satin collar that her mother had give
her for Christmas, Sam absently brushe
her damp hair while she rewatched the videotape she
made of Mack's statement to the press outside the apar
ment building, and then Mayor Edelman's statemen
which followed an hour after Mack's.

Mack had obviously managed to persuade the may
that Michael Valente was innocent and that the may
needed to distance himself from Trumanti immediatel
Smiling, she watched Edelman make his statement agai
"The investigation into Logan Manning's death reache
a sad, but final conclusion tonight when Lieutena
Mitchell McCord and his team interrupted Jane Sebrin
attempt to murder Mrs. Manning at Mrs. Manning's apa
ment," Edelman said. "Before Miss Sebring fired h
weapon at the police who'd entered the apartme
apparently she admitted to murdering Logan Manning, a
well as psychiatrist Dr. Sheila Winters, whose body w
discovered this afternoon in her office. According to t

olice they returned Miss Sebring's fire, and she died
nstantly."

The first and only question Mayor Edelman took after
is brief statement was the inevitable one about Michael
alente's involvement. To that, the mayor replied emphati-
ally, "Michael Valente had nothing whatsoever to do with
ogan Manning's death. He was, however, responsible for
ssisting Lieutenant McCord's team in the investigation,
nd it is my clear understanding that, tonight, Mr. Valente
sked his own life to save Mrs. Manning's life when shots
ere being fired.

"Tomorrow morning, my office will institute an inves-
gation into all prior charges brought against Michael Va-
nte by the City of New York. I have asked Lieutenant
cCord to head up that investigation, and I'm awaiting his
cision. In the meantime, I have asked for—and re-
ived—the resignation of Commissioner William Tru-
anti, effective immediately.

"My office will have no further statements to make on
is subject until the investigation is completed. However,
 this time, I am already in possession of enough informa-
n to ascertain that an apology is owed to Michael Valente
r some grievous injustices done to him in the name of 'jus-
e.' When I campaigned for this office, I promised the citi-
ns of New York City that I would take a hard line against
isuse of power and privilege by city officials at all levels,
d I'm making good on that promise tonight."

Sam pressed the *rewind* button, rewound the tape all
e way, and then watched Mack making his much shorter
d, typically, more direct statement to the press outside
e Mannings' apartment building. He was brusque, and so
hally, ruggedly handsome that she thought the mayor
emed insignificant and puny in comparison.

Clad in his leather jacket and open-collared black shirt,

Mack looked straight at the cameras and said what he had to say: "Jane Sebring was shot and killed in the Mannings apartment tonight while she was attempting to murder Mrs. Leigh Manning. Before her death, Miss Sebring implicated herself in the murders of Logan Manning and Dr. Sheila Winters. Two of Mrs. Manning's employees were more fortunate. Joseph O'Hara and Hilda Brunner were taken to the hospital a short while ago and are expected to make a full recovery."

He paused, waiting for the excited reporters to grow completely silent; then he said, "Throughout our investigation, Michael Valente was incorrectly targeted and treated as a primary suspect. Despite that, tonight he aided us in our investigation; then he risked his own life to save the life of Mrs. Manning, and in so doing, he may well have saved the lives of those of us who were present during the exchange of gunshots. I understand the mayor is preparing a statement regarding Mr. Valente, which he will make shortly. In the meantime, I would like to express my gratitude for Mr. Valente's assistance . . . and my admiration for his unbelievable forbearance." Finished, he looked up at the crowd and said, "I have time for three questions and no more."

"Lieutenant McCord," a reporter shouted, "are you trying to tell us that Michael Valente should never have been a suspect in Logan Manning's murder?"

Sam giggled at Mack's quick, incisive response. Instead of answering, Mack looked at his audience and said with amused disgust, "Does anyone have an *intelligent* question?"

"Exactly what was Michael Valente's involvement in Manning's murder?" another reporter yelled.

"Does anyone here know the *definition* of 'intelligent'?" Mack countered. "Last question," he warned.

"Lieutenant McCord," a woman's voice called, "would
ou care to speculate on the current relationship between
Michael Valente and Leigh Manning?"

Mack's grin was lazy, baffled, and mocking. "Can you
hink of any reason on earth why I *would* care to do that?"

With that, he moved away from the microphones and
trode off through the crowd, his broad shoulders clearing
path through the crush of reporters, photographers, and
nlookers.

Sam pressed the *rewind* button again while she con-
mplated this recent proof that Mack did not suffer fools
ghtly. Her smile faded a little as she wondered if he was
erhaps equally intolerant and unforgiving of a subordi-
ate—namely, her—who'd knowingly circumvented his
ishes tonight by telling Shrader and Womack the details of
e Trumanti-Valente issue.

She was still wondering uneasily about that when the
uzzer at her apartment door rang. It had to be Mack, she
ought as she raced through the living room. Her door-
an would have stopped anyone without a badge and in-
sted on phoning her first before letting someone up to
m's apartment.

Forgetting that she was wearing a robe, she glanced
t the peephole while she unlocked her apartment door;
en she yanked it open.

Mack was standing there, his right hand braced high
;ainst the doorframe, his expression as enigmatic as his
ening remark. "Don't you normally check to see who's
anding out here before you open your door?"

"I knew it was you," Sam explained.

"Good, because I'd hate to think you open your door to
st anyone wearing—" His gaze dipped to the expanse of
100th bare skin above her satin lapels. "—that."

Sam self-consciously pulled the lapels closer over her

breasts and tightened the belt. "It's a robe," she explained foolishly and defensively. Then she smiled at her own absurdity and stepped back. "Would you like to come in?" she asked, certain that he would say yes.

"No," he said.

Sam looked at him in surprise. "Then why are you here?"

He took his hand down from the doorframe, and she saw her cell phone in his palm. "I came to return this," he said evenly. "And also to make sure you were doing all right after—what happened tonight."

Sam wasn't certain whether he was referring to what happened to Jane Sebring or to his attitude toward her after she told Shrader and Womack about Trumanti. She studied him in silence, wondering why all her expertise on male never worked when Mack was involved. The Manning case was over, therefore, they could begin, but evidently Mack wanted to rethink the matter—or else he wanted to nurse grudge for what she'd done. Or else he was simply exhausted from an incredibly long, stressful day. Whatever the case, she gave him the only answer she felt was appropriate: "I'm fine," she assured him, taking her cell phone from his outstretched hand, but she gave conversation on last try. "I saw your interview and the mayor's statement," she said softly, smiling. "It looks like you've won your battle with city hall already."

He nodded, his gaze shifting momentarily to the hair spilling over her shoulder; then he stepped back away from the door. "That's the way it looks," he agreed.

Mentally, Sam decided to let the unpredictable male her hall walk away and the hell with being in love with him so she was understandably startled when she heard herself say, "Are you angry with me for telling Shrader and Womack about what Trumanti did?"

"I was," he admitted, "earlier."

That did it. Sam never lost her temper—except with 〔h〕. Folding her arms over her chest, she leaned against 〔the〕 doorframe. "Then it's just as well we never got started, 〔Ma〕ck, because there's something about me you don't 〔kno〕w."

"What's that?"

"I have a brain," she informed him. "Every morning 〔wh〕en I wake up, it wakes up, too, and starts working. I 〔don〕't know why, but it just does. Since you had not specifi〔cal〕ly ordered me never to tell Shrader and Womack about 〔Va〕manti, my brain decided tonight—rightly or wrongly— 〔tha〕t it was the correct thing to do. I'm sorry," she said, feel〔ing〕 suddenly sick and eager to retreat to her apartment. "I 〔rea〕lly am. Thanks for coming by and returning this—" She 〔ju〕ggled the cell phone in her hand, smiled to show him 〔tha〕t she wasn't upset; then she stepped back into the apart〔me〕nt and started to close the door.

He stopped it with his hand. "Now let me ask you a 〔que〕stion. In fact, I have two questions to ask you. First, by 〔any〕 chance, are you upset because I'm not coming in?"

"No," Sam lied emphatically.

"Good," he retorted. "Because I am trying my damnd〔est〕 to live up to the spirit of the bargain I made with you 〔yest〕erday. I gave you until the Manning case was over to de〔cid〕e if you wanted to be with me, but I never imagined it 〔wou〕ld be over so soon. And while I'm on the subject, I 〔thin〕k that after what happened between us last night, your 〔rem〕ark just now that 'it's just as well we never got started' 〔was〕 either heartlessly flippant or else it was a final decision. 〔Whi〕ch was it?" he demanded shortly.

Sam felt an almost uncontrollable urge to laugh hysteri〔call〕y because she could not seem to maintain a grasp on 〔wha〕t was happening.

"I'm waiting for an answer, Sam."

"In that case," she replied, "I would have to pick 'hea
lessly flippant.'"

His jaw relaxed a little. "Don't do it again," he warne

"Don't give me orders, Lieutenant," she shot ba
smoothly. "Not on personal matters. You said you had t
questions; what was your second question?"

"Are you naked under that robe?"

Sam blinked at him, more disconcerted and m
amused than ever. "Yes. And what possible difference d
that make?"

He shook his head and backed up a step. "I can't
lieve you can ask me that. Last night, I barely managed
keep things under control when I had several impera
reasons to stop. Now I have none of those reasons exc
that we had a bargain, and I intend to keep it. Take y
time deciding about us, Sam, and when you've made
your mind, *then* you can invite me in."

"Is that all?" Sam asked dryly, "or do you have any ot
orders to give me?"

"One," he said. "The next time you invite me in w
you're wearing a robe, you'd better be damned sure
want me to stay." His gaze dipped to her lips, droppe
the shallow cleft above the crossed lapels of her robe; t
he lifted his smoldering gaze to hers and shook his he
"I'm going home now, while I'm still fit to drive."

Sam finally, completely, understood what he was
ing . . . and doing. The look she gave him back was ev
bit as warmly intimate as his had been, and it was just a
liberate. "Good night," she said softly, biting her bottom
to hold back her smile. "I'll let you know when I've m
up my mind and I'm ready to invite you in, Mack,"
promised sweetly, closing the door.

Holding her cell phone in her hand, Sam pressed
numbers for *his* cell phone, but not the button that w

ke the call go through and his phone vibrate. She waited
re than a full minute to do that . . . long enough for him
have taken the elevator down to the lobby . . . then she
:ssed the *send* button on her phone.

He answered almost instantly with his name, his deep
ce clipped and businesslike. "McCord."

"Mack?"

"Yes?"

"I've made up my mind."

"Open your door."

Sam turned the knob; then she stepped back in shock.
was standing exactly as he'd been when she opened the
or the last time—with his hand braced high on the door-
ne, only this time he was holding his own cell phone in
hand. He wasn't laughing; he was looking at her in-
tly, and Sam felt her voice shake at the enormity of what
was telling her solemnly with his eyes.

"Would you like to come in?" she asked unsteadily.

His arm dropped from the doorframe. He nodded
wly, twice.

Sam stepped back. He stepped forward.

He closed the door. She opened her robe and let it slide
he floor.

His burning gaze followed it down; then he pulled her
tly into his arms. "You just ran out of time, Sam," he
ned, his lips slowly lowering to hers.

"Time for what?" she whispered, sliding her hands
r his shoulders and around his neck.

"To change your mind about us."

"I'll never change it," she promised him achingly—a
ment before she lost the ability to use her mind at all.

HE HOSPITAL WAITING ROOM, Michael stood in front of
television set, his hands shoved into his pants pockets,

watching the rerun of McCord's brief press conference the late-night news: *"I understand the mayor is prepar a statement regarding Mr. Valente, which he will me shortly,"* McCord said. *"In the meantime, I would like to press my gratitude for Mr. Valente's assistance . . . and admiration for his unbelievable forbearance."*

Beside him, Leigh slipped her hand through his a and smilingly said, "I think we should send him and Sam tha Littleton tickets to the play next week, and then t them out to dinner, don't you?"

"In Paris," Michael agreed with a chuckle.

CHAPTER 75

"What a fantastic place!" Courtney exclaimed when O'Hara let her into the living room of Michael's penthouse apartment on Central Park West. After Jane Sebring's death three weeks before, Leigh had moved out of her old apartment, and she'd insisted that O'Hara and Hilda come with her so that she could oversee their recuperation. "I phoned Leigh this morning and asked if I could come over. Is she here?"

"She's in the kitchen, trying to convince Hilda to leave the dust on the top of the doorframes until Hilda feels better," Joe replied irritably.

"Didn't Mr. Valente have a housekeeper of his own?"

"Sure, but Hilda ran her off a week ago. That woman spot dust where there is no dust."

"How are you feeling?" Courtney asked him.

"Foolish," O'Hara replied. "I barely got winged with that bullet and I got a heart attack over it."

"No, you didn't," Courtney argued, and with a rare show of affection, she linked her hand through his arm as

they strolled toward the dining room. "You got a heart
tack because you thought Hilda was dead. I think you
sweet on her."

"I am not. She's the bossiest woman I've ever met.
at least she lets me cut the cards when we play gin."

"You never bothered to cut them when we played,
stopped asking you."

"That's because I was in a hurry to lose all my money
you and get it over with," he joked. "At least with Hilda,
got a fair chance of winning."

Courtney nodded, but her mind was on someth
else, and she sobered. "I got my invitation to Leigh
Michael's wedding. It's still three weeks away, bu
brought one of their wedding presents with me. They'll
ther like it or hate me for the rest of my life."

Joe stopped short. "What do you mean? What sor
present is it?"

"It's a newspaper," Courtney replied vaguely; then
put on a determinedly happy face and walked into
kitchen, where she said to Hilda, "O'Hara told me he's
ured out a way to cheat at gin when he cuts the cards."

Hilda swung slowly around, her hands on her hips,
brows drawn together into an irate frown that didn't q
reach her eyes. "I'll keep a close eye on him after this."

"Good idea," Courtney replied, sliding onto a chai
the kitchen table, where Leigh was going through the m
"Where's Brenna? Why isn't she handling the mail?"

Leigh enfolded her in a quick hug and shoved the
aside. "She had a lunch date."

"How are the wedding plans coming?"

Leigh laughed. "We invited one hundred people
we seem to have one hundred and eight attending. Ma
and Mrs. Edelman and Senator and Mrs. Hollenbeck
going to be there, and the manager at the Plaza is de

ed to provide special security, which the mayor and the
ator don't want. The banquet director is convinced we
uld move the event to a larger room, which I don't
at. The chef is tearing his hair out over some of my spe-
requests, and Michael's aunt is threatening to cater the
nt herself." When Courtney didn't smile or reply, Leigh
lied her for a moment and then said, "What's up?"

"Nothing. Well—something is." Reaching into her
rsize shoulder bag, Courtney pulled out several type-
tten sheets of paper and a copy of *USA Today*. She
ded Leigh the typewritten sheets, but kept the newspa-
folded on her lap. "Two weeks ago," she explained,
er I interviewed Lieutenant McCord, I finished my arti-
about Michael for my investigative journalism class. I
ught you might like to see it."

"I'd love to see it," Leigh said, puzzled by the teenager's
sual apprehension. Leaning back in her chair, Leigh
l the article written by a teenager for a special journal-
class for the intellectually gifted:

> Among citizens of the United States, there is a
> widely held, fundamental belief that the criminal
> justice system exists to protect law-abiding citi-
> zens, and that when this system errs, it errs on the
> side of leniency to the guilty, rather than deliber-
> ate persecution of the innocent.
>
> Most of us believe in this premise as surely as
> we believe that a person must be considered inno-
> cent until he has been proven guilty beyond a rea-
> sonable doubt; that "double jeopardy" prevents
> anyone from being tried over and over again for
> the same crime and that once a debt has been paid
> to society, the debt is . . . paid in full.
>
> But there are those among us who have reason

to doubt all those concepts, and their doubts are based on bitter experience, rather than intellectual self-deception and wistful philosophy. Michael Valente is one of these people.

Michael Valente is not an easy man to know. And until you know him, he is not an easy man to like. But like everyone else who reads the newspapers or watches the news, I thought I knew all about him long before I met him. And so I did not like him.

I like him now.

More than that, I admire and respect him. I wish he were my friend, my brother, or my uncle. I wish I were older or he were younger, because, as I've seen for myself, when Michael Valente loves a woman, he does it unselfishly, gallantly, and unconditionally. He does it permanently, forever.

Of course, there is one small drawback to being loved by him: It apparently allows the entire criminal justice system a license to spy, to malign, to misrepresent, and to persecute—not only him, but you as well. It allows them to violate every civil right the Constitution promises and that they have sworn to uphold.

From that point on, Courtney's article was fact rather than emotional, and it documented several of cases brought against Michael. By the time Leigh finish reading, Courtney had gotten an apple and was munch it while stealing worried glances at her.

Leigh was so touched by the article that she reac out and laid her hand over Courtney's.

"What do you think of it?" Courtney asked.

"I think it's wonderful," Leigh said softly. "And I think you're wonderful, too."

"Hold that thought," Courtney said obliquely.

"Why?" When Courtney hesitated, Leigh thought the problem must have been that Courtney's journalism professor hadn't liked it, so Leigh asked what he'd thought.

Before replying, Courtney took another bite of apple. "Well, he wasn't quite as enthusiastic as you are. He busted me for displaying a flagrant bias in favor of my subject, and for using a writing style that was 'so gushingly sentimental that it couldn't be digested on an empty stomach.' He said the only connection between investigative journalism and what I wrote was that I used paper to write it on."

"I don't think that's fair—" Leigh exclaimed loyally.

"Why not? He was absolutely right on target. I knew he'd say stuff like that."

"Then why did you write it that way?"

Courtney took another bite of apple and chewed it while she contemplated her answer. "I wanted to set the record straight on Michael Valente."

"I know you did, and I appreciate that. But I also remember that your professor was only going to give out one A in the class, and I know how much you wanted to get it."

"I did get it."

"You did? How?"

"I got major points for 'Degree of difficulty of access to the subject' and for 'Fresh point of view.'"

"I can believe that," Leigh said with a smile.

"But there was one other little thing that practically guaranteed me that A."

"What was it?" Leigh asked, trying to fathom Courtney's hesitant expression.

In answer, Courtney pulled a new issue of USA Today out of her lap, opened it to an inside page, and folded it;

then she slid it across the table to Leigh. "I even got my own byline on the story."

Leigh's eyes widened with a mixture of alarm and horrified amusement as she transferred her gaze to the open newspaper. "Oh, my God."

"Honestly—I didn't realize our professor was going to submit all the articles to the news services, just to see what might happen," Courtney explained, "but when I heard my article was the one they chose, I really felt that since Michael was maligned in the national media, that's where the situation ought to be corrected. I mean, he's already sort of a hero in New York City to anyone who's ever been hassled by a rude cop over a traffic ticket. But I wanted to set the record straight everywhere else."

She seemed to run out of words in her own defense, and her shoulders slumped. "What do you think Michael will say? I mean, it's sort of an invasion of his privacy, particularly when I never actually interviewed him—formally, I mean."

Unaware that Hilda and O'Hara were also looking worriedly at her, Leigh tried to imagine how Michael would feel about the article. "He's never cared what other people think of him," she said after a moment. "He didn't care when the newspapers blackened his reputation, so I doubt that he'll be any more concerned that you've shined it all up for him."

CHAPTER 76

With her cheek resting atop the muscled warmth of Michael's chest, Leigh glanced at the clock on his nightstand and realized it was almost time to start getting dressed for their wedding. But first she had something to tell him, and she decided on an indirect approach. "There's something very hedonistic about making love right *before* you go to your wedding," she remarked softly.

Michael smiled, completely contented, lazily tracing his fingers over the curve of her shoulder and down her arm. "Nice word, 'hedonistic.'"

"Actually, there's a section in our contract that relates to that subject."

"To the pursuit of pleasure?"

She nodded, her cheek rubbing against his chest.

"I don't remember that section," he teased. "What does say?"

"It says that in your diligent pursuit of pleasure, certain results may occur that require amending one of the other clauses."

"Which clause needs to be amended?"

"I think you said it was Clause 1, Section C—the one that's headed, *'Someone to Watch Over Me.'*"

"Mmm," Michael replied. "Have I failed to live up to that clause?"

"Not at all," Leigh hastily told him. "But the clause needs to be amended because the pronoun is no longer correct."

"Really?" Michael asked, his smile already widening in anticipation of her answer. "What should that clause say now?"

"It should say, *'Someone to Watch Over Us.'*"

She was telling him she was pregnant, and Michael's joy made his voice husky. "Renegotiating a prior, binding contract can be a complicated, lengthy procedure. When will that particular clause need to be changed?"

"In about seven and a half months."

He gazed at the ceiling for a moment, calculating dates and his smile turned to a grin. "Really? The first night?"

"Probably so."

"A baby," he sighed. "What a *perfect* wedding present!"

She buried her laughing face against his chest. "I knew you would see it that way."

"Have you picked out names yet?"

She laughed harder. "No. Have you?"

"No," he admitted, "but in anticipation of this moment—" He paused to reach over to his nightstand and open the drawer. "—I got one of these a few days ago." Into Leigh's hand he placed a tiny, delicately crocheted infant bootie. It was yellow, with blue laces up the front and interlocking pink and green circles on the side.

"You only got one of them?" Leigh asked, her eyes swimming with tears of mirth as she lifted them to his.

He nodded.

"Don't you think you should have gotten two?"

"There's something inside that," he explained.

Leigh felt it then—a hard object in the bottom. "Please tell me it isn't a toe," she joked.

Beneath her cheek, his chest shook with laughter as she turned the bootie upside down.

An exact replica of the bootie dropped out, perfect in every detail and color. It was made of diamonds.

CHAPTER 77

With his tuxedo jacket slung over his shoulder, Michael headed toward the bar, intending to open a bottle of champagne while Leigh was getting dressed for their wedding. They still had almost two hours to go, and the Plaza was only a few blocks away, but Jason Solomon had phoned a while ago and said he needed a ride from the theater on Broadway to the Plaza. For some reason, Leigh had agreed to go all the way down to the theater district to pick him up, instead of telling him to take a cab or phone a car service.

Michael was in the process of opening a bottle of Dom Pérignon when he heard O'Hara answer the phone in the kitchen. A moment later, O'Hara appeared and said, "Lieutenant McCord is downstairs in the lobby with Detective Littleton. Is it okay to let them come up?"

"It's fine," Michael said, but he was understandably puzzled by the arrival at his home of two of his wedding guests, whom he expected to see later, at the Plaza, instead.

As Leigh had suggested at the hospital, they'd sent M

Cord two front-row tickets to Leigh's play, and McCord had escorted Samantha Littleton. After the play, Michael took everyone to the Essex House for dinner at Alain Ducasse, and during their three-hour meal, a sudden friendship had sprung up between the two women. On the surface, they had little in common except two things: They were both about the same age, and they were both in love with men who were unapologetically in love with them. Within minutes after sitting down to dinner, Michael had sensed that McCord was completely hooked on the pretty brunette detective, and when Michael made a pointed, joking remark about that, McCord hadn't denied it.

That at least gave Michael something in common with McCord, which was a good thing, because Michael had the distinct impression that Leigh and Sam Littleton wanted McCord and him to be friends; though, at the time, he couldn't imagine why two intelligent, lovely women would think that he and McCord had anything whatsoever in common. Nevertheless, Michael went along with their scheme because he sensed that Leigh wanted to forge new friendships of their own, as part of her life with him, rather than drawing him into all her old friendships, many of which were tainted with memories of Logan.

Since McCord was heading up the mayor's investigation into all the charges brought against Michael by the City of New York, McCord and he were required to meet periodically to discuss all that, so they'd actually seen quite a lot of each other in the last three weeks. To Michael's secret amusement, he was actually developing a wary liking for his former enemy, and he knew McCord felt the same way about him.

As he thought about that, he heard O'Hara letting them in and he poured champagne into four glasses. He handed the first one to Sam Littleton, who gave him a smile and a quick hug. "You look very handsome," she told him. "I don't know how you do it, but you and Mack both manage to look macho and rugged in tuxedos, instead of like penguins."

"Thank you," Michael replied with a lazy grin. "And may I say that you look extremely feminine in that gown, even though I know the bulge in your beaded handbag is probably a large, loaded, semiautomatic weapon."

"You're right, it is." She laughed. "Where's Leigh?" she asked, accepting the glass of champagne he was handing to her.

"Getting dressed," Michael said.

"I'll go see if she needs any help," Sam said, and Michael handed her another glass of champagne to take to Leigh.

He gave the last glass to McCord along with an inquiring look, which McCord understood. "I'm here to deliver a wedding gift from the mayor," he explained.

Since McCord had a glass of champagne in his right hand and his left hand was in the pocket of his black tuxedo trousers, Michael said, "What gift?"

"You have to look out the window to see it," McCord replied, strolling over to the wall of glass that overlooked Central Park West. "Look down there on the street."

Michael did, and what he saw, twenty-eight floors below, was his limousine surrounded by a bevy of uniformed police officers on motorcycles. "Oh, good," he said dryly. "Cops. Just what I always wanted."

"It's a motorcycle escort," McCord clarified with a chuckle. "Compliments of His Honor, the Mayor."

"Really? From up here, with those helmets on, I thought they might be skeet, and I was going to ask to borrow your gun."

Together they strolled back to the bar. The granite

countertop was high enough for Michael to comfortably lean his right forearm on it, which he did while keeping his eye on the living room, waiting for his first glimpse of Leigh in her wedding dress. "We have to leave early," Michael said idly, taking a sip of champagne. "We're picking Solomon and Eric Ingram up at the theater and taking them to the hotel."

McCord walked around to the other side of the bar and leaned his left forearm on the granite countertop. "Why?" he asked, lifting his own glass to his mouth.

Michael shook his head, his voice filled with tolerant amusement. "I have no idea why Leigh agreed to pick them up there, but she did. Do you want to ride with us?"

"We'll pass," McCord replied. "Solomon is in a snit because the IRS is auditing him. He thinks it's because we questioned him about Manning's two-hundred-thousand-dollar cash deposit, and then sent the IRS after him. He's written a stern letter of protest to the governor."

Michael chuckled and sardonically said, "That will do him a hell of a lot of good."

"Sam and I are getting married," McCord said quietly.

Michael glanced over his shoulder and quirked a brow at him in mock surprise. "What kind of drug did you use on her to get her to agree to that?"

"A slightly less potent one than you used on your bride, I imagine," McCord replied unconcernedly.

"I own a château in France. If you actually get that beautiful woman to marry you, instead of shooting you, you could use it for your honeymoon."

"Sam's a hell of a marksman," McCord remarked proudly, taking another sip of champagne.

"In that case, be sure you never let her go to bed with you when she's angry," Michael replied with a chuckle, taking a swallow of his drink.

"She'd love a honeymoon in a French château, I think So would I."

Michael nodded. "Let me know the dates you want it and I'll make sure it's staffed and ready."

Sam and Leigh emerged from the bedroom, started across the living room, and then stopped in amused sur prise at the sight of the two men at the bar. They were both leaning on a forearm, drinking champagne, and regarding each other over their shoulders. "They are so much alike! Sam whispered with a laugh. "I realized it a long time ago."

"So did I," Leigh replied. "But they don't think they're anything alike."

Sam was quiet for a moment, thinking of an analog that fit them. "A pair of lions," she said aloud.

Leigh nodded, looking at Michael. "They would have made terrible foes."

At the sound of their voices, Michael looked up and hi breath caught at the sight of Leigh walking toward him in long, strapless cream sheath covered in French lace. At he throat she was wearing the diamond-and-pearl choker he' given her. Deep inside her slender body, she was shelterin his child.

She handed him the aquamarine velvet wrap she wa carrying over her arm, and she turned around. He draped over her shoulders; then he slid his hand protectively ove her flat abdomen. "Thank you," he whispered.

She covered his hand with hers and gave him a meltin smile over her shoulder. "I was going to say the same thin to you."

CHAPTER 78

It was twilight when the motorcade turned onto Broadway, and O'Hara slowed the limousine down. On the street, pedestrians turned to watch them go by, trying to see inside the darkened windows of the long Mercedes.

In the backseat, Michael glanced out the window, automatically waiting to see the name "Leigh Kendall" lit up in the marquee above Solomon's theater. It was a habit of his—this watching for her name on theater marquees. He'd been doing it for years, consciously and unconsciously, whenever he happened to be on Broadway. Invariably, the sight of her name there had given him a surge of nostalgia followed by a plunge into fatalistic reality because he'd passed up his long-ago chance with her.

But fate had given him a second chance, Michael thought with an inner grin, and he hadn't let this one slip past, nor had he wasted a moment's time. Three months ago, Leigh had been Logan Manning's wife. Since then, Michael had swept her from widow to bride—with a stop for motherhood in between.

Only twelve weeks ago, she'd stood in front of him at a party wearing a red dress and hiding her disdain behind a polite mask. Tonight, she was sitting beside him in his car wearing a gorgeous wedding gown and holding his hand. In a little over an hour, she was going to stand beside him in front of a supreme court judge and voluntarily join her life with his. And seven and a half months from now, she was going to give him his first child.

He had, of course, been aided in all that by an attraction between them that was so strong, and so vital, that it had sprung instantly to life after being dormant for fourteen years.

"What are you thinking about?" Leigh asked him.

"Second chances," he said with a smile at her upturned face. "I was thinking about fate and second chances. I was also thinking that if Solomon isn't ready and waiting for us at the theater, I will haul him bodily into this car in whatever state of dress—or undress—he's in when I find him."

Leigh laughed at his threat and nodded out the car window. "We're almost there now, and I can already see Jason on the sidewalk, but it looks like he's having lighting problems again."

Michael looked out the window and saw that the marquee above Solomon's theater was lit up with the words *BLIND SPOT*, but Leigh's name was dark. Solomon was standing on the sidewalk in a tuxedo, his head tipped back toward the marquee, a cell phone at his ear. Eric Ingram was standing a few yards back, also in a tuxedo, looking up at the marquee. At the box office, people were already lining up in hope of buying unclaimed tickets to the show if any became available at the last minute.

"Poor Jason," Leigh explained with a sympathetic little sigh. "He's been plagued with lighting problems of one kind or another since opening night."

Michael's mind was on marriage, not marquees, so he missed the odd, tender note in her tone when she said, Could we get out for a minute? Otherwise, he'll stand here forever, frustrating himself and yelling at the lighting supervisor on his phone."

He nodded, resigned and amused that when show business was involved, lighting problems evidently took precedence over everything else, including impending marriages. Raising his voice a little, he said to O'Hara, "Pull over in front of the theater as close to the curb as you can get us. We're going to get out. Solomon has lighting problems."

"You gotta be kidding!" O'Hara exclaimed, gaping at Michael in the rearview mirror. "You're both in your wedding clothes, and I've got four cops on motorcycles in front of me and four more behind me. Can't Solomon call an electrician like everybody else does?"

"Evidently not," Michael said wryly.

A moment later, eight police motorcycles and one limousine bearing a bride and groom in formal wedding attire all pulled slowly over to the curb—because Jason Solomon had lighting problems.

The maneuver caused a traffic jam as motorists tried to move out around the halting cavalcade and also get a look at who was in it and why it was stopping at a theater two hours before most Broadway shows began.

Michael helped Leigh out of the car; then they walked over to Solomon and stood beside him on the sidewalk, all three of them looking up at the marquee. "I'll have it fixed in a minute, I think," Solomon assured them.

In the street, the cops on the motorcycles started looking up at the marquee and so did pedestrians, who began gathering into groups. The people in line at the box office couldn't see what everyone else was staring at, so they stared at the growing spectacle on the sidewalk.

Suddenly one of the women in line to buy tickets recognized Leigh and called out her name. "Miss Kendall!" she cried excitedly. "Could my daughter and I have your autograph?"

"I'll be right back," Leigh said with an apologetic glance at Michael; then she walked over to sign autographs.

He looked at his watch. They still had plenty of time thanks to their motorcycle escort, but he was running out of patience with Solomon. "What the hell is wrong with the lights?" he demanded.

Solomon gave him a distracted smile as he gazed up at the marquee and stepped back a few paces to see it better. "We've got it now," he said. To whoever was on the phone with him, Jason added, "Light it up. One at a time."

A moment later, Michael watched Leigh's name begin to flash on in bright white lights . . .

L—E—I—G—H
V—A—L—E—N—T—E

He slowly lowered his gaze from the marquee, an unfamiliar constriction tightening his throat.

Beside him, Solomon said, "There's something you should know—something that makes Leigh's decision to use your name very significant."

"I can't imagine anything that could possibly make it seem more significant than it does now," he said gruffly.

"You'll change your mind about that," Solomon predicted, "when I tell you that Leigh made that decision the night we met at the St. Regis. You went to make a phone call, and she insisted that I be ready to switch her name to yours."

The constriction in Michael's throat doubled.

"At the time," Solomon reminded him needlessly, "you

ame was not one to be proud of, but she was proud of it, ven then."

Michael didn't hear another onlooker call out and ask if he could take his picture with Leigh, and he didn't see he woman raise her camera. All he saw was Leigh walking p to him, smiling at him, her eyes glowing with love.

He pulled her into his arms almost roughly and pressed er face to his heart. "I adore you," he whispered hoarsely.